Racing North

Geneviève Montcombroux

Whippoorwill Solitude Publishing

ISBN 978-1-987946-25-3

Cover: Getcovers.com

Published by Solitude Publishing

solitudepublishing@gmail.com

To Michel

For his undying support

Contents

CHAPTER ONE

"Okay, Scott Walsh, where the devil are you?"

Chris watched her breath form a plume in the still air. The bus had long since sped off down the unpaved road, swallowed up by the gathering October dusk. An icy cold cut through her parka and blue woolly toque.

In a nervous gesture, she tugged her collar over her ears. Serious second thoughts about her crazy adventure swirled through her mind. Whatever had possessed her to reply to the ad in the online dog mushing magazine? URGENT! it had read, Sled dog handler wanted. Experience necessary. Able to take on Iditarod training responsibilities.

If only she could have spoken to him by phone before setting out. But the email, which was sent from a certain Byron Murdoch, contained no phone number. An internet search revealed that remote cabins in the Yukon lacked the luxury of cell phones or landlines. When she tried to get a phone number from that Byron Murdoch, she only got the Conservation office in Fletcher Creek. Undeterred, she had attached her resume to the email reply. It had to do. Though the written word could never convey her passion for working with dogs.

Tapping one booted foot against the other hoping to restore the circulation to her numbed toes, she silently cursed her new boss. Maybe his reputation for being ornery was well deserved. If he had been desperate enough to hire someone, he ought to have been here to meet her off the bus.

Fletcher Creek was a place so small she couldn't even find it on the map. It hadn't deterred her. Racing mushers lived with their dogs in the most out of the way places. She glanced at her phone, just in case it worked in this town. The flashing red light told her there was no cell service. A sigh later, she compiled the positive aspects of her being in this godforsaken place. It had been the chance of a lifetime to get hired to learn the fine art of sled dog driving over long distances under the tutelage of the best of the best musher, something she had planned to do ever since the death of her father, himself a champion sled dog racer.

After dispatching her application, days dragged by without a reply, she'd grown discouraged. Then one afternoon, right out of the blue, the office receptionist had dropped an email printout on her desk.

"This arrived in my inbox. I guess this is your dream come true, Chris."

Hardly able to contain her excitement, she snatched up the message and read it over and over again. The note was crisp to the point of being blunt: Chris. Hired. Meet October 18. Bus depot Fletcher Creek, Yukon Territory. Scott Walsh. Scott Walsh! She thanked her lucky star. Being hired by such a pro was her ticket to success. Since no hour was mentioned, she assumed that in such a remote location, there must be only one bus per day. That proved correct.

Now, standing on the edge of what passed for Fletcher Creek's main street, the feeling of being alone and very much let down, washed over her. She envied the handful of people who had got off the bus with her. By now, each one of them would be toasting themselves in front of a roaring stove in the cozy cabins she had seen from the bus windows before the darkness had closed in. Too late now to ask them about her new boss. There was no one in the street. The light dusting of snow and the clumps of withered grass rendered the scene even bleaker. Her nostrils twitched as she sensed the peculiar feel in the air that precedes a heavy snowfall.

She looked around again at the scattered houses forming the settlement. Trapper Jake's Lodge - Open 24 hours June 1 to Sept 10, read the signboard of a bigger building set back from the road, its windows boarded up. The only bright lights in the town came from a ramshackle log building across the street, Ida's Diner. Oddly out of place in the semi-wilderness, its gaudy neon sign hung at a drunken angle above the door. Another five minutes and she'd go in and inquire. A 'closed' sign on the door of a general store gave a forlorn look to the neatly kept building.

A shiver raked her body. Then again, it might be better to walk down to the gas station and motel she could see to her left. But even if they knew Scott Walsh, there was little they could do. The damn man appeared not to possess a phone. Even if he did, there was no reception. Helplessness began to creep in. Was it an insidious regret that pushed at her mind? Coming all this way to try to fulfill a dream may turn out to be the worst decision of her life.

Had she stayed at home in New Brunswick, she could, right now, be enjoying the resplendent fall colors and the rich smell of the quiet woods. The farmers would be hurrying to bring in the last of the crops. Here in this bleak northern land, the ground was already frozen. Only the dank odor of shadowy pine forests marching up the steep slopes alleviated the sterile chill in the air.

In her hurry to pack, she had overlooked the fact that winter comes early to northern Canada. She'd gladly trade her fashionable light boots for her insulated snow boots, but she wasn't going to start unpacking in the middle of the street. Shoulders hunched against the cold, she glanced around and back to make sure she wasn't missing a waiting man.

While she moved her shoulders in a circular motion to create muscle heat, she mentally tallied what she knew about her boss. Scott Walsh hailed from Nova Scotia, and had moved to the Yukon, because it guaranteed him snow eight months of the year. He was one of sled dog racing's greatest mushers. He was equally well-known for his fiery temper and his legendary outbursts at the press and spectators.

Yet he had not always been a media bad boy. There was a time when he was their favorite, a man who won races. For the last few years, he had only managed to scrape a finish 'in the money', as they called it, but he no longer took any of the big prizes. That meant an end to corporate sponsorship. Corporations liked winners.

The troubling thought that perhaps her scheme was not such a good idea after all pushed at her mind. Not because of Walsh's personality. That, she could handle. To race sled dogs stirred painful memories, like of the day her father, mother, aunt and uncle climbed into the truck with the dog-transporter on the back, to drive to a major sled dog race. As he set out on that fateful trip five years ago, her father had been brimming with confidence, race fever in his eyes. He was within a few points of the championship. Only, he never even reached the starting line. A drunk's car swiped the truck on an icy turn. It ended up at the bottom of a steep ravine. All the occupants were killed instantly, along with ten of their fifteen dogs in the transporter.

At the time, she had been a starry-eyed twenty-two-year-old. Her boyfriend shared her love of dogs and enjoyed the thrill of the competition. After her parents' horrendous accident, the young man rapidly lost interest in her. She didn't blame him. Few could have coped with such a tragedy. Later, however, she came to realize he'd been more attracted by the celebrity status of her father and how he could exploit it to his own advantage than any genuine interest in her as a person.

"So, Scott Walsh, you're letting me down." The sound of her own voice startled her. Only crazy people talk to themselves. Right now, she needed to hear a human sound in this spooky darkness. No wonder people got cabin fever when the sun set so early and didn't rise until late, only shining for a couple of hours.

Without saying as much to her face, her friends had hinted she was crazy to go through with her plan. She didn't mind. They didn't understand the depth of her love for dogs or why she should want to leave the comforts of the city to go to the frozen North. They'd never appreciate what running a superb team of huskies brought to a person. To them, it was merely being tugged along by a bunch of dogs. When she explained that her ambition was to enter the fabled Iditarod Trail race, their eyes started from their heads. Entering a thousand-mile sled dog race somewhere at the wrong end of the North American continent was beyond their comprehension. And for a woman to think of doing so was sheer lunacy.

A pickup screeched to a halt in front of the gas pump. A door slammed. A man sprinted across the road to the diner. The scene passed in front of her eyes as if it were on a movie screen.

A moment later, voices from out of the gloom broke into her thoughts. She peered across the road. Two men were standing in the eatery's doorway. Voices carry far in the cold air.

"Heck, Byron, I tell you that young guy I hired should've been on that bus!"

"Well, I tell you he wasn't," the other man replied. "I was here when it came in. The only person who got off that I didn't know was that young woman over there." He jerked his head in Chris's direction. "I guess she's waiting for someone. She's been hanging around since the bus pulled out."

"Damn me! You just can't trust anyone these days. I'd never have thought Guy Taylor's son would leave me stranded without a handler. What a lousy start to the race season."

At the mention of her father's name, Chris snapped fully alert, her cold hands forgotten. She stared at the man who spoke with so much anger in his voice.

By the light of a solitary street lamp, she made out the figure of the man waving his arms and speaking with much animation. He and his companion turned to cross the dusty thoroughfare to the waiting pickup at the gas station. A knife edged gust of wind blew open his unzipped parka. She glimpsed a plaid wool shirt molded over a muscled chest. He was an inch or two taller than the man beside him and radiated an aura of strength and agility. By the way he walked, lightly, as though springing on the balls of his feet, she recognized a conditioned athlete, which was what all top-racing mushers were.

When the pair drew level with her, the man looked in her direction. In contrast to the other man, he wore no hat. A lock of dark hair fluttered over his forehead.

As he drew closer to the light, she noted the knitted brows and the complete absence of a smile from his full lips, turned down at the corners. This and something about his resentful stare confirmed he must be the man she had come north to meet.

A tiny inner voice urged her to look away and to pretend that she was waiting for someone else. It was not too late to turn her back on this unwelcoming place and catch the next bus home. Instead, she stepped forward as the men reached the edge of the rickety boardwalk.

"Hi, Mr. Walsh? I'm Chris Taylor. You were supposed to meet me off the bus. I've been waiting for half an hour."

Walsh halted in his tracks, one foot on the boardwalk. His jaw dropped. The dim light threw his features into sharp relief. A smile she couldn't suppress reached her lips when she saw the man's perplexed expression. She was also aware of even white teeth framed by the most sensual lips she had ever seen on a man, and of smoke gray eyes that bore into her with a disturbing intensity.

There was a moment of awkward silence while man and woman sized each other up. She moistened her lips with the tip of her tongue. Scott Walsh's gaze followed the tiny movement. Mechanically, she pushed her toque further back on her head. Her gleaming chestnut hair spilled onto her shoulder.

"Chris Taylor? But you're a girl."

Her laughter bubbled to the surface. "How wonderfully observant of you, Mr. Walsh."

"I didn't hire a female."

"It seems that's exactly what you've done."

"You didn't say you were a girl. And what the hell are you laughing for? It isn't funny."

"I didn't hide anything. It was plain enough from my resume. Or didn't you read it carefully enough? Maybe you were only too glad to hire someone, anyone, that you didn't even bother to look closely at my application." She was enjoying his discomfort. It made up for the time she had to wait out in the cold.

The man identified as Byron cut in. "Just a minute, Scott. Don't get so het up. Chris is a girl's name just as much as a boy's. Why the hell did you automatically assume she was a guy?"

"I never thought for one moment a female would bother to reply to my ad. That's why." His features hardened in a scowl.

"Well, maybe you should've spoken to her on the phone?"

"You know damn well I'm too busy with the dogs to come down to use your phone." He spoke defiantly. "It's bad enough having to trek to town to send an email. I'm shorthanded. I've been working round the clock."

He drew his hand over his face. The glowering anger in his eyes had not diminished.

"And in the ad, Mr. Walsh, you didn't specify what gender the applicant had to be," she said.

"Of course not. It's understood–"

"No, it's not. There are a lot of women handlers and mushers nowadays. I'm very sorry to disappoint you that I'm not a man, but you hired me in good faith. You're not going to rat on the contract, are you?" She dropped the bantering tone. Her anger mounted.

"The problem is that a woman wouldn't be able to cope with the work."

"Why not? I have every confidence that I can do all that's required."

Byron interrupted the rancorous exchange by stepping with his carton of groceries between the protagonists. "Look, how about continuing this enlightened discussion in my kitchen? At least it's warmer there."

"Okay, let's go. I'll move the truck."

Byron picked up one of her bags with his free hand and strode toward a log house screened by a clump of pines. "Follow me."

She snatched up the rest of her luggage and followed. What would Walsh do now that he had found out she wasn't a man? For her part, she had no intention of quitting before she had even begun, not after traveling a few thousand miles. Any doubts she had only moments ago volatilized in the cold air. Besides, she had resigned from her job at the office.

Once inside, Byron dumped his burden on the table and went to the sink to fill the kettle. "I'll make some coffee, then we can discuss this problem rationally." He held out his hand to Chris. "Pleased to meet you. I'm Byron Murdoch, Government Wildlife Conservation Officer for the region."

She shook his hand. As well as a comforting warmth, she detected an amused twinkle in his brown eyes.

Scott Walsh pushed in through the door and slammed it shut. Byron turned to his friend. "You know Scott, I think Chris's right when she says she can do the work. And it's true what she says about women handlers and mushers. Some of them are darned good.

Every bit as capable as a man. Aren't you forgetting that a couple of women have even won the Iditarod? You need a handler in a bad way."

"Okay. I agree. Maybe she can cope with the physical work. But there's another problem. She can't stay at the cabin."

"I knew I wasn't coming to a luxury condominium, Mr. Walsh. As far as dog handling goes, I'm as good as anyone, and probably better." Her tilted chin showed her determination.

"Pretty modest, isn't she?"

Scott's sarcastic tone was not lost on her.

"If I don't say so, who's going to say it for me?" She stiffened her back and held her head up as a sign that she had no intention of letting this macho curmudgeon put her down.

Convulsed with laughter, Byron sank into an armchair.

Scott grew red in the face. "Shut up, Murdoch." He swung round to face her. "Don't be so hasty. You haven't seen the cabin. It's small. No running water. No electricity and only one bedroom. Mine!"

"You promised room and board in your ad. Therefore, you must have arranged accommodation for whoever you hired."

Scott mimicked a woman's voice. "Accommodation?" He dropped the silly tone. "Yeah, everyone who comes to the cabin bunks down in front of the stove. I don't have a fancy boudoir for you."

His gaze raked her slender body. A gleam lit up his eyes for an instant, but he promptly lowered his eyelids. Still, she caught the glint and a strange tremor shook her.

"I don't expect a fancy boudoir, as you put it. So I'll just put up with what there is. I'd like to remind you it's not me that's making the fuss." She reached out to take one of the mugs of coffee Byron had placed on the table. Her fingers came into contact with Scott's who was reaching for the same cup. They pulled back as if scorched. A quiver of excitement swelled through her.

A deep breath settled her nerves. This job was already more of a challenge than she'd imagined. She could tolerate the stubborn attitude that had earned him his reputation. What she hadn't bargained on was reacting physically to him. One accidental touch of his fingers and lightning had shot up her arm. Had Byron not been there, he might have completely lost his temper. Unless he'd have grabbed her to kiss her. He looked just as startled as she did.

Rumor had it Scott hid himself away like a recluse between races. The smoldering look he had just given her was proof enough that he was no hermit and was far from being immune to feminine charms.

"You're maybe not making a fuss, but I happen to live in that cabin, and it's just not set up for visitors, let alone a woman." His growling tone exuded hostility.

"That's not a problem for me. Why should it be for you?" She fought to keep her tone even.

Scott looked toward Byron. "And she's opinionated too!"

"For goodness' sake, Walsh, cut it out! You're acting like a mean old bear in one of my traps."

"I don't like company. I'm fixed in my ways."

"So am I, Mr. Walsh. The difference being that I need a job. And you need a handler. Don't worry about me. I'll keep to myself. If I feel the need for conversation, I'll talk to the dogs. You won't be bothered."

He scowled. With his brows knitted, he both scared and fascinated her. His clenched jaw sharpened the planes of his face. Yet she was determined not to be intimidated by his surly behavior.

Byron pounced on what he saw was a lull in the hostilities. "As far as I can see, you're both perfectly suited to each other. The dogs are going to improve their conversational skills, and you two will live in harmonious silence. There're no arguments in a Trappist monastery. But to make things easier, I suggest you let her have the bedroom, Walsh. You can bed down in front of the stove."

"That suits me," she said.

More than ever, she was ready to put up with anything, his raw temper included, though she didn't know why. She threw him a rebellious glance. The warm current she had experienced earlier returned. Under his wool shirt, she guessed there wasn't an ounce of fat on his sinewy body. Bitterness etched lines around his mouth, which she instinctively longed to soothe.

At least, she was thankful that Byron seemed to be on her side. He possessed the rugged frame of a man who spent his life outdoors. His black hair parted on the side and the way his mouth curled easily into a smile gave him a boyish air. He struck her as levelheaded and, in marked contrast to Scott Walsh, friendly.

Byron stood up and slapped his friend on the shoulder. "You old rogue. I reckon you've got no choice but to accept your new employee. Personally, I think Chris is a terrific young lady." He grinned at her and added, "If he throws you out, honey, just come here. The door is never locked."

He gave an exaggerated wink. His eyes shone with warmth. She rewarded him with a smile. Her anxiety began to slip away. Scott Walsh drank his coffee in silence. This round was hers. But she was not fooled into thinking she'd won him over.

He set down his empty cup. "I hope you've brought more suitable clothes than that citified parka."

"All my mushing gear is in my bag."

He pulled a felt cap out of his pocket and jammed it onto his head, a gesture of annoyance if ever she'd seen one.

"The truck's outside. Let's get going."

Byron plucked her sleeve as they followed him out. "The old bruin is grumpy," he whispered. "He doesn't bite, though."

Scott stopped, the door half open. "I heard that, Murdoch." He punched him in the ribs. "If it wasn't for the Iditarod..."

Once in the truck, he threw his cap in the back seat. He didn't speak, and neither did she. She didn't mind, used as she was to long solitary journeys on the back of the sled where the only spoken words were the commands to the dogs. If this was the way Scott Walsh wanted it, it was fine by her. At least they had one thing in common, their love of dogs.

She stole a glance at her new employer's chiseled features as he hunched over the wheel. With his eyes riveted on the road, she could only see the profile of a shuttered face.

Eventually he must have become conscious of being watched, for he raked his fingers through his thick hair, but studiously refrained from turning to look at her.

After several miles of empty road, he swerved off the main highway and gunned the truck up a rough trail that snaked steeply through the dense pine forest. She may have been mistaken, but she felt he was taking an evil pleasure in pushing his four-wheel drive to the maximum. Assuming he was doing it expressly to unnerve her, she forced herself to remain unruffled.

After one ferocious bump, she turned to him. "I hate to mention it, but I think you've just lost the box of things from the back of the pickup."

"Hell!" He slammed on the brakes so hard that her seat belt locked and bit into her shoulder.

With another muttered oath, he backed up slowly, jumped out, and began gathering the cans and packets of food scattered along the darkened path. She opened the passenger door and slid out, massaging her bruised shoulder. A raw wind sapped her breath for a second.

He didn't look up. "You don't have to help. It was my stupid fault."

Crabby he was, but he had integrity and didn't hesitate to take responsibility for his mistake. He went up a notch in her esteem.

"I want to. From the look of it, that's also my dinner you've dropped in the dust. I figure I'd better lend a hand."

"I've found the cardboard box. Now, where on earth is the tarp?"

"Hooked on that tree. That's what caught my eye when it flew off."

"Thanks."

"You're welcome."

He glared at her and opened his mouth, but shut it saying nothing more. She leaned against the side of the truck, content to observe his temper work itself out as he picked up the last of the spilled goods.

From his distorted features, it was easy to see that a battle was raging inside him. Out of frustration, he kicked at a stone, only to find it firmly embedded in the frozen ground. She winced. His toe must be hurting. A curse escaped his lips.

Something deep inside her stirred as she watched him effortlessly pitch the heavy box of and other items into the back of the pickup.

The task completed, he climbed in the back to secure the load. Taut, powerful muscles on a deceptively lithe frame gave him the fluid movement of a mountain lion. She smiled at the wry association of wild cats and the big dogs he ran. But, yes, he did remind her of a cougar she had once seen. Close up, he was probably just as dangerous.

"Something funny?"

"This whole situation, I guess."

"Why did you come? You must have heard I was a loner."

"This late in the season, yours was the only want ad in the magazine and on the Racing Sled Dogs website. Apart from that, I wasn't free any earlier." She tried not to sound too flippant.

"You really know how to flatter a guy. Do you always have such sharp answers for everything?" His tone was dry, a sharp contrast to his natural deep mellow voice she heard briefly when he talked to Byron Murdoch.

"Sorry. I didn't mean to sound smart. When I discovered it was you, I thought I was in luck. I'd be learning from the best."

"Not the best anymore, not since..." He looked away. "Never mind. Get back in the truck."

"You have qualities and experience—"

"Let's go. It's going to snow."

Undeterred by his gruff tone, she clambered into the warmth of the cab. This was not the time to ask questions. He drove more carefully now. A strange feeling welled up from deep within her, a desire to comfort and appease, but she was loath to break the heavy silence. The moment for it slipped by.

Several bumpy miles up the road, he stopped in front of a log cabin. A deafening chorus of howls greeted her as she stepped down from the truck. Once her eyes became accustomed to the darkness, she made out wolfish shapes all around her. Dogs, dozens of them, sat perched on their boxy log houses. As if on cue, they stopped their serenade. Only the thump of tails on the flat wooden roofs continued.

There was no mistaking the affection in his sonorous voice as he called out each dog's name and told them to go back to sleep. Fortunately, the shadows hid her look of bewilderment. This man had two very different sides to him.

He switched on a flashlight, freed a big black dog from a nearby enclosure, and went into the cabin without a word. Undismayed, she retrieved her bags from the pickup, put on her headlamp and followed him in, the dog at her heels. Inside, the animal shook his thick fur free of ice crystals. The dog turned to sniff the newcomer, then wagged his bushy, curled up tail. She let him inspect her hand, then tickled him under the chin, obeying the rule never to approach an unknown dog from above to pat his head. Scratching gently, her fingers sank into the soft neck hair, so dense she couldn't feel his skin. The dog raised his muzzle and licked her face.

"That's Renoir."

She laughed, gazing into the limpid pools of his dark amber eyes. "Such a big, tough dog, Renoir, but you're as soft as my heart. And you're so handsome with your black face and those two white spots above the eyes."

Talking to the dog earned her an irritated glance from under knitted brows. For a moment, she wondered whether all his dogs were named after impressionists painters. Now was not the moment to ask. He lit an oil lamp and hooked it to a nail on the low beam overhead. A warm glow bathed the cabin's interior. The paper and kindling already laid in the cast iron cook stove sprang to life with the touch of a match and soon threw out a comforting heat.

Her fingers trailing along the sturdy chinked logs that formed the walls of the cabin, she approached a small window, devoid of curtains, that looked out over what she determined was the kennel area. A few cupboards and a tiny counter with a sink without faucets, and a white plastic pail underneath to catch the run off, made up the kitchen corner. The lack of running water didn't discourage her. In her history courses, pioneer life had fascinated her. If those brave women could do it, so could she.

On the other side of the cabin, a partition enclosed what was obviously the solitary bedroom, its doorway screened by a curtain. Another curtain concealed the door to an alcove. Which she presumed must be what passed for a bathroom. A plain wooden table, a few mismatched chairs, an armchair, and a battered couch gave the place a masculine, lived-in appearance.

The black husky lay curled up on the couch, its tail over its nose, completely oblivious of the two humans staring at each other across the untidy room.

"Now that you've seen the palace I live in, I imagine you can't wait to get back to civilization. The bus back to Whitehorse comes through Fletcher at seven-thirty in the morning."

"Fine. I'll be on it sometime next April or May. What's for dinner? I'm starving."

Her remark threw him off guard. Inside her, she scored a point. He'd really expected her, a refined young woman, to be horrified by his primitive living conditions. This would be like camping in a wooden tent, and camping held no secrets for her. His obvious annoyance didn't fluster her.

"You'll find some frozen pizzas in that box I brought in."

"That sounds great. I presume you keep baking sheets under the counter."

She unwrapped a pizza and slid it onto a flat cookie sheet. He fed more logs into the cookstove. Compassion overcame her. Lit by the dancing flames, his handsome face was creased with bitterness and fatigue. An urge filled her to smooth his forehead. She reined in her emotions and decided to drop the attack-is-the-best-defense attitude she had adopted on first meeting him.

"How about if I put one in for you? There's room for another pizza next to mine."

"Thanks."

That concession, she reckoned, must have cost him dearly. His shoulders sagged under the burden of sorrow and resentment he appeared to carry. On the road, while picking up the spilled groceries, he had been about to confide what bothered him. But he had changed his mind and retreated into silence. She quickly slid the pizzas into the oven.

He must have suffered at the hands of a woman. Only an unhappy love affair could warp a man that way. There had been many magazine photos of him crossing the finish line and being embraced by a woman. A wife or lover, maybe. Maybe not a wife. There was never any shortage of pretty women on hand to kiss a race winner in the glare of the flashbulbs.

Could she remain immune to such a good-looking man? With his bristling hostility, there was little danger of anything romantic developing between them. And that was the way she wanted it. She shook her head, amazed that she was even thinking such thoughts. Her cheeks reddened. That was due to the heat of the stove, but she couldn't fool herself. The need to settle, to claim her part of this territory, swelled through her, and she busied herself with her bags. Since she received no instructions, she hung her parka on one of the wooden pegs aligned into the log wall.

"I guess you'd better take the room."

"There's no need to–"

"I said you take the bedroom!" The words sliced through the air like a hatchet.

"Is that an order, boss?"

"I'll sleep on the couch. I'm an early riser."

"So am I."

Their eyes locked, and they stared mutely at each other. Silence persisted.

He shook off the torpor. "If we are going to work together, how about if we stop being at each other's throats? It's only fair you should enjoy the privacy of the bedroom. I'll move my stuff out tomorrow."

"I appreciate the gesture. Both the sleeping arrangements and the peace treaty. Judging by the smell, I'd say the pizzas must be done. Shall I make coffee?" She struggled to keep her voice level despite the panicky feeling that he was about to kiss her.

Perhaps the easing of hostilities was not such a good idea. It was too dangerous to feel sorry for a man who had been hurt by another woman, if that was what it was. It had to be. He wouldn't be so miserable or hostile otherwise. Losing races might make an ambitious man testy but more driven than ever. Financial woes would make anyone worried, but not ready to bite off someone's head. Especially if that someone was essential to help refloat the money boat. Her curiosity had been piqued. Later, during the long nights of winter, he might ease his torment by telling her what troubled him. Unfortunately, intimacy in front of a fire might just be too romantic for words. It was up to her to keep their relationship strictly on a business footing.

The effects of her long journey began to catch up with her. She tried to concentrate on her food, but her thoughts wandered back to him.

Before leaving home, she had checked the race results for the last couple of years. He claimed he hadn't won a race in a long time, yet he finished moderately well in every event he entered. Though, of course, finishing well didn't carry the thrill of winning first place. Some people just couldn't accept to be less than number one.

He had lost that certain something which makes a top rate racer out of a merely competent one. The greatest of the great had vanished. If she could find out what was gnawing at him, she might be able to give him the right encouragement.

For now, she was looking forward to sinking into a warm bed and closing her eyes. When she did retire to the bedroom, all she could see was an empty road bordered by endless fir-covered mountains. Just as she was sinking into sleep, the dog pushed under the curtain and joined her on the bed.

"Renoir! Get out here, boy." The dog ignored his whispered command, stretched out on the bed and let out an enormous sigh of contentment. On his second more insistent call, the big black dog yawned, gave her face a friendly lick and went back to his master.

Chapter Two

S cott dropped on the couch. He couldn't understand how the woman had managed to worm her way into his life so easily, so quickly. Now he was stuck with her for the next six or eight months. When he received her resume in which she said she had handled for her father Guy Taylor, he hadn't read further or made any other inquiries. No matter how hotly she denied it, she had duped him. Despite all his efforts to keep women at arm's length, this smiling creature, who looked so innocent, had succeeded in slipping through his defenses.

He would be forced to put up with her because nobody wanted to work for him anymore, not since word about his difficult character had become common knowledge in the dog mushing community. There was also the small matter of a signed contract. If he broke it, she could wipe him out of the little money he had left.

What a crummy start to the day! He had already made himself look foolish in front of this auburn-haired woman. Things were going from bad to worse. In addition, his body had suddenly woken up and was clamoring with want. Chris Taylor was just too attractive for her own good.

The sight through the window of the rim of the valley, velvet black against the luminous dark of the sky, brought some peace to his mind. Yet he tasted bilious anger in his mouth. In a short instant, he had almost emptied his heart to a stranger, a woman at that!

What was she doing to him, anyway? He just met her and had been on the verge of letting out what he suppressed from his conscious memory for the last five years.

Renoir thrust his wet nose against his hand. He patted the broad head. "Okay, let's go out." Dog and man stepped into the cold night. Her image in the golden light of the lamp came between him and the quiet of nature. His jaw tightened. Signed contract or not, she'd have to leave. His whole body tensed. The delicate profile of her face, the satiny skin glowing from a healthy outdoor life, and those steady green eyes had quickened his pulse.

Just thinking about her made him want to kiss her and bury himself in her. He gritted his teeth to ward off the wild, familiar feeling. There was a time when, young and stupid, he considered any attractive female fair game for his masculine prowess. But not this beautiful young woman, who radiated a strong will and determination enough to match his own. He checked himself and mentally corrected it to the will and determination he used to have.

A long sigh later, he clipped a leash to Renoir's collar and took him back to his pen. Afterwards, he stared up at the stars until the cold drove him inside. He blew out the lamp and crawled under the covers. Sleep didn't come for a long time. This arrangement would never work.

Chapter Three

C hris awoke with a start. For an instant, she didn't know where she was. It was still dark. Then the vague shapes in the room and the howling of the dogs from outside brought her back to reality.

Fascinated, she listened to the rising and falling song of the dogs. When it stopped, the stillness of the night was all the more profound. From afar, she heard an answering call. Her ears strained to hear. Wolves! It had to be. There was an unearthly beauty in the sound. As if on cue, the dogs replied with the same primitive complaint. The wilderness seemed to be all-encompassing, enveloping her in its mystery. She sighed with a sense of exhilaration that comes from being in an utterly isolated place, at one with nature.

The dogs ceased their moonlight serenade. A feeling of peace and solitude settled over her. She listened intently to the sounds in the night. In the wilds, absolute silence does not exist. Scurrying animals, the splintering of ice in a stream and the creaking of the log cabin as its members contracted from the cold made up the thousand tiny noises of silence.

Gingerly, she crept from under the covers and tiptoed over the rough-hewn floor to peer out of the window. As Scott had predicted, snow had fallen during the night. A fresh mantle of sparkling white weighted the pine boughs. In the sharp moonlight reflected from the snow, she could make out a trail leading down through the pines to where a frozen creek sparkled.

Her eyes caught the shadowy figure of a man half hidden by a big tree. Scott too was watching the long shadows thrown on the fresh snow by the trees. After a few minutes, he shrugged as to shake off the spell and turned toward the kennels. The cold from the floor crept up her bare legs. She rummaged in her bag for her toilet things. It was time to get ready for work.

Her eyes became accustomed to the darkened room. The bathroom, she had discovered the previous evening, was tiny, consisting of a composting toilet, which took up most of the space, and an old-fashioned bowl and pitcher. Not the most practical arrangement for sharing with someone, but the bathing facilities were the last thing she was going to complain about. In the dark, she held out her hand, expecting to make contact with the curtain. Instead, she collided with a solid door.

Strange. This wasn't here last night. Yet a well-fitted door it was. He must have got up early and noiselessly slipped it into the hinges she had noticed the night before. Inside, her hand found a box of matches and a candle in a holder. By the flickering light, she looked at a partially built shower stall in one corner. The pipes suggested he intended to bring in running water. For a moment, she wondered how. But for now, she was content to give herself a sponge bath in the enamel basin, using hot water from the stove's boiler.

A good breakfast to start the day had always been her mantra. Since the boss was already out caring for the dogs, she felt she should be out, too. Breakfast would have to wait. Taking down a can of whole milk powder from the kitchen shelf, she mixed herself a quick drink with water from a five-gallon container. Then she pulled on her parka and boots, drew the headband of her headlamp over her toque, and went outside to join him. The cold air mingled with the subtle scent of pine to assail her nostrils. She took a long gulp of the scented air. Her body tingled with energy.

Her arrival was greeted by a renewed chorus of howls. Renoir came bounding to greet her, his pink tongue lolling from his black face. The powerful animal raised himself and put his front paws on her shoulders to lick her chin.

"Good dog!" She scratched him under the collar.

A flash of light swept the ground in front of her. Scott's voice drawled behind her. "You're making the others jealous."

"Oh, I intend to go round and say hello to them all. Isn't that what you to do every morning?"

"You have a quick tongue, young lady."

She laughed. Among her office colleagues, she'd been the quiet one. Not so at the dog sled races, where the animation and the easy familiarity of the mushers made everyone feel like family.

"I'm only trying to get to know how things work around here."

"At least you've hit it off with old Renoir."

It was a grudging admission.

An uncomfortable feeling spread over her as his eyes roved over her figure revealed by the unfastened parka.

"Could you please explain the routine?"

"The routine? All right. First thing in the morning, I come out to greet the dogs and check that everything is okay. Then I have breakfast. Back to the kennels, I give them a snack of fat. They get their main meal in the evening. While I'm in the pen, I clean up. By the time I finish, the dogs going out have digested their snack and I hitch them to the sled. When there's no snow, I hitch the team to the ATV."

"So you really do visit with the dogs."

"Yes, of course. Why wouldn't I? I love them." His voice softened over his last words.

Once again, she had glimpsed the human side of the man whom the media had nicknamed Old Grizzly because of his ungracious refusal to cooperate. It left her perplexed.

She advanced among the dogs staked out on twelve-foot chains. The animals were quiet now, lying with their noses on their front paws.

"They're a pretty contented lot."

He walked beside her. "Uh? Oh, yes."

"I see you've made some enclosures over there."

"I'm building more. I'd rather have the dogs in pens than tethered."

"My father and uncle used to house their dogs in big pens. Many mushers simply stake out their dogs. Usually on too short a chain."

"Dog mushing sure isn't what it used to be."

"Like everything else, it's evolving. I've attended several seminars on nutrition and athletic conditioning over the last couple of years. The technical advances alone are quite remarkable." Her enthusiastic tone was genuine.

He raised a skeptical eyebrow. "I keep the pups in this big pen, along with the pack made up of their parents and the rest of the team. I only separate the pups from the adults at meal times to ensure they get enough to eat. They're six months old."

"They're beautiful! Huge for six months." She crouched among the rowdy, jumping dogs. "Black and white, cinnamon and white, a gray one and a white one, so many different coat colors."

"These are Canadian Inuit dogs from the high Arctic. They've been bred randomly in the North for thousands of years. The coat never got fixed, as it did with other breeds. Random breeding has kept them free of genetic disorders."

"True. It prevents recessive genes coming to the fore to cause diseases."

"Where did you learn all that?"

She shrugged. "I studied biology."

The pups tugged at her clothes, licked her face, jumped on her and pushed her until she lost her balance laughing without restraint.

Scott intervened. "Okay, you pups, sit!"

Five of them obeyed his firm voice, two remained standing, looking at him cheekily. He repeated the command, but they didn't budge. He put his hand to his pocket and the two pups sat in haste. They all craned their necks expectantly and took tiny pieces of dried meat from his fingers. He repeated the sit command to those who could not wait any longer and were trying to get served before their turn.

There was an unexpected gentleness in his actions. Nothing like the man of yesterday. A new sense of wonder came over her. Finally, they left the pups to their play.

"Since Renoir is allowed to run loose, I presume he is the boss dog."

"Right. He's the Alpha male and the sire of the pups. But he is only the boss of the working huskies. The old dogs live in that enclosure over there and are never to mix with the working ones, only with the pups. There can only be one boss and the younger one would try to kill the old one unless he submitted, which old Palootok would never do. Come over here and I'll show you the kennel building." At a short distance from the main cabin stood another log structure. Inside, bags of dog food were stacked along one wall. An orderly array of harnesses, ropes, snow hooks and dog collars hung near the door. One corner of the room was fenced off to form two pens.

"Indoor pens?"

"The big one is a birthing pen. Pups stay there with their mother until they're ready to live outside. They could be born outside, but I believe in maximum well-being for them to grow strong and healthy. The other pen doubles as an infirmary, if necessary. Over here is where you'll prepare the food."

A propane stove stood in a corner.

"I believe in strict hygiene. That's where you'll wash the bowls." He pointed to a sink with a faucet set in a counter against the opposite wall. A heap of stainless steel bowls waited in readiness on the counter.

"Makes sense."

"If everything is clean, we have no bacterial problems. I'm one of a number of mushers who go to such lengths. Others think I'm overly fussy, but I think it's worth it."

A kerosene heater, vented through the roof, stood in the middle of the room. She tested its warmth.

"The heater is a nice luxury."

"Not a luxury, a necessity. It's kept on low heat. There's a well under the building and the heater is needed so the pressure tank doesn't freeze. The pump operates with a generator. This way we have running water year round. Otherwise, it takes too long to thaw blocks of ice each morning to water the dogs. In a pinch, you can come and get water here for the house, but otherwise go down to the creek."

"Perfect." She was not in the least surprised to find more amenities for the dogs than for the humans. It fitted with his austere code, too.

"Not asking why I carry water from the creek?"

"Let me think. The well water must be good or you wouldn't give it to the dogs. So, could it be the generator?"

He smiled. "Right. I'm trying to save on the gas. It's darned expensive up here."

"That's smart."

"And damaging to the environment."

"Are you planning on a wind mill?"

"I am. Now you've seen everything, how about breakfast? Ours, that is."

"Wonderful! My stomach is clamoring for something. It's still dark. When does daylight appear?"

"About ten at the moment. Until the winter solstice, the days get shorter and shorter till there's all of three hours of daylight. If the prospect of almost twenty-four hours of darkness is more than you can handle, you'd better pack. I'll drive you to town."

"Get off that old refrain, will you? I merely inquired about the time of day and night because I know it's the land of the midnight sun in summer and perpetual darkness in winter."

"Some people go crazy in the depths of winter."

"And I imagine plenty more don't. People go crazy everywhere. They don't need darkness to do it."

A grunt was the only answer she received as they made their way back to the cabin. Her arm brushed his while negotiating the rough ground. The jolt of electricity between them was almost tangible in the crisp morning air despite the heavy clothing. On the tour of the kennels, she had sensed the attachment he had to his dogs. In unguarded moments, she caught him looking intently at her. She was beginning to think she had judged him too harshly.

Obviously, he was still in shock after discovering that she was not the man he had been expecting. He certainly was trying hard to make things difficult for her. At least they had similar ideas when it came to dog care. So long as she confined herself to learning sledding techniques and dog handling in big races, everything should remain uncomplicated. No doubt she could squelch the physical attraction that troubled her last night. He was a handsome man. It was normal for her to react like any other woman would.

"What's that small shed raised on wooden posts?"

"A food cache. We must keep all the meat up there out of reach of wild animals."

They walked on.

"Apart from the pens, I see you're planning to build something else." She pointed to a stack of lumber, now under a layer of snow.

Her remark touched a raw nerve. He growled something and hurried into the cabin. Baffled by his sudden change of mood, she ran to the door before it closed in her face. Renoir pushed in behind her. Puzzled by his unexplained gruffness, she shrugged and closed the porch door behind her. After all, she wasn't here to solve puzzles.

"Is Renoir allowed in or not?"

"Let him stay. When he's too warm, he'll ask out." He had his back to her and was busy loading wood into the stove.

"What are you having for breakfast?" Her attempt at being casual while setting plates and cups on the table worked.

"Let me see what there is." He opened a small hatch in the wall. "How about bacon and eggs with hash browns?"

Looking over his shoulder, she saw that the door opened onto a large cupboard. He met her quizzical look.

"A cold room built on the outside but within the porch. It's as good as a fridge, which you must have noticed we don't have." His tone was now more amiable.

"How clever. I'll join you for bacon, eggs and hash browns. What do you want to drink? Milk or coffee?"

"Milk. It's powdered milk."

"I know, I found it."

"Powdered eggs too. I guess you're going to miss not having a convenience store round the corner where you can buy fresh stuff."

Her chin rose a notch in defiance. "Not at all. I've not always lived in the city. I know about life in the bush, even if mine was a little closer to civilization than this."

He chuckled. "I'm glad you've got plenty of spirit. You'll need it. When I'm away, you'll have to cut wood and haul water."

"That's no problem. I've used a chainsaw before." She spoke tartly, omitting to say that it had been at least five years ago and then only once under her father's supervision. "As for the water, I don't see that as a major inconvenience."

She found a jug and measured out the milk powder. As she worked, she felt his eyes boring into her back.

"Shall I cook? I'm no chef, but I'm a wiz with a frying pan."

"Suits me." He stepped back from the cook stove. "Tell me, after the... accident, did you have to sell your father's dogs?"

"Most of them. Our racing friends offered to buy them. My cousin and I sold the young ones. We kept the older dogs and four one-year-old dogs that I had raised and trained myself."

"How many do you have now?"

"We still have eight, four dogs eleven years of age and the pups. They're six, but we still call them pups. We exercise them after work and on weekends."

"That must cut into your social life." Cynicism pierced his tone.

"I never even gave it a thought." Her reply was quick and sharp.

"You mean you live in a big city and never go out?"

"We don't live in the city, only work there." Mentally, she thumbed her nose at him.

"I see."

"No, you don't see." She felt the need to explain. "After my parents' death, I sold the house with the land and the kennels, and bought a cottage on eighty acres an hour's drive outside the city. We commute." Her words carried a tinge of sadness.

"We?"

"My cousin and I."

"This cousin, is he very close to you?"

The sudden abruptness in his voice surprised her. He didn't look pleased at the mention of her living with her cousin.

"She. Marcia's quite definitely a woman." A teasing laugh escaped her. What difference would it have been to him if her cousin had been a man? If the idea wasn't so patently absurd, she'd say he was jealous.

"Just the two of you out there? No man around?"

His rasping tone startled her. She looked up from the cooking.

"Marcia's father was with mine in the car, as well as our mothers, when the accident happened."

"I'm sorry... You must miss your folks."

"Yes, I do, but life must go on. I'd wanted to learn how to be a top ranking musher and a racer. My father insisted I go to college first before joining him on the racing circuit. So I missed out on a whole lot of his teaching while I was away. After that... well, it was too late." She tried to keep the grief she still carried out of her voice.

He scowled and averted his gaze. She replaced the cups with glasses.

"You can have coffee if you want."

"No thanks, I've got to work outside. Coffee is too dehydrating."

"You mean it makes you run to the outhouse."

"Precisely."

The ghost of a smile that crossed his lips was not lost on her. So he did have something of a sense of humor. They sat opposite each other at the table and ate in silence until the plates were cleared.

"We'll go back to the kennel room where I've got all the feeding instructions written out. I'll take care of the team I'm taking out this morning. I expect to be back in the early afternoon." He stood up.

"Did you pack a lunch?"

"Lunch? No time for such niceties."

The touch of scorn in his tone annoyed her, but she brushed it aside. "You nourish the dogs, you must do the same for yourself. Sled dogs are athletes, so is the musher. The body doesn't perform well on a deficit diet. Do you have an emergency pack?"

"What's this, a survival 101 exam?"

"I just hope you don't break a leg in the mountains and have to overnight until someone can get to you."

Her bantering tone didn't hide the underlying seriousness of her words. They stared at each other. He blinked first.

"I've gone out for days on end without anyone caring whether or not I carried survival gear or extra rations. Why should you?"

"There are many ways to kill yourself. This one seems awfully convoluted. You should know that even the best mushers can be stranded."

"How about if you mind your..." He clamped his jaw. "Oh, just forget it. Yes, I've got a survival pack. I'll toss it in the sled."

She handed him a package.

"Lunch. Bacon sandwiches." She immediately turned and washed the dishes to head off any protest from him.

"Uh... Thanks."

He stood as if hypnotized for a moment, then followed her to the bedroom, where she retrieved her coveralls from her bag.

"What do you...?"

He never finished his sentence, but she heard the animosity in his voice. She deliberately ignored him while she zipped up her overpants. He filled the door frame, a brooding giant of a man. Stormy brows contrasting with his full, sensitive lips.

"Excuse me, please. I have to go and work." Her outward calm was put on. She really had pushed him too far, yet it was only common sense.

His response was to grab her arm as she brushed past him. Their bodies met. A tremor rippled down her spine. Instinctively, she raised her face to his, her lips trembling in anticipation.

For one glorious moment, she was oblivious of everything, save the feel of his muscular chest pressing against her softness. She was filled with a yearning to have him hold her in his arms and kiss her. Warning signals went off in her head. Her breathing shortened. She wrenched her arm free.

It took all her strength to step back, still struggling to regain control and unable to comprehend what was happening to her. His dark gray gaze caressed the creamy smoothness of her cheek and neck. He moved aside to let her pass, looking every bit as troubled as she did.

Chapter Four

They grabbed their parkas and went outside. An uneasy silence hovered over them. In the kennel room, she read the instructions and pocketed a plan of the kennels with the dogs' names on it. Knowing all their names was essential if she wanted them to obey her commands. He busied himself rearranging the already orderly dog harnesses.

A low whistle escaped her lips.

"Something wrong?"

"Nope, just the complicated schedule. It looks like a battle plan."

"You can leave now if you think the work's too much for you."

"That's out of the question. Actually, I admire the mind that worked all this out."

He was about to reply. She waited, but he checked himself. With a deep breath, he resumed the task of sorting his gear on the other side of the room. The pups were fed twice a day. She'd start with the pups and gathered up the bowls.

Her attempt to get them to sit wasn't successful. All around her, the howls changed to a frenzy. She glanced over her shoulder. A sled was sitting in the middle of the path. Two dogs were already hitched to it. He must have reckoned that the snow was thick enough for sledding. The pups were torn between running to the fence and the bowls she was holding. Not wanting to distress the young dogs further, she gave in. Their breakfast could wait. She put the bowls onto the plank shelf nailed to a post.

Accompanied by a horde of juvenile dogs, she went to the fence. Laughing, she cuddled the two closest to her, so young and already so eager to run with the pack.

Another of her duties was to take the pups out for an afternoon walk to begin teaching them trail commands. She would also have to sled with some of the adults. According to the schedule, dogs would be exercised on alternate days. From the look of it, she was going to enjoy her job.

He hitched two more dogs and commanded them to sit. He pulled up a second sled ahead of the first and hitched four dogs to it.

"Come over here!"

"Me?"

"Who else?"

She hesitated. This sounded much like a test. In a flash, she plucked the bowls off the shelf and put them down without getting the pups to sit. They rushed to the food, slurping the meat hungrily.

"You're not trusting me with a team on my own, are you?"

"The dogs you're to help train are Canadian Inuit dogs. They're freighters, which, as you should know, means they can pull huge loads effortlessly. You don't weigh much. I have to be sure you can handle them."

A curt reply came to her lips, but she bit her tongue to stop it. All he needed to do was to tell her, then let her harness the dogs on her own. But no, this infuriating man had to go and hitch the sled for her. He made her feel like a rookie being checked out.

"Fair enough. What's the name of the lead dogs?"

"Capitor and Tekoone."

Remembering fondly her father's first teachings, she didn't step on the sled runners immediately. Instead, she asked each dog's name. Then she patted the dogs and checked the harnesses and lines.

"All in order here."

She felt proud of the professional way in which she had checked the equipment and acquainted herself with her team. But she was sure his male pride prevented him from telling her so.

"You go on ahead. The trail slopes down for a short distance, then up. After that, it turns sharp right."

So he was checking her out. Calmly, she put her foot on the brake, pulled up the snow hook anchor and wedged it into its holster. The dogs felt the movement and took up the slack on the lines. She released the brake, and the team bounded forward. The sled shot over the fresh powdery snow. Although she had expected the quick start, she had to cling to the sled's handlebar to maintain her balance, so great was the power of that four-dog team. He was probably disappointed that she hadn't fallen off.

In the exhilarating burst of speed, she forgot he was behind her, watching her every move. The air rushed past her face, tugging at her long hair straying from underneath her toque. A deep joy swept through her as trees became a mere blur on each side of the trail and the sled left a cloud of snow in its wake. The only sounds were the swish of the runners and the eager panting of the dogs. The sky had grown lighter, though the sun wouldn't appear for another couple of hours.

She glanced over her shoulder and saw his sled following a few hundred yards behind. Their encounter this morning surfaced in her mind. Despite the cold, the memory of his touch brought a flush to her cheeks. Reason quickly took over. There was no denying the attraction to each other. They were both adults. It was normal. She could live with it, just like the harmless flirting and exchanges that took place among the young men and women at the races she used to attend. A deep friendship with him might not be possible, at least not in the foreseeable future. She would treat the attraction in the same way as she did with her male friends... lightly.

Wrapped in thought, she failed to pay attention to what the speeding sled was doing. Her eyes scanned the trail ahead, too late to avoid a big bump directly in her path. The left runner hit it and the sled jumped a foot in the air. She gripped the handlebar to stop herself from being pitched off.

Damn! That was what happened when she let her mind wander. If she wanted to make a success of her stay in the North, she'd better not think about Scott in any other way than a man whose skills would be useful to her. All those other wayward ideas she had must be curbed. The job came first.

Almost immediately after surviving the near spill, the sharp bend in the trail was upon her. Her foot missed the bar between the runners that lowered the two brake paddles with their metal points. The command she yelled to the dogs had no effect. They never slackened their pace. In their enthusiasm, they probably didn't even hear her. Doing what they enjoyed most, running in the crisp air with the wind in their fur, was all that mattered to them.

Instinct took over; she bent her knees to give herself more leverage and leaned into the bend. Just as the sled was about to shoot off into the bush, she gave a powerful kick with her left foot, at the same time twisting the handlebar to her right.

With the strength of the kick, the sled was thrown back onto both runners. The dogs accelerated out of the turn, and she let out the deep breath she had been holding.

That was too close for comfort. She bit her lip. Her heel smarted from striking the frozen ground. It would hurt for a few days. At least she hadn't lost the sled and plunged headlong into the snow. In the end, she relaxed, and hoped her boss hadn't been near enough to see her stylish maneuver.

The rest of the outing was an anticlimax in comparison. On her arrival back at the kennels, she brought her team to a halt. With the sled secured by its snow hook, she went up to her lead dogs.

"Good dog, Capitor. Good dog Tekoone. That was great! I think we're going to get along just fine, you and I."

She straightened just as he pulled into the yard.

"What the hell do you think you were doing back there?"

Even the dogs didn't snarl as nastily as he did.

"Back where?" Her innocent look masked her agitation. He was sure to chew her out. "At the bend."

"I didn't realize it was so close until I was right on it."

"You weren't focused on the task. It was obvious." Fury tainted his voice.

"Okay. So I got a little distracted." She heated up. "I managed to stay on the runners, didn't I? Besides, it was my first time out on an unknown trail."

"Which brings me to the real question. Why did you want to come and learn with me when you obviously can handle a sled even when you're not paying attention?"

Anger flared in his eyes. His scowl etched the rugged lines of his face deeper. She took a breath, refusing to be influenced by how magnificent he looked in his anger.

"Why? We seem to have been through this before. It's getting kind of stale. I came because you hired me in response to your ad. How was I to know it was you? You didn't even put your name in it." Her heart was beating fast and not simply from the exhilaration of the ride. "Rather than criticize me, maybe you should tell me how I can improve my technique."

His features relaxed. His anger appeared to evaporate in the face of her unruffled logic. He glanced away for an instant. "First, you must constantly monitor the trail ahead. Watch the lead dogs. They're running more than twenty-four feet up front. When they begin to swing to one side, you know then you have to use the brake and keep the sled straight halfway into the turn before shifting your weight. You must be prepared for anything that's ahead."

She nodded her agreement.

His momentary calm dissipated in a blink of an eye. "Damn it all, woman! Of course you know it! Tell me, what's your real reason for coming here?"

"I'll say it again. I always wanted to take a handler's job and learn more about dog management and long distance racing. One day, I intend to enter the Iditarod." She did her best to ignore his angry outburst and thought she saw a flicker of a smile hover over his lips.

"You don't fool me. Nobody gives up a good job to come and work for a pittance in what amounts to a slave labor camp."

Her laughter burst out. "One person's labor camp is another person's professional development school. I love dogs and sledding and racing. I'm also aware that it's become big business. Nowadays, only competitors with solid training make the grade and win races. And with that comes the sponsorships. Fate decided I wasn't going to get that training from my dad."

A short silence followed her words.

"Yes. And I'm sorry about that. But, I'm not like your father."

"I'm well aware of that." Startled, she looked at him. No, he was unlike any father figure she could imagine. And she didn't react to him in that way. Her breath rasped in her chest. She held his smoke-gray stare, then let her eyes roam over the lean planes of his face. A touch of frost clung to his eyebrows. She blushed and concentrated on unhitching the team.

"So why me? There are plenty of other mushers. Some of them are women."

"How many times to do we have to go over this? Yours was the only ad in the magazine."

"But I signed the email. Once you knew it was me, why didn't you change your mind? Since you seem to know everything, you must have heard that I'm a difficult old cuss. Those jerks from the media are always going on about it."

"Why should I have changed my mind? You confirmed I was hired. I saw no reason to back out. I'm here because of the dogs. Everything else is secondary, something I can work around. Now, if you'll excuse me, I've got to take care of my team."

She sensed his eyes boring into her back as she moved to the wheel-dogs standing quietly in front of the brush bow of the sled.

"It wouldn't bother me if you decided to quit right now. I'm a loser anyway," he said.

Her head snapped up. "People are only losers if they believe they are."

"Very smart." His tone was bitter and sarcastic.

"Smart, but true. If you want to turn things round, you must concentrate on your training. Like right now, not when the snow melts."

His jaw dropped. "This season's got off to a lousy start." He grumbled loud enough for her to hear him. "No snow till yesterday, and I've got myself a sassy female handler who's an expert in psychoanalysis."

She stifled her angry reply. Or maybe the laughter that wanted to erupt. He wanted her to lose her temper, and she was determined not to let him have that satisfaction. He gave her every reason to hate him. No doubt he would derive some twisted pleasure from seeing her storm off to pack her things and leave him to his misery. Nobody was going to cower her in that way.

If it were possible to measure it, her stubbornness probably equaled his own. Never before had she backed down from a challenge, and she was not about to do so now. Yes, there were other mushers, possibly more mild-mannered ones, but something about Scott Walsh appealed to her. Underneath his churlish exterior was a strong, vibrant man, a man she was drawn to despite everything, despite herself. To discover that other man became an obsession. She walked over to the kennel building and came back with a bowl of fat.

His sled fully loaded, he headed down the trail in the direction of the creek on his routine run. Sunshine spilled over the mountains and valleys. The snow-laden pines sparkled with a million needlepoints of light, like so many precious stones carelessly scattered by an invisible hand.

Her eyes followed him until he disappeared. The serene beauty began to appease the jumble of emotions he had left her with. To keep her mind off her recurring thoughts, she threw herself into her new duties. She was here to do a job, to learn all she could, but it was difficult to concentrate.

After a few minutes, she stopped work and leaned on the shovel she was using. Of course, she could give in to his demands and return home. But then she'd have to admit to being a complete failure. True, she could buy fresh dogs and enter the racing circuit without the benefit of his expert instruction. It would take a while longer to get to the top, since she would doubtless make every mistake in the book, but she was confident she'd eventually work her way up to the Iditarod. Yet, she was adamant about staying the course. She told herself it was because she had a contract to honor, but that was only fooling herself. Although she was reluctant to admit it, the real reason why she was still here was because of the intriguing man she had seen vanish over the distant snow-covered ridge.

"Don't be stupid, Chris." Speaking aloud to herself delighted the dogs, who howled a reply. She resumed her duties and got more acquainted with her charges.

Early in the afternoon, the light rapidly dimmed and nightfall approached fast. Anxiety began to gnaw at her. He hadn't returned yet. Carefully measuring broth water and meat, she fed all the dogs before going into the cabin to prepare dinner.

The kitchen tasks soothed her nerves, but the calm didn't last long. She soon found herself glancing out of the window, and straining to hear the sound of his return.

CHAPTER FIVE

Scott tipped the dregs of his hot chocolate into the snow and looked up at the darkening sky. No matter how he tried, he couldn't shake Chris from his mind. Never before had he encountered such a stubbornly opinionated young woman. Panic rose in him. He didn't want her here. His peaceful existence was being disturbed. But there was no other way. He had to accept the situation. A musher can't race without a handler. These past couple of years had been hellish.

The dogs responded to her as if she had always been there to take care of them, and that rankled. Her ease with the boisterous dogs served to remind him that lately he had been less than patient with them. A feeling akin to shame swept over him. He walked to the dogs laying in the snow and hugged each of them, murmuring soothing words. They reacted eagerly. Love for his furry companions brought him a measure of contentment. He promised himself he wouldn't let anything interfere with his relationship with them and set off on the homeward trail.

***

Scott's return created a ruckus in the kennels. The cabin door opened and light spilled out in the yard. He watched her slim silhouette as she shrugged into her parka. Hunched over the sled, he applied the brake. By the look of it, she'd been waiting for him, but that was what a good handler was supposed to do, wasn't it? Nothing more.

She came forward to meet him.

"Hi there! I was getting worried."

He gulped cold air and began unhitching the dogs. Only after the dogs were in their pens, watered and fed, did he mumble an acknowledgment of her presence. "Thanks for coming out to help."

"Don't mention it." She headed for the cabin and called over her shoulder. "Supper is on the go."

Her nerves were frayed, he reckoned. He recognized a certain eloquence in her back. She must be biting her tongue to stop herself from putting him in his place. The idea that she must be truly concerned because he was late unsettled him.

He shuffled around the cabin, picking up items and setting them down again and again. There was only so much he could do after he added wood to the stove and trimmed the wick in the oil lamp. Anything to take his mind off the question that had gnawed at him all day. Why was he bothered by the presence of this woman?

No one would know he had spent most of his time sitting on a fallen tree by the creek. His mind had been trying to come up with the best way of telling Chris Taylor she must leave. Now that he was here with her, watching her bend over the cookstove, and admiring how the lamplight fell on the coppery sheen of her hair, he couldn't put the words together.

No doubt, he was turning into the deadbeat musher the media painted him. As soon as they'd discover a girl worked for him, they'll crucify him. Already he could hear taunts of Scott Walsh is incapable of hiring a man to handle his dogs.

His eyes stole a glance at her, irremediably drawn to the graceful curves of her legs, utterly feminine despite the thick wool pants she wore. His hands almost crushed a can he was holding. It was all he could do to curb the urge to reach out and touch the hair that cascaded to her shoulders. A craving to kiss her overwhelmed him. He fidgeted.

Still with her back to him, she said, "That's three times you've picked up that can of jam. Do you want me to open it for you?"

The unexpected sound of her voice jolted him.

"Uh?"

"Why don't you wash up? The dinner is almost ready. I hope you're hungry. I've made a mountain of hamburgers and mashed potatoes. There's a rice pudding in the oven. Unfortunately, I didn't find any raisins to put in it."

"I hate raisins."

"Funny. Me too."

He almost laughed. The table was quickly set. They ate in silence for a while.

"You said you'd be gone two hours." She spoke casually. "Why so late?"

"Why so concerned?"

"I was beginning to think I might have to call out the Royal Canadian Mounted Police."

"Very clever." He threw her a dark look and returned his attention to his plate. He cleared his throat. "If you must know, I stopped awhile to think. We've got to talk."

"Whenever you feel like it."

Her flippant tone hit home. His jaw contracted. Undeterred, she went to the stove to refill their coffee cups.

The aromatic smell tantalized his nostrils. He took a sip. "I'll give you that. You make the best coffee this side of the Elias Range."

"Thank you for the compliment, sir."

He focused his attention on the oil lamp, which threw their two strangely shaped shadows on the log wall behind them. A cloak of unhappiness settled over him, painfully aware that something was missing from his life. He couldn't even remember the last time he had held a woman in his arms. A powerful need to bury his face in the silken fragrance of her hair came over him.

In a gesture of irritation, he ran his fingers through his hair and pushed back his chair. He was going soft. That's what domestication did to a man.

"Look, I... I don't think this is going to work out."

"The job? I think it will."

"No. You don't understand. You're a woman."

"That, I'm already aware of."

"And I am a man."

"Yes. I noticed that too."

His tanned face took on a darker shade.

"You're being deliberately awkward."

"No, I'm not. Not any more than you. If you mean we cannot live side by side in this cabin, you're mistaken. People to do it all the time. When Marcia and I were in our senior year at college, we shared a house with two guys. Despite what you might think, nothing happened. If doesn't bother me, I don't see why it should bother you."

"Sharing a big house in the city is one thing. How do you account for the needs of a male and female in a cramped cabin like this?"

"You think our base animal instincts will get the better of us? Are you assuming I won't be able to resist an urge to go to bed with you?"

"Perhaps. Or, if I want to go to bed with you."

"I don't recall that being part of my job description, Mr. Walsh."

"You're a very attractive woman."

"Would you have preferred if I'd been lumpy and warty?"

"Frankly, yes."

"Well, I think you're a handsome man. Now that we've recognized that we're mutually attracted... I mean attractive, could we talk business?"

"Sure. I'll agree to pay your expenses and give you a month's salary. Get packed. I'll drive you to town. I'll even pay for a room at the motel. Like that, you'll be right there when the bus comes through in the morning on its way back to Whitehorse."

She blanched. "The lodge is closed and I'm not leaving. There's absolutely no reason for me to go. You can't have any complaints about my ability to do the job, so you have no reason to fire me. Discrimination on sexist grounds is against the constitution."

"Nothing like that in the constitution."

"How do you know there is not? Nobody reads it except lawyers."

"This is getting crazy!"

"Quite definitely. And as you've recognized already, I'm just as stubborn as you."

He ran his fingers through his hair. "We're totally isolated here. There are no amenities nearby."

"There's Fletcher Creek down the road."

"Fletcher Creek is deader than dead in winter. It has one store and one closed lodge."

"Anyway, who said I wanted amenities?"

"All women do."

"Really? On what does Professor Scott Walsh base such a scientific observation? You've made a lifelong study of women's needs, I presume?"

"It wasn't necessary. The reason is you're driving me mad!" His voice rose a notch.

"I'm sorry. That was not my intention. And please, don't yell."

"What if something happens between us?" He dropped his voice to a hoarse whisper.

She remained silent for a full minute. Renoir, unused to raised voices, got up and came to nuzzle her hand. To calm him, she stroked his rough-textured fur. "Nothing need happen between us. I'll attend strictly to my duties and for the rest of the time, I'll keep out of your way. We can eat separately, if that would make you feel better."

He stared at her and Renoir at her side.

"Even my dog is siding with you. Since it looks as though you're staying... for the time being at any rate, we'd better work things out. We must go over my training schedule."

"Good."

"I'll be away most of the time." He spoke as if being away was the most appealing idea he'd had all day.

He took a sheaf of papers from a drawer. For the next half hour, they forgot their heated exchange and worked on the kennel routine. They discussed rotating the young dogs and the experienced dogs on the teams and argued about various combinations. Renoir sat at his side and put his paw on his thigh.

"Okay, pal, we're all friends again." He stroked the dog's broad head.

In the end, he threw down his pen in exasperation. "It's no good. I just don't have enough dogs to operate a real training program, let alone enter a big race."

"But the dogs you have are first rate. Just select which race is most important for you to win, and forget about the others."

"Important for me to win?" He echoed her last words as if hearing the expression for the first time. "You expect me to win after the losing streak I've gone through?"

"Of course! Why else are we doing all this hard work?"

"If you must know, I haven't won a race in years." He gave the sigh of a defeated man.

"You've got to believe in yourself and your dogs. Otherwise, they'll sense your lack of spirit and will just trot along mechanically."

"Do you charge extra for the pep talk?" A grim smile stretched his lips.

"See, I knew you had the will. All you need to do now is get out of that negative groove you've gotten yourself into."

"What do you know about things like that?"

"How do you think I felt after burying my father and mother, along with my aunt and uncle? And the injured dogs we had to put down. Before the tragedy, I used to sing to my dog team when I took part in the junior races. And the dogs ran like the wind. The first time I stepped on the runners after the accident, I couldn't sing. The dogs didn't understand why, and turned to look at me. I saw the unconditional love in their eyes. Because of that, I made the effort. I sang again."

"I used to sing to my dogs. Haven't done so in a long time."

"Tomorrow, take a team out and sing to them as you go along. Tell yourself and them over and over that you're going to win the Iditarod. I know you will. I have faith in you."

"Although I've signed on, it's not certain I can even enter the Iditarod Trail race. I've only got twelve huskies I can put in the race. Nowadays, mushers run fourteen nowadays. I just couldn't afford to breed more dogs the past couple of years."

"Can't your Canadian Inuit dogs run too? You have fourteen adults."

"Thirteen available actually. Arnavik has been bred. She'll have her pups in mid-December."

"Oh great! A whole bunch of new puppies."

"Yeah. The problem is that Inuit dogs are much slower than Alaskans and Siberian huskies. They'll go on forever under even the worst conditions, but they aren't built for speed. I have them because of an idea of establishing an outfitting business. You know, taking tourists out by dog sled. People pay good money to come to the North for wilderness adventures. A woman is doing it over by Donek Lake. She has a good business."

"You sound like you've given up on the idea."

He shrugged his broad shoulders. "On my own? Not feasible."

"Concentrate on racing this year while planning your business."

"Stupidly enough, I signed on for the Yukon Quest. The toughest sled dog race on earth. Can't do."

"Why not? The Yukon Quest is in February and the Iditarod starts the first weekend of March. You'd have three weeks and a bit in between."

"Chris, you make it sound so easy, but I still only have twelve dogs and need fourteen."

It was the first time he had said her name, and it surprised him to find he liked it.

"Twelve good dogs are better than fourteen mediocre ones. My father always criticized mushers who start with a lot of dogs, just so they can drop off those who get injured or aren't running fast enough, so they finish with only those who can keep up the pace. In fact, they're really wasting time at the beginning. A team goes only as fast as its slowest dog. But if you have high-ranking dogs, you don't need to drop any of them off and readjust the team."

"Your father taught you all that?" His admiration was sincere.

"Yes. And I've watched the Iditarod on TV. And I handled for my father when he and my uncle were racing in it."

"What the hell do you need me for? You can learn everything you want on your own. You wouldn't have to put up with my grouchy moods." He'd said the same words before, but this time there was a touch of ironic humor in his voice. His repressed rage had faded.

"Forget about my going away, will you? I may have picked up a few useful ideas along the way, but nothing can replace hands on experience."

"The dogs might be too tired to do both races."

"Why don't you take your Inuit dog team for the Yukon Quest?"

"Do you realize I'd be competing against mushers with the fastest Alaskan huskies in the North?"

"It's a difficult race over rough terrain. Maybe the slower, more reliable Canadian Inuit dogs would do better in the long haul than the lighter huskies."

"Nobody has raced them before."

"Maybe not raced but generations of nomadic Inuit people used them to travel the Arctic. They raced between themselves for fun. Nothing new on this earth, people and animals always race to be first. I think the dogs have all the stamina you need. When you're racing across a thousand miles of snow, ice and bad weather, endurance is more important than speed. Isn't twelve the maximum on a team?"

"It's been brought up to fourteen."

"To cater to the less resistant huskies, I suppose. So you'd have thirteen."

"You're a pretty convincing talker, you know that, Ms. Taylor? All the same, I can train one team thoroughly, but not two."

"What about me? Isn't that why I'm here?"

"And who'd look after the pups and the older dogs? There aren't enough hours in the day."

"I can get up earlier in the mornings. According to your schedule, the pups are to run behind a sled pulled by the five veterans. You don't race those, correct?"

He nodded his head.

"Since we don't go very far, it doesn't take up too much time. On that day, the racing team can have a short run, with no weight in the sled. We can concentrate on speed. The next day, the pups and veterans rest, and I take the Alaskans for a long, fully loaded run."

"But I'll be away as much as one week at a time."

"Great! Like that, we won't fight so much."

He gave a dry laugh. "You've got ready answers for everything, don't you?"

"Somebody's got to make things happen. If not, we may as well just limit ourselves to giving sled rides down at the seniors' home. It's about time you faced up to the situation and got to work."

"See what I mean?" This time, there was a twinkle in his gray eyes.

"It's agreed, then? I train one team."

"How big a team can you manage?"

"That I don't know until I try."

"Until the huskies learn to obey the commands from you, you should start with only four at a time. I'll take your advice and take the Inuit dogs to the Yukon Quest, since it's the first to be run. Hell! I'd like to see what those dogs can do. These arctic dogs could pull heavy loads for hours and think nothing of it. We'll give it all we've got."

"Hallelujah!" She stood up and moved away from the table. "Since we've agreed to start earlier, I guess I'd better turn in."

Amazed, he watched her disappear into her room. For the first time in months, his spirits were lifted. The blood tingled in his veins. An insane desire to hold her in his arms swept over him. He knew she'd respond to him. He had read it in her sea-colored eyes.

He returned to the problem of racing the Yukon Quest. To no avail. A dull fury rose in him. This was impossible. He had to be able to devote himself to nothing but strategy. And here he was dreaming about the auburn-haired woman in the other room. This was no way to win races. He had sworn never to fall again under the spell of a woman.

Yet it was a woman who had rekindled his excitement for racing. Sending her away wasn't going to help. In silence, he rolled her name on his lips. A name with a sharp edge to it, though belonging to a woman so soft it drove him wild.

He loaded wood into the stove, then took Renoir back outside to his pen. Training, training, he repeated to himself. Nothing else. Don't think, just train. When he settled down for the night, stretched out on the couch, he kept tossing and turning, repeating the mantra, train, train. An hour later, his brain was finally numb enough to let him sink into a deep, dreamless sleep.

Chapter Six

S leep eluded her, too. Systematically reviewing the evening's conversation, she wanted to figure out what had happened to her boss. Maybe she overstepped the mark by taking over cooking duties. He was clearly a man long used to living on his own. In a way, there was nothing else she could have done. It was absurd not to fix a meal for two, knowing he'd be back soon, ravenously hungry. No, that was not it. Nor was it because she had been so anxious about him. She had hidden that feeling well, and he couldn't have seen how she had wanted to reach out and smooth away the creases marring his forehead.

A tremor quivered deep inside her. A battle won was not the end of the war. The last thing she intended to do was quit or be forced out simply because she was a woman. Already she felt she belonged. But if he made her name sound like a caress every time he called her, she might come undone. At the memory of the way he looked at her, heat suffused her skin. Her cheeks reddened. That was silly, stupid even, since she was alone in the privacy of the bedroom.

With her provocative remarks, she had rekindled some fire in him. It was enough for her to hope he was finally accepting her. His enthusiastic talk about the races, his entrusting her with the race training of a team, was a giant step toward a sound working arrangement.

***

The darkness studded with thousands of diamonds reigned over the mountains. They finished the first round of the kennels. They bumped into each other as together they reached the door of the cabin.

Scott grinned, "After you."

The hoarseness in his voice didn't go unnoticed by her ears. She hurried inside and removed her headlamp and her parka.

While she busied herself with the breakfast, she searched for something neutral to say, something that would not break the fragile truce. Although he hadn't yet spoken a word, he didn't appear to be having second thoughts after last night's discussion.

A small hope in her heart, she put sausages in the pan and picked up the bread knife. His eyes followed her. Immediately, she was struck by the domesticity of the scene. Her imagination ran wild for a second while she imagined herself living like this forever. When her brain responded with an unequivocal yes, she became frightened. She scolded herself and asked silently, What on earth am I doing?

He broke the silence. "I've decided to do a short run with the Yukon Quest team. One day out, one day back."

That's not what he had agreed to last night, but she sensed his agitation and didn't object. He wasn't talking about sending her away, but he doubtless felt the need to get away, to put some distance between them.

"Very well. While you're gone, I'll take teams of four Alaskan Huskies each day for two hours. In that way, all of them will run at least once and I'll learn their characters. Which dogs can lead?"

"Singarnak and Pinghasuet, but only when they are together. Itirit is a smart little female, but I haven't had time to try her out. There's Nunii. He shows leadership qualities, but he is a bit young to go in front of a team."

"What about Tioralak?"

"He's shy. He gets nervous when he's got dogs behind him. He likes being in the wheel position so there's only the sled behind him."

"I guess I'll find out who's okay in front. Maybe I'll have to train more leaders."

"It's a big job training leaders."

"Not really. Dogs are always eager to please their teacher."

After a pensive silence, he looked up. "True, but it doesn't mean they can all stand at the front for a long run."

"Let me try."

"Sure."

They sat in companionable silence. She noticed he kept stealing glances at her.

"Your hair...."

"My hair?"

"Is that your natural color?"

"Dark auburn? Yes, of course. That's what I was born with. And I don't wear make up."

A repressed smile puckered his lips, and she burst out laughing.

He looked abashed. "Alright, I'm a jerk, but it's so shiny, I was wondering..."

"It's usually women who do want to know what brand I use to color it."

Now he was going to say something about being beautiful. All men did.

But not him.

"I'll pack what I need. Go ahead and do your work."

About to utter a tart reply, she pursed her lips, remembering her promise to put up with anything, or almost anything.

"Let me prepare you two days of rations. I saw some dehydrated dinners in the cupboard. If you'd mentioned it last night, I could have opened some cans and frozen the contents in wax cloth bags."

"Cloth bags?"

"Much lighter and easier to pack than cans. Reusable, so better for the environment."

He looked stunned. "Next time. Thanks all the same."

"Do you have your cell phone?"

He looked at her as if she came from Mars. Then laughed. "Ain't that city girl talk!"

She frowned. "Oh... sorry. I forgot. No reception."

"No reception, nothing, zip. This is the wilderness, not the city."

Red crept up her face. "So, I forgot for a moment." She took a deep breath. "Don't forget to leave me an itinerary of your trip."

"I'm not a kid, for hell's sake!"

But she was already outside. She zipped her parka and jammed her toque onto her head. Her heart beat faster. The temptation to go back in and face him was strong. The man had been on his own for so long, he wasn't used to leaving an itinerary behind as a safety precaution, or to have someone care for his material welfare. She'd ignore his outburst. The headlamp cord kept brushing her face. In annoyance, she removed the headband to untangle it. Momentarily blind, she tripped over Nunii's chain and sprawled ungracefully in the snow. The big dog jumped up and pawed and licked her. Her laughter encouraged the dog even more. "Okay, okay! Down boy! That'll teach me to keep my mind on task, right, Nunnii?" She regained her feet, only to be caught in the glare of her boss' headlamp.

"You hurt?"

"Of course not. I just didn't expect so much friendly attention."

"You're not heavy enough. The dogs can easily knock you down."

Did she detect a note of concern under the fierceness of his tone? "I tripped, if you want to know. It could happen to anyone in the dark."

Gathering up her lamp, she stormed off to the kennel building. Inside its friendly warmth, she touched a match to the oil lamp and turned the wick up a notch to throw more light. In no time, she had water for the broth boiling on the propane stove.

The door opened and Scott came in, along with a burst of cold air. He hung his parka on a nail and began collecting the dog food he intended taking on the trip.

Despite herself, her eyes drifted to his tall, muscular frame. He scooped up the forty-pound box of frozen meat with the effortless grace of a well-coordinated athlete.

He looked at her. "Something the matter?"

His brusque question made her flinch.

"Uh... I wanted to ask about refilling the kerosene stove."

"The fuel is in the lean-to next door. There's a funnel on the peg above it. Switch off the stove first. One tank lasts thirty hours, but it's best to refill every night. And don't forget to check the diesel level in the generator."

A lesson followed on how to switch off and relight the stove, as well as how to restart the generator. To avoid making a mistake, she carefully wrote down the instructions.

When the necessary food and equipment were stowed in the sled bag, he hitched up the dogs and let them mill around at the end of their long lines.

"Why aren't you hitching them up two by two, in tandem?"

He smiled. "They like the fan hitch better. The first seven dogs are hooked directly to the sled with different lengths of lines so they can regroup in twos when we're on a narrow trail and open up when we're on a lake or river. The other six are tied in the same fashion to the end of the long, central gangline."

"Don't they get tangled up?"

"Not too much. They stick to their places pretty well."

"That's the way the Inuit people hitch their dogs, isn't it?"

"Yes, but on the open tundra they don't have to worry about narrow trails, so all the lines are tied directly to the sled and almost all are of equal length."

"I'm amazed they're not agitating to get going."

"That's the way they are. I've also reinforced that in their training. They know we're going. They also know how to conserve energy and pace themselves. When I give the signal, they'll give a burst of speed for about a quarter mile, then they'll settle into their cruising gait."

"That will carry them for miles and miles."

"You got it."

His pride in his dogs showed on his face. She saw a fleeting happiness on his face at her admiration for his well-trained team.

He whistled twice. The dogs' ears pricked up and all of a sudden, snow was sprayed in all directions as they leaned into the harnesses. Excited yelps only rose from those dogs not going out. The team of Canadian Inuit dogs made their spectacular departure in total silence.

For a long while, she stared after him down the now empty trail, until the biting cold cut short her reverie. "I care for the man, yet he's the most obnoxious person I've ever met. How do you figure that out, dogs?" A few delighted throaty sounds answered her. The dogs kept up the conversation until they were all fed and watered.

When she went into the cabin after running one team, she found his scribbled route on the table. She smiled at this small victory. Aware of the short daylight, she snatched a sandwich and a glass of milk. Tomorrow, she'd pack herself a lunch so she wouldn't interrupt her day.

It was only the next day, after she'd returned with the last team of huskies, that she realized the cabin was low on firewood. She looked in the woodshed. The smell of resin filled her nostrils. Two chainsaws sat on a bench. Apart from that, the shed was empty. Outside, a tall stack of heavy logs extended to the trees on the far side of the yard.

The smaller chainsaw would do her well. She inspected it, trying to recall the starting instructions. It was simple, really. Switch on the choke and pull the starter cord. Nothing happened. She tried again, and again. Her arm became sore and sweat pearled on her forehead. The saw stubbornly refused to start. She repeated the operation with the other machine, with the same lack of success. Discouraged, she leaned against the door frame to recover her breath and think of what to do next.

She unhooked the lantern and examined the ground. Some small pieces lay here and there, not quite enough to fill the wood box, though enough to burn for a few hours. The weather had turned relatively mild. As long as there was some heat, she'd survive.

Gathering the small pieces of wood took longer than she had expected. In the end, the supply in the wood box was still depressingly low. Finally, she took an ax, her headlamp, and went into the forest. Surely she would find some dead wood. Luck was with her when she found a fallen tree with enough branches of a size she could cut. Back home, she often cut the frozen meat for the dogs up in that fashion, just like it was here, so she was familiar enough with the use of an ax.

With a good store of wood, she was just beginning to relax enough to think about making dinner, when a crackling sound came from the corner of the room. Puzzled, she looked up and saw a light on the radiophone. She had recognized it as such on her arrival and meant to ask her boss if he was collecting antiques. To her amazement, this one worked.

A voice came from the speaker. "Hi Boreal Kennels! Byron Murdoch, Omega Beta calling. Is anyone there? Over."

A museum she had visited a long time ago had given a demonstration of a radiophone. This was no museum piece. She smiled and picked up the mike. "Oh, hi Byron! It's Chris Taylor here. Reading you loud and clear."

"I repeat. Boreal Kennels? This is Byron Murdoch, Omega Beta calling. Is anyone there? Over."

"Yes, Chris here," she shouted.

"Chris, if you can hear me, press the talk button on the microphone, then speak. Over."

Red-faced, she promptly pressed her finger on the button on the hand piece of the mike. "Hi Byron! It's me, Chris. Sorry. I didn't know how to use the thing." There was a moment of silence. "Byron, are you still there?"

"Well, howdy-do, Chris! You've got to say 'over' when you've done speaking, otherwise I don't know when you're in receiving mode and let go of the button. Over."

"Okay, I get the hang of it now. Over."

"Good. What's the old bear doing? Over."

"Gone for two days. He's due back tonight, fortunately. Over."

"Why fortunately? Something wrong? Over."

"I've a confession to make. I don't know how to start the chainsaw."

"If you're out of wood, I'll come up and show you how to use the chainsaw."

"I was a girl scout in a previous life. I went into the forest and picked up dead wood."

"That's my girl! I knew you would manage no matter what. Have you heard from Charlie yet?"

"Who's Charlie?"

"He's our resident radio watchdog. A nice old guy who runs a regular sked. He calls every isolated cabin once a day to make sure no one's in need."

"He may have called last night when I was out watching the northern lights."

"It was quite a sight, wasn't it? If you need help with the wood, let me know."

"I sure will. Once I know how the thing starts, I can do the rest. How do I work this radiophone? I don't want to look stupid again."

"You never looked stupid."

"Oh yeah, I did, like when I asked him if he had his cell phone."

Byron couldn't hide his mirth. "He has something about technology, not that it matters around here, since we have no reception except for the office. Conservation has its own tower. He won't even carry a satellite emergency beacon on the Iditarod."

He went over the instructions for operating the set. Still laughing at Byron's humorous parting remarks, she set down the microphone.

"That thing's not a toy!" Scott's voice boomed across the room.

Her shoulders stiffened.

"If you miss gossiping on the phone, you better consider leaving. The radio is only used for essential calls and in emergencies."

"What's the good is it if I don't know how to use it? Which is what I've just learned from your friend Byron. Had a good trip?"

Her honey-peppered-with-sarcasm tone was meant to combat his aggressive mood. Her heart rate sped up as she stared at his wind-tousled hair, ruddy cheeks and a two-day growth on his chin. His powerful presence dominated the room.

He raked his hair with his hand. "The trip? Good, I guess." He abruptly crossed the room to the bathroom.

She grinned and filled a jug from the stove's hot water tank. "I've got warm water for you to wash up."

His hand came out and took the jug from her. The door closed behind him.

"You're welcome."

The door reopened, wider this time. His head appeared. "Thanks." The door shut again.

She added wood to the stove and examined the cold storeroom to see what she could prepare for dinner. If she wasn't mistaken, he had been overcome by the insane desire to kiss her, but obviously his willpower quenched it.

Chapter Seven

Scott splashed the water into the basin and set about removing two days' worth of trail grime and stubble. He washed vigorously, as if wanting to erase his inner turmoil.

Her taunting smile was imprinted on his mind. Try as he may, he couldn't suppress the desire to take her in his arms. It was infuriating! He was, and always had been, in control... until she arrived. To let her stay on was a big mistake. But he couldn't race if she wasn't there to help. He couldn't always rely on the kindness of Byron to look after the dogs while away on training runs. The local youths weren't interested in working for him, not since he no longer was the conquering hero, not since he chewed their heads off a few times too many.

Grudgingly, he recognized that she had revived long dormant hopes in him. Her calm assurance that he could again win had shaken him out of his depressed state. She made him ashamed of his former negative attitude.

The melodious tones of her voice filtered through the door. For a second, he thought she must be talking aloud. Then he remembered it must be the time for Charlie's sked. He opened the door intending to tell her about Charlie and checked himself in time; he was naked. He closed the door none too gently, but not without getting a whiff of meat stew. No need to bother to explain the radio calls to her. The woman worked everything out for herself as it was. And he mustn't forget that he was no longer the sole occupant of the cabin. His stomach rumbled with hunger.

When her laughter reached his ears, he bit his lip and pressed his forehead against the wall, overcome by an ardent desire to throw the door open and seize her...

Enough! He shook himself and looked at the unfinished shower stall. Perhaps he could fix a bucket of cold water to the top. He was going to need it if he had to live so close to such a tantalizing woman.

She was setting the table when he emerged from the bathroom.

"How did the team perform?"

"Just fine. The dogs didn't want to stop, and when we did, they were up and eager to go long before the rest period was over."

"Where are you going tomorrow?"

"Do I detect a wish to get rid of me?"

"Oh sure. I think I like my solitude better than your long face."

His features tightened. Though he didn't believe she meant to be unkind, it hurt. When she reached out, he expected her to caress his face. Instead, she took the salt shaker from the shelf beside him.

A strained silence followed while they ate their food. She had to remind herself that this was what she had accepted. In good time, he'd talk about his trip. For now, patience was going to be her most needed virtue. Well, maybe not the only one. A slow heat was spreading through her body, setting it ablaze.

From under lowered lashes, she watched him get up from the table. His wide shoulders tapering to narrow hips above long legs sent a quiver in her stomach. Her heart beat faster at his blatant, raw masculinity. She ought to gather the dishes and wash them, but she didn't trust herself to stand close to him.

The meal over, he crouched by the sink, picked up the pail that caught the drain water and carried it outside. No point in starting the dishes until he brought it back.

When he returned, he had a toolbox in one hand and a length of pipe in the other. Half his body disappeared under the sink. For the next half hour, only the clatter of a wrench interspersed by grunts and the odd, muffled curse could be heard. She thought it wise to remove herself to the couch. Strong fumes of adhesive filled the room. To avoid being poisoned, she stood up to open the window to let in the cool pine-scented night air.

He came out grinning from under the sink.

"There we are. Connected to the outside drain. That's the end of carrying that slop pail."

"Wonderful! It's going to be more efficient and save me time."

"I should've done it a long time ago. Since I've got my tools here, I'll go and connect up the washbasin in the bathroom."

While he was fighting with plastic pipes and drain fittings, she washed the dishes. She didn't pull the plug until the bathroom was finished. His hair streaked with a smudge of yellow glue, he came out grinning.

"Can I use the drain now?"

"Go ahead, I'll check for leaks."

With some trepidation, she removed the plug. The dishwater gurgled down the drain hole.

"Wow! No leak!" He danced a few steps.

"Congratulations!"

They looked each other in the eye and laughed at the absurdity of being so excited about a piece of plumbing. That instant imprinted itself on her mind.

"As a matter of fact, I'm staying here tomorrow. I reckon we need some wood cut. Did you hack those spindly pieces from the woodpile?"

"From the forest."

"Why didn't you cut some logs?"

"The..."

"Oh! I bet you didn't know how to use the chainsaw." A smug smile flitted across his lips.

Nettled by his remark, she fired back, "Neither of the confounded things would start."

"You did check the gas, of course?"

Her face turned crimson. Gas! She mentally kicked herself for being so stupid.

"Never mind. I'll show you tomorrow."

Unwilling to trust her voice, she nodded. Their gaze met and held. A fire danced in his eyes. Unable to trust herself, she rose to go to her room. He stood up and blocked her path.

"Tell me, why are you doing all this for me?" His soft voice sent shivers down her back.

"It's my job."

"That's not the whole of it." He put out his hand.

Panic seized her. If he touched her, all her best resolutions would crumble like dry sand. But she didn't move away. His hand took her chin. His thumb gently stroked her smooth skin. Her breath came in short gasps. Without haste, he bent his head. His lips hovered close to hers.

Spellbound, she watched his eyelids grow heavy, his angular features soften. A trembling began deep within her. Alarm bells buzzed in her mind. She opened her lips and murmured against his, "This is not in the contract."

"To hell with the damned contract." His lips had barely grazed hers when he stopped and pressed his eyes closed. She saw him struggle against his mounting passion. With a supreme effort of will, he pulled back. "You're right. You're right." He was mumbling and made an effort to square his shoulders. "Though I can see you want to kiss me as much as I want to kiss you."

"Maybe, but we must stop before..."

"What are you scared of?"

"The attraction between us. I'm here to do a job."

"You're right again. I apologize for trying to take advantage of you."

Astonished that he had caved in without protest, she retired for the night. Her emotions drained, she sat in the center of the big bed. It was the truth. She had wanted that kiss as much as he did, but reason had to prevail.

***

Breakfast and the morning chores passed in a neutral atmosphere, without unnecessary words. Only the discordant call of a jay and the harsh cry of a raven perched on a dog fence could be heard. She watched as he took his team on the trail heading north. She then directed her team toward the south.

A shallow depression in the snow indicated where the trail was. The sled sped up on the virgin trail. Up front, her four huskies, pulling only a light load, easily ate up the miles. Filled with the joy of being in the outdoors, she launched into a song. A couple of dogs turned their heads and gave her a curious look. Nunii in the lead with young Namatuk slackened the pace. She laughed and called to them, "Good dog, Nunii. That's fine, Namatuk."

The huskies resumed the gallop, and she took up her song once more. Later, she lapsed into a contented silence and let the team fall into a lope. Eventually, she ordered a halt.

The two snow hooks dug in, she secured the sled's snub rope to a nearby tree. Not wanting to leave anything to chance, she made doubly sure the knots were all secure. Next, she took stainless steel bowls from the sled bag, scooped snow from beside the trail and half filled them. The dogs' mouth drooled in anticipation as they watched her pour rich broth from the thermos into each bowl.

For a minute or two, the dogs lapped the liquid. Once refreshed, they crouched in the snow, their heads resting on their outstretched paws. From away in the bushes came the animated chatter of whiskey jays.

The thoughts about her boss didn't want to go away. The lack of sleep was confusing her mind. It wasn't that she was shocked or even surprised that he had wanted to kiss her.

What troubled her was why it made her feel so vulnerable. Sitting close to him, her body had clamored for much more than a simple kiss. The emotions he provoked were entirely new to her. Never before had a man affected her this way. He wasn't the first male to make a pass at her, but no other man moved her as deeply as he did.

In the past, she had found it easy to deflect the often inept advances of the men she'd dated. This situation was different. Scott was impossible to ignore. If only her insides wouldn't turn to mush each time he brushed against her or simply looked at her, she might be able to brazen it out. Maybe he sensed how badly she wanted him to kiss her.

Her sketchy experience was no help in knowing how she ought to react. If they made love, should she treat it as a bonus on top of all the professional expertise he was teaching her or consider it as the beginning of a relationship. She shook her head. The first option didn't sit well with her principles. The second was premature and heading for trouble. Life had become very complicated.

With a sigh, she set about picking up the empty bowls. When everything was stowed in the sled bag, she pulled out the snow hooks and pulled the snub rope free. On the return journey, the sun had long dipped below the distant ridge. The once sharply lit landscape had dimmed to a world of blurred shapes.

Somehow, the dogs knew they were homeward bound and trotted with renewed energy. Only the occasional hoot of a snowy owl and the steady swish of the slender runners over the packed snow broke the silence that had settled over the land.

The waning moon threw little light. A dark shadow blotted the white trail ahead. Out of caution, she applied the brake. The dogs were already alerted and were slowing down. She screwed up her eyes. The somber form moved toward them. It had to be a wolf. She clicked the beam of her headlamp on low to avoid spooking him. Without undue movements, she put down a snow hook and pressed it into the snow with her foot.

A wolf! She had never seen a real live wolf before. Fear touched her a fraction of time, then dissipated. There were many fanciful accounts of wolves attacking dogs and people. She remembered distinctly reading in a biology book that wolves stay away from humans. No musher had ever reported being attacked by a wolf, but the dogs might decide to take a run at it. Silently, she dropped the second anchor for added security and stood with both feet on the brake.

The animal advanced to within twenty feet of her lead dogs. The majestic creature stopped and stared directly at her, regal and unblinking. This was his territory, and he was king.

His muzzle appeared gray and white, coated with frost. His eyes, shining a metallic blue in the beam of light, were unwavering. Like the dogs, he had to have dark amber eyes. In the light, they appeared blue. The wolf held his head high, unafraid and disdainful of the dogs. Joy bubbled up inside her. An exhilaration set her pulse beating faster. The primeval beauty of the scene touched her heart. Here in this vast wilderness, this lone wolf was accepting her into his domain.

After several minutes of inspection, the nonchalant wolf stepped off the trail and melted into the trees as silently as he had appeared. For a while longer, she remained enthralled. Her mind superimposed Scott's image on the spot where the wolf had stood. The man, like the regal wolf, possessed a dark, untamed spirit, one that made her shiver with its latent power.

Then, just as quickly, the spell was broken. At a hidden signal, known only to them, the dogs strained in their harness. She yanked out the snow hooks and the sled shot forward. When they reached the spot where the wolf had disappeared, the dogs swerved off the trail and would have followed its tracks had she not yelled a straight ahead command. Her leader, Nunii, tossed her a mischievous glance, hesitated a split second and obeyed. The team wavered and came back into line. The leaders pulled on. The others followed and kept up a furious pace until the dark shape of the cabin appeared in the distance. All the way home, her mind remained filled with the wonder of her encounter with the wolf.

A chorus of envious howls greeted her return. Watering her team, making sure she stroked and patted every dog in the kennel, took up time. His dogs were in the pen. He was back.

The steady whine of a chainsaw from beside the woodshed attracted her attention. Working by the yellowish light of the storm lantern, he was stripped to his pants and thermal undershirt despite the sub-zero temperature. She watched him lift a log from the stack, muscles rippling across his broad chest. The chainsaw sent wood chips flying. The rebel lock of hair that she found so irresistible hung over his forehead. When the log was reduced to stove size, he put the chainsaw down and took up a long-handle splitting ax. Her mouth went dry. She watched him effortlessly split the logs. There was an invisible connection between the fiercely independent wolf she had seen earlier on the trail and the fiercely independent man at work.

When he finished, he threw down the ax and looked up. He grinned when he saw her watching him. "You're back! Did you want to learn how to use the saw?"

"Of course." She dropped her backpack and stepped closer.

"First, check the gas here." He unscrewed a cap for her to peer in the reservoir. "And the chain oil in this one. Put it on the ground and grip the front handle with your left hand. Apply the choke and grip the saw by putting the toe of your boot through the handle at the rear. Now pull on the starter cord."

She bit her lips and did as he said. The chainsaw fired and stopped.

"Good. Take off the choke. It should start this time."

One more tug and the machine burst into life. The next ten minutes were spent in practicing under his critical eye.

"For a woman, you handle that thing pretty well. Let's stack the wood in the shed."

She looked in dismay at the mountain of wood he had cut. Her stomach contracted with hunger. Her legs buckled beneath her.

"Have you watered the dogs?" She hoped he hadn't.

"Yes, all done. I also took the last of the meat out of the freezer."

"What freezer?"

"The one in the lean-to. It's plugged into the generator during the summer."

"I thought you kept the meat in the cache."

"Not in summer, we can't. That's why I have the freezer. Let's get that wood in."

"All right." Her words sounded just as weak as she was.

Steeling herself against the pangs of hunger, she began picking up the cut wood. It was going to be a long job.

Beyond the circle of light, night shrouded the earth in its mystery. The penetrating scent of the freshly split pine logs brought her a measure of comfort.

"What's the matter? You're slowing down." His voice penetrated the fog that was numbing her brain.

"Uh... I need to answer a call of nature."

"Well, you don't need to ask my permission." He was laughing at her.

Nettled, she tried hard to keep her tone light. "I was trying to finish the wood before making dinner."

"I've started it. Dried fish and potatoes. It's all in the oven."

"Good. I'll be back."

"I'll finish this."

"I'm not tired, really."

The defiance in her tone made him smile. "I can see you're dropping with fatigue."

With a shrug, she picked up her pack and ran to the cabin. On opening the door, she was welcomed by a savory smell. Near the stove, rising bread dough was almost overflowing its pan. For a guy who claims he didn't know how to cook, he did pretty well. As she tore open the tinfoil to test the fish with a fork, fragrant steam escaped. Cooked to perfection. So were the potatoes. She removed the crock and put it in the warming oven, then slid the bread pan in. Since bread needs a hot oven, she added more wood to the firebox.

When she finally joined him, in the hope he had finished, he was still stacking the logs in the shed.

"I've taken the food out of the oven and put the bread in. I didn't know you made your own bread."

"Yes. Store bought bread tastes like pasteboard. I like solid, well-risen slices for a sandwich. Unfortunately, I don't always have time to bake."

"If you teach me, I'll be willing to do it. My aunt used to make bread. It was always such a marvelous treat."

He looked at her intently, was about to say something, but apparently changed his mind.

Noting with relief that the heap was almost gone, she picked up a couple more logs. In a matter of minutes, the last piece of wood was brought into the shed. She sighed with relief when he extinguished the lantern and closed the woodshed door.

He picked up his flannel shirt and cap and placed his free hand on her shoulder. "Look at the northern lights."

Their bodies, heated by the hard work, drew together of their own accord. She raised her eyes and gasped as waves of green, pink and white light swept the sky above the mountains. The rapidly moving veils changed color before spreading out to encompass the universe. The mystical dance of the skies with its fairytale display was hypnotizing her, a mere mortal below.

His hand on her shoulder, almost a gesture of possession, sent tremors down her spine. Anguished by her reaction, she had to break the spell.

"I saw a wolf this afternoon out on the trail."

"And you were scared?" His voice betrayed a hint of amusement.

His tone annoyed her. "My only fear was that the dogs would attack it."

"I didn't mean to sound sarcastic."

"It was impressive to see such a wonderful creature close up like that." Her quiet words made him look at her. "And yes, there was fear. Fear of something greater than me, greater than people or things. It was something I couldn't quite grasp. There was a beauty about that proud animal that words can't describe."

"This is the essence of the untamed North."

The eagerness in his voice told her he was sincere and conveyed his love of the land. In that instant, a tacit understanding bonded them. She shivered. He turned her into his arms. His lips searched for hers. His warm breath caressed her cool skin.

This time, she didn't move away. The aurora borealis wove its spell over them, the lights framing his dark head in a halo of swirling color. Waves of delightful sensations rippled through her.

With eyes closed to retain forever the bewitching moment, she heard a faraway howl. A wolf. The eternal song of the North.

Close by, a dog rattled its chain. She shuddered. Her reason fought against her attraction to the man holding her. His lips barely touched hers, but a million volts coursed through her body. The effort to speak came from some unknown recess of her mind.

"The bread's in the oven." What a lame way to break the magic.

He grinned, but maintained his grasp for a second longer, then released her. "Let's go inside."

Only too happy to stay with his people, Renoir pushed past her legs. With the dog underfoot, serving dinner was difficult. She assigned Scott the task of keeping the dog's nose out of the food on the table.

In his arms, it had taken every scrap of her willpower to break the enchantment. Her body had betrayed her. Even now, she was stabbed by unbearable shafts of cravings. A glance over her shoulder caught his face, a closed mask, bent over the dog he was petting.

The two humans ate in silence, their every move watched by the patient canine. Any resentment she may have briefly experienced had disappeared. What had happened out there in the wood yard was natural, the attraction of two healthy young people. Clearly, the contact had troubled him, too. She wasn't ready to give in to her clamoring body, not to a man like him, a man who scorned any notion of commitment. Nor would he even speak of it. His belligerent attitude and his lifestyle were his statement. A man like him would burn her till she was reduced to a small heap of cinders.

He interrupted her thoughts. "Look, we can't go on like this. I wanted to kiss you out there. Hell, I still do. It's just no good. I'll be honest with you. I don't want to be snared in the web of a relationship. I've had my fill of being pinned like a bug to a board."

The bitterness in his voice took her aback. A deep breath steadied her. "Who's talking about a relationship? I won't deny I thought you were going to kiss me, but it was me that broke away. In fact, the last thing I want is a relationship, and I don't go in for cheap sex."

To hide her confusion, she bit into a potato and burned her mouth. She forced herself to look into his eyes while pretending nothing had happened.

A smile of amusement softened his lips. "I'm thankful you don't... go in for cheap sex, that is. You don't have to scald your tongue to prove it."

His reply only riled her further. "I'd like to point out that you made the first move."

"And I apologize. Any man would have difficulty ignoring a beautiful woman like you. But it's only physical. I'll get over it."

She received the compliment with a grimace. "Thanks! I'm just a worker, your employee. Don't forget it."

"How can I? Having you here has completely changed my life."

Unsure whether to take his declaration as a compliment or a criticism, she firmly gripped the tip of her tongue between her teeth. Keep busy, she told herself, and stood up to clear the dishes.

The crackling of the radiophone came as a welcome diversion. Charlie's cheery voice rose above the static. While Scott spoke to him, she hurriedly washed the dishes, then took refuge in her room.

CHAPTER EIGHT

With Scott away on a two-day training run, she had to admit she missed him. Working beside him filled her with contentment, but that made her wary. She was constantly on guard to avoid a repetition of their earlier intimacy, especially since she had caught him stealing glances at her. More than once, she, too, had been guilty of gazing in his direction. His handsome profile, the half smile that sometimes played on his lips, set her heart aflutter. At other less happy times, he wore his old morose expression, tempting her to kiss him until he smiled.

That afternoon, she intended to run the pups on foot to test their obedience. About to open the gate, she pushed back the bolt. A flash of white on the far side of the yard alerted her that something was wrong. With the intuition born of years around dogs, she knew it must be a dog on the loose. She ran over to see if all the dogs were in their enclosure or properly picketed. An empty collar was still attached to a chain. Her lips attempted to whistle the "come-here" command, but her whistling skills weren't up to it. A sharp little face poked from behind the compound fence close to the pine trees.

"Aqua! Come here, Aqua!"

The light-haired dog slunk toward her. She promptly pulled a treat out of her pocket. Aqua came close enough to sniff it. As she was reaching for her, the dog jumped back.

Crouched, treat in hand, she called again. Three times, Aqua came within touching distance, yet not close enough to be caught.

"Patience, patience." She said aloud to herself as much as to the dog. "The next time you almost touch my hand, I'm going to tackle you in the best football style. Now come on, dearest Aqua..."

The shy female approached, neck extended toward the treat. Chris lunged... and missed, landing flat in the snow. Aqua scampered off toward the trees. She picked herself up and brushed the crust of snow from her face. Hoping the escapee would join in, she began to run the other way, calling, "Come'n Aqua. Where's your chasing spirit? Aqua! Here, girl!"

The dog had other priorities in mind and disappeared down the trail. With heart pounding in her chest, she ran to the cabin and snatched up the microphone with shaking hands.

"Hi Charlie! This is Chris, Alpha Dog calling. Do you read me? Over." Please be there, she prayed silently. She repeated the message and pushed the button to the listening mode. Static fizzled in the speaker and Charlie's voice came on.

"Hello, Chris. I read you. You have a problem? Over."

"I've lost a dog. She ran onto the north trail and into the forest. Over."

"Okay. You want me to pass the word around? Over."

"Can you, please? It's young Aqua. She's white with some gray over her back."

"Oh, yes, we know that little hound. She's always running off someplace. A real Houdini. I'll get onto it and tell everyone to keep an eye out for her."

"Thank you so much, Charlie. I'll take a team and go after her. She might come to us and follow. Over and out."

The button back to the listening mode again, she grabbed some food and a thermos of water. Methodically, she packed spare clothes and batteries. Not that she expected to be out long, but she followed common sense safety rules. There were overflows on some creeks and if she had to take a ducking to round up her runaway, she wanted to have dry clothes in reserve.

The choice of dogs for the team was critical. She put dependable Nunii next to Itirit in the lead. Those two were demonstrating remarkable leadership qualities. Then Navut, as Aqua, had a particular liking for him and was tethered next to him. Soon, she had six reliable dogs hitched up. Just as she was about to set off, a snowmobile driven by Byron roared into the yard.

"Byron! I don't have time to talk. I've got a missing dog."

"I know. I heard it over the radio. That's why I'm here. Did you want to go with me on the snowmobile?"

"I've got my team hitched up. Aqua is likely to come to the dogs. The noisy machine might scare her off."

"You're right. I'll come with you. Can you spare a few dogs? If need be, we can split and cover two directions."

"Thanks. Take Pinghasuet and Singarnak in the lead, but leave Namatuk. She doesn't get along with Aqua."

"She doesn't get along with anybody."

"I ran her in front of three males and she went like the wind."

"Showing off for her admirers. The poor suckers. She's spayed." Byron's good humor eased some of her anxiety.

"Are you ready to go?"

"I've got my emergency pack and spare boots."

Between them, they assembled a second team. She returned to her own sled and pulled up the snow hook. "Search, Itirit. Search!" she called.

Time to see if she'd been right in varying the training, playing search games with some of the dogs. Smart Itirit had come through with flying colors. In her opinion, the games made the dogs sharper and wiser. But at this moment, she feared for Aqua's safety should she meet up with a pack of wolves or coyotes. A lone dog would be no match for them and could not outrun them even if she tried. A lone wolf, likely to ignore a team, might get curious about a solitary dog and ignore it, but a pack's behavior wasn't predictable.

Until now, she hadn't realized how attached she had grown to the dogs. A pang of nostalgia pierced her heart at the thought of her faithful huskies back home in the care of her cousin. Scott would be devastated if Aqua was not found. He loved every one of his dogs. She felt guilty for not having checked her collar and chain more carefully.

"I have to find you, Aqua. Aqua! Aqua! Search Itirit, good girl."

Itirit was running nose to the ground. The farther the team ran, the heavier her heart sank. Maybe Aqua had run deep into the thick forest, rather than follow the trail. Itirit was perhaps following a false scent. The dogs had traveled the same trail only a few days ago. The light snowfall since then would not have obliterated whatever it was that dogs seemed to follow unerringly. Itirit made a sharp turn on a narrow, little-used trail. Chris's heart beat faster.

Byron was following. From time to time he gave a shrill whistle, the come-here signal she wished she could master. In between, she called out Aqua's name and encouraged Itirit to search.

When she thought she may not find the young female, panic rose in her chest. Beside the emotional drain it would be, he couldn't afford to lose a dog, particularly a top rate racer like Aqua, an ideal dog for the tough Iditarod race. Grief and anger at the unnecessary loss of one of his dogs might undo all the progress he had made since her arrival. Tears welled up in her eyes, blurring her vision.

She braked the team to a halt when she came to a fork in the trail where snowmobiles had passed. One branch headed in a westerly direction, toward the border with Alaska, the other swung toward the north-east. Once the sled was firmly anchored, she unhitched Itirit. Her lead dog sniffed both parts of the trail and grew excited on the north-east fork.

Byron drew up alongside.

"I guess I'll follow Itirit's nose. I'm not sure if she can really find Aqua's track, but I'll give it a try."

"She looks like she knows her business. This north-east trail turns south farther on. I'll follow the other one toward the Alaskan border. Turn home when it's dark. There's no point in staying out all night."

Darkness was less than two hours away. "I know looking for a dog in the dark is pretty useless, but it's hard when you know she's out there somewhere."

"We'll find her. She won't go far. She knows where to get fabulous food, not to mention lots of love."

"I hope you're right."

They parted. She hitched Itirit back onto the line. Her fears came back in a rush. Without Byron's comforting presence behind her, she became acutely aware of her solitude.

The sky was losing its brightness when Itirit gave a sharp yelp.

"Whoa!" The team stopped and Itirit yelped again. Her nose quivered in the direction of a clearing in the spruce forest. Navut sat and gave a series of short, sad howls. A moment later, a ghostly shape emerged from the dense bush. Her heart leaped.

"Aqua, Aqua," she called softly. The young female approached cautiously, though not close enough to be caught. She lifted the snow hook but kept her foot dragging the brake. The team started slowly. Navut made throaty sounds and turned his head toward his favorite mate. Aqua wagged her tail and fell into step next to him.

It was better to let Aqua run free next to her male companion rather than stop and try to snare her. That was her chance to see how her obedience training had been absorbed. She prayed Aqua would now run alongside while they headed for home. A moment of cold fear ran down her back. By concentrating on the search, she hadn't paid much attention to the fact that, now in the dark, she was heading into what for her was completely new terrain.

Panic hit her, and she closed her eyes. Reason took over. The dogs always find their way home and Nunii and Itirit were running with assurance. As long as she refrained from giving any command, she trusted Itirit would lead them straight home. Smaller than the others, the white female was proving herself to be an ace dog. Scott had told her how he almost sold her as a pup, but relented because she was so affectionate. Not all pups grew to become racing dogs. It took a staunch attitude and eagerness to run, as well as the right body shape.

Several miles later, she breathed a sigh of relief when she recognized a familiar landmark. They were close to the cabin. Night had closed in at its darkest when the team finally pulled into the yard. Her first move was to secure Aqua to her picket with a new collar. The dog licked her face and pushed her nose inside the open parka, looking for a treat. Half laughing, half crying, she cuddled her and gave her the piece of dried meat she had tempted her with.

Byron arrived as she was finishing to unhitch the team.

A joyful shout erupted from her throat. "I've got her!"

"I see that. Good for you."

"I didn't do the work. Itirit and Navut did."

"But that's because you train the dogs that way. Next time we have a missing person, I'll borrow Itirit."

They chuckled while they unhitched the second team and tethered the dogs. When the harness and equipment were returned to the kennel room, the dogs fed and watered, she invited her helper into the cabin. Emotionally exhausted, she dropped onto a chair.

"Will you stay for dinner, Byron?"

"I should really go."

"And eat cold beans on your own? The least I can do to thank you for coming out is to share my stew with you."

She jumped up and set the pan on the stove.

Byron chortled. "Put like that, I can hardly refuse. Where's Old Grizzly?"

"I wish you wouldn't call him that."

"Sorry. Where's the boss, then?"

"Gone for two days."

"How is he these days?"

"We're getting along fine. We've got a working arrangement, a truce. And it's holding, if that's what you're asking."

"He's so lucky to have you around."

"I better call Charlie and tell him Aqua's back."

In no time, everyone in the area would know the reassuring news. The radiophone was anything but private.

Byron mopped up the last of the stew from his plate with a chunk of bread. He caught her eye. "Not the best manners, I know, but this stew is too good to waste. What did you tempt my palate with? Or shouldn't one ask?"

"I chopped up a piece of dark red meat I found in the storeroom and the last of the fresh potatoes. Since I don't know what kind of meat it is, I called the dish Boeuf Bourguignon."

"My, my, gourmet dishes in the wilds. Dark red meat, you say? It's got to be moose."

"Thanks. I didn't really want to know."

"Ah! But moose meat is delicious. As equally delicious as you." His impish tone made her smile.

The slamming of the cabin door startled them both. Scott towered in the door frame. He dropped his bag noisily on the floor. His dark eyes fell on the remains of the meal on the table. "So busy entertaining were you that you didn't even hear me come back? Don't worry, I took care of the dogs on my own."

"The kennel dogs never made a sound, except when the wolves howled. Nor did they utter a peep when your team came back."

Her protest was ignored.

"What are you doing here, Murdoch?" He grumbled something else inaudible.

Byron stretched. "Having dinner. Chris made Beef-something-or-other. A true culinary delight. We've left you some. Sit yourself down, Walsh, and tell us about your trip. And how come you're back so soon? Chris said you were gone for a couple of days."

At his friend's bantering tone, his face darkened and his mood sank another notch.

Chris bit the inside of her cheek.

"Did something go wrong? I wasn't expecting you back until tomorrow or the day after."

"Is that why you were throwing this dinner party?"

"You sly old dog! If I didn't know any better, I'd say you're jealous."

An angry growl was Scott's only answer to Byron's smirk.

"I believe this is my cue to exit," said Byron. "Chris, I thank you for the best meal I've had in a year."

"And thanks for your help this afternoon." A smile floated on her lips.

Byron pulled on his parka and left. The door closed behind him. In the cabin, the tense atmosphere was almost palpable. Scott still didn't move or say anything.

She wondered why she should feel so guilty. He sat at the table. Now he was going to ask her the reason for Byron's visit.

He didn't.

Yet she could see conflicting emotions darkening his face. Jealous? A chuckle rose to her lips. No, that couldn't be. Not him.

To break the awkwardness of the moment, she went to the stove and took the lid off the pot of stew.

His nostrils twitched at the rich aroma. "I see the lady's man has made a conquest."

None too gently, she dumped the pan on the table in front of him. "Why should it bother you?"

Without warning, he scraped back his chair and pulled her into his arms. His mouth descended on hers and plundered its softness. She stiffened with surprise, but just as quick, she relaxed under the onslaught. Her body sought his hard contours and molded itself to them.

Her hands linked about his neck. He drew her closer. Strong fingers burned a path down her spine. He groaned and tightened his hold. Her fingers raked his hair, pulling him to her. She tasted the outdoors, pine and wood smoke on him. He lifted his head to permit them to breathe. Hesitant fingers unfastened the clasp of her hair. The auburn glory tumbled to her shoulders. He sank his hands into its silken mass.

"I've wanted to do this for a long time."

"But it doesn't lead us anywhere." She sighed.

"Oh, no?" He began to pull her toward the bedroom.

Her body stiffened. It was her last bit of willpower. He stepped back. Flushed and troubled, she wrapped her arms around herself. Heat still radiated between them. She stumbled back, forcing her legs to move. With effort, she lifted her head to look at him. Heavy with repressed desire, his eyes bore into hers. For one sublime moment, time was suspended, during which she was aware that they both were resisting the inexorable attraction which threatened to trap them in a web of passion.

"N-no..." she stammered.

His hand paused in midair. His trembling fingers betrayed the violent battle raging within him. Abruptly, he lowered his hand and stalked out, slamming the cabin door behind him.

She retrieved her clasp and fastened her hair. Still shaking from the kiss, she replaced the pan on the stove. Her shaking hands poured a glass of ice-cold water which she gulped down. Slightly more composed, she debated whether to go to her room or face him when he returned. It didn't matter which. There was no point in hiding what they both knew. They would kiss again. It seemed inevitable. She threw up her arms in a fatalistic gesture and resolved to cling to her resolution for as long as she could. Beyond that... she'd cross whatever bridges lay ahead when and if she reached them. Some dog harnesses needed repairs, so she began work.

When he returned, she was sitting under the lamp, sewing a red strap on a harness. She stood and took the food off the stove.

"I don't need to be served." His tone carried a trace of resentment.

"Suit yourself. I wanted to be friends, but I suppose we aren't any more." The pan clattered onto the stove and she threw him the oven glove.

"Look, I'm sorry."

"No, you aren't. I'm not either."

He chuckled. "I don't know if we can be friends, but we could be lovers."

"Don't even think of it."

Their eyes met and held. She retrieved the pan from the stove and dumped the stew on a plate in front of him.

"We have a problem."

"I know. As long as I have two ounces of brain in my head, I'll stay away from you and your kisses. And you can keep your distance too." She tried to appear nonchalant, though that was not how she felt inside.

"I'll do my best. By the way, this is delicious."

"Thank you."

Visibly fighting with himself, he asked, "Why did Byron come up?"

"Aqua escaped this morning. He came to help find her. We took two teams out."

His hand froze in the air.

"Is she...?"

"Itirit found her. Aqua followed us back home."

The relief in his voice was tangible. He gave her a grateful smile and released the breath he'd been holding. "What do you mean, Itirit found her?"

"I've been trying to teach the huskies to search. Just for fun. They aren't simply running machines, so..." She looked at him, wondering if he approved.

"You mean search and rescue techniques?"

"Sort of. I take some dogs out. Then the next ones have to track them. Sometimes we go off the trail and around trees. Most of the dogs get the right idea, more or less. Itirit's the best, though."

"Interesting. But if you want that team to learn speed and long distance, they have to run to full capacity all the time."

"That's the theory. I'm sorry that you don't approve. From now on, I'll drop the games."

A smile softened his lips. Crowfoot lines formed at the corners of his eyes. "No. Come to think of it, the dogs probably like it. Happy dogs put more effort into their work."

"Is that why you don't have one of those training machines?"

"You mean like a treadmill?"

"Right."

"I think that's ridiculous. Dogs are meant to run on a trail, paws digging in the snow, feel the wind on their faces. They are meant to learn the wilds, sense danger of thin ice, find the best way around an overflow. They don't learn that when they are inside on a treadmill. That's for city folks."

The vehemence in his tone denoted his passion for the dogs, the outdoors and his understanding of the symbiotic relationship between dogs and men. She nodded in full agreement.

Nothing more was said. He finished his meal. Eventually, she spoke with caution. "What made you come back today?"

"I don't rightly know. All of a sudden, I didn't want to be away. I'll go out again tomorrow for the day."

His voice muted, he shook his head. She wondered whether a strange kind of bond with his dogs made him feel something was amiss.

Unless... no, he didn't come back because of her. Of course, not. Once he was on the trail with the team, he no longer thought about anything else.

Charlie's voice came booming from the speakers. She went to the radio to answer and her sparkling voice filled the room until she signed off.

"Chris...?"

"Good night. It's early rising tomorrow."

His disappointed groan served as a goodnight. At least, that's what she guessed it meant. It had taken her all her strength to break the magnetic force. She prepared for bed, taking care to make the least noise possible. Sleep should have taken over, but it didn't.

She heard him move to put wood into the stove. The couch creaked under his weight. One boot fell. She waited for the other. The clock had marked another minute when the boot dropped. She pulled the pillow over her ears, more to dampen her wanton imagination than to muffle the rustle of fabric. "I'll survive," she whispered into the pillow.

***

Scott's eyes drifted to the window and focused on the twinkling of the stars. A beam of white light shot through the dark sky. The northern lights were dancing. He sighed, involuntarily murmuring, "Chris." She was the reason he had cut short his trip. He needed to see her, to hear her. His worry had grown and overtaken reason. A force was pulling him toward home and he surrendered to it. Now, he wished he was miles away for the sole reason that it was unbearable not being able to touch her.

He gritted his teeth. A long time ago, he had vowed that no woman would ever again turn his life upside down. He had better stick to that resolution, starting right now.

He was impressed she had had the presence of mind to alert Charlie when Aqua took off. Not many habitations around these parts beyond the few oddball prospectors in the summer and those who lived off the land in remote cabins, though any of them would turn out to help, and a few mushers at the head of the valley.

Then there were also men like Byron, whose twin passions were nature and women, but would never sacrifice one for the other. Most of the other sled dog racers lived on the other side of the valley, or closer to the territory's capital. He knew most of them and met them from time to time while out training. Companionship was important, but he also dearly loved the quiet peace and isolation of his forest retreat.

Another sigh escaped his chest. He couldn't see two ways about it. He needed her... for the kennel and the racing, he added mentally.

CHAPTER NINE

They completed the early morning chores in the dark. Afterwards, he got ready to leave. This time, he intended to finish the entire trip and not let his urges get the better of him.

"Here's my plan. I aim to do some night running, not just camp while I'm out. I should be away for three days at the most. Will you be okay?"

"Of course, I will." She smiled despite her misgivings. Three days was an awful long time to be without him.

"And Chris..." He didn't finish his sentence. His face hardened. His shoulders tensed.

She waited beside the sled to see him off. Scattered snowflakes landed on her upturned face. He turned his back abruptly, but almost as soon, turned again to reach for her, drawing her tightly against him. He brushed the flakes off her eyelashes with his lips and trailed kisses down to her mouth.

"Do take care," she whispered.

The thinning darkness swallowed him up, but still, she remained rooted to the spot. For a long time, the beam of his headlamp bobbed in the distance. Deep down, she knew he had gone because if he hadn't, he would have made love to her. And she would have been unable to say no. Would that be so terribly immoral? People did it all the time.

Other people, yes, but not her. Not unless she loved the man. That thought made her gasp. She had almost given in. After all, she was a healthy woman with healthy needs, but it wasn't love. Her breath caught in her throat. She couldn't possibly love him. Compassion for his hurt, certainly, but not love. Love was something that was shared. He was only lusting.

The unrelenting cold brought her back to reality. Somewhere behind her, a pup gave a plaintive whine, a reminder that she had a training schedule to attend to.

It was past noon when she went back to the cabin for a bite to eat. A cursory inspection of the cupboards revealed a dismal lack of food. The last of the meat for the dogs was in an insulated box. The cache was equally bare. Not that she was fussy, but food was a necessity. She made a list and estimated quantities for at least two weeks. He had omitted to tell her what groceries she should get or whether she could use the truck. Since the track to the cabin hadn't been plowed, she was hesitant to drive. A sled dog team, however, would have no problem negotiating it. Not wanting to trust her memory to find the road to the village, she picked up the detailed map of the area from the bookshelf. It showed a faint, hand-drawn trail from the cabin down to Fletcher Creek, and she immediately decided to hitch up her veteran dogs to the toboggan sled. The team could easily pull her there and back with a load of groceries.

Her arrival in the community caused quite a stir. It was recess at the local one-room school and the kids flocked to her. The pretty woman teacher introduced herself.

"Hello. You must be Chris Taylor. I'm Vicky Peters. Nice to meet you."

"You know who I am."

Vicky smiled. "Of course. In a small place like this, everyone knows everyone else. You're a most talked about person for miles around."

"I am? Heavens, what for?"

"For daring to work for Scott Walsh. The bet was you wouldn't last three days. It was revised to three weeks, and now stands at three months." She shook with uncontrollable merriment as she tucked blond tresses back under her fake fur hat.

"Then tell the gamblers to call the bet off. I'm staying till the end of the season, whether he likes it or not."

Vicky laughed louder. "That's what Byron tried to tell them. Nice to see you come to town, and with the dogs."

"Town?" She did her best to hide her amusement.

"I agree. It's funny to call this place a town. Like you, I come from the south. To the locals, Fletcher Creek is a big metropolis. It's home."

"Yes, I suppose it's home." A dreamy look crossed her face. "I came because we need groceries. I feel more confident driving a sled than the truck."

"Can't blame you. There must be quite a bit of snow around your place. Your road doesn't get plowed."

"Scott doesn't pay his taxes?"

Vicky burst out laughing. "The tracks to cabins off the main road get plowed at the owners' request and expense."

"I suppose the municipality saves money that way since most of them are gone with their dogs anyway."

A dozen children had gathered to pet the panting dogs. She had to answer a torrent of questions and explain how the harnesses and lines worked.

"The big red dog is called Palootok. He's seven years old, and he is the boss. The others are also about the same age. That's old for a sled dog."

"Do you race them?" asked one child.

"Not anymore. But this team must have won many races." A little white lie wouldn't hurt, she thought, since she didn't know whether those big heavy dogs did race or not.

The youngsters' eyes widened in admiration.

"All right, children," Vicky announced. "Recess over. Time to get back to class and let Ms. Taylor do her shopping." As she shepherded her charges back into the school building, she said, "I hope we can get together sometime soon. I imagine you'd welcome a change of company from time to time."

She laughed but felt saddened that the inhabitants of Fletcher Creek should have such a low opinion of Scott. The dogs went enthusiastically down the street to the grocery store. "Whoa! You fellows must have been here before judging by the way you ran down here." They immediately lay down, accustomed as they were to conserving their energy. The snub rope secured to a convenient utility pole, she entered the store.

It was unexpectedly large and stacked to the ceiling with goods. The odor of spices and leather mingled with other less identifiable smells. A small woman, her white hair pulled into a tight bun, came from behind the counter.

"You must be Chris. I'm Mary Foster. My husband over there is Fred." She gave her a broad smile. "Here's a letter for you. From a Marcia. Lovely handwriting she has. We're the post office as well as the general store. I was wondering when you'd get hungry enough to come in for supplies. I know Scott doesn't believe in buying much food. It's about time somebody looked after him properly. So, what do we need today?"

Overwhelmed by such a friendly welcome and slightly amused at the lack of privacy, she pocketed Marcia's letter. Small towns! Everyone knew everything about everybody. Next, the dear old lady would try to find out who Marcia was. She handed Mary her shopping list.

Mary's gray-haired husband joined them at the counter. "Don't bother with the food for the dogs. I'll get Warren to bring it up tonight or tomorrow, since you say Walsh's not home. Tell you what. Leave the flour, rice and potatoes too. No sense in burdening yourself down. I'll get someone to go up and deliver it."

"What dog food is that? I didn't know Scott used kibble."

"Not kibble. It's a ground up cooked mixture of rice, corn, vitamins and some herbs like rosemary for preservation, all rolled in with some premium fat to keep it together. It's made by an artisan musher."

"That sounds good. There was none in the kennel. I just fed meat and fat to my charges."

Mary gave an exaggerated sigh. "Scott forgot to order. I didn't order because I thought perhaps he still had enough."

In no time, they had placed most of the two weeks' supply of groceries into the sled bag. Fresh produce was stashed in a couple of insulated bags. Butter and frozen local fish and meat needed no protection. She secured the load with a tarpaulin and rope. The dogs stretched themselves. Palootok turned round to sniff the sled.

"There, big boy." Fred came out of the store again to hand out a treat to each dog. "These are the nicest dogs I've ever known. Okay boys, sit. Gentle."

The dogs sat and took the treat delicately from the old man's fingers. "Some dogs take your fingers off with it, but not these. They've been doing the grocery run for the last couple of years and they know they get a treat. Only had to tell them once."

"So Scott comes here by dog sled too?"

"Sure does. Why pay for gas when you've got so much four-legged power?"

Finally, the team was ready to go. Under the watchful gaze of the patrons, looking on from the window, the dogs made an impressive U-turn and headed back up the street and out of town.

Darkness had already invaded the valley, but soon a full moon illuminated the clear, starry sky. The snow reflected the silvery light, and darkness receded. There was no need of a headlamp to find the way. The sound of the sled runners skimming the snow and the panting of the dogs were magnified by the quiet of the wilderness. She breathed in the pristine air with a deep sense of contentment. An owl hooted in the distance.

She wondered if he was also running his team by moonlight. Behind her warm scarf, her lips tingled as though remembering his kiss. Chasing the memory away took most of her energy.

Back at the cabin, after feeding the dogs, she snatched a moment to read Marcia's letter. Chris felt a pang of remorse for not having given much thought to her cousin and their former life together. Marcia's writing was full of longing. She had broken up with her boyfriend and was wishing she, too, had found an interesting job in some exotic location. Chris smiled. Exotic location, indeed! With a tinge of nostalgia, she folded the letter and went outside to water the dogs. Time to write to her cousin later that evening.

The next day passed quickly enough. To soothe her impatience in waiting for Scott's return, she took old Palootok for a walk with a couple of pups. Long before she did, the dogs heard the noise of the truck toiling in a four-wheel drive up the slope toward the cabin. Perched on the flat roofs of the doghouses, the kennel sent up a combined howl of welcome while she was still some distance from the cabin. Hurrying, she arrived to see a man unloading a stack of heavy cartons at the foot of the cache ladder.

The man straightened his back. "Hi, I'm Warren. I've brought dog meat. Only sixteen hundred pounds of it."

"Scott didn't tell me about any meat delivery." She eyed the cartons.

"Walsh not around?"

"He's out on a training run. Won't be back till the day after tomorrow."

"This lot had better be put up into the cache before the coyotes or wolverines get at it."

"How many boxes are there?"

"Forty for today. We're short at the moment. I'll be bringing out the rest of the order next week."

"Forty... that's forty pounds a carton."

"Yep, that's right. They're our standard pack. I'd like to stay and give you a hand but I've got to make a delivery at Robertson's an' that's another two hours' drive north of here."

She closed her eyes a fraction second, then smiled. "That's all right, Warren. I'll manage just fine."

"Okay. Tell Walsh he can pay me next week when I come back with the rest."

He climbed into the cab of the truck, fired the motor, and set off.

"Goodbye, Warren."

Her parka was in the way, so she dropped it on the ground, and hoisted the first carton onto her shoulder. Balancing herself, she carefully tackled the ladder. At the top, she realized it would have been easier if she had opened the cache door before climbing up. One sure thing, she was not going down again. Breathing steadily, she moved her free hand carefully to unhook the latch. She teetered on the last rung as the door swung open with a creak. A heave of her shoulder and she dumped the box of frozen meat onto the floor of the cache, then crawled in and pulled the carton to one side. Climbing down was a lot easier. As long as she took her time and moved cautiously, she would make it. Only thirty-nine to go. She corrected that to thirty-eight as she decided to drag one box into the kennel building.

After ten cartons, she was shaking with fatigue and had to sit in the snow to recover. At this rate, the work was going to take the rest of the evening and probably most of the night. Perspiration streamed down her forehead. Her empty stomach growled. If she wanted to finish this grueling task, she'd have to eat. And she still had to feed the dogs. Just then, the canine chorus signaled the arrival of another visitor.

She groaned. Not more heavy stuff to carry. I'm out. The unmistakable sound of a snowmobile pulling a loaded toboggan came closer and closer. It appeared and swung into the yard. Two men got off. They removed their helmets.

"Hey! What a welcome committee!" Byron made a theatrical gesture toward the second man. "Chris, I'd like you to meet Conrad Windett, my fellow Conservation Officer."

The newcomer was as tall and as rugged as Byron. He brushed back a mane of dark blond hair. Blue eyes sparkled in his tanned face. This North country certainly bred big strong men, came to her mind. She shook Conrad's outstretched hand.

"Byron promised me I'd meet the most beautiful woman in the Yukon. And he wasn't kidding."

"You're embarrassing me."

"And you'll catch your death of cold if you don't put your parka on," Byron said.

"There's no chance of that happening. I've got to get back to putting the meat away."

Byron placed an arm around her shoulder. "Why do you think we're here? I saw Warren's truck in town loaded with frozen dog chow. Then I remembered Walsh saying he'd ordered his regular supply of meat. Knowing the old rogue had skipped out and left you with the chores, I roped Conrad here into coming to help. And anyway, Mary threatened to cut my supply of mint drops if I didn't take some stuff to you. Now, get yourself something on and relax."

"This is really good of you both."

"You don't think we could leave a gorgeous lady like you wilt under all these boxes." Conrad bowed like a nineteenth-century gentleman.

The gallant banter lifted her spirits. The two men didn't let her help. In short order, all dog food was properly stowed in the high cache, and the groceries in the cabin.

"We were thinking we should celebrate," said Conrad. "You work too hard. You need some time off, some fun in your life."

Her eyes brightened in the space of an instant. "Sounds good, but I'm awfully busy."

"We know how much of a slave driver old Walsh can be," said Byron. "One evening, after you've finished with your dogs, we'll throw you the welcoming party you never got."

"I can't say anything until I've talked to Scott."

"Don't let him make a drudge out of you," Conrad said.

"He's got to share!" Byron said.

They all laughed.

"A party would do Scott good, too. Loosen up his mood. It's about time he came out of his shell." Although Byron spoke in a jocular way, he sounded serious.

"I'll try, but I can't promise anything."

"You must come and visit the Conservation office," Conrad said.

"Unfortunately, we've got to go back now. We're after a poacher. Heard any shots today?" Byron asked.

"No. Not around here."

"I didn't think he'd come anywhere close because of the dogs. They sound the alarm as soon as someone's a mile away."

"Don't lots of people hunt for food?"

"They can only do so during the hunting season or in an emergency. But some poachers often hunt at night with a light and sell the meat in the city, and that we don't let pass."

"With a light?"

"A powerful flashlight. Animals are attracted to the light and easy to shoot."

"Worse is the trafficking of animals parts, antlers, gall bladders, bear paws and the like," Conrad said.

"That's terrible!"

"Those poachers only take the parts they need and leave the carcass to rot. It's big bucks for them, so these guys take risks." Byron shook his head. "We haven't half the manpower we need. We've got to rely on tips from the public."

"Walsh nailed one of them last summer when out with his team and a wheeled cart. He approached without noise. The dogs blocked the damn guy's ATV. He tried to run, but Scott tackled him. When the dogs jumped up, he was so scared he wetted his pants." Conrad couldn't repress his laughter.

Although she laughed with them, her heart still beat faster thinking about the danger he might have been in while arresting the poacher.

"Won't you have a cup of coffee before you go?"

Byron's face lit up. "That'd be welcome."

Over coffee, the time passed quickly in lighthearted conversation. Byron and Conrad stood up and zipped up their parkas.

"Stay in or you'll freeze," Conrad said.

"I have to feed the dogs, anyhow. But I'm really grateful for your help."

"You were doing just fine, honey," Byron said.

Howls interrupted them. "Another visitor?" She frowned. There had been no engine noise.

"Looks like Scott's back," said Byron. "Hell, we could have left all those cartons for him to lug into the cache."

"We could always take them down again," Conrad said.

They grinned and went to greet the incoming team. Scott said a brief hello to his friends and turned back to the dogs.

"Okay, we're off."

They waved farewell. A moment later, the snowmobile roared off. She helped Scott unharness the dogs and water them, then fed all the dogs. Happiness rose in her heart. He came back two days earlier than expected. Now she realized how much she had missed him, though he had cut his trip short and that wasn't a good training practice.

He glowered. "Can't wait to get your men friends up here as soon as I'm gone, can you?"

"Did something go wrong to make you grouchy like that?" She pushed open the cabin door.

At a glance, he took in the empty coffee cups and empty cookie dish on the table.

"I seemed to have interrupted a cozy gathering."

Her elation at his return slipped down a notch. She shrugged at his sarcasm and winced as pain shot through her shoulders. Jaws set hard, she raised the wick of the lamp for more light and cleared the table. Her back to him, she began to prepare the evening meal. He stood and watched her. Catching sight of him reflected in the window glass, she smothered a sigh. Both Conrad and Byron, although big men, had not dwarfed the room the way he alone did. Her heart pounded in her chest.

After a lengthy silence, he said, "I came back because I remembered Warren was to deliver the meat. I'm glad he didn't."

"For your information, Mr. Walsh, Warren did make his delivery."

"Heck! Where's the meat, then?"

"All in the cache." She spoke modestly, with eyes lowered toward the floor, anticipating her punch line.

"In the...? You didn't get the whole lot up there on your own?"

"That's the cozy gathering I had with Byron and Conrad. My men friends, as you put it."

"Oh!" He glanced away, shamefaced.

"There's no need to apologize for being so insensitive." She savored her minor triumph.

He took her by the shoulders. "I'm sorry if I act like a real rube sometimes."

"Ouch!" His fingers were digging into her skin. Her attempted smile turned into a grimace.

"What's the matter? Are you hurt?"

"I got ten of the cartons into the cache myself before Byron and Conrad showed up."

"You did what? You must be sore as hell. Here, let me massage your shoulders."

His strong hands began easing her aching muscles. A warmth invaded her that had nothing to do with the relief of her soreness. The circular motion of his thumbs soothed the pain and sent shivers up and down her spine. His breath fanned her neck. Once or twice, his hands faltered. His lips touched her ear. He turned her in his arms. His lips trailed from her forehead to the end of her nose before kissing her waiting mouth. She let herself go against his hard frame and encircled his waist with her arms.

The pressure of his lips increased. Shivers rippled through her body while disturbing tremors ran through her. A tantalizing scent clung to his skin and made her lightheaded. He lifted his head to look into her dreamy eyes.

He lifted her in his arms and carried her to the bedroom.

Much later, he kissed her lips lightly. Abruptly, he sat up.

"It was wonderful," she murmured.

A sudden chill fell in the room. He rolled to the edge of the bed and sat, his head in his hands. "I've taken advantage of you. This is the last thing I meant to happen."

"But it did. I'm not sorry."

"Well, I am! I had no right to do that. It mustn't happen again. And it won't."

His back stiffened. The temptation to caress the rigid set of his shoulders burned her fingertips, but she didn't move.

"You enjoyed it. I enjoyed it. There's no problem."

"There is. You just don't understand."

"Try me. I'm a mature adult."

A feeling of weariness settled over her. All the enchanted excitement had subsided, but she wanted to reach out and tell him she loved him. Shock went through her. No, she didn't, couldn't. It wasn't possible. It must be the glow of their lovemaking that made her mind hazy.

"I knew it wasn't going to work. I knew it!"

Hearing the anguish in his voice made her cringe. "Let's put it behind us, then, and concentrate on the work of getting you to win races."

"Damn!" He stood abruptly, picked up his clothes, and strode out of the bedroom.

Her fist pressing on her eyes stemmed back the tears which flooded under her eyelids.

Chapter Ten

I n the morning, she heard the dogs in the compound and reasoned that he must be already outside. The early morning, opaque and gloomy, no star showing, hung like a bad omen.

A slight hesitation before she swung her legs over the edge of the bed and then she inhaled deeply, resolute to face the day. Her jumbled brain didn't know how she should behave today or what his reaction would be. Why had he been furious and unhappy last night after they had made love remained a mystery. Last night... How tender and gentle he'd been. So considerate, yet so passionate. The memory of it came rushing back. Her pulse quickened. They could never be the same with each other again. Their working together was seriously compromised. She pulled on her clothes and went outside.

The older dogs raised their heads and gave a brief howl of greeting but didn't come out of their houses. Only the younger dogs jumped eagerly to the fence before curling up again on their springy beds of pine twigs. The pups made the most noise and played in their pen long after the humans had gone back to the cabin.

Strained silence presided over breakfast. The atmosphere in the cabin was so oppressive, she sought a way to lighten it. Talking about dogs was neutral ground.

"Do you have a particular reason to check on the dogs before starting work?"

"Yes. I check if everyone is there. A dog could slip its collar, like Aqua did the other day, or find a way through the fence. Something might have happened to one of the old veterans during the night. That would change the plans for the day."

A nod was all she could muster. The heavy silence returned. By the time breakfast was over, she noticed it was snowing hard.

His chin pointed at the scene outside. "Do you fancy taking a team out in that?"

Surprised by the question, she made a guarded answer. "I'm game for anything."

"We'll go up to the head of the valley, to Ashin Point. It's a two-hour round trip."

A rush of excitement lifted her mood. Not only was he now talking normally, but had actually invited her to go with him. Floating on the edge of unreality, she prepared a bagged lunch and a thermos of cocoa.

They each readied their own team. The pleasurable anticipation of a rare outing with him tingled in her veins. Champagne would have had the same effect. It'd be tough going through deep virgin snow, though so exhilarating as they overcame the obstacles. Most of all, he would be with her. Since he had made the invitation, perhaps he wasn't angry with her after all.

He led the way with his sturdy Canadian Inuit dogs. She was happy to follow in his tracks with the huskies. Because of the worsening weather, it took them more than the hour to reach Ashin Point. They stopped to rest the dogs and give them some of the broth she had prepared. Their strength restored, the dogs were soon eager to get back on the trail, but he lingered. He poured cocoa in a cup and handed it to her.

"There's nothing better than a cup of hot chocolate on the trail."

"Even better in a storm when the snowflakes fall right into the cup to cool it down."

They chuckled and put the cups and thermos back in the sled bag.

"You take the lead on the way home."

She looked at him. "You mean that?"

"You'd better get some experience finding your way in a storm."

"I'd let the dogs find their way. I trust them."

"I do too, but it's a good idea to see if you agree with them. But let's make it better. When you get to Lone Pine corner, you take the east trail and get us home from there."

"I'll have to turn south again, won't I?"

"Yes. See if you can find the trail. You've been on it once from the other side, and I've sledded over it a couple of times. Look at the snow, it'll be uneven compared with the undisturbed snow elsewhere."

The snow was falling thicker now. Her lead dogs disappeared occasionally in the swirling snow. From time to time, she called out to Singarnak and Pinghasuet to keep heading home. The tracks of their outward passage had already filled with fresh snow. Navigation wasn't difficult until they reached Lone Pine, a huge spruce standing by itself on the edge of a small frozen lake. After the turn, finding the right trail was more difficult.

Her eyes strained to see the slight indentations left by earlier sleds and dogs. No matter where she looked, she was blinded by driving snow. To her relief, she found a depression, even though it was nothing more than a space between the trees. By her estimate, it had to be the right one. It ran east, or at least appeared to do so. Without the sun for orientation, she relied on the lay of the land that she remembered from studying the map. He said she had been on this trail before from the other side, though. Through the thick curtain of white, it was near impossible to spot any landmarks which, in any case, she would hardly be able to recognize since she'd see them from a different angle. The team turned just as she was giving the command. In fact, she could have sworn the lead dogs hadn't waited for her order. The trail twisted again, and she assumed it was going south.

For no apparent reason, the team gave a spurt. From afar, faint howls were heard. They were nearing home.

"Thanks. That was a good exercise. In the south, we don't have this kind of weather." She spoke while unhitching her team. "But if we did, we're not likely to go out."

"I know."

Of course! It was a trial run. That's why he had asked her out this morning. Not for the fun of sledding. Solely because he wanted to test her skills and her endurance. All the same, they had shared a companionable time. She sighed and watched him lead two dogs to their pen, his long legs slicing a path through the fresh blanket of snow.

A spiral of longing began in the pit of her stomach, but she released her breath and tried to ignore it by busying herself with her dogs.

Back in the cabin, they ate a quick snack of bread and cheese. He remained silent. Occasionally, he looked through the window at the falling snow. At other times, she caught his eyes on her.

"I'm going to chop up some frozen meat for tomorrow." He left the table and was gone before she could reply. Shrugging, she turned her attention to the bread she had started that morning. The dough was ready to knead. She turned it onto the table, sprinkled it with flour, and folded it. Soon, she discovered how therapeutic pounding dough was. A great outlet for her frustration.

His businesslike attitude stung to see him treating their wonderful moment of intimacy as though it never happened. Of course, she didn't expect him to fall in love with her. The only love he seemed capable of was the love of his dogs, but still she expected him to treat her with some affection, respect, not like some woman he'd picked up in a bar. If only she could find out what made him so angry, so defensive, she could help him overcome it. At least she thought she could.

When it came time to feed the dogs, he still hadn't returned to the cabin. She pulled on her boots and zipped up her parka. He was just outside the porch, shoveling a path to the dog pens and the kennel house. The rhythmic bending of his powerful body that sent the snow flying triggered her longing once again. Closing her eyes, she took a deep breath and stepped forward. Renoir leaped at her from out of the deep snow. She grabbed his head and rubbed it.

She turned to Scott. "Dinner's ready whenever you are."

"Thanks. I've fed and watered the dogs. I'll be in shortly."

His curt words cut, but at least he spoke. Renoir took advantage of the partly open door to dash into the comfort of the cabin. The big black dog shook the snow and ice from his coat in front of the stove.

"Renoir, you infuriating dog! Couldn't you have done that outside?" She wasn't really angry, seeing the dog smile at her, a huge pink petal of a tongue lolling from his mouth. After a pat on his head, she set the table.

To occupy her hands until they were ready to eat, she picked up a length of blue polypropylene rope and started on a new gangline by weaving the ends into a loop. A smile came to her lips as she held the aluminum splicing fid in her hand. The design of the tool hadn't changed since the first sailors invented the slender hollow cone to splice the ropes for sails several centuries earlier. Of course, now the fids were hollow and made of aluminum. Originally, they were a solid wooden cone with a cleat to hold the rope at the hollowed out top.

When he came in, her hands wavered and dropped the fid. His looking so devastatingly handsome, with a crown of snow on his dark hair, unraveled her composure.

Her heart skipped a merry dance against her ribs. The room was intimate and warm, with the smell of fresh baked bread tickling her taste buds. For a fleeting moment, she had stepped back in time to a simpler age.

Throughout the meal, he brooded and limited his conversation to a couple of thank-you. Several times, she opened her mouth to speak, then closed it again. Unable to break the impasse, she finally wished him goodnight and retired to her room. Stretched out under the covers, she remained awake, longing to go to him, to tell him she wanted him to make love to her. He'd certainly reject her. Regret over their intimate encounter was written on his stern face.

Yet during those glorious moments, he had revealed a different man beneath that forbidding exterior. She could easily love that other man. Perhaps she already did. No, she didn't, didn't want to. It was the effects of isolation. Cabin fever. That was it. Cabin fever.

In the morning, he was still cold. When she opened the door, she saw that the snow had stopped. It lay in a thick mantle over the yard, having erased the path he had dug out the previous day. He handed her a pair of snowshoes. Although she wanted to laugh at the novelty of wearing snowshoes to go and take care of the dogs, she refrained. The animals had dug tunnels from their houses and were busy frolicking in the snow. "If anyone ever doubted that they love the white stuff, they should see them now," she said.

"Or when we bring harnesses out."

She hadn't realized he was so close. He had prepared a pack for his sledding run. The task of hitching the dogs helped calm her erratic heartbeat. The rebel lock of hair swept his forehead. The man rarely wore a hat as far as she could see. A shiver traveled down her spine. When he had kissed her, his soft hair had caressed her skin, imprinting him on her.

Moments later, he was set to go. A ghost of a smile softened his lips. A sigh escaped her chest. That's where all his love went, to his dogs and his wilderness. Without warning, he took her in his arms. His fevered mouth kissed her trembling lips. Then, just as fast, he let her go. "Bye, sweetie." In no time, he and his team were gone.

For a long while, she stood motionless, staring at the indentation in the snow where the sled and the dogs' feet had broken the powder snow. Bye, sweetie. Two little words that raced around and around her mind. Her lips burned from the unexpected kiss. It took all her willpower to shake the bewitching memory.

Thankfully, her morning duties absorbed most of her thoughts and energy. Her most impossible task was trying to forget about him. He was an invisible presence, always at her side. When she paused, she could hear his voice, feel his arms around her. It was obvious he was fighting a battle between wanting to make love to her and keeping his distance. They were two mature adults and should enjoy each other. That was what she told him. But something perturbed him deeply enough that he resisted his own urges.

CHAPTER ELEVEN

B y the end of the morning, the sky cleared and the sun came out. The frosty air smelled clean and fresh. The pine branches were bowed down under their new load of snow. She hummed while preparing to take out a team of six huskies. They'd be challenged by the deep snow, but she didn't plan to go very far. In case she'd have to break a trail for her dogs, she lashed the snowshoes on top of the sled bag.

For a while, she forgot everything but the delight of the huskies' panting as they plowed through the powder snow. The sharp air turned her cheeks a healthy rose color. She adjusted her goggles to protect her eyes from the dazzling expanse of white.

The trail narrowed in a forest of mixed spruce and aspen. A sluggish arctic owl rose from in front of the team, and the dogs sped up and jumped as one. In vain. The bird flew onto a high branch. A daydream whether she was in love or not blunted her senses. The strident whine of an oncoming snowmobile startled her back to the present. Not wanting to take any chances of having an accident, she ordered her team off the trail and secured the snub rope to a tree. This was her first encounter with a snowmobile on the trail. She hurried to her lead dogs and held them by the collar.

At that moment, a gleaming black missile crested the ridge and headed directly toward her and her team. Standing at the front of the team, she waved her arms, screaming at the top of her lungs.

A band of fear tightened across her chest. Only at the very last moment did the driver see them. The snowmobile swerved right and left. It continued, zigzagging into the trees. It ricocheted off a stout fir and overturned. Free of its load, the motor shrieked and dropped into the idle mode. Her heart in her mouth, she ran back the few steps to check her dogs. Tioralak emerged from the snow and shook himself. Bobijo cowered under cover of a pine bough. She stepped over the lines, calling his name. He stood, his eyes wild with panic. The front dogs were shaking. They were used to the noise but not a big black mass so close.

Guilt overcame her. Here she was concerned about her dogs, when there was a human also in need.

How would Scott have acted in her place? Exactly how she had done, her inner voice murmured. The dogs didn't understand what was happening. They could panic and try to run off, perhaps killing a dog unable to run with his line tangled around a tree. In this remote wilderness, the musher's life depended on the dogs. Like it did over a century ago, before the invention of the snowmobile. She had to secure and comfort her team. Only when every dog was reassured and settled with a treat did she turn toward the upturned snowmobile.

A glance at it showed no sign of movement. Adrenalin still pounding in her ears, she felt her anger rise. "Damn the crazy driver!"

Carefully approaching the overturned machine, she called out. No response. She skirted the machine and saw a figure laying in the snow a few feet away. With caution, she looked under the snowmobile, saw the key, and cut the ignition. The noise died instantly. Rage and fear warred inside her brain as she went back to the man. He was now moving, attempting to sit up. She was relieved he was not dead, though an insidious thought tugged at her mind wishing that he were.

"What did you think you were doing, driving like that?" Anger colored her shouting even as she bent to help him up.

"Hell!" he groaned. "My leg hurts."

She glanced at the oddly twisted leg. "It's broken."

The man gave a maniacal laugh, then spluttered and coughed. His voice was slurred like that of a drunk. "Stupid bitch!"

A smell of sour alcohol wafted up her nose. "Look, mister! If you call me names, I leave you right here with your injured leg." Fury seethed inside her. Drunk! Waves of anger nearly had her hit the man on the head. For the first time in her life, she had to struggle to restrain her temper and not whack him across the head.

Broken leg or not, she had no sympathy for him. She stood up and walked back to her dogs.

"Ouch! No, don't leave me!" the man yelled after her.

"Just stay put and don't move. I've got to attend to my dogs, because without them, we're both stuck here."

For a few more minutes, she talked to the dogs to restore their confidence and calm her own nerves. Her rescue options were limited. She could either make the stranger as comfortable as possible and sled to Fletcher Creek, which must be about a good hour's distance away, or she could load him on the sled and take him there. The latter was probably the better choice, though with this fresh snow the going was going to be arduous.

There were splints for dogs in her first aid kit, but they wouldn't do for a man. Perhaps a snowshoe would do, but she was likely to need the snowshoes to break trail now that the sled was going to carry a heavy load. One way or another, he was going to be hurt.

"I'm going to have to get you into the sled," she told the man. "But you've got to help me."

"Can't move."

"Well, you better try or else you'll have to wait here until I come back with help. Though the wolves might find you first." There was no disguising the disgust in her voice.

"Don't leave me!" he cried.

"Then, grit your teeth. I'll move the sled closer."

The dogs were now calm. They cooperated as she made them back up. The sled now next to the man, she unloaded her gear. The man made incoherent sounds.

"Quiet, you drunkard!"

"I need a drink."

That was all she needed to rekindle her white fury.

"You prefer to wait here?"

"No! Don't leave me."

A deep breath calmed her nerves while she slipped her snowshoe under the broken leg, trying not to move it too much, and gripped him under the arms. She started pulling him out of the brush. He screamed in pain. The man wasn't tall, but he was stocky. He let all his weight fall on her. Panting from the effort, she tugged until he was alongside the sled.

At that point, the dogs decided to investigate. They pawed and nudged him, expecting a pat in return. The man let out a piercing wail. "Wolves! Wolves!"

"Why did I get myself a drunk!" Still fuming, she debated the easiest method of lifting him into the sled.

The trembling man was sitting with his arms over his head, trying to shoo away the dogs sniffing all around him.

"No, don't leave me."

"Okay, sit," she commanded her dogs.

They sat more or less obediently. She turned her attention to the man. "Now, you, help by pushing on your hands to get into the sled."

Instead, the man grabbed her legs. Caught by surprise, she hollered at him. Her yell must have acted as a signal. Snarling, Itirit moved in on the man, immediately joined by the rest of the pack. What was happening to her friendly dogs? She shouted at them and waded among them. They stood, a defiant, growling mob of dogs, their fiery eyes trained on the man. He sobered up in an instant and sat up straight.

The man sank back. All hostility had been knocked out of him. He heaved himself on his hands while she leaned the sled sideways under his rear end. He grabbed the stanchions and heaved himself inside. As carefully as she could, she lifted the snowshoe under the broken leg and moved the leg into the sled. Now that the man was calm, she gently withdrew the snowshoe. The man lifted his good leg in without being told. His snowmobile suit was ripped, but there was nothing she could do about that. She rearranged the sled's contents around the broken leg to immobilize it as best as she could. The sleeping bag would cushion the inevitable bumping on the trail. After she closed the flap of the sled bag around him, leaving only his head sticking out, she patted each dog to reassure them. Itirit flattened her ears and, prancing, licked her chin. She swung her backpack with her thermos on her back.

Persuaded the dogs understood the silent transmission of thoughts, she thanked them silently.

"Okay, hike slow."

A quick glance at her compass confirmed her position. Her mind recalled the map of the area. There was no direct trail to the village from where she was, which meant she'd have to break one. That wasn't a good option, but she was sure there was a snowmobile trail somewhere nearby. A small detour. Worthwhile though, as the trail would be packed. In the meantime, she'd have to break trail.

Now came a tricky maneuver, one she had never practiced. Snowshoes strapped on, she had to release the anchors before she could be in front of the team. Everything now depended on her leaders.

"Itirit sit. Stay." The dog obeyed, so did the rest of the team. Relieved, she quickly moved ahead and started the long trek through the deep, fresh snow. Apprehension of what the dogs might do next gnawed at her. If they decided to overtake her or run in another direction, there was nothing she could readily do.

The going was extremely arduous. The sun had dipped below the horizon when she halted. She reached for the thermos and drunk avidly. In all honesty, she knew she should also have given the man a drink of water, but she was the one working hard. Her lack of empathy didn't even trouble her, even though her anger had subsided.

Directly in front, she saw snowmobile tracks in the beam of her headlamp. After a quick check of the compass, she promptly removed her snowshoes and hurried back to regain control of the sled. The dogs sped up the moment they reached the snowmobile tracks.

Her patient remained motionless. Eyes closed, his head hung to one side and his nostrils were pinched and white. Standing on the runners enabled her to rest her legs. After her exertion, they were beginning to feel like lead.

The whine of a snowmobile broke the silence. "Not again!" She rolled her eyes while directing the team into a small clearing on the edge of the trail.

The machine slowed and stopped alongside. Even before the operator removed his helmet, she recognized Byron.

"Out on patrol, Byron?"

"Yes. We saw the overturned machine, the dog tracks and the churned up snow. I was frantic with worry. Thank Heavens, you're safe."

"The guy is drunk. He nearly plowed into us."

"We've had reports of our poacher in these parts. Saw some tracks. We were following him."

"I think I've got your man. He's got a broken leg."

Byron went over to the sled and examined the passed out man. "Conrad's taking pics of the accident scene. He'll be here in a moment."

Minutes later, Conrad pulled in beside them.

"Better make camp. Want to go and get the toboggan, Byron?"

"You can go. I'll build a fire here."

Conrad disappeared and Byron set to build the fire.

"It would've been easier for you to leave him back there and sled to the post, you know."

"I feared he might get hypothermia if I left him, even in my sleeping bag. He is quite drunk!"

"You're mighty generous. It must have been real punishment to break trail."

"Chalk it up to keeping fit exercise."

They laughed and shared a cup of hot chocolate. Soon after that, Conrad reappeared with the medical toboggan. The two conservation officers cut away the man's pants leg after removing his boot and slipped a cradle under the broken bone. The man whimpered. They worked efficiently. The injured man came to and looked about him, wide-eyed. "Those dogs attacked me! I'll sue!"

They transferred the man to the rescue toboggan.

"Shut up, you crazy idiot! One more peep out of you and you won't be able to sue anyone." Conrad's growl was fierce. He grinned at her and said. "I just hate drunk drivers, on the road or on the snow trails."

"You checked his snowmobile?" asked Byron.

"Sure did. Guess what I found?" Conrad's face was a mixture of satisfaction and disgust.

"Parts."

Byron's answer was terse with anger seething underneath. The man shrunk down in the toboggan and remained silent.

"Yeah, hide, you scumbag." Byron spoke in a deceptively soft voice. "You're going to be put away for a long time."

The man shrunk farther down.

"He celebrated his moose kill with Jack Daniels."

It drew a snort from Byron. Lips pinched in disgust, Chris shook her head. Alcohol the killer. Images of her family sprung up, but she had exhausted her anger. Right now, she had to untangle her dogs.

Conrad set off. Byron helped her straighten the gangline. "Since I'm here, would you like me to break a trail for you to the cabin?"

"That's good of you. I can manage now that I've had a rest. You've got work to do with your poacher."

"Conrad will take over. The Mounties will want to interview our man before he's sent on to Whitehorse to get fixed. They should leave it crooked so he'll never hunt again. I'll break trail."

"Thanks. It's been hard getting here."

When they arrived back at the kennels, Byron helped her unhitch and care for the dogs.

"Want to come in for a cup of coffee?"

"I'd settle for a thank you kiss."

"I don't have any to spare." It troubled her that Byron had grown very fond of her and tried to keep her tone light.

"Saving them for Scott?"

His forthright question caught her unawares. She stooped to clip the tie chain to Nunii's collar, knowing the truth must be plain on her face. Marcia always told her she was transparent.

"Scott's not interested in me." She hid her confusion with a nervous laugh.

"Don't try to fool me. Why else would he bite my head off every time he finds me here? He acts like one really jealous guy."

"It's not what you think. At the beginning, he was reluctant to accept me. You saw that for yourself. Now that I'm here, he's scared he might lose me. Not because I'm a woman, but because he recognizes that I'm indispensable for his training program. He needs a handler."

Sadness choked on her words. That's what Scott had become, a calculating manipulator. He needed a handler, not a woman. Had she listened to her voice of reason, she'd have seen through him earlier. His lovemaking, with all its tenderness, was his way of keeping control of her. He wanted to ensure she didn't fall in love with some other man and leave. Pain stabbed her heart. No matter that he spurned her, she couldn't throw herself at another man. Anyway, she was unable to look at another man, not even someone as kind as Byron.

"You know, a man could fall for a woman like you." He led Itirit to her place.

"It wouldn't do him any good." Her tone was light, but her insides were churning.

"Does that mean a fellow shouldn't try?"

"A wise man might decide to look elsewhere." Scott's image danced in front of her eyes.

"Still, he might not get discouraged."

"I don't like nice people getting hurt on my account."

"You're so sweet, you know that?" Byron gave a wistful smile. "You've got it bad, haven't you?"

Her denial was too feeble and didn't conceal the tears welling up in her eyes. She brushed back her hair with her fingers. "It sounds crazy, I know. I tried reasoning with myself, without success."

"Look, honey, Scott's been my friend since I came here four years ago. I've never seen him so positive and possessive at the same time." Byron placed a comforting hand on her arm. "You've transformed him."

"But it doesn't lead anywhere."

"I hate to say this because I'm half crazy about you myself, but I think he really loves you. He's just too damned afraid to admit it."

"If I had the slightest reason to believe that, I'd propose to him." A sad smile fluttered on her lips.

The dogs started howling. "Talking about the devil, look who's arriving."

His headlamp bobbed on the trail and a moment later, his team pulled up in front of them.

"You're not expecting him?"

"No, she's not," Scott snapped. He threw the anchor down. "This cavorting is becoming a habit."

Byron held the lead dogs. "Well, well, still going round with a sore head?" Byron stretched his tall frame.

"Are you looking for a fight or something? Anyway, what are you doing here?" Scott grumbled and unhitched the wheel dogs.

"Waiting to help you."

They quickly cared for the dogs.

Scott's simmering temper got the better of him. "So what's the excuse today for being here instead of attending to your duties?"

"I broke trail ahead of Chris and her team."

A bubble of laughter came up to her lips. Her friend was teasing Scott, and he fell for it.

"Why the hell did you do that for? If she takes a team out, she can snowshoe the trail!"

"My, I hadn't thought of that!" Her taunt hardly masked her rising displeasure. Yet some other emotion drowned out her annoyance. Her eyes devoured his face, his rugged features contorted by some intense inner turmoil.

"I'll leave Chris to tell you the epic tale. She's the heroine of the day, my friend. Be proud of her."

"No, please don't leave. Stay while I explain to my boss what happened."

In a few words, she related her encounter with the snowmobile.

"Who is the guy?" His belligerent tone brook no good should he ever meet the man.

"Why? Are you planning to bust his other leg? He's a new guy from the village. Conrad drove him to the nursing station. The Mounties will handle the rest. They'll charge him with everything they can, including overdue library books. They're getting pretty darned sick of impaired snowmobile drivers who go round poaching animal parts. Which reminds me, they'll want a statement from you, Chris."

She smiled and nodded.

Byron waved. "I'd better go now. We'll have to get back and salvage the meat. Talk to you later." Byron turned to her and dropped a light kiss on her nose. "I think this guy'll keep trying. I may be wrong after all."

The roar of the departing snowmobile shattered the stillness of the night. After the dogs had been fed, Scott stood aside to let her enter the cabin. The soft lamplight heightened the somber expression in his eyes. He tossed his parka over a hook.

"So, what's going on? Are you trying Byron out too?" The disdain in his voice cut her to the quick, though she wasn't going to admit it.

"It's a free country, isn't it?" Her tart answer startled him, but it didn't give her any satisfaction.

He whirled and crushed her against him. His mouth came down to possess hers. Faint tremors began in the pit of her stomach, growing in wider and wider circles.

He pulled away. "Does he kiss any better?" A bitter challenge colored his voice. Dazed from the sudden onslaught, she stared at him in mute amazement. He raked his hand through his hair. Making a visible effort, he stepped back. "No. Forget I just said that."

"That was a ridiculous question to ask. I wouldn't answer, anyway." Her breathing had steadied, but the desperate yearning inside persisted.

He threw himself onto the couch and watched her pick up her backpack from beside the door and disappear into her room.

***

Eyes fixed on the red glow of the woodstove, he chastised himself. He had sworn he wouldn't let another woman into his life. Not only had he let this one through his defenses, he had actually wanted to possess her with such intensity he couldn't stop himself. But more, he needed all of her, her vivacious personality, her sassy tongue. No, this wouldn't do. The auburn-haired woman in the other room did not differ from the others in his life. True, she shared his passion for racing. So had Alina, only, her interest had been short-lived and a mere sham.

Nothing had been good enough for Alina. He hadn't seen her for what she was until too late. Bitterness colored his thoughts. The charm of living in the northland quickly wore thin. Her sexy diamond-in-the-rough, as she called him, became a boor under her acid tongue. To Scott, she rapidly became a shrew. The ensuing custody battle over their baby drained him financially and emotionally. No one, not even Chris, was going to put him through that hell again.

Maybe he should just give up everything and go and live deeper in the mountains, the way old Hiram did. Scott had met the white-haired hermit in the store one day. The old man came out of seclusion only once a year, driving his team of equally ancient dogs to buy his meager supplies.

His mind came back to Chris. How different she was from his ex-wife. No nonsense Chris had instilled in him a new confidence. Of course, she scoffed at the lack of modern conveniences because at season's end, she'd leave to go and get her own team and disappear from his life. Full of knowledge and experience, she'd join the racing circuit and be a winner and quickly forget about the ill-tempered man who had given her the break she needed. She couldn't care for him. No sane woman would. One evening of great sex meant nothing to a hot-blooded woman like her, determined as she was to succeed. To women like her, sex was just another weapon to enslave men. That he'd never allow to happen to him again.

She stepped back into the room to prepare dinner. The thoughts churning through his mind vanished as his eyes followed her every movement.

CHAPTER TWELVE

At breakfast, Chris tried to find some way to bring Scott out of the cloak of silence he had wrapped himself in. The only weak chink in his armor was his love of dogs. "I don't want to impose on your busy schedule, but I think you should spend some time with the pups. If you don't, they'll grow up without knowing you."

He flinched. His face hardened. The dishes rattled when he brought his hand down in a fist on the table. Without bothering with a coat, he strode out of the cabin.

The door slammed shut behind him. His reaction to her suggestion astounded her. So angry. It didn't fit. Usually, the mention of the pups was met with sympathetic understanding. The suffering etched on his face made her regret her choice of words, or maybe the tone she used. Not meaning to, she may have injected a note of reproach in it, a challenge even in her voice. A sigh escaped her. Living with him wasn't easy.

His parka over her arm, she went outside. The sub-zero temperature hit her squarely in the face, but she knew where to find him. Crouched among the pups, he let them jumped all over him, paw him, lick him. Her heart beat faster to see how relaxed he seemed. Anxious not to break the fragile spell, she let herself into the pen as quietly as she could. The pups turned their exuberant attention on her. He accepted the parka with a brief thanks.

"Let's take them out to see what you have taught them. More games, I bet."

"Right." Relief flooded her at his change of mood.

Amazed, he watched while she put the young dogs through their paces.

"Let's take them out on the trail."

It was her turn to admire as he ran and jumped with the pups. His tall, powerful frame was so agile, so vibrant, that she was filled with renewed hope. She wished she'd never have to leave this remote valley or leave the man presently making a fool of himself with a bunch of young dogs. A strong sense of belonging engulfed her.

The rest of the day passed like a dream. She sang as she worked with the dogs and later replenished the wood box. With him there, it was as if she were on vacation. The beautiful winter landscape around them was a picture postcard backdrop to her happiness.

After dinner, he busied himself sharpening the points of the sled brake, while she finished a new harness for one of the big pups.

To avoid disturbing the mood, she chose her words with care. "By the way, Conrad and Byron want to throw a party. They asked if you would come."

"A party! What's the matter? Missing the bright lights?"

She quashed her sigh, realizing that she'd chosen the wrong moment to speak. Again.

"I couldn't care about the bright lights. Your friends have suggested a small gathering. You can't shun the rest of the world all the time." She bit her lip.

His face was a closed mask. "Fine. If you feel like that, you go. Take up with someone else while you're at it."

"Grow up, will you?" Her face colored. "I'm talking about a social outing. One relaxed evening of fun wouldn't hurt you."

His voice hardened. "I've chosen my way of life. If it doesn't suit you, then go. All women are alike. All of them! I should never have let you stay on here."

No way was she going to rise to his bait. Instead, she shrugged and went to her room. Once more, she had blundered into forbidden territory. If she needed more proof that a woman had almost destroyed that man, she now had it. Hatred surged for that unknown woman who hadn't loved him enough or at all.

***

Alone once more, he sat staring at the stove. Bitter memories flooded his mind. Alina had loved parties more than anything else. Then she was pregnant. Of course, she'd been prompt to blame him for not taking precautions. But he'd insisted the baby was precious and had married her. When the racing season was about to start, he had brought her north, with the promise he'd build her a big house fitted with all the luxuries of city life. By the time the baby was born, she'd have everything. Too impatient to wait, it hadn't taken her long to loath the cramped cabin and the simple lifestyle. She fled back to California, leaving their newborn baby with him.

At first, she appeared different. The outdoors, the dogs, the routine of race training, all what made up his life, Chris also liked. Alina, too, had claimed to love the dogs, but she also told him she didn't want anything to do with them.

The fact that Chris wanted to go to a party was not, in itself, so awful. But it represented the first step down a slippery slope. Soon, he'd be enmeshed in a social whirl he wasn't prepared for. That would be the end of his rigorous training.

He didn't know why he should be so obsessed with her. He had to admit she worked well, and his dogs adored her. Despite her denials, she was truly a splendid cook, and he was enjoying the best bread any man could wish for.

An unwelcome heat overwhelmed him. He slapped his head! Did she have to be beautiful as well? That soft feminine exterior was a deception; it hid the conditioned body of an athlete. His hands ached to touch her again. Such delicate features and smooth skin didn't belong in the wilderness. Yet she fitted in here as if she'd been born to it. With her at his side, his days were brighter and the long hours of darkness were less somber.

Disturbed by thoughts of simmering passion and unfulfilled longing, he went outside into the frigid, starlit night. Thousand of sounds in the forest whispered that not all creatures were asleep. The hoot of an owl, the squeak of a rodent, an old tree cracking in the cold, the faraway howls of wolves made up the eternal song of this untamed north country. It appeased his soul.

***

When Chris awoke in the morning, he was already out. That didn't surprise her, since he often was first up. Yet there was no sign of him in the dog compound. There was no light in the kennel building. A sled and a team were gone. Vexed that he had made a night start without telling her, and without breakfast, she went about her daily tasks, then took a team out. On her way back, she heard a deep baritone voice singing off key. Noises, particularly the human voice, carry far in the cold, still air. Although she was too surprised to believe it, it had to be him. Other mushers didn't venture much around these parts.

She halted her team and waited. Her dogs had heard him, too. Their ears turned as one toward the sound. He was closer now, and she thought it'd be unwise to surprise him on the trail.

"Hike!" she commanded. Reluctantly, the huskies resumed the trek home. The singing had stopped. A moment later, his team broke from the cover of trees and drew alongside hers. Automatically, she called her team over to the side to permit him to pass.

"No, no. We'll run together. It's good for the dogs. They're too isolated. We need to meet more teams."

"How about running some local races?"

"Too far to go for just a day's run. Anyway, my freighters wouldn't stand a chance in those sprint races. I don't want to break their spirit by losing."

A smile floated on her lips. He could have taken the huskies to the local races, but he hadn't left any room for it in the training schedule. Winning the Yukon Quest was now his one and only goal, and nothing was going to distract him from it. His pride had returned, and that, she believed, was an achievement.

They traveled in company. Close enough for her to reach out and touch him. Taking deep breaths to curb the urge, she pulled her tuque down over her ears. Aware of her scrutiny, he turned and smiled, a devastating smile. His eyes, grayer than the winter sky, brimmed with affection. Hope swelled in her heart.

Her team running parallel to his paid scant attention to hers. Both teams strained to get ahead. The trail was almost too narrow for two teams abreast, but for a brief moment, she imagined she was shoulder to shoulder with a rival competing in the famed Iditarod. They were racing to the finish line in Nome, Alaska, with her sliding in under the burled arch, and the crowds going wild.

Without warning, she burst into a yodeling song. Itirit in the lead pricked up her ears and leaned into her harness. The rest of the team members were already in tune with their leader and ran like demons. Her team arrived home a whole length in front of his. An impish smile on her lips, rosy and breathless, she greeted him. "I believe I won that heat."

"You did! Where the heck did you learn to yodel like that?"

"I haven't the faintest idea. Most times I just make a gargling noise. Whether it's a song or my version of yodeling doesn't seem to bother the dogs."

"Far from it. It makes them run like the wind."

They laughed and went to take care of their respective teams. They did the evening chores together. In the future, she'd choose her words carefully in case she damaged the wonderful yet fragile harmony that had so unexpectedly been re-established.

The dogs' howling, followed by a knock on the door, interrupted their table talk. Byron entered, a broad grin on his face.

"There's a letter for you, Chris." He handed her an envelope.

"Thanks. You didn't come up especially to deliver this, did you?"

"I called in at the store and Mary badgered me into delivering it. I couldn't refuse. Besides, the Fletcher Creek singles set has proposed we all celebrate Christmas Eve together at my place. Pot luck. Everyone brings something." Byron gave a smirk. "Scott, you'll bring Chris?"

"No. I won't be available." His terse tone chilled the air.

"Come on, you need a little R & R."

"I tell you, I will not be here."

Byron's coaxing had no effect. A pang of disappointment tugged at her. Training was important, but she had hoped he would stay home for Christmas. A shiver shook her. Home... She must stop making these associations, but there was no denying that the cabin had become just as much home to her as the big house she had grown up in.

Byron smiled at her and said. "Then, if he's busy elsewhere, honey, I'll come and fetch you."

Scott's expression turned sour. The earlier relaxed atmosphere vanished. She almost groaned out loud, dismayed at how little it took to switch his mood back to the old bristling attitude.

"I've a letter to post. Would you be so kind as to mail it for me?"

"My pleasure. Just give me a call whenever you have mail to pick up."

"She can go to town any time she wants. She doesn't need you to handle her mail."

"Well, thank you for telling me." A touch of irony laced her words. "I wasn't planning a trip to Fletcher Creek for at least a couple of days."

"The keys are always in the truck."

"Actually, I prefer to take the team of older dogs to town. It's a nice run for them."

"Oh, you found the back trail to town." There was a hint of respect in his tone, yet he frowned as if annoyed.

Byron coughed. "Well, I have to be off. Give me your letter and I'll see it catches the next outgoing mail."

The noise of Byron's snowmobile faded into the distance, and the cabin settled back into silence. It was pointless to expect Scott to revert to the happy state he was in before Byron's visit. The irritated expression had returned. She knew she could talk him out of it. A couple of shelves of books hung near the door.

"You don't mind if I read some of your books?"

His face brightened. "Of course not. Try this book. It's My Life of Adventure, by Norman D. Vaughan. You'll discover he's quite a character. He was in his late eighties when he ran the Iditarod for the nth time."

She took the book from his hand and read the first sentence three times over before admitting to herself that she couldn't concentrate. Without shifting her eyes from the page, she was aware of his gaze on her, a hungry gaze that expressed his primitive longing. A familiar warmth spread throughout her. If only they could be honest and open with each other. The tension between them rose a few more degrees.

When she did look at him, he was writing in a notebook. He avoided meeting her eyes. Exasperated, she closed the book and wished him goodnight.

***

His self-control slipped when she left the room. A surge of fire spread through his body already tense with unfulfilled need. The point of his pencil broke under his hard grip. Only one word on the page: Chris. He wasn't sure why he told her he wouldn't be there for Christmas. Alina might or might not let him see his son. The number of times she had an excuse to cancel his visits was too numerous to remember. He was aware of her game. The only time it was convenient to schedule a visit coincided exactly with the most important races he had to enter in order to earn enough money to survive. And in summer, she was traveling to far-flung countries where she knew he couldn't afford to fly. A knot gripped his throat. There was no need for him to take it out on Chris, but he couldn't help wanting her desperately and, at the same time, wanting her miles away. He just didn't understand the turbulent feelings he was experiencing.

***

In the days that followed, they behaved like two boxers in the ring, each wary of making the first contact. If they happened to collide while handling the dogs, they recoiled with mumbled apologies.

Before setting off with his team, he finally exploded. "Damn it! This pussyfooting around is killing me. I want you."

Without letting her reply, he took her in his arms and invaded her willing mouth. A jealous dog thrust itself between the two humans and brought them back to the present. The kiss ended as if lightning had fallen between them.

Afterwards, he struggled with himself to behave as if nothing had happened. He looked at his team. "Can you take Arnavik to the maternity ward? She's due any time from now on." His voice, heavy with thinly controlled passion, wavered.

"Certainly."

His departure didn't bring her peace. His kiss had set her body afire, although the trembling had subsided. No doubt he would come back early. Arnavik came over and nuzzled her hand. The once trim dog waddled somewhat ungainly at her side. In the large pen inside the kennel building, Chris lay out more straw. Arnavik walked around and around until the straw was flattened to her satisfaction. Then she settled down and went to sleep.

After dinner that evening, she and Scott went to check on Arnavik's progress. They sat together on a bale of straw in one corner of the pen and observed the canine mother to be. He talked gently, and Arnavik responded by rubbing her head against his hand. The dog's heavy panting was the only sign that something was about to happen.

Several minutes later, the dog turned her head toward her back end and brought her first pup out. Well licked but still damp, and protesting vigorously, it found its way to a teat to suckle greedily. Scott pulled out his notebook and recorded the birth. When a second pup appeared, he picked up the first one, weighed it and placed it in the open front of his jacket to keep it warm while its mother was busy with the newborn. Then he put it back to nurse alongside the second pup.

The pups, all seven of them, arrived at intervals. She marveled at his gentle manner. There was an expression of quiet on his face, as though this was the first time he had seen the miracle of birth, yet she knew it wasn't. He placed a black and white pup in her hands. She looked down at the tiny creature, blind, deaf and so utterly dependent. She kissed its moist little head and put it back with his mother to suckle.

When the new mother ceased labor, Scott checked her over and left water for her in the pen.

"No need to give her food. She won't eat for the next couple of days. All those placentas she gobbled are nourishing her so she can stay with her pups when they are at their most vulnerable."

Smiling with satisfaction, he extended his hand to her to help her up. Taking it sent millions of delightful miniature shocks up her arm. She stretched her cramped limbs and turned off the lamp. The door securely closed, they walked to the cabin.

As she removed her outer clothes, she threw him a tender glance. "It's always wonderful to be present at a birth, isn't it?"

"It never fails." He loaded wood into the stove. "I always feel privileged to see the creation of a new life."

The softness in his voice tugged at her heartstrings. No doubt he would have the same sense of wonderment at the birth of his own child. How wonderful he'd make his wife feel. Somewhere in the world, there had to be a woman who could win his love and smooth the stress off his brow. Better not think about that since she wouldn't be around to witness it. Her throat constricted. Don't think about that. He needs someone soft and pliable. Yet, she wanted to be that woman. No matter how much she chided herself, she still wanted to be that woman.

Standing side by side with him at the kitchen counter was enough to send quivers down her spine. For the moment, a sense of having truly come home flooded her with hope.

To occupy her hands, she poured milk into a saucepan. He picked up the can of cocoa. Their eyes met. His head tilted slowly toward her and his lips touched hers. The pressure on her lips increased. She raised herself on tiptoe to press closer to him. He let the cocoa can fall as he encircled her waist.

"Scott, the cocoa..."

"Who the hell needs cocoa?"

A wild, primeval force swelled between them as he pulled her into his arms. His scent, so redolent of this mysterious northern land, intoxicated her. His hand pulled the clasp from her hair and let the silken tresses tumble over her shoulder.

"You are too tempting for a sane man. You're utterly irresistible. I have to make love to you."

He buried his face for a moment in the wildflower fragrance of her hair. She smoothed the anxious lines on his forehead.

"I want you too."

His passion rising, he lifted her in his arms and carried her to the bed.

For the longest time, they held each other close. Lulled by the distant cry of wolves, they drifted into sleep.

They rose late next morning. Gentleness expressed itself in his every gesture. They set about the day's work. His finger raked his hair as he announced he didn't want to be away. They would run the teams together and arrange to have their two teams meet and pass on the same trail, so the dogs would get used to passing other teams.

As his sled passed hers in the opposite direction, he stole a frozen kiss from her. Laughter echoed among the pines. Gray jays sat on the end of branches and looked on with curiosity. Back in the cabin, Chris cooked their meal. Happiness filled the air.

A sticky mess of dough and apples out of the oven in her hands, she tilted her head. "I reckon I wasn't concentrating." She grimaced. "I'd best throw it away."

He stayed her arm just as she was about to empty the pan's contents into the trash pail. "Don't. It's perfectly edible. All good ingredients." He tried his best to suppress a smile.

"Even though my mom kept saying there's nothing to cooking, I still create regular disasters."

"Don't put yourself down. You're a great cook... most of the time." His eyes shone.

Humor sparkled all around them. "At least the dogs don't complain about my cooking. But then, with raw meat and bagged food, I can hardly go wrong."

"Your broth is delicious." His face remained deadpan.

"You haven't tried it, so don't speak."

"Oh, but I did. One day, I'd spilled my thermos. I was too lazy to set up the stove to melt snow, so I drank some of the dogs' broth."

They shared a moment of carefree laughter.

"You must miss not having your dogs around."

"I've got plenty of others here."

"That's not the same."

"Agreed. I do miss those old dogs of mine. But it's only a temporary absence."

A silence fell. A temporary absence. Suddenly, she realized that eventually she'd have to leave. Not to see him again would quell the flame of happiness she had kindled with such care.

An overwhelming elation surged through her. And shock too. For the first time, she freely admitted to herself the depth of her feelings for him. That all-encompassing emotion which submerged her could be nothing else but love. It was love that made her watch anxiously at the window when he was late returning. Love that overflowed into such wondrous excitement when he smiled.

The flip side of being in love with him was that he didn't love her. Lust, yes. Love, no. Last night, they had glimpsed paradise. But during those idyllic moments, he had not been able to say the magic words *I love you*.

"How about getting your dogs up here? There's room for them."

"That's very nice of you to offer, but then Marcia would also miss them. Besides, I can't afford the cost of transport."

"We could arrange that. My friend Jerome comes up every year to race the Yukon Quest. He could bring them."

"I'd feel like a heel taking them from Marcia. Anyway, two of them are hers, and we couldn't possibly separate the dogs. They'd die of grief."

"Yes, I know how they get so attached to one another. Sometimes they don't survive the death of a lifelong companion."

Charlie's sked, on cue as usual, interrupted them. While Scott talked to him, she occupied herself by tidying the cabin. Her mind kept returning to whether they would again share a night of passion. The very idea kept her on edge. But she mustn't think of it as the beginning of a relationship. Perhaps he could learn to love her. Perhaps not. Love and commitment weren't in his vocabulary. It wasn't in most men's vocabulary. She had learned that the hard way. It took very little to throw him back into a bleak mood. She ought not to be dreaming, but she'd take all she could in the meantime, starting with a goodnight kiss.

He watched the curtain fall back and almost jumped up to follow her, but he needed her to keep up his spirits, keep him centered on the task of preparing for the big race. Her quiet assertiveness and her feminine presence had become indispensable. Her jauntiness spiced up their daily routine. There had to be a way to keep her with him at the end of the season. He shook his head. No need to think about that just yet. Ideas crowded his brain, nonetheless.

A smile lingered on his lips while he loaded the stove for the night. With one last look around to make sure everything was in order, he blew out the lamp. He stretched and looked toward the linen curtain. A feeble moonlight shone through it. A battle raged inside him while he took his cabin boots off.

They had established a peaceful work atmosphere. If he succumbed to his desire to make love to her, it might destroy the fragile truce. He threw his sweater on the couch and sighed. Without him being aware, he had taken the few steps to the bedroom. He lifted the curtain.

Half-undressed, she turned round and smiled at him. The soft light of her oil lamp threw a golden glow over her skin and set sparkles of fire in her hair. Mesmerized, he stood still for a moment before reaching for her.

Chapter Thirteen

L ulled by the steady pace of the huskies up front, Chris breathed the cold air as it rushed past her face. Darkness had already crept over the valley. A shimmering mantle of snow reflected the tranquil light of the moon and stars.

Only a few days before Christmas. A genuine friendship had blossomed between them, but she was preoccupied with how she could change his mind about the party at Byron's. She took a deep breath under her neck warmer and murmured to the wind. Lovemaking it was, but still not love. He had made no further mention of being away at Christmas, and the training was going well. Surely, he could skip one day without setting the team back. Rest periods were also part of thorough training.

When she pulled into the dog yard, she saw immediately that he was back. Her heart leaped with joy. She quickly finished her chores so that she could sit for a while with the new puppies. They had grown. Their eyes had now opened onto the world.

He was talking on the radiophone when she entered the cabin, probably ordering dog food.

A line creased his forehead and his smile was strained as he set down the mike. "Had a good run?"

"Yes, it was fine, thanks."

Although she would deny it, she wasn't surprised that he'd cut his trip short.

He broke the short silence. "The dogs were impatient to turn back."

An impish smile lit her features. "Were they? Just the dogs?"

"Well, their musher too. Don't think I'd push my dogs just because I want to kiss you."

"I hope not, Mr. Walsh." She went and raised herself on tiptoe, offering him her lips.

"I've missed you." He engulfed her in his powerful arms. His stubble chin rasped her cheek as the kiss lengthened. A tremor shook her and she reluctantly pulled apart.

"I must go and feed the dogs."

"Don't take too long. I'll wash and shave."

Dressing rapidly, she let herself out, but hadn't gone far when she thought she heard the call on the radiophone. Charlie must be early.

Once the dogs were fed and watered, she hurried back to the cabin. A smile floated on her lips as she watched the northern lights dancing in the sky. The scratch of paws on the snow, the subtle scent of pine smoke drifting skyward, Scott waiting in the cozy cabin, their common goal and the dogs, all that was home. Home wasn't a house or any place. Home was where the heart found love.

The moment she stepped into the cabin, she was aware his mood had changed. The old shuttered look was back. Her heart sank. His mood flipping with such rapidity remained a mystery. They'd shared some beautiful moments over the past couple of weeks. She was careful not to make any demands on him. He went on with his usual training program, being away for two or three days at a time, coming back impatient and ardent.

At the beginning of the evening, he'd been happy, carefree almost. Something had happened that he couldn't confide in her. Unless it was something Charlie had passed on, but then if something had happened in the far-ranging community, he'd share it with her. It definitely had to do with the call.

"I've got to catch the bus tomorrow morning. Will you drive me to town?"

Only with the utmost willpower did she prevent her jaw from dropping.

"The bus...? Yes, of course. While I'm in Fletcher Creek, I'll get some groceries. It'll save me a trip later." She was babbling.

The silence hung heavy with all that was not said. Since he wasn't willing to share his travel plans, she wasn't going to ask in case it completely broke the magic that had enchanted them earlier in the evening. His face showed signs of the old hostility. Standing by the window and looking out into the night, he didn't say another word.

Puzzled, she put the meal on the table. They ate in silence. She dealt with the domestic chores, then retired to her room. The certainty he wouldn't be joining her tonight weighed heavily on her. A sudden weariness tinged with sadness crept into her bones. As she had often done of late, she wondered where this relationship was going. He had responded, if not with love, at least with passion. Hostility had given way to tenderness. Yet, tonight, he'd once again withdrawn into his shell. At the heart of the sublime emotion she felt for him was the numbing realization that she had given herself to a fickle man. Her earlier happiness clutched at her heart as it disintegrated.

Evidently, their recent intimacy meant little to him. In that respect, he was the stereotype of a male. He took what he wanted and walked away. Now he sought to put distance between them, literally and figuratively, by taking the bus to goodness knows where, at Christmas of all times. A need to paint him dark gnawed at her. The more she could conjure up faults, the lighter her heart would feel. But it didn't work.

Lip biting didn't help. Following her own advice and resisting the attraction between them had failed miserably. It was too late now to undo the past and just as useless to regret it. Though regret it, she would, and bitterly. An uneasiness rose in her when the thought she could be pregnant came to her. Contraception had not even crossed their minds. She shrugged and hummed *Que Sera Sera. Whatever will be, The future's not ours to see...*

Thoughts swirled in her mind and prevented her from sleeping for a while. After a long while, she sank into an abyss of oblivion.

The night was short. The sound of movement in the cabin woke her up. Scott! A sudden rush of emotion caught in her throat. He was preparing to leave. Leaving without confiding in her. For no reason she could think of, he had shut her out of his life, even after those wonderful moments spent together, not just making love but sharing and working together.

Despite the thick comforter, the cold crept around her and brought about an acute sense of abandon. So different was this from the previous departures with their joyful teams of huskies. Of course, he said he was going for a few days only. Then he'd be back because of the dogs and the race training. Perhaps a little because of her.

He looked up when she came out of her room. His face registered nothing, but she read the signs.

"Good-morning." His voice sounded awkward, stilted. He resumed packing his bag.

The frying pan was already on the stove. The last two eggs soon sizzled in the pan.

"I don't need breakfast. We should get going."

"Well, I need to eat. I'm not driving on an empty stomach."

No way was she going to be cowed by his aggressive manner. He shrugged and went outside. As before, he took refuge with the dogs. She prepared the food for them both and served two plates. When he came back in, she waved him to a chair.

"There's no need to sulk. Eat."

A grumble about wanting to be away passed his lips, but he ate. "You sure you can take care of things while I'm away?"

"Of course, that's why you hired me, isn't it?" A faint trace of mockery tinged her voice.

He frowned but made no reply.

A glance at the clock confirmed that he was right. There was no time to waste if he was to catch the seven-thirty bus. The dishes could wait. With one jump, she got into the truck. The motor was already running. He drove the four-by-four in low gear through the deep snow until they reached the main highway. She breathed easier and wished she didn't have to come back alone to tackle their snow-filled track.

The bus hadn't arrived, but she didn't wait. No point in a lingering goodbye, not when he was morose and silent. He didn't even look at her. Despite the hour, the store was open since it also served as the bus depot. Her shopping didn't take long. When she came out, the bus had come and gone.

So had Scott.

On the return trip up to the cabin, the fight to keep the truck on the road took her mind off her sorrows. Once home, she resolved not to give him another thought. Maybe she lacked realism, but from now on, it was going to be strictly a business relationship. In order to convince herself, she repeated it several times.

The work took her mind off the hurt, but it troubled her he had left bristling with suppressed anger. She wanted to share his worries, to soothe and encourage him, but he wouldn't let her near him. Not even after the beautiful moments they'd shared, right until that phone call.

Later in the day, the dogs signaled the approach of someone on the road. She listened. The booming noise of an engine made her anxious. It couldn't be a delivery truck. The rest of the dog meat order had been stored in the cache while he was home. She remembered wistfully how their laughter had lightened the task of carrying the heavy cartons. The vehicle eventually came into view. A huge snowplow blasted its way into the yard. It stopped, and a man jumped down from the cab. She went out to meet him.

"Hi! I'm Devon Santoni. Byron said I'd better plow your road so you could get to the Christmas celebrations in town. Is Old Grizzly here?"

"He caught the bus out this morning."

"Darn! I wanted to know if he'd sell me a couple of pups. When will he be back?"

"That I don't know."

Tall, dark eyed, and broad-shouldered, black hair protruding from under a wool toque, Devon looked as though he'd stepped off the cover of a men's fashion magazine.

"Do you mind if I take a look at the dogs? I never come up without visiting them." He flashed her a devastating smile. "I'm in the market for pups."

"Good. Did you want a couple of the seven-month-old pups?"

"Yes, that's right. I got rid of my wife," he said. "I want to rebuild my sledding team. Recreational only, I'm not into racing."

It took her a moment to absorb his off-the-cuff remark. "What do you mean, you got rid of your wife?"

"The wife didn't like my dogs. I gave them away and regretted it ever after. Then she decided she hated it up here. She left and went back south." Devon pointed out a lively pup rolling an ice ball around the pen. "This black male is a beauty. Do you think Scott would part with him?"

"Charcoal? Quite possibly. I noticed this particular pup stays on the edge of the pack. He never seems to join in with the others. See how he plays on his own? He'd make an excellent sled dog on a small team."

"Would he get along with my old Bruno? The guy who took him has offered to give him back to me."

The emotion in his dark eyes touched her. She guessed the pain he suffered when he had to give away his faithful companions. All that for a woman who didn't appreciate his sacrifice, didn't understand his love, and selfishly moved on with her life.

"I'm sure he would. He gets along fine with our older dogs. And he's got a very friendly nature. The little white female with a black head is bonded with Charcoal."

"Good, I'd love them both. Don't tell me she's called Snow White."

She laughed. "You bet! But I had nothing to do with naming them."

When the laughter subsided, Devon said, "By the way, while I'm here, would you like me to clear your yard? I see you're getting a little choked up with snow."

"That would be great. I find it hard to move about and there's too much to clear with a shovel."

"Your road isn't on the schedule to be plowed for free, but what the Public Works Department don't know won't hurt them. I'll be back later for my pups."

They shared an easy chuckle. She watched as he skillfully maneuvered the big machine, removing several weeks' accumulation of snow and dumping it on the downslope at the edge of the compound. He waved goodbye to her from the cab and sent the powerful machine down the incline and back along the track.

Overwhelmed by the noise and Devon's whirlwind visit, she walked to the forest edge and gathered spruce boughs to make a Christmas wreath. Back in the cabin, she cut a length of tin foil into narrow strips and wove them through the clumps of fragrant green needles.

The result was so pleasing she decided to do some more decorating. By the end of the evening, she'd made garlands of spruce and small tin-foil bells to lend a festive touch to the cabin.

Total darkness prevailed when she went out to check on the dogs and let Renoir out of the pen. "Come along, big fellow, she said. You miss him, and so do I. We'll keep each other company."

The black dog bounded inside and ran straight to the couch. Though when she went to her room, Renoir had no hesitation in following her in and curling up on the mat beside the bed. After a moment, he stood and put his muzzle on the bedcover. She reached over and scratched him behind his ears. By way of thanks, he held out his paw. Laughing softly, she shook it, then kissed his broad head. The dog lay back down and gave a sigh of sheer contentment. He definitely was a people's dog.

However, at two in the morning, he wanted to go back to his pen. Renoir wasn't a house dog. She had almost forgotten it, though she didn't mind her outing. Twinkling stars crowded the sky. A flame of red shot from behind the trees, curled back and hooked a green veil to dance back and forth. Hypnotized, she watched the northern lights till the cold began to hurt.

Chapter Fourteen

In a fit of mild exasperation, Chris dumped the contents of her bag on the bed. Makeup. It was unthinkable to go to a party without makeup, even here in the back of beyond. Now she had to find it.

After a long search, she located the few items that made up her cosmetic kit and placed them in readiness by the mirror. She then turned her attention to the old-fashioned flatiron heating on the stove. Gingerly, she tested the heavy iron by holding it close to her cheek. With even greater caution, she touched it to the damp cloth laid over her one and only dress, a pretty outfit in fine burgundy wool.

Before dressing, she applied soft brown eye shadow to her eyelids and enhanced her long eyelashes with dark mascara. A bit of pink gloss outlined her lips. Then she wriggled into the sleeveless dress. The clinging fabric with its elegant but simple cut outlined her slender figure. In the restricted bathroom space, she performed a pirouette to flare the calf-length skirt. Scott's shaving mirror didn't give her a full view, but that's all there was. Thinking of him made her wonder what he would say if he could see her now, dressed in all her finery. It'd be enough to jolt him out of his touchy mood, though maybe not.

From her bag, she took a gold-mounted topaz pendant that had been her mother's favorite and fastened the thin gold chain around her neck. The lamplight glittered on the jewel. She pressed her lips together to ward off the wave of longing that engulfed her. If only he could see her...

Just as she finished, the lights of Byron's truck lit up the windows. A knock followed, and Byron himself filled the door frame. His mouth gaped.

"Wow! Princess, where have you been hiding all this time? You look absolutely gorgeous."

"Thank you, sir."

"That dress does wonder for you. You should wear it more often."

"Can you imagine me sledding in this getup?"

"Why not? Right now, my imagination is running wild."

She laughed. "In that case, you should go outside and cool it off in the snow."

"Won't I just gloat when the guys see me with you on my arm. Seriously, I'm the luckiest man on this side of the mountains."

"Have you been lacking feminine company, by any chance?"

"You can say that again. Shall we go?"

"Give me a minute to get my outdoor gear on over my dress and I'll be right with you."

Byron didn't react immediately. His eyes traveled down her body from head to toe and back again. "A man could die for a touch of that long hair of yours," he said at last.

"It's the night for compliments? I suppose as a woman I should be happy to hear them."

"Aren't you?"

Her eyes met his. "Don't take me wrong, I love it. I'm just out of practice. Now let's move if we're going to the party."

"I could think of some alternatives." Byron gave a devilish grin.

"So could I. There's frozen meat to be chopped up for tomorrow's dog chow, and a whole stack of wood waiting to be split."

Byron laughed at her quick wit. She pulled on her insulated snow boots, a wool tunic which reached her knees and zipped her down-filled parka. In one hand, she carried her silver high-heeled sandals and, in the other, the container of cookies she had been asked to provide for the party. "Okay, I'm ready."

He walked her to the truck and helped her up the high step. Always considerate, he wrapped a blanket around her legs.

"Thanks. A party dress isn't made for this weather, even with my leggings underneath."

The noise of the party hit them the moment they climbed down in front of Byron's log house, one of Fletcher Creek's finer residences. They took off their outer gear. Smiling faces greeted her when she entered the living room. To her relief, Vicky Peters was waiting for her.

"Hi Chris! I'm so glad you could come."

Conrad came forward to greet her. "And isn't she elegant?"

Vicky dug him in the ribs. "How can you judge? You spend your life in the backwoods, so I don't think you know what a woman looks like."

"I'd recognize a nice pair of legs anywhere."

Vicky took her by the arm. "Come along. Let me rescue you from these uncouth men. I'll show you the house first."

Back in the living room, Vicky introduced her to several other guests. Except for a handful of older and married women, Nicole Lantell, a beautiful First Nations woman, was the only other young one.

"Make yourself at home. Here, have some of the punch the men made. It's supposed to be non-alcoholic since Fletcher Creek is a dry community, but it's got a terrific kick to it," Nicole said.

Conrad leaned over and whispered in Chris's ear. "The secret is the half-bottle of Tabasco sauce I threw in."

Like the punch, the party turned out to be lively. Devon was in high spirits and cranked up the music to dance. Byron dragged Chris, laughing and smiling, over to the space that had been cleared for dancing at the end of the room. Other couples soon joined them. For a large part of the evening, she found herself dancing almost nonstop.

"My feet!" she groaned. A sofa welcomed her with its thick cushions.

"What else do you expect in a place where men outnumber the women by three to one?" Byron said.

The respite didn't last long before Byron pleaded with her to dance with him again. While she swayed to the music and talked easily with him, her thoughts were on Scott, wondering where he was at that precise moment. He hadn't shared his destination, and she had feared his reaction if she asked, so she hadn't. His puzzling and abrupt coldness after such wonderful days of intimacy still baffled her.

In spite of the carefree laughter and talk all around her, a dull pain settled in her heart. If she had to fall in love, she should have done so with an uncomplicated man like Byron. He was happily flirting with her. His adoring eyes followed her whenever she wasn't at his side. Unfortunately, when he held her on the dance floor, his touch didn't bring her alive the way Scott had.

"Are you enjoying yourself?" Byron asked. They filled their plates at the buffet table.

"Terrific. I just hope I can get up tomorrow, or rather later this morning, to care for the dogs."

"When you're ready to go, just say the word. I'll drive you home."

Children had fallen asleep on chairs, and parents were scooping them up. Even the die-hard were showing signs of fatigue.

"I guess it's time we went," she said.

The farewells were warm and the feelings genuine. The guests exchanged promises to meet again soon. Byron made a point of helping her on with her parka. That was when she noticed Vicky's wistful gaze on him and immediately felt like an intruder.

When they arrived at the cabin, she wished she had thought about leaving a light burning. In the dark, the cabin appeared deserted were it not for the chorus that greeted them the moment the dogs heard the approach of the truck.

"Just a minute, before you get out," Byron said. "I've got a flashlight here somewhere. I don't want you to trip over something in your finery."

He helped her light the lamp in the cool cabin and coax the embers into a roaring blaze.

"Would you care for something to drink? You'll not be surprised that the choice here runs to coffee, tea or hot chocolate. We do have good water too."

"Coffee would be nice. And Chris..."

Something in the way he said her name sent a jolt of alarm through her mind. She finished preparing the coffee before turning round.

"How is it going with Scott?"

"Professionally, very well."

"Emotionally?"

There, she knew where the conversation was leading but couldn't find the words to deflect it. "It's all right. I had a great time tonight. Thanks for a lovely party."

"You didn't answer my question. I asked, because I've grown more than fond of you. Since I met you, my heart has been turning somersaults."

She bit her lip. "I'm not a heart specialist, so can't give you any advice for that serious condition of yours."

Byron had the good grace to smile. "I know you don't want to hear this, but I love you. I did the moment I saw you standing on the road in the twilight."

Shaking her head, looked down. "I'm so sorry."

"I know. I've just been hoping that maybe you didn't really love him."

Her voice strained. "For all the good it does."

A silence lengthened between them.

"I'd better go and let you catch some sleep. Unlike the rest of us, you have work to do in the morning."

She stood and gave him a shaky smile.

"Actually, I should come up and help you with the dogs."

"Thanks, Byron, but you don't have to. It isn't a difficult task and the busier I'm, the better I like it."

"Okay, I have my marching orders."

"Can I still count on you to be my friend?"

"You bet. Any time you need me, I'll be there for you."

He'd already donned his parka and set his fur cap on his head when he bent his head toward her. The kiss was light. It didn't evoke a response in her.

A moment later, he was gone. She stood by the window until the red taillights disappeared down the hill. Tears she couldn't controlled rolled down her cheeks. The emptiness of the cabin closed in around her.

After a few hours of sleep, she got up, surprised how fresh she was. After a simple breakfast, she was deciding which dogs she would take out for a run, when she was alerted by the approach of a snowmobile.

Her heart leaped in her chest in the hope that it might be Scott. It wouldn't have been the first time he'd returned unexpectedly. It was not one, but two snowmobiles. Both drivers had a passenger on the seat, and the second machine was pulling a toboggan with two children. They drew to a halt in the yard. She went out to meet the visitors.

"Season's greetings!" Byron pulled off his helmet. "Meet Cindy and Mike. They weren't at the party last night. Cindy is Mary and Fred's daughter. These two scamps, eight-year-old Jack and six-year-old Danny, are Mike and Cindy's kids. They're up from the city. They've never seen sled dogs before, so I thought it might be fun for them. I hope you don't mind the impromptu visit."

"Merry Christmas, everybody! I'm delighted to have company, even though I've nothing much in the house to offer you."

"Don't worry, Mom sent a Christmas cake for you," Cindy said.

"Thank you. How about a sled ride? I was about to take a team out."

"The kids would love that, if it's not too much trouble."

"Not at all. It's excellent training for the dogs. Do you want to take a team and come along, Byron?"

"Okay. I'll take Jack and Cindy in my sled. You take Conrad and the kids. That should equalize the weight."

Conrad gave a good-natured growl. "Hey! I'm not riding in one of those!"

She chuckled. "Yes, you are. I need the ballast. These freighting dogs can really pull."

"Byron, you devil, you didn't warn me about this when you dragged me up here. Right now, I could be sleeping in."

"The fresh air will do you good." Byron laughed while preparing the gangline and the sled bag.

Soon, seven Canadian Inuit dogs were hitched to Chris's sled and six to Byron's. The passengers settled themselves in. The dogs turned round and came to inspect the helpless travelers, generously kissing them with wet tongues. Satisfied with their cargo, the dogs tightened the lines and waited for the order to hike.

The dogs sensed this was a special run. They started at top speed, kicking up the snow behind them. Shrieks of laughter burst from the children. A short way down the trail, the dogs settled into their cruising speed.

The impressive silence of the wild nature awed the young visitors, and no one wanted to spoil it with a human voice. She watched closely in case the children were cooling down, but saw only happy smiles. The party arrived back at the kennel with cries of excitement.

Conrad joked and rubbed his backside with exaggerated gestures. "That damned sled needs its shock absorbers testing."

"Bring a cushion next time."

"Is it hard to drive that bunch of dogs?" Conrad adopted a more serious tone.

"Easy enough," she replied.

"I think I could like that."

"See, I told you. We'll give it a try sometime," Byron said.

The men took care of the dog chores while she explained the work to the children, then she showed them the new puppies. Later, she made hot chocolate for everyone and even discovered some leftover cookies in the cupboard. Only the children accepted a slice of their grandmother's cake. Conrad regaled the visitors with outlandish tales of the wilderness.

Long after her guests were swallowed up by the darkness down the road, Chris stood in the yard. It had been a fun day, and for a while, her mind hadn't been filled with disturbing thoughts about Scott. The pain came back quickly enough. She recalled the conversation she'd had with Byron, in which she'd almost admitted that Scott must have exploited her feelings for him to keep her here. That wouldn't have been fair, as at no time had she even thought about leaving. Chewing her lip didn't solve her problem. Well, Chris, old girl, it's too late now to think about curbing your feelings. You did rather behave like an adolescent with runaway hormones. She sighed and went into the cabin to make more cookies, just in case she had other holiday visitors. The task would keep her from worrying about him.

Next day, she was shouldering her day pack when the radiophone crackled.

"Hello Boreal Kennels. Are you there, Chris? Over."

She ran to the microphone.

"Hi Byron. I'm about to take a team out. What's up?"

"Would you be willing to take some out-of-season tourists on a sledding excursion into the wilderness?"

"You're serious?"

"Of course. I'm not joking."

"I haven't done it before."

"There's nothing to it. You have the dogs, and you know the trails. It's the same as taking out Mary's grandkids."

"Tourists in winter won't have the winter clothes needed."

"We'll scrounge something."

"But when and how would I get them?"

"That's my secret."

"Alright. Let's do it. It's good for the dogs."

"That's my girl. We'll be there in half an hour. Over and out."

She pursed her lips. It'd be futile to press Byron to find out what he had in mind. If he said he'd bring tourists, he would. In the meantime, she should think about how to feed those potential visitors. This was a rare opportunity to do something different, and almost as important, it would take her mind off Scott.

Byron brought two middle age couples as well as a load of groceries. While working side by side, she and Byron discussed the possibility of running a dog sledding tour business. Byron was adamant she could do it. He had set the fee, which she thought was too high, but she couldn't argue with him. While the tourists were out of earshot, he confirmed that he researched the business and the fee was right. "Same price as Tapiskoot Tours charge, over in the Donek valley."

"Fine, but how will Scott react when he finds out?"

"Walsh needs money. You know what it costs to feed dogs. He can't possibly complain."

"Where do you find the clients?"

"My secret. For the moment, let's keep it quiet until we see if it's viable."

The tourists had a great time, so did she when the check went into the empty dog shaped crock Scott used for keeping his money

Two days after Christmas, she prepared a team and went to pick up her pack in the cabin. The warm smell of fresh baking floated in the air and made her hungry. Just then, the radiophone crackled.

"Listen, Chris. There're a couple of American tourists in town. I reckon they must have gotten lost to be up here at this time of year. They really would love to see something of the backcountry. It would make a memorable stay if you'd take them for a sled ride. Over."

In his roundabout way, Byron announced clients without informing the whole neighborhood about their attempt to start a tour business. She played along and chuckled.

"That sounds like fun. Bring them up, but make sure you find them some warm clothes. Over."

"Don't worry, hon, we're outfitting them with parkas and boots. I'll bring along the bear skin too."

"Great. We could take them to Ashin Point and back."

"Splendid. See you in a half-hour or so. Over and out."

She packed a thermos and cookies, then went to prepare the sleds.

The tourists, an older couple from Texas, climbed out of Byron's truck.

The man extended his hand to Chris. "Ms. Taylor? I'm Rex the Texan, and here is Daphne, my wife of forty years."

The jovial Texan shook her hand vigorously. Tall and slim, he swam in his borrowed parka. Daphne's fitted better. She was beaming.

"We must look the height of fashion, but I'm sure the dogs won't mind. Can we see them?"

"Certainly. Come with me."

She gave the visitors a tour of Boreal kennels and explained about training and racing.

"So, if you're entering that thousand-mile race, you have to run the dogs a thousand miles before?" Daphne asked.

"Not in one go. First, we run the dogs for a few hours, then progressively we augment the time and distance. One day we train for speed, so we have a light sled and encourage the dogs to go as fast as they are willing."

"What if they aren't?" Rex asked.

"We go back home and try to figure out why they're not willing and correct the cause. Those dogs love nothing better than to run. When they don't, we have to find out if they're ailing or something."

"Of course, it's just like with kids. Then, after that?" Daphne, intensely curious, was impatient with her husband.

"The next day, we load the sled with all the stuff we'd need in the race plus some, and we run at a steady pace for weight training. As the date approaches, we camp out, day and night, to simulate the race schedule."

"Marvelous dedication." Rex looked impressed.

When they got to see the puppies, she thought they might not get anywhere soon, until Byron reminded the visitors that the daylight lasted only three hours.

After the couple had been shown how to put a harness on a dog, the party was on its way. Byron drove the second sled. On the return leg, both Rex and Daphne had to try standing on the runners. There were some hilarious moments, but the team made it back without tipping the sleds.

They enjoyed themselves so much they pressed a generous check into her hand in payment for their outing. She was about to protest, but Byron waved her into silence.

"They're happy," he whispered.

The couple insisted on inspecting the pups once more.

Byron motioned to the guests. "You could easily do this as business, if you had a mind to, and charge twice that amount. The clients would still be happy. It's a unique experience for them."

"I guess you're right. Scott had thought about developing something on those lines."

"Yeah, I remember him saying so. A long time ago. Never did anything about it, though."

The visitors came back in. "Thank you, Ms. Taylor." The Texan gave her a broad smile. "You've been most hospitable. I can't wait to tell the folks back home and show them the photos. It's going to make them green with envy."

Alone again, she hid the check in the crock in which Danny and Jack had, with the excitement of childhood, dropped a few coins to help with the dog food. Pride of having earned some money from dog sledding boosted her morale. It had been fun too, and moreover, Scott needed it.

True to his prediction, Byron brought a young family out for a short tour the next day. They too left a contribution in the crock. The family was followed the day after by others. The stream of visitors didn't end until New Year's Eve.

"How did you manage to find all those people wanting sled rides, Byron?"

"Nothing to it. I just spread the rumor that a former Miss America was willing to take people out on sledding excursions. The phone didn't stop ringing."

She choked trying to contain her laughter. "Miss America indeed! No wonder they insisted on posing for photos with me. And I thought my cookies were the attraction."

Byron departed along with the last guests. Her mind drifted back to the void created by Scott's absence. Her throat tightened. Shaking the gloom from her mind, she finished her chores.

Somehow, seeing in the New Year without Scott didn't feel right. She had become far too emotionally dependent on him. One of her New Year's resolutions was going to break free of that emotional reliance. It wouldn't be easy, but if she didn't, she was going to be hurt even more. Renoir, lounging on the couch, pricked up his ears and jumped down. She looked up from the dishes she was washing. "What do you want... Oh! Someone's coming. Not more visitors at this time of night?"

Three snowmobiles came to a halt by the cabin door. Six people in all climbed off the machines and stretched. Through the kitchen window, she immediately recognized Byron and Conrad. She dried her hands and went to welcome them.

"Hello, Byron. Come in out of the cold. And who have you brought this time?"

"Friends," Byron said.

Smiling, Vicky and Nicole came up behind him.

"Since you're stuck out here on your own, we all thought we'd bring the New Year to you," Vicky said.

"My goodness! I'd quite forgotten it was New Year's Eve." That was a lie, but she wasn't about to tell them how despondent she'd felt earlier on.

Vicky pushed a young woman in front of her. "Meet Summer Monroe, also called Little Star. She's brought her accordion too."

Little Star smiled shyly. "May I leave my squeeze box in the house for now so it doesn't get too cold?"

Chris showed her the way while more snowmobiles and trucks pulled into the yard.

A tall man carried a box into the middle of the yard.

"Hi, Mr. Weiman. You came all the way from Agate Rock, Devon told me."

"The name's Dexter. Indeed, I bought a cabin there on the other side of the valley."

"Are you going to get a team?"

He rubbed his chin. "That's under consideration, but my work can take me away for weeks at a time."

"How about a cookout?" Devon interrupted. "We've got steak, potatoes, wieners, marshmallows and I don't know what else."

"That's a great idea! Let me put on my parka and a toque."

In no time, they had a fire going. Conrad rummaged in the shed and found an iron grill to use as a makeshift barbecue for the steaks and wieners. She brought a huge pot of steaming coffee from the cabin. Renoir made off with a mouthful of wieners. Peels of laughter rose to the overhanging pine branches and were echoed by a howl from the dogs. To prevent further trouble, she tied the thief to his line by the door.

"I hope you don't mind, but we've invited two other guys along, Byron said. They should be here soon. Peter and Craig. You probably remember them from the Christmas party."

"The two wildlife officers from Agate Rock, right?"

"Correct. They had to attend a meeting in the capital, otherwise they'd have been here already. Poor suckers! Can you imagine anyone scheduling a meeting on New Year's Eve?"

He had barely spoken when the dogs announced the arrival of the missing guests.

"What a racket the dogs make!" Nicole put her hands over her ears hidden by a wooly toque.

"It takes some getting used to," Conrad yelled over the din. "But they sure make an excellent early warning system."

A government truck appeared over the crest of the hill and parked between the cabin and the dogs' compound. Peter and Craig jumped out.

Chris gasped in surprise when a third man emerged from the truck and shot an angry glance at the group around the fire. "Scott!" she shouted.

He acknowledged her presence with an awkward wave of the hand, turned and yanked his bag from the back of the truck. Without giving her or the revelers a second glance, he strode toward the cabin. She caught up with him. He turned.

"Is this what you've been doing while I've been away, entertaining the entire neighborhood?" He left her dumbfounded in the snow. At the cabin door, he bent down and released Renoir. Master and dog disappeared inside. Undeterred, she pushed her way in.

"Scott, it's New Year's Eve. I don't know why you're getting so hot under the collar. Our friends decided to come up and spend it with me. There's lots of good food. Please, come and join us." She regretted the words the moment they escaped. In addition, it sounded so absurd, inviting him into his own home.

He tossed his parka on the couch. "I've got things to attend to."

"Attend to them next year. You can't stay in the cabin while your friends are outside."

He whirled on her. "Just watch me!" He ripped off his shirt.

The sight of muscles cording across his broad back as he bent to unzip his bag sent a liquid shiver over her skin. She shook her head in disbelief and leaned against the doorjamb. All the joy that Byron and the others had brought was snuffed out.

Overshadowing her misery, her body clamored for his touch. Her heart cried out for the buoyant and carefree days before his departure. She craved a kind word, a look from him, anything that could give her hope. He ignored her pleading eyes and stomped off to the bathroom. The door slammed shut behind him.

Little Star slipped into the cabin. On her way out with her accordion, she gave Chris a sad nod. With a big breath, Chris smoothed her palms over her eyes in a desperate gesture to ease her wretchedness. Waiting for him would be pointless. She rejoined the merrymakers around the fire. With the happy sound of music, the laughter and welcoming cheers to the New Year exploded around her. The northern lights danced in tune with the music across the dark sky overhead.

"It's too bad we don't have mistletoe," Byron said in her ear

"Mistletoe is for Christmas. We're celebrating the New Year."

"Who cares? You're evading me." His casual tone carried an underlying streak of seriousness.

"We're not back on that, are we?"

"You can't fault a guy for trying. What's got into old Walsh?"

"Have you ever seen him relaxed and ready to enjoy life?"

He looked thoughtful for a second. "Yes. Just before he went off, he really seemed to be happy."

"As you can see, it didn't last long, did it?"

"How come Scott isn't out here?" Conrad asked.

"A bit tired, that's all," Byron replied.

"Is he giving you a rough time, Chris? Maybe Peter should have left him at the bus depot in the capital."

"I'm glad your friend gave him a ride. It saved me a trip." Mentally, she added, I think I prefer to put up with his black moods as long as I can breathe the same air as he does.

When the friends concluded they had truly welcomed in the brand new year, the men doused the fire. The women carried the leftover food into the cabin. She opened the door cautiously. There on the couch lay Scott's inert form, shrouded in a comforter. Vicky and Nicole looked at each other and shook their heads. Chris motioned them not to leave the food on the table, pointing to Renoir's expectant face. They stowed it in the cool cabinet.

After everyone left, she took Renoir back to his pen. He licked her face and curled up in the snow while the other dogs poked their noses out of their houses. Seeing that no food was offered, the noses retreated. When she went back to the cabin, she saw he hadn't moved. Making no noise, she got ready for bed, hoping he would be in a more reasonable state of mind in the morning.

CHAPTER FIFTEEN

In the quiet morning, Chris willed herself to wake before Scott. For the first time ever, she was successful. Noiselessly, she went to check on the dogs. On her return, he was up, slouched on the edge of the sofa. His hair was awry and his chin sported two days of growth. The sight of him, even disheveled as he was, made her heart thump.

"Good morning. Do you have any plans for today?"

"Maybe I should ask you what social events you've got organized?"

His belligerent tone cut her to the quick. The temptation to lash out at him in an equally bad-tempered way was strong, but she refrained. Instead, a wicked smile lit up her face. "As a matter of fact, I've arranged to take all twelve huskies right around Mount McKinley and party with some real hunks of Alaskan mushers."

The look he gave her altered subtly while the silence stretched.

"Okay, okay. You win. I'm sorry I'm such lousy company. You know, it's not too late to change your mind about working for me. If you want to go, you can. You don't have to put up with my surly moods."

She watched him wrestle with some powerful emotion. "I thought you'd learned by now I'm not the kind of person who reneges on a promise, let alone a contract. In some funny, twisted way, I've got used to you by now."

Her remark was met by a flicker of amusement in his eyes. It vanished in a blink. He propped his chin on his hands, not looking at her. "I just don't think I can run those races. It'd be too much for the Canadian Inuit dogs."

"No way. They're simply raring to go. You can't give up now. There're only four weeks before the Yukon Quest."

"In which case, I'll take the huskies. The maximum allowed is fourteen. And I'll simply scrap the Iditarod."

"That's not right, either. You need to enter both races. Your two teams are ready." Resolve heightened her voice.

He shook his head. "No. I won't be able to run both. I never discussed it with you before, but I don't have enough money to afford the expenses of both races. If I cancel now, I'll get back some of the registration fees. You've got wages coming to you."

For a brief instant, she was too surprised to speak. "Wages? You don't need to worry about paying me. I live here free, as it is."

"Handlers are supposed to get paid for their work."

"Well, I'm not your average handler."

"Don't I know that!" A touch of grim humor colored his voice.

"If you forget about my salary, you can cover the race expenses, correct?"

"Wrong."

She dropped to his side on the couch, caressed his hands, his hair, and drew his face toward her, touching his lips with hers. Reluctantly, his mouth moved to possess hers, then he stood up. Confusion beset her.

"No, we can't–" his words were cut short by the radiophone bursting to life. He made no move to answer the call.

Hurt by his rejection, she went to the phone as Byron's voice boomed from the speaker. "Hi, anyone at home? It's Byron, here. Over."

"Yes. Chris speaking."

"Great. Sweetheart, there are two parties of southerners in town. Can I bring them up?"

"Certainly. Give me an hour to prepare. How many?"

"Six in all. They'd like to have a taste of the wilds."

"We could take them to the old prospector's encampment and back. We'd return by five or six o'clock tonight. I'll pack some food."

"Good. We've rounded up some clothes for them. See you in an hour. Over and out."

She put the microphone back in its cradle with a satisfied smile.

"What the hell's all that about?"

She ignored his angry explosion. "Boreal Dogsledding Adventures Company. Your new business venture."

"Are you crazy? I've got training to do. And what do you think you're doing, feeding six people?" His brows knitted fiercely.

"They pay." She grabbed the old earthenware crock from the counter and banged it on the table. "Take a peek inside."

With a quizzical look in her direction, he removed the lid. A pile of checks and bills spilled onto the table. His jaw sagged. "Where did all this money come from?"

"From satisfied customers."

"We're training dogs to race. Pleasure excursions will ruin them." Despite his outburst, his eyes remained fixed on the money, an expression of disbelief spread over his rugged features.

She remained unperturbed. "I think we agreed before that the dogs are not merely running machines. They need variety to keep in top form. I don't see what's the problem. Their training is not suffering. They go out with a full weight, more than you'd carry in the race, so it certainly helps build up their strength and stamina. The money from the tourists will pay for the race expenses."

"What about the dogs' speed?"

"The freighters keep going at the same pace. I think we should take a team of Alaskan huskies on today's outing and see how they handle it. I presume you'll want to drive a sled. Byron will drive one and I'll take another."

He raked his hands through his hair, looked at the money again, and shook his head. "I don't know what to think."

"Then don't bother to think. Just accept it. Oh, by the way, I've sold two of the older pups to Devon Santoni. That is, unless you disapprove. But you know Charcoal wouldn't make the racing team and Snow White couldn't live without him, so I think it's better that way and Devon's happy. Get dressed. I'll cook us some breakfast."

He hesitated, then picked up his gear and disappeared into the bathroom.

Neither of them lingered over breakfast. Out in the compound, he didn't protest when she told him what to do. An air of amazement still marked his face.

Exactly one hour after the call, Byron's truck, closely followed by a car full of visitors, pulled into the yard. Scott fumed silently to see the easy familiarity between her and his best friend, although his respect for her soared as he watched how graciously she welcomed the visitors and took them on a tour of the kennel.

"Murdoch, whose damned idea was it? These tours?"

"Nobody's. Though you did think of it sometime in the past. It happened quite by accident. First, it was Mary and Fred's grandkids wanting to go for a little outing, then a couple of Texans."

"She didn't make Mary's grandkids pay, did she?"

"No, of course not. The kids enjoyed themselves so much, they wanted to help buy food for the dogs. We couldn't stop them from dropping their allowance in the pot. As for the other people, they were only too happy to pay for the excursions."

"They pay well from what I saw."

"They sure do. Of course, there was no question of them wanting a free ride. Chris sure knows how to operate an efficient business. Customer satisfaction all the way."

"What about you? You've got your own job to attend to. You can't come and drive a sled for nothing." His dry tone resonated in the cool air.

Byron suppressed a laugh. "I love being out with the dogs. We're not too busy right now at the office. I don't mind using some of my free time and days off to help out here. I love being out with the dogs. One day..."

Inwardly, Scott, still seething, had no doubt about the reason his friend was so eager to help, but he composed himself.

"How do you manage to round up all these people?"

"Trade secret. Actually, my brother and his wife run a travel agency. I just happened to mention sled rides to them."

"You're taken with her, aren't you?" He couldn't disguise the anguish that gripped him.

"Chris? Of course I am. Who wouldn't be?"

His smug look provoked Scott, but a glance at the tourists reminded him it wasn't the moment to have it out with his friend. Anyway, without him, he wouldn't be earning that extra cash. He sighed and shook his head.

Everything was ready, and the passengers installed in the sleds. She flushed with pleasure when he motioned her to take the lead. Driving the team of ten huskies, she had thought wise to leave troublemaker Namatuk and a friend at the kennel, she kept a close eye on their performance. Mostly, she thought about Scott bringing up the rear with half the freighters. He was smiling again, a marked contrast to the night before.

Part of his problem was a shortage of funds, so much so that he'd thought of pulling out of one of the big races. With the money she was making from the tourist excursions, optimism blossomed once more.

By Lake Tootkoo, the halfway point in the tour, the party stopped and built a fire of dead pine branches.

"What are those big tracks? Is that a bear?" The visitor didn't disguise the anxiety in her voice.

A half smile lit up Scott's face. "Bears hibernate in winter. This is a wolf following close in the tracks of a moose."

A woman's shriek turned everyone's head. "Sorry. You said the ride wasn't dangerous. But there are wolves. I read about them in Call of the Wild."

"You mustn't believe the stories Jack London wrote. They are fiction. Wolves are actually shy of people and will run away as soon as they sense you, long before you can see them. In fact, sighting a wolf is a rare occurrence."

"Still, I don't think I'd like to camp out."

Her companions chuckled and closed around her. Comforted, she sighed with relief. Byron pointed to the far shore of the lake. All eyes focused on the dark shape.

"Caribou," he said.

Chris pulled out a pair of binoculars and passed them to the guests. For a long while, they watched the heavily antlered animals paw the snow to reach lichens and grasses beneath.

Later that evening, after Byron left to escort the tired but contented tourists back to town, Scott sat at the kitchen table. His eyes were glued to the check in front of him. He could hardly believe the figure. Long ago, he'd vaguely sensed that a winter tourism business could be developed. That was as far as he had taken the idea. Now, almost without effort, Chris had started it, right under his nose. Next spring, though, she'd be gone, and he would slide back into his old negative rut.

"Is there enough to cover both races?" Her voice interrupted his thoughts.

"Just about."

"Good. I'll bet we get a few more tourists in the next couple of weeks."

"The travel agent will be wanting a cut of the profits."

"Not at the moment. All the sister-in-law does is give out Byron's phone number. If we go one step further and set up a formal business, then she'd treat us just like any other vacation package and charge a commission. Her husband reckons the market is unlimited."

"What would setting up properly entail?" He was testing her, wanting to hear her describe the dream he himself had relinquished.

"Print brochures. Have a remote website——"

"What do you mean, remote website?"

"Hire a website manager in Whitehorse to run the marketing according to the information we provide."

"Hire? But it costs money."

"Right. The benefits of an internet marketing will pay back and more. We'll offer tours of various lengths and so on. Naturally, we'd have to supply warm clothes, boots and other equipment. Some tourists might like to ski alongside the sled. Then there are those who might want to try skijoring. The idea of being towed along the trails on skis by a dog or two really appeals to some people. Everything involves planning and a wise investment of capital. It can only help finance the racing. Down the road, we might think about providing accommodation by building a few log cabins for the guests."

"You're saying we should go into the hotel business?" His face became genuinely alarmed.

She laughed. "Not right away. At first, we could get a couple of wall tents and put wood stoves in them. It wouldn't suit everybody, but a lot of people like to feel close to nature. They don't expect a real hotel. More of a wilderness lodge."

He loved it each time she used the word 'we' in her plans. This fascinating woman had a way of weaving her spell about him, enmeshing him with soft words. The craving for her flared again in him. She must have read his mind, for he saw a pink blush invade her cheeks. They fell silent, each looking into the eyes of the other. Was she gripped by the same urges as he was? Memories of their lovemaking surged into his brain. Fists clenched to prevent himself from reaching out to her, he shook his head. In the morning, they would both regret their actions. But how he loved to see her smile.

His stomach tensed again. The yearning for her rolled over him. And she was there, vibrantly close yet so distant. He had to keep her at arm's length, otherwise he'd make a fool of himself. Now that he had admitted that racing no longer provided him with enough of an income, reason was telling him to push it aside and get a job somewhere in a city.

Then he'd be able to claim his son for the holidays. Maybe the wilderness adventures could bring in good money, but that'd be barely enough. The hospitality business, tightly linked to the economic health and the weather, knew ups and downs. The judge made himself clear on the matter. If he couldn't pay child support, he couldn't visit either. The amount he was ordered to pay was way beyond what he could earn with his dogs. But if he had a regular employment in the city, the payment would only be a percentage of his wages. The income would increase his chances of obtaining custody. In the course of the past week, he got an inkling that Alina was no longer so keen to have permanent custody of their son. Her animosity appeared to have dropped. A young child going to school was no longer as interesting as a beautiful baby and a smart toddler for her friends. Now she had finally recovered her figure, she had no more need to brag about the greatness of motherhood against her lost model body. A substantial alimony hadn't materialized, and the child was preventing her from resuming a modeling career.

He couldn't drag Chris into all this mess. She had to go on with her racing career. The beautiful dream of a sledding tour business would remain just that, a dream. Giving up his child was unthinkable. Something indefinable pulled him toward the little tyke. It was just like bonding with a puppy.

The moment he had held the infant in his arms, a strange new feeling overpowered him. For the first year, it was he who had fed, changed, smiled at and talked to the baby, saw his first steps and his first words. It was he who had bundled him into the sled and camped out when his babysitter wasn't available. And baby Cody, totally unafraid of the big dogs, had loved it. He grasped his forehead, pressed hard on his eyeballs, remembering how gentle the dogs were when they licked Cody's face, and how much the baby laughed. The year had been one of tremendous happiness. With his young friend Jerome acting both as a handler and babysitter, he won a few major races. The money flowed.

Everything came crashing down when Alina reappeared. Living in the cabin was not for her. One day, she had gone and taken their son with her. He shook his head to clear the bitterness of the long custody battle that ensued, one that he had lost.

One day, his son would grow up and ask questions. He wanted to be part of his life until then and afterward.

For now, he had to tell Chris about his lightning trip to California, tell her this was his last season, tell her there'd never be a Boreal Dogsledding Adventures Company. The pain gouged a raw path through his heart.

Eyes closed, he held his breath. The only sounds were the ticking of the clock and the burning logs shifting in the stove.

Even though it took all the willpower he could muster, he stifled his craving. He had to make sure that she didn't get attached to him. The first thing to do was to put an end to the short training runs that permitted him to be back by evening. That was a legitimate excuse. Close to the big race, he could ill afford any distraction from his schedule. It was imperative that he distance himself from her, stop lusting for her, and stop making love to her.

Unmoving for a long while, he threw off his stupor to go outside in the cold to clear his head. That was the northern version of a cold shower. She stood up at the same time.

With a few inches between them, the heat rose to an unbearable degree. He pulled her to him. One last time, he told himself. His mouth came down hard on hers. Only a meek cry of protest escaped her lips before responding to his kiss.

His hands held her against him. He lifted his head. Heavy-lidded eyes burned with unspoken passion.

A sharp gasp broke the heavy silence. He dropped his hands and stepped back. With a will he didn't know he possessed, he drew back, pushing her away. She stumbled toward her room with a soft goodnight.

Chapter Sixteen

Abandoned, her thirst for him flushed red on her skin. His rebuff stung, but a wild hope that he'd relent slowed her steps even more.

After a moment of hesitation, she lifted the curtain.

The room was empty.

Unable to comprehend his rejection, her mind reasoned that it was better not to indulge in lovemaking. She hungered for him. Not just his body, she wanted to possess his heart.

When he had shared his love of nature with the tourists, gentle, knowledgeable, so friendly, she had been proud. This was a side of him she hadn't seen before, only guessing at its existence. Along with the pride, there was another feeling, that of quiet desperation. If only he would love her.

***

Awakened from an uneasy sleep, she slipped out to check on the dogs. With the breakfast underway, she wondered whether she should speak up. A look at his troubled features discouraged her. Silent and somber, he bolted his food, grabbed his pack and left the cabin.

A long sigh, almost a sob in its intensity, relieved the pressure in her chest. She admonished herself. Something upsetting had happened to him during his brief absence. It must have been traumatic for him to take her in his arms and then recoil. Since he didn't want to discuss the problem, she could do nothing more than treat him as her boss.

The jolt of that resolution shook her to the core. She wasn't one to turn love on and off, and that was exactly what she was trying to do. It was fortunate, he had only seen the physical attraction, not suspecting for one moment she harbored deep feelings for him.

It might be difficult, but she'd restrain the impulses to make love, especially never saying out loud how much she loved him.

When spring came and with it the end of racing, she'd have to pack her bags and go. Living with unrequited love was not healthy.

Right now, the pups required her attention. She gave herself fully to her furry companions and the tasks in the kennel. More tourists came and kept her busy.

Three days later, Scott returned. The dark stubble on his chin made her forget her resolve for one short moment. An aroma of wood smoke pervaded the room as he removed his parka. A picture of the solitary man, brooding by a campfire, passed through her mind, but she dismissed it. Only a log crackling in the stove and the bubbling of the cooking pot broke the silence. Soon, the smell of butter and garlic invaded the cabin, mingling oddly with outdoor scents.

She served moose stew and the pasta she had made earlier in the day. After a few days on the trail, a musher is quite ready to down a healthy serving of solid food. His first words were to thank her. For the first time, he appeared to relax while she set about to clear the dishes.

He got to his feet. "I'll wash."

"Thanks, I'll dry."

She didn't know whether to laugh or cry. At least he was being civil. Maybe he'd talk as they sat down after stoking the fire.

He examined the ganglines she had made.

"Pretty fancy handiwork." His approval was genuine. He opened his old race notebooks and appeared to concentrate on comparing the race strategies he had used. She picked up a book.

On the couch, Renoir rolled over and snuggled with consummate enjoyment deeper into the bed comforter. Of everyone in the cabin, only the dog was perfectly at ease. The humans both sensed the tension in the air.

Scott chewed the end of his pen, but still didn't talk. Finally, he bit the pen so hard the plastic cracked in his mouth. In disgust, he spat out the fragments.

She looked up from her book. "Anything I can help with?"

He hesitated. "Not at the moment."

Palpable stress filled the room. She curbed her spontaneous nature just in time to prevent herself from asking what was troubling him. The lights of an approaching vehicle distracted her. "Surely, we can't be having tourists at this hour?"

They stepped to the window. "It looks like there are two trucks."

Together they watched the headlights catch the sparkle of snow on the pines boughs as the vehicles negotiated the steep, winding path toward them.

"Three trucks."

"I bet you it's Byron." A trace of displeasure echoed in his voice.

Her keen eyes focused on the second truck, caught in the lights of the third vehicle. "No, it's not. It's a dog transporter. Who could be coming here with sled dogs?" Her excited voice caught his full attention.

"It must be my buddy, Jerome." He broke into a grin.

They shrugged into their parkas and ran outside. The trucks came to a halt. Byron leaped out of the lead vehicle. He waved at Chris. "Hey, honey! Wait till you see who we've brought for you."

She spun around just as a figure of a young woman jumped out of the third truck and dashed toward her. A moment later, she was swept up in a wild embrace.

"Marcia! It's really you!" She laughed and cried at the same time.

"We thought we'd surprise you."

"You certainly have. I'm speechless."

The young woman with flowing blond hair lifted her sparkling blue eyes to a smiling Scott. "Well, my dear cousin, aren't you going to introduce me to your hunk of a boss?"

Chris spun to face Scott. "Did you know Marcia was coming? If you did, how come you didn't tell me?"

Hands thrust into his pockets, he looked at the ground like a bashful college kid. He grinned at her and lifted his hands in a fatalistic gesture.

"And wait till you see what we have in the dog boxes," Marcia said.

"You... you don't mean you've brought our dogs along, as well?" She held her breath.

"That's right. The whole bunch of them." Marcia laughed happily.

"But..." Chris turned to Scott. "You didn't..."

Overwhelmed, she didn't try to stem the tears. She dashed to the truck and peered through the small windows of the dog carrier. Familiar snuffles from the individual compartments greeted her.

"Let's close the gate in the middle of the big pen and round up our dogs at one end. Then you can put your dogs on the other side. But before we do, I'd like you to meet Jerome Renard."

She held out her hand to a wiry, young musher with an easy smile. "Please to meet you. Scott has told me so much about you."

"Oh, heck! There goes my reputation!"

The men went down to the pen while she reacquainted herself with her beloved dogs, overjoyed to see her. Byron helped Jerome picket his team at one end of the compound while the two young women led their dogs in the enclosure. When all the dogs were settled, watered and fed, she led Marcia and the men into the cabin. She paused at the door and pulled Scott aside. "Thank you! Thanks for being so thoughtful." A surge of love and gratitude welled up inside her.

Under the light of the lamp, she could hardly take her eyes off her vivacious cousin. She must be dreaming. "This is so...so..." She struggled with her emotions. "I can't put words to my feelings. I'm going to cry again."

"I'm glad my scheming has a happy outcome," Scott said. He looked so very pleased with himself.

"How long can you stay, Marcia?" Chris asked.

"I don't intend going back. I've rented out the house and the kennel to a musher. There must be a job I can get around here."

"How about being my handler? You've helped me magnificently all during the long drive." Jerome, his brown eyes twinkling, made the offer in earnest.

"Okay. It's a deal. I had hoped you'd ask," Marcia replied. "Until you go back south at the end of the season."

She smiled at her cousin, then at the handsome Jerome, with his incredibly curly mop of dark hair.

"I suppose we can arrange the sleeping accommodation," Chris said. "The cabin's pretty cramped with just the two of us, but we'll cope somehow. Marcia can share with me. Maybe the kennel house could do for–"

Byron gave a wave of the hand. "Don't worry about it. I've got two spare bedrooms. Jerome and Marcia can bunk at my place. It doesn't take too long to drive up here."

"Are you sure?"

"Everybody needs a good night's sleep to train properly. Athletes do. Mushers are no different."

She would have liked her cousin to stay at the cabin, but she saw the wisdom of Byron's argument. During the day, the presence of Jerome and Marcia would act as a buffer between her and Scott. Though that still left the evenings when she'd be alone with him.

That was a mixed blessing.

As the animated group ate an impromptu dinner, Chris surreptitiously glanced at Scott. Some of the hardness was gone from his face. While he discussed details of race strategy with Jerome, he looked like the real Scott, the man she loved deeply. Conflicting sensations, some comforting, others disturbing, coursed through her body.

Leaning her chin on her hand, she turned away from him to hide the reddening in her cheeks. Marcia brought her up-to-date on news from home. Although delighted with her cousin's lively chatter, her mind was with Scott. A glance at Byron and she saw he was aware of it. He gave a resigned sigh and fetched himself more coffee from the stove.

"What about you Marcia," Byron asked. "Do you want to race?"

"Good gracious, no! I love my dogs and I'll take them for rides, but that's all. Racing's not for me."

Byron resumed his seat next to her. "You're like me. I'm not keen on racing, either. Don't let on to Scott. He thinks anybody who doesn't want to race sled dogs must be weak in the head. I like to be out in the wilds with a team of dogs, though I don't particularly want to own any at this time."

Byron's gaze drifted toward Chris. Marcia brushed back her mane of blond hair. "I guess those three will be out on the trails most of the time. Which means I won't see much of Chris."

"She'll be at home every evening because she has to care for the dogs," replied Byron.

"If I know my cousin, the moment she gets behind a team of dogs, she has no time for anything else. And if she's involved with a race, that's all she thinks about."

Byron looked into the young woman's luminous blue eyes. "You really believe in her, don't you?"

"If she enters a race, you bet she'll win. She succeeds at everything she does."

"What about you?"

"Me? I'm a dreamer. I'm not a great one for action."

"I'm kinda the same way, too." They both shared a laugh that could only be described as conspiratorial.

Before the evening wore on too much, the new arrivals stood up to go. Chris gave a final wave to Marcia as the truck left for town. "I must thank you again. I'm so happy she came."

He held the cabin door open for her. "It was nothing."

"Nothing? How did you convince her to give up everything to come here?"

A grin spread across his face. "Mary remembered the address." He laughed. They both knew Mary's inquisitiveness had probably led her to record the address. "I wrote her letter. After that, one call clinched it. She knew that once you were up in the North, you weren't likely to be returning home anytime soon. Your enthusiasm is infectious. I gave her the invitation and told her Jerome would travel with her. There was no stopping her after that."

"She had written to me saying she wished she could cast off and do something else, go somewhere exotic."

"Well, Fletcher Creek is exotic for other people. When she's finished with Jerome, she could probably find a job in the area with a musher or open up a business. Work for my.. our business..." A frown marred his features, and he promptly turned his head.

She looked up. Had she heard correctly? If she interpreted his words rightly, the fact Marcia would stay on meant she, too, would stay on. He might consider keeping her on as a handler. The thought was too enormous. But no, she should be realistic. It'd be utterly self-destructing to spend her life next to a man who only saw her as the best employee he ever had, one that assuaged his manly needs, too. When he won races again, he could very well find himself a compatible wife. Then where would that leave her? It'd leave her in the depths of desolation, with the daily torture of seeing him love someone else. She'd go in the spring. Enough see-sawing, stay, go, stay. The best thing she could do for herself was to go. But...

When he looked back again, the joy went out of his eyes. His jaw hardened. The transformation meant one thing, he had been about to reach out to kiss her. Something had stopped him.

The agony of not knowing stabbed at her. His unsmiling lips contrasted with the memory of the burning trail they'd once left on her skin. Longing to touch the stubble chin and to bury her fingers in his thick hair overwhelmed her. Tentatively, she put her hand on his chest. He closed his eyes and held his breath. The only sounds were the spluttering of the logs in the stove. Between the man and the woman, awareness grew to explosive proportions.

All of a sudden, he threw off his stupor, pulled her to him and kissed her hard before softening to a caress. Her nostrils flared at his heady outdoors scent.

The tension escalated. Their bodies fit one against the other. He lifted his head, his eyes heavy with passion. Her thirst for him flushed red on her skin.

He dropped his hands and stepped back. The rigid set of his shoulders told her of his inner turmoil.

What was the past hurt that had him so fiercely rejecting her, reject an admission of love, reject the idea of a shared commitment? There had to be a woman behind it.

CHAPTER SEVENTEEN

Snow fluttered down when they went out to the kennel. Scott surprised her by announcing he was not going on a training run, but intended taking care of the things that needed doing at home, like splitting logs for the stove.

The next day, he was silent and introspective, and she was almost glad when he and Jerome left for the day's training.

Marcia stared after the disappearing teams. "What's bothering your boss?"

"If only I knew." If Chris hadn't been bent over to adjust a dog's collar, Marcia would have seen the distress written on her face.

"He was okay yesterday. What happened? Caught a bug or something?" Marcia emphasized the final word and gave her cousin a sly grin.

Chris shrugged. "Your guess is as good as mine. That's how he is most of the time. On top of the world one minute, down in the dumps, the next. Though it's really nice when he's happy."

"I can see that. You two are arcing sparks the moment you're together. Bedtime must be terrific."

"But didn't last. Something's eating at him." She changed the subject. "It's so good to have you here."

"Which brings me to my next item. You're training the Alaskan huskies for the Iditarod, but you haven't been able to take them out at night or camp out with them. They'll need to have some camp experience for the race."

"True."

"So now that I'm here, you should do it."

Chris perched herself on a doghouse, her legs dangling over the edge. Nunii jumped up and rested his furry nose on her shoulder. She circled his neck with her arm. He rubbed his face against hers.

"There would be time when Scott comes back after racing the Yukon Quest, but it'd be better if I'd already done a few night runs to have the dogs conditioned." Nunii's pink tongue snaked out to lick her nose. "If you must, lick me under the chin, you big dope." The loving tone of her voice was all the dog needed. He pawed her thigh and wriggled himself closer before snuggling his head on her lap.

"If I'm going to take care of things here, you'll have to explain the routine."

"The whole day's work? Actually, I should go for a night run when Scott is away. Like that, there'll be fewer dogs to care for."

"Let's do it. Is it always this dark? Unless my watch has gone haywire, it's mid-morning and still no daylight."

Chris jumped down, much to Nunii's chagrin. "The days are getting longer now. We're getting three and a half hours of daylight."

"No kidding! Let's have lunch. I'm frozen and starved."

"I forgot to tell you, it gets far colder than this. We'll have lunch, then you can sit by the stove while I take a team out." A hint of mischief sounded in her tone.

"Maybe I should get myself acclimatized by running our old dogs."

"Don't start feeling guilty. They'll need a couple of days to adapt to the change of climate."

Marcia looked relieved. "I'll prepare your dinner while you're out. Like that, you and Scott can eat immediately when you get back."

"It's a deal, but only if you agree to share it with us."

"Alas, I can't. I promised Byron I'd do the cooking in lieu of rent."

"Lucky him, gourmet cooking. That's what I missed the most. Do you realize I'm cooking here?"

"Would that account for Scott's mood swings?"

Their laughter echoed from the cabin's low roof beams.

In the late evening, Scott and Jerome returned, frost clinging to their parkas.

Marcia shivered when the men brought a blast of cold air in with them. "Yikes! It's like standing in front of an open refrigerator." She hugged the stove.

When Jerome and Marcia departed for Fletcher Creek, Scott occupied himself hauling logs into the cabin. It took only so long, then there was nothing more for him to do. This situation was becoming impossible. She didn't need to be a clairvoyant to see the torment he was going through. Holding her own nerves in check, she stood up and went to her room.

Her breathing settled. She sat on the bed and slowly sank back onto the mattress. Secretly, she hoped he would come to her, but at the same time, she was determined not to give in to her weakness. Her peace of mind demanded that she never let herself be as vulnerable as she had been. Hours later, she calmed down sufficiently to fall asleep.

***

The closer the date of the Yukon Quest Race neared, the more intensified the training became. Although it was impossible not to fall over each other in the small cabin, they did their best to keep some distance between them. She was grateful for the times, often several nights in a row, that the men spent camping out on the trail in preparation for the grueling thousand-mile event.

During one such extended run, she decided to do her own overnight camping trip.

"Don't forget we're having tourists on Saturday and Sunday," Marcia reminded her.

Her foot firmly on the sled brake, Chris nodded. "I'll be back tomorrow, and so will the men. They won't forget."

"Unlikely! Scott asks where you are the minute he arrives."

"He doesn't, does he?" A little flutter in her heart sent warmth through her body.

"If he can't see you, the guy wants to know where you are. He's nuts over you."

"No, he's not. As far as he's concerned, I'm nothing more than a convenient helper."

"That's not my reading of the situation. Do I detect a hint of bitterness? You can't deny you feel something for him."

"What I feel doesn't matter. Not to him, anyway."

"I thought it was pretty decent of him to arrange for my trip here with our dogs."

"I agree. He can be considerate at times. He's a complex individual."

"I'm positive he loves you."

She sighed. "When you know him better, you'll understand that he doesn't know the difference between love and lust. He's never told me as much, but I suspect a woman has hurt badly him in the past. That accounts for his grumpiness around females... of the human variety, that is."

"If we go on discussing the man, we'll be here all night. You have to get going."

"You're right. Talking about men, Marcia, you seem on very friendly terms with Jerome. Is there more than meets the eyes?"

Marcia tossed back her hair and laughed. "Jerome has what you might call seasonal girlfriends. Every summer, he takes up with one only to ditch her when romance gets in the way of serious race training. That's not what I'm interested in. We've become good friends, that's all. For me, real love must be forever, not something that lasts a month or two."

"I understand. What about Byron? I see the looks you give him."

"We get along fine, but he's got his sights set on you."

She heard a telltale catch in her cousin's voice. "Byron is reluctant to muscle in on what he thinks is Scott's domain. What he doesn't realize is that Scott isn't interested in me. As much as I like Byron as a friend, I'm not looking to get involved with any man, no matter how handsome. I told him so. Surely, he had to have noticed you. You're so striking, with your blond hair and blue eyes."

Marcia wiggled her shoulders. "Being pretty hasn't always been such a wonderful asset. I can vouch from personal experience. Anyway, let's not talk about men. They drive you insane. Do you need all that gear for just one night out?"

"Having a powerhouse of twelve huskies in front of the sled is akin to a jet engine. I need some weight so I don't fly off into the trees."

"I should have guessed. Nothing like our good old dogs."

"I'm off. See you tomorrow." She called to her dogs, "Okay, hike!"

The team set off at a lively pace. A half-mile down the trail, they fell into their steady cruising gait. The moon was still up and reflecting on the snow. She dispensed with her headlamp to enjoy the mystical luminosity and spooky shadows.

By early afternoon, the sun had ended its brief appearance. The landscape returned to darkness. Miles later, she emerged from a line of trees and noticed a speck of light in the distance. From the way it bobbed up and down, it could only be that of a musher coming toward her. It was an eerie sight. The ghostly outline of the dog team glided over the surface of the snow without a sound.

After what seemed like an age, the light gradually drew close. She assumed the driver had not seen her, for he made no effort to slow down, so she pulled off the trail to avoid meeting the other team head on and promptly switch her headlamp on. When the gap between her and the other musher closed to a matter of yards, her lamp lit up the sleeve of his parka. It was Jerome.

Her heart fluttered. If this was Jerome, Scott must be somewhere behind him.

When their two teams were almost level, Jerome yelled, "Whoa!"

"Hi Jerome!" She jammed on her sled brake. "Are you looking for a good spot to camp?"

"Chris! What a surprise. I must have been half asleep. I never saw you until I was right on you. I was supposed to meet up with Scott somewhere along here. Have you seen him?"

Her spirits sank. "No. There's been no one on this trail all the time I've been on it."

"Damn! I must have taken the wrong turn."

"That's all too easy to do."

"Okay. Maybe I should set up camp in the hope he'll figure out where I am. Do you know a good place?"

"If you continue straight ahead for a couple of miles, you'll come to a sheltered valley by the grandiose name of Little Valley. There's plenty of wood there to build a fire."

"Do you want to stop?"

"I've already rested my dogs. I'd prefer to keep running for another three to four hours."

"This is great sledding country. I'd like to join you, but I must take a breather. We started at three this morning."

"Then we'll part here. See you tomorrow back at the cabin."

Her impatient team shot forward the moment she lifted the brake, and they got back on the packed trail. When she managed to catch her breath, she looked back. The darkness had swallowed Jerome and his team up.

Her well-trained team dashed over the frozen ground. Although the sled was laden with camping gear and food, its weight was of no hindrance to her sturdy huskies. Occasionally, she shone her headlight to check for limping dogs and tangled traces. Tongues lolling, their breath condensing in streamers, the dogs were in their element. This was what they lived for, being in the vast open spaces, running in concert with their pack mates, with each one trying to out-pull the other.

After working their way up a slope, the dogs crested a ridge. She decided it was as good a place as any to camp for the night. Just as she came to a halt, she heard a wolf howl off in the darkness. A sense of wonderment filled her. That plaintive sound embodied the northland, the hunt and the hunted, life and death. Others took the howl up. Up at the front of her team, Itirit sat, lifted her muzzle and howled to her distant cousins. The remainder of the dogs immediately joined in.

"Down!"

The dogs paid scant attention. Obliged to let the dialogue between the wild and the domestic canines continue, she firmly buried her two snow hooks. She needed the dogs' full attention before she dared step off the sled to secure a snub rope to a tree.

Tioralak, her sturdy red dog in the wheel position, fell silent first. At this signal, the others quit howling. For several seconds, silence prevailed until one lone wolf took up the challenge again, followed by others.

"Is that another pack? It's coming from a different direction."

She cocked her head to listen. "Oh no, not wolves. I know those voices. They're dogs, sled dogs. Our Canadian Inuit dogs! I'm glad no one's with me. I ought to be ashamed not to have recognized the difference right away. On the other hand, even experts can't tell the difference between those arctic dogs and wolves, at least not right away."

The dogs looked at her when she spoke aloud. Then, as one, they turned their attention to the trail and showed every sign of wanting to press on.

"Forget it, you guys! I'm bushed even if you're not. This is where we camp."

Her words made no impression on the dogs. Every nose and every ear pointed toward the howls. Without relaxing her vigilance for a second, she used her lamp to consult the sketch map of her route. Farther on was a small lake. That was where the sounds came from. A feeling of excitement gripped her. Those dogs were Scott's. Separated from Jerome, he probably decided to camp for the night.

As if reading her thoughts, her dogs again took up the howl, filling the air with their primeval song.

The strength of the team was becoming too much for the sled anchors. She had to take a snap decision or the team would take off on its own accord... without her. In the nick of time, she lifted the snow hooks and grasped the handlebar before the sled was careening madly down the slope.

Oblivious of the miles they'd already covered that day, the dogs streaked toward the lake at breakneck speed. She stood both feet on the brake to prevent the sled from running over the dogs and sending her flying backward. It barely slowed the team. In the distance, she saw a flickering glow. It grew as she came closer. The campfire now acting as a beacon for the team on the frozen shore. A line of picketed dogs appeared. They were howling frantically. No doubt about the distinctly wolfish howl of the Inuit sled dogs. No wonder she first mistook them for wolves. Now she wasn't sure whether she had heard wolves or not.

Pleasure rushed through her. Out in this vast wilderness, devoid of any human habitation and where a person could easily become hopelessly lost, she'd stumbled on him and his team. Blindly, she directed her team across the lake, dogs and woman floundering through deep virgin drifts.

Scott ran to meet the incoming team. She pulled up a few yards from his dogs.

"Chris! What the hell...?"

"Nice to meet you."

He did his best to hide his grin. "What are you doing here?"

"Do you want me to go back?"

"No. Of course not. I expected Jerome."

"I know. I met him this afternoon. He missed the turning. His dogs were too tired to turn back. He's camped in Little Valley. I never thought I'd find you, not out here, at night."

"You mean you didn't know I was here?"

"No. I was going to make camp back on the ridge when your team howled."

"So you came!"

"I really didn't have much choice. I simply tagged along behind."

Her dry humor provoked a flash of white teeth. He helped her picket her dogs a short distance from his own.

"I was just melting the broth for the dogs. I haven't been here long."

"Did I hear a wolf pack before your dogs started howling?"

"They serenaded us. They're over on that hill. If you look carefully, you can see them."

For a while, they both watched the wolves, black silhouettes against the lighter sky. A brief howl, and they all disappeared over the other side.

"Must have spotted a prey."

They returned to their chores. With a habit schooled by experience, she set up the stove to warm the pan of broth for her team. This was a time she loved, with the companionship and the expectant looks of the dogs watching her every move.

Once the teams had been cared for, she turned her attention to nourishment for of the humans.

"What do you have left in the way of food?"

"Just dehydrated."

"Want to share some delectable fresh meat, precooked potatoes and carrots?"

"That beats what I was planning. Did you bring along any of your special cookies?"

"Is that why you're being so friendly?"

Her teasing drew a chuckle. She bent over the hissing spirit stove. Hours of exertion in the cold had sharpened her appetite. They ate in silence. He melted snow for water to rinse the dishes and pots.

"I'll put up my tent," she said.

"Need a hand?"

"No thanks. I'll manage. What about yours?"

"I sleep under the stars."

"Sleeping out isn't all that great an idea. The body cools down more than it needs to and the cold saps the energy you need in the morning."

"I like seeing the stars over my head."

"Stubborn must be your middle name. So suit yourself. But you can share mine if you want."

The moment the words were out, she regretted them. This was an invitation that she hadn't meant to issue. Too late now. Erecting a tent in the dark had become second nature. When the last long peg, specially designed for snow, was pushed home, she unzipped the entrance door and crept inside. A double-thickness sleeping bag over an insulated foam mat provided a comfortable bed.

One luxury she allowed herself was a tent heater. She stretched a line between the poles and hung her mittens and socks to dry. Inside the tent, the temperature had now risen enough for her to get undressed. Before doing so, though, she switched off the lantern. No need to put on an old-fashioned lantern show while she put on fresh bamboo-silk underwear and a thermal outfit. She sat on the bedroll, toasting her toes by the tent heater, and idly reflected how nothing keeps a body as warm as bamboo-silk, except perhaps... A sigh of regret escaped her lips.

Scott's voice startled her at the door of the tent. "Chris?"

"Yes?"

"Is it okay if I join you?"

She pursed her lip. This wasn't a good idea at all. "Sure. Come on in." She lit the lantern.

His bivvy bag under his arm, he crawled in. His unexpected presence made the tent seem very small.

"I took your advice." His humble tone didn't sound like him.

A quiver of excitement ran down her back, followed by an erratic pounding of her heart. She snuggled deeper into her sleeping bag.

"Well, don't stay on top of your bag."

His hand reached for the zipper of her sleeping bag.

"We have an agreement."

"I didn't make any such agreement. I want you. That's no secret." The rasp in his voice affected her in ways she couldn't resist.

"A physical relationship complicates everything." She kept her voice level. "You have to reason with yourself."

"Why don't you admit you want me as much as I want you?"

"That's not the point." She was fighting the storm inside her.

"Just relax and listen to your body." He propped himself on one elbow to study her better.

"For me, a relationship has to be meaningful."

"Women are meant to love, but their heads are stuffed full of romantic fantasy. Why does it always have to be so deadly serious?"

"Some women are paid for that, no romantic fantasy there. That's where you should turn your lust to and leave women like me alone. It's too bad there isn't any of this feminine company for you out here in the wilds. If there were, you wouldn't look twice at me." She fought against the rising haze of heat that threatened to engulf her.

A rumble came from his throat. "That's where you're quite wrong. I find you irresistible."

"Thank you. What about Marcia? She's a stunningly good-looking woman and has all the right curves, too."

"So do you." His hand reached out to caress her cheek.

"When you win the Yukon Quest, you'll have a gaggle of women around you, all wanting to offer their charms to you."

"Maybe I'm not interested in a bunch of groupies."

His dry, forceful tone alarmed her. "Sorry, I didn't intend to be so mean spirited. Let's talk about something else."

Both his hands raked his hair. "I don't know. My life has changed so much. Since you've been here, I set myself new goals. I want to win the races again before I quit. What do you want from life?"

"I want to win..." an inner voice urged her to say, *your love*, but instead, she concluded, "... the Iditarod Trail race."

Her answer made him think for a moment. "Okay. Then what?"

She frowned, knowing he was leading her into a trap. "I don't know. This is one dream I've had since I was a little girl. I never thought beyond it."

"Take it from one who's been there. Winning races is not all that it's cracked up to be. You end up with a cold bed at night."

The seduction in his voice unsettled her. "If I need to keep warm, I'll buy an electric blanket." Her words were more forceful than she intimated.

"I love it when you get angry. Your eyes flash fire."

"I've extinguished the fire. Now sleep until morning." The quaver in her voice betrayed her.

He turned toward her. Defensively, she pulled her bag over her head. When she shut her eyes, a shower of meteors exploded in her head. She wanted to tell him to move away before her resolve crumbled, but the words died in her throat. She hoped that by remaining passive, she would discourage him. Her plan failed miserably.

With a delicate hand, he lifted the edge of her bag and dropped butterfly light kisses on her lips.

Somewhere in the distant reaches of her brain, alarm bells, very tiny ones, sounded. For a while longer, she resisted the inevitable. "No. We mustn't." Her words slurred drunkenly.

"Why not? You want this as much as I do. No matter what you say, your body doesn't lie."

"Please, let go. We agreed we'd have a business relationship only." The fear that trembled in her voice was directed at herself. She knew she would weaken if he kissed her again.

"You give the orders, boss." A resigned tone and a sigh ended the conversation.

The moment he rolled back to his side, relief inundated her. With a low growl of dissatisfaction, he doused the lantern.

In the morning, she went about the task of watering the dogs and feeding them their rations of fat. They spoke only as much as necessary. He had a preoccupied look. Over a simple breakfast, they agreed that he'd set off first and she, with her faster huskies, would overtake him later.

The sight of his face shadowed by a couple of day's growth tugged at her heart. Sleep had eluded her for hours after she had rejected him. Now in the haunting light of an arctic predawn, she wished she hadn't.

After he'd gone in the morning, she erased all traces of their camp and loaded her sled. With a final pensive glance at the flattened patch of snow where their tent had rested, she gave the dogs the departure signal. The exhilaration of the wind in her face, well muffled against the bitter cold, raised her spirits. In the semi-darkness, the sled glided smoothly over the snow as she followed his tracks. Having another team to pursue was a great incentive for the dogs. It was not long before they were trailing close behind him.

Growing impatient of plodding along behind, she called out "on-by", the signal to overtake and her dogs gave a burst of speed that sent the blood singing in her veins. They passed his team without a second glance. She waved a greeting while he raised his hand in salute.

CHAPTER EIGHTEEN

An unmistakable tightening in his belly stirred up unfulfilled longings as Scott watched Chris's lithe figure balance effortlessly on the runners of the sled. The fatigue that came from hours behind his team didn't help him forget about her. More difficult was to overcome the need to have her close, the need to hear her cheerful words of encouragement.

Although it was still a long way off, he was dreading the day at the end of the season when she'd go her own way. He couldn't tempt her to stay, not when he was making plans to sell up and get a job in the city. And if he didn't, he'd lose his chance to get custody of his son. Besides, she had learned to resist his advances. They couldn't even develop a relationship that might keep her with him. She wanted to race. Women like her possessed iron-clad willpower. In spite of the certainty he'd lose her, his respect for her grew with every passing day. Her ability to handle the dogs set her apart from any other females he had known.

When he finally arrived at the cabin, she had already taken care of her team. She hastened forward to help him with his. As they stumbled in the pale light, they laughed and joked. He couldn't take his eyes off her. Before, he used to curse the perpetual darkness. When she was with him, it became enchanting. With her by his side, he scoffed at numbing sub-zero temperatures. This attachment to her was proving dangerous. Winning was all that counted. If his mind was filled with fantasies, he couldn't win.

***

Training came to an end in the week before the start of the annual Yukon Quest Race, which that year started on the first weekend of February in Fairbanks, Alaska, and ended in Whitehorse, Yukon Territory. For a few days, the dogs were allowed to frolic and play, running free in small groups or sledding just a few miles a day. The dogs chased each other and cavorted in the fresh snow, but the sight of a harness attracted them to the gate, raring to go.

Jerome and Marcia had set out earlier in the week for Fairbanks. From there, she would come back to Whitehorse and drive the truck to the half-way Dawson City checkpoint, the only stopover in the race where handlers were allowed to help the mushers.

Scott and Chris spent most of their time packaging food for both canines and humans. Then he drove the load to Whitehorse. From there, it would be flown to the various checkpoints.

Unlike Jerome, he wouldn't have his handler in Dawson City. She couldn't leave the remaining dogs unattended.

Although the atmosphere had been one of companionable work, she sensed a reserve in him she couldn't explain. A whole day without him was becoming a welcome respite. He had not long gone when she heard a snowmobile rush up the trail. Her mood lifted. She darted outside to greet her visitor.

"Hello Byron! Have you been hiding?"

"No, just busy. The territory we have to cover is huge. How's the big man?"

"Gone to the capital."

"Ah! Getting the food out. Is he still grouchy?"

"It's peace. He's trying to make an effort to be sociable."

Byron shrugged helplessly. "He baffles me."

"I think he has a problem, but won't share it."

"I don't know how you put up with him when you could have a guy like me."

She laughed and opened her mouth to speak. Byron cut her off. "No, don't say it. I know, but I can't help wondering if love doesn't wear a little thin when it's always brushed off."

A long sigh was her only reply.

"Anyway, I'll be here to help with eight tourists on Saturday. It's going to be tight."

"We'll manage. Thanks for helping. You didn't come up just to tell me that."

"Okay, it was just an excuse to see you."

"Tsk, tsk, Byron!" She shook her head. "Since you're here, come see the pups. I was about to take them a little way down the trail before it gets totally dark."

"How can I refuse?"

Carefree laughter and yipping sounds echoed among the pines. Snowballs made good toys for pups to run after, grab and then drop in disgust. Back in their pen with the reward of a biscuit, they scooped big mouthfuls of snow.

With a nostalgic look in his eyes, Byron took his leave.

The day of Scott's departure for the big race arrived. They drove the Canadian Inuit dogs to Whitehorse. His friend Mark had offered to fly him and the dogs from Whitehorse to Fairbanks in his private Cessna Titan II.

When the dogs were loaded, Mark closed the cargo door. "There, all set."

"You be careful, now," she said.

"I sure will. Your precious dogs are safe with me. That's what you're concerned about, isn't it?"

His teasing brought a smile to her lips. "Right. Do you always fly supplies to those big races?"

"I've been part of the Iditarod Air Force for years."

They laughed.

"Who decided on the name?"

"I don't really know. One of those things that starts as a joke and then sticks."

"It's well named for the number of planes that help the racers."

"I treat it as my vacation. You know what they say in Alaska?"

"Tell me."

"There are three holidays: Christmas, New Year and the Iditarod."

She laughed. "What exactly do you do after you get there?"

"Myself and the other volunteers fly in the supplies. We patrol the length of the race trail, checking on racers and teams. Make sure everyone is safe. We fly out injured or tired dogs. We carry the media types. You name it, I've done it. A bit different with the Yukon Quest, but us volunteers are always ready to go."

"It makes you wonder how they coped in the early years of the race, no snowmobile to groom the trail, no satellite beacons, no planes, no advance party leaving food at the checkpoints."

"You could say they were like acrobats without a safety net. They were tough guys who could live off land. Not that the modern mushers are soft, but they rely on an awful lot of technology, state-of-the-art clothing and equipment."

"I think I'd have liked the old-fashioned race." A wistful look passed in her eyes.

"It's different. In the old days, mushers had only their own resources and knowledge of the land. The dogs were freighters, bred for strength and endurance, as most of the racers operated a trap line. Now they are bred for speed only."

"Right, they're so light they need a coat. Scott's Iditarod dogs are a little bigger and more furry than most. But for the Yukon Quest, his Inuit dogs won't need any gear."

He smiled. "My kind of dogs."

"They're not fast, though. I hope the Quest is as tough and difficult as it is said to be, both in terrain and weather. If it is, he has a chance with his freighters."

"It really is a tough and difficult race with long stretches of nothing. I agree he has a good chance. At least, I'm confident he'll make it in the money."

"I want him to win. What's different with the Yukon Quest?"

"We make food drops to the nine checkpoints, that's all. Nine stops in a one-thousand miles race. We're on standby, though, in case of emergency. The Quest is still a rugged, no-frills race. Man against untamed nature."

"What about woman against untamed nature?"

Mark gave a sheepish grin. "That too. A few women have taken part in that race. But as far as I know, only Ally Zirkle has won it."

"She received the Golden Harness Award in 2000. And Michelle Phillips placed second. Makes me dream."

"One day, it'll be your turn." He glanced at a figure leaving the terminal. "Here's the boss coming now."

Mark climbed into the cockpit and fired up the engines. She stepped back. Her pulse fluttered as she watched Scott stride across the tarmac. As usual, he was bareheaded, his parka open to the wind. He came up to her and pulled her against him. The wash from the propeller blew her hair in his face. Quivering with anticipation, she waited for his kiss. He hungrily took her offered lips. For one exquisite moment, time and the outside world stood still. "Good luck!" she whispered.

"Thanks. See you back here in Whitehorse."

"I'll expect to greet a winner."

He smiled. Her heart leaped in her chest, the airstrip suddenly illuminated, clouds lifted, music sang in her ears. He put a finger on her lips, then on his and clambered aboard. The door slammed shut, and the plane taxied to the end of the runway. She climbed to the windswept observation deck to watch the plane carrying him and the Canadian Inuit dogs she was so fond of gather speed and lift into the air. It banked steeply and pointed its nose toward Alaska. When the tiny speck disappeared into the clear northern sky, she retraced her steps to the truck.

It was just a good luck kiss. The refrain went around in her head. Just a good luck kiss. On her way back home, she stopped at the Fletcher Creek store for supplies and called on Byron.

"The race will be covered on radio, won't it?" she asked.

"Sure thing. And on tv, but here the reception isn't as good and it isn't live. Still, it's a big event up here."

"There's a small set at the cabin. The only problem is that we get such lousy reception, even with new batteries. Scott says it's due to the shielding effect of the mountains. So we never put it on." She reddened, realizing how easily she used 'we' to describe her life in the cabin.

Byron must have noticed, for he gave her a grin. "You can always come down here to take in the coverage."

"Thanks, I might do that."

"Don't forget to pick up the battery for the radiophone at the store. It's all charged up again."

With her thoughts focused on Scott, she went about her work. In the evenings, her duties done, she'd drive to Fletcher Creek to listen to the race reports with Byron. Some nights when the temperatures plummeted, and the truck refused to start, she covered the distance by dog sled.

"How is this cold weather affecting the race?" she asked.

Byron pulled a face. "It's not a happy picture. Two mushers scratched today. A few others are about to."

"The race won't be canceled, will it?"

"Unlikely. Most teams are doing well. Walsh is still among the front runners. There are about ten of them, all jockeying for position."

The special race report came on the radio. She glued her ear to the speaker, impatient to catch any mention of Scott. There was good news and bad. The front racers had left Eagle, Alaska, the last checkpoint before Dawson City, and were toiling over Eagle Summit before winding their way down to the ice-covered Yukon River. From there, the race trail followed the river to the Canadian border. The bad news was that the fierce blizzard sweeping the area showed no sign of abating. Part way along the lonely trail was a cabin, whose occupants served the mushers hot drinks as they passed through. Otherwise, it was pure wilderness all the way.

Chris closed her eyes. In her mind, she willed Scott to move ahead. You can do it. You can do it.

Chapter Nineteen

I n the swirling snow, Scott had trouble seeing the reflective trail markers. From time to time, a scrap of fluorescent ribbon reassured him he was on track. Without slackening their pace, the dogs kept their noses to the ground. He wondered what Chris would say under such conditions. Keep awake and put your trust in the dogs, most likely. The image of her smiling green eyes danced before him like a beautiful mirage.

Heartened by the thought that she was possibly thinking of him at that very moment, he drove on into the worsening storm. He came upon a team halted on the side. He slowed his dogs to a crawl. "Everything okay?" His voice hardly carried above the shriek of the wind.

The other musher raised a hand in recognition. "Yeah, Walsh, my dogs are protesting. I'm low on food."

"I can spare you a bag."

"Thanks so much, but you need it for your dogs."

Scott pulled a bag of kibble from his sled. "Here, my dogs don't like kibble, anyway. I've got enough mush."

"I reckon I'm going to bivouac down right here until it eases off."

"You're probably smarter than I am. I feel the urge to push on. My dogs are eager to run." He pulled up the anchors and lifted his foot off the brake. His dogs bent once more into their harnesses.

An hour later, he was forced to stop again when he came across a team blocking the way. He anchored his sled and ordered the dogs to lie down. He stepped off the runners and approached the musher.

"Trouble?"

The other musher's face was haggard with fatigue. "Got to take a rest. I took a tumble on the hill. Can't get my tent up in this wind."

It dawned on him that the man he was helping was Hans Reesink. The reigning champion.

"Let's secure the dogs first. I'll help."

Words translated themselves into immediate action.

"Thanks, Walsh. Do you want to share with me until this crazy storm dies out?"

"Thanks, no." He tugged his parka hood strings tighter to protect his face and pulled his neck warmer to cover his nose. He climbed back onto the runners of his sled and set off again. Hans had been in the lead. Scott could hardly believe that now there was now no one left between him and the Dawson City checkpoint.

Smiling at his dogs, he called out, "All right, my friends, this is your kind of weather and we're up in front." His leaders, Capitor and Tekoone, were barely visible through the curtain of thick snow. For the race, he ran the dogs two-by-two in tandem formation but without necklines. The dogs were linked to the center gangline only by the lines attached to their harnesses. They were less restricted and, as a result, pulled harder. It wasn't the accepted practice, but as long as the dogs stayed in their places, he didn't think anyone would complain.

His lack of sleep eventually began to take its toll. A long-distance dog musher had many tasks to accomplish during the short rest periods. The race schedule must be adapted to the dogs' requirements, not his own. He could hear Chris telling him, when you feed the dogs, feed yourself. Shamefully, he had not followed that precept over the last two days. Now the effects of lack of nourishment and rest were showing. He removed one hand from its mitten and fumbled in the sled bag in search of cookies and dried bananas. The high-sugar food gave him a new burst of energy. He even sang to his team over the roar of the tempest.

The dogs' sudden change of direction almost pitched him off the sled. As if of one mind, the entire team swerved off the trail and hurtled down a steep slope. His shouts were futile to stop the runaway dogs. In the deep snow, the sled brake had minimal effect.

Out of desperation, he was about to flip the sled over to drag the team to a halt when he saw the dark shape of a man laying face down in the snow. The dogs slackened their stride and stopped by the motionless figure. Scott recognized that the man wasn't a race competitor. There were no signs of a team or sled tracks. He jumped off and ran to him. The dogs sniffed and nosed the man. Tekoone pawed him in the back. Scott turned him over.

"Hey! Wake up! Are you hurt?"

"I dunno," the man groaned. "I'm awful tired."

"You're freezing to death."

"I got lost in the storm. Say, you're Scott Walsh. Remember me? I'm Rob Larter, a photojournalist with Federated Press."

"I seem to recall we've exchanged a few choice words in the past. Let's get you back on your feet. You're hypothermic. How come you're here at the bottom of a ravine?"

"Stupid snowmobile broke down."

"Where is it?"

While he talked, he rearranged the load on the sled and bundled Rob Larter into the Mylar emergency blanket.

"I abandoned the piece of junk back a way. Figured I'd hike to the next checkpoint."

"Hike? Have you the slightest idea how far it is to Dawson City?"

Larter smiled lamely, his speech slurring. "I was hoping to hitch a ride."

Scott groaned. The damned fool! His former irritation toward the media flared briefly. "Get in the sled bag. You've got hypothermia."

The man did as he was told and stumbled into the sled. Scott finished wrapping his sleeping bag around the journalist and made him drink from one of the thermos bottles he carried.

"That's good. Warms me up already."

"Now don't fall asleep. Talk, or sing, but keep up the noise. Tell me, how did you end up in this gully?"

"The snowmobile slid down."

Then, Scott turned his attention to getting his team and their load out of the ravine. He stepped into his snowshoes. The dogs were fully responsive to his commands. They stretched themselves, and with him pushing from behind, they dragged the heavy sled back up the slope.

CHAPTER TWENTY

To fill the void left by Scott's absence, Chris spent more time than perhaps she ought to playing with the young pups. No one could feel depressed when surrounded by seven exuberant baby dogs.

The chores finished, she was about to go in when pitiful cries reached her ears. The pups! She turned and ran to the kennel house. The cries came from behind the swinging door to the outside pen. Laughing, she lifted the door and scooped up the puppy.

He wriggled in her arms as she returned him to his concerned mother. "You're almost big enough to live outside, but we'll wait until the weather warms up a bit. In the meantime, try not to get stuck again in the exit tunnel." Disregarding her injunction, the pup dashed back into the tunnel, followed by his littermates. Nine weeks old and already so independent and cocky. Arnavik, made guttural sounds to call her offspring. They pushed on the swinging door and rushed to nuzzle her mouth in the hope she'd regurgitate some food for them. With a soulful sigh, Chris left them to their play.

In the cabin, someone was trying to get through on the radiophone. She picked up the mike. "Hello. This is Boreal Kennel, Alpha Dog. Over."

A shrill feminine voice came through. "Who am I speaking to? Over."

"Chris Taylor. Mr. Walsh's dog handler. Over."

"Put Scott on."

"Who's calling?" The woman's hostile tone grated on her nerves, but she made an effort to be polite.

There was a throaty laugh at the other end. "Alina. Scott's wife, that's who."

Chris's jaw dropped. She gripped the edge of the counter, unable to believe what she'd just heard.

"Hello? Are you still there? Press the talk button."

She took a deep breath. "I'm sorry. I'm not used to this machine."

"Yeah. Stupid contraption. I never got the hang of it, either. Now let me speak to my husband."

"He's away in a race. May I take a message?" She was amazed she could still talk. Married! Shock wrapped itself around her in an icy cloud.

"You sound young. You must be his latest girlfriend."

"No, I'm not!" She yelled back before she realized she hadn't pressed the send button. A steel vise tightened around her chest. "No, I'm not his girlfriend." She repeated without shouting, but in a forceful voice. "I only work for him." Well, she wasn't his girlfriend. They only had sex. Call it therapy.

"All the same, my husband has quite an eye for a cute little behind. Funny, he didn't mention anyone called Chris over Christmas, or that he'd got himself a new handler."

"He must have had other things on his mind." She leaned against the cabin wall. Another piece of the Scott Walsh puzzle just dropped into place. The mystery of where he'd spent Christmas had been solved.

"You can say that again. I have to speak to him to tell him that I'm sending Cody. It'll do the kid good to spend some time with him."

"Cody?"

"Our kid. Scott's son."

The restriction cramping her ribs tightened another notch. Scott's son!

"Does Mr. Walsh know about the arrangement?" The effort to be polite brought beads of perspiration to her forehead. "He didn't mention anything."

"I wouldn't expect him to discuss his private life with you. But, no, he doesn't. I've changed my mind about Cody visiting his father."

"When are you sending the child? It may be some time before Mr. Walsh gets back."

"Cody's on a flight north tomorrow. He's due in Whitehorse at three in the afternoon. Tell my husband he's got to meet him at the airport."

"Impossible! Mr. Walsh is running the Yukon Quest. He's still on the trail in the middle of nowhere."

"Quit stalling, won't you, girl? Get a message to him. They've got helicopters for an emergency. That's what this is. He's got to accept his responsibilities. I'm flying off to New York with a good friend an hour after Cody boards his plane."

Chris was at a loss. If she put up an objection, Scott's wife would start phoning the race organizers. There was no saying what might happen then. The rancor in the woman's voice hinted that she was capable of anything.

Hurriedly, and hiding her panic, she articulated, "Don't worry. I'll meet Cody at the airport."

"Are you capable of looking after a child?"

"I look after forty-seven dogs and puppies. I guess I can care for a child. How old is he?"

"Six. He's used to babysitters. You have to watch out for that pesky asthma of his. It's a real nuisance."

The brittle tone from the speaker did nothing to inspire Chris's sympathy.

"I'll do my best." The woman cut off the transmission without the slightest word of thanks.

Chris collapsed on the couch, her head buried in her hands.

Scott with a wife and a child! That explained his behavior. That explained why he didn't want to be tied down. He already was! A long distance relationship may suit two people with opposite dreams. Nothing really strange about that. Some couples did it and were happy.

Shock gradually gave way to fury. The cushions absorbed her pounding fists. Damn the man for putting her through such emotional turmoil, for making her fall in love with him! Damn the man for his adultery!

Her fit of anger eventually ran out of steam. It gave way to worry over practical problems. Now, she was committed to going to the capital tomorrow to meet this young boy. Below a certain temperature, a truck engine simply refused to start, not unless it was kept warm by an electric block heater. The motor might be fitted with one, but the cabin had no electricity. Undaunted, she went out and tried to start the truck. "Just what I expected!"

Back inside, she called Byron on the radiophone.

"I need to start the truck. It's frozen."

"Use a tiger torch. The boss is bound to have one."

"What's a tiger torch?"

"It's a... Look, hang on, I'll come up. See you shortly."

When she heard the whine of his snowmobile, she put on her outdoor clothes and went out to meet him.

"Sorry to force you out on a cold evening."

"No problem. It doesn't bother me. There must be a tiger torch in the kennel room, plus a tank of propane."

With her flashlight to light the way, they walked to the building. In one corner of the kennel room, Byron found what he was looking for.

"This is a tiger torch. It's nothing more than a metal pipe with a handle on one end and a burner on the other. Connect the rubber hose to the propane cylinder and light the burner. When it's going properly, you crawl under the truck and heat up the oil pan on the motor. Simple."

"Isn't it dangerous?"

"Not as long as you don't touch any wires or fuel lines. Here, I'll light it up and start that beast of a truck for you. So, you're taking me up on my advice to go and meet Scott at Dawson?"

Fearful of imposing on her friend, she hadn't yet accepted his offer to look after the dogs, though she'd love to be at the checkpoint to see Scott and take care of the dogs for him while he rested. Now, with the arrival of the child, that was out of the question.

"I can't."

"You can if I take care of the place while you're gone. This bad weather is slowing down the race. Scott is still up in front, but anything can happen on the final run to the finish line in Whitehorse. If you're in Dawson to help him, that might be enough to give him the winning edge. He'd be able to get a good night's rest. Sometimes a race is won not just by the dogs but because the musher has all his wits about him."

"You don't know the all of it. Scott's wife just phoned. Their six-year-old son is arriving in Whitehorse by plane tomorrow afternoon. I'm in shock. I didn't know he was even married."

Byron gave a low whistle. "He is what? That's a whopper! And I thought I was his buddy! He never told you?"

"Not a word."

"What are you going to do?"

"About the kid? I don't have any choice but to be at the airport to meet him."

"Then what will you do with him?"

"Keep him here with me, I guess. That's why he's going to have to cope on his own in Dawson City."

"Just hang on a minute. We might just be able to do something. What if Vicky looked after him until you came back?"

"I can't ask Vicky to look after the kid. She can't take time off teaching just for us."

"Saturday tomorrow. No school. Vicky's a mother hen. Monday, she'll take him to school and love every moment of it."

"I ought to ask her first."

"Consider it done. I know. She is the sweetest person ever. And I've got vacation days due so I can take some time off work to help."

"That's really generous of you, but–"

"No buts. We'll do it."

The warmth in Byron's voice boosted her spirit. "Scott is not expecting me."

"All the better."

"I don't know how to thank you. His... wife said the boy has asthma. That's pretty serious. It can be life threatening."

"Yes, especially when he takes a few gulps of refrigerated Yukon air. I hope he has medication with him. Why don't you ask Vicky? She must have experience of asthma among her schoolkids."

"I'll do that."

"But first, we gotta get this truck warmed up."

Byron slid partly under the engine and trained the propane torch on the motor's oil pan. After a few minutes, he cut off the propane, climbed into the driver's seat and turned the ignition. The engine protested, but cranked over and burst into life.

"There, you're all set. We'll just let it run for a while. It should start fine for you in the morning if you give it a couple of minutes with the tiger torch."

"Thanks."

"Call in at my place. Vicky and I'll follow you to Whitehorse in my truck."

"You need not do that."

"Better if we're all together to meet the boy. Besides, you'd cut it a bit short to get on the road to Dawson."

"Are you sure I'm not foisting a lot on Vicky?"

"I wouldn't offer if I wasn't. Don't worry, we'll look after... What's his name?"

"Cody."

"The first mushers are expected in Dawson Sunday evening at the earliest. If you leave straight on from Whitehorse, you'll get there in good time and can get camp and billet organized for him. You don't mind driving through the night?"

"No. It doesn't make much difference since it's dark most of the day."

"Up here, folks help one another out. We're all friends. You must have learned that by now."

"I know and appreciate it."

"Start the truck in the morning and let it run a bit. Call if you need help."

"Have you had dinner?"

"Not yet. When I received the damsel-in-distress call, I leaped on my black charger and came to the rescue."

"Thanks, Sir Knight. You're really great! Step this way for a frontier style dinner."

The tantalizing smell of dinner filled the cabin. Byron sprawled on the couch.

"Do you know Dawson?"

"No, I meant to read up about it, but I've been busy. It seems that the cold slows me down."

"It does. You're using more energy. Imagine the stampeders more than a century ago, during the Klondike Gold Rush. They didn't have the benefit of our high-tech clothes."

"But they wore wool clothes and wool keeps you warm even when wet."

Byron laughed. "True." He then affected the serious tone of a travelogue narrator. "In those days, Dawson's dusty streets echoed to the clamor of miners, prospectors and dance hall girls. Today, it's a sleepy town of a thousand souls, until it relives some of its former glory twice a year," he said.

She couldn't stop laughing. "All the ads talk about the short summer under the midnight sun and the hordes of tourists who come to soak up the glamor of the gold rush days. What else?"

Byron raised a finger. "The other time is the Quest."

"Don't tourists come in for winter sports the rest of the winter?"

"They're biased. They don't think life exists when the winter descends on the Klondike. But they come for the Quest."

"We're going to change that with Boreal Dogsledding Adventures." She spoke tongue-in-cheek.

He slowly nodded. "You could, especially that the Quest wakes everybody up and does bring people out. So on their way back Outside they could just drop by for a sled ride."

"Outside? Oh yes, the world outside the North, right?"

"Right. For us sourdoughs everywhere else is Outside."

"Am I a sourdough yet?"

"Nope, still a cheechako. If you survive one winter up here, you officially become a sourdough. But a bit of advice on the road to Dawson. There are few settlements or roadside facilities. Travelers have to be self-contained. So make sure you pack well and have a full tank of gas and a jerrycan."

"I'll do that."

"I'm off now. Dinner was great."

"You're welcome, and thank you for the tiger torch lesson."

After he left, she prepared food and camping equipment for her long drive north to Dawson City. In addition to provisions, she packed extra clothes for herself and Scott, as well as a selection of spare harnesses and lines. The race was hard on men, dogs and equipment. In case he was running low on dog food, she loaded the surplus frozen dog food that they had prepared before his departure. Nothing could be taken for granted, nothing left to chance.

In the event she'd need to bring back an exhausted or hurt dog, she checked the truck's dog transporter. The last thing she did was to replenish the soft spruce boughs that lined the individual compartments. In one compartment, she loaded enough of them to lie on the ground where the team would be resting. Though they would be supplied with one bale of straw, nothing insulates a body from the frozen ground like spruce boughs.

The six-year-old child remained at the forefront of her thoughts. She packed several bags of dried fruit and nuts, filled two thermoses and took several packets of instant hot chocolate. On the spur of the moment, she threw the sweater and parka she used to care for the dogs on top of the bag. It was already stained with spilled broth and marked by dog paws. She wouldn't have to worry about keeping it clean.

CHAPTER TWENTY-ONE

Next morning, she started the truck, and after letting the engine warm up in the sub-zero temperature, she left for her rendezvous with Vicky and Byron.

While they waited at the airport, Byron gave news of the race. "The blizzard almost immobilized the mushers. The latest news is that Scott didn't stop and appears to be in first position. Hans Reesink is two hours behind him."

"Can he catch up?"

"Maybe, maybe not. A lot depends on the trail. Scott's dogs are strong and his team is still intact. Reesink has had to drop another dog. He's now down to eleven."

The territory's airport was not large compared to those in big cities, but after the tranquility of her wilderness cabin, the noise and frantic activity assaulted her ears.

From the terminal window, she watched the arriving jet taxi to the apron. A flight attendant holding a young boy by the hand and a plane blanket in the other was one of the first to disembark. At the bottom of the steps, the attendant scooped him up into the blanket and ran inside.

Chris hurried to greet them. Her heart missed a beat. The boy's gray eyes and dark hair, the shape of his chin and nose, were Scott's in miniature.

Byron and Vicky gasped. "Shorts and T-shirt?"

"And a light jacket. I can't believe it," Chris said. "He's blue!"

"In shock because of the cold. Who is stupid enough to send him in this getup?" Byron's angry voice drew some attention.

"Ms. Chris Taylor?" the flight attendant asked.

"Yes, that's me."

"Here is your charge. I'm sorry. The best I could do was this blanket. He transferred to us at the Calgary international airport. He comes from California. No one there had any idea how cold it would be up here. Do you have clothing for him?"

"We'll get him some right away," Vicky said.

"Good. This pouch contains his medicine and instructions in case of an asthma attack."

"Thank you. I was wondering about that."

"He was fine on the plane. No symptoms of distress. You won't miss his case on the baggage carousel. It has a big blue label with his name."

The young woman crouched down. "Goodbye, Cody, I must go back to the plane."

The child clung to the woman's hand, looking at her with pleading eyes.

"This nice lady, Ms. Taylor, is going to take care of you now. 'Bye, Cody."

"Hello, Cody. I'm Chris. Did your mommy tell you about me?"

The youngster gave a shy nod. He reached for her hand. She gave his a squeeze. Cody relaxed.

"Did you like flying in the airplane?" They waited for his baggage.

"Yes."

"That's good. Cody, I want you to meet my friends, Byron and Vicky. Vicky is a schoolteacher."

Cody looked at them timidly, but did not return their greeting.

"Do you go to school?" Vicky asked.

Cody didn't answer. Instead, he lowered his gaze. "Where's my daddy?"

"He wanted to be here, but right now he's racing his dogs. That's why I came to pick you up," Chris spoke in a gentle voice.

"I want my daddy." Tears pearled at the corners of his eyes.

"He'll finish the race soon. Let's see how many fingers do you have?" Vicky said.

He didn't answer.

"There is one sleep for each finger on this one hand. That's when your daddy will come back."

Cody looked down at his hand, then at her. "I can count."

Chris smiled at him. "Very good. For now, would you like to go with Vicky and Byron?"

"No!"

In the meantime, Byron had retrieved Cody's suitcase. The little boy kept his eyes lowered, clutching her hand. They moved to the nearest chairs and looked inside the case. The adults looked at each other in dismay.

"Do you have a coat in your bag?"

Cody stared at her and pulled on his short poplin jacket. "I've got my coat on."

"Heck, the flight attendant just said he's from California. They don't need coats down there," Byron said.

"We can't take Cody outside dressed like that!" Vicky sounded alarmed.

Byron raised his shoulders in a gesture of futility. "I'll tell you what. Let's get out of here and go and have a hamburger."

"Is there not something warm in the case?"

They carefully searched the packed clothes. The only garments of some use were a pair of long pants and a light sweater.

"That won't do," Vicky exclaimed.

"We can start with those," Chris said. "I've got some warm things in the truck. Cody, you wait here with Byron and Vicky. I'll only be a minute."

Cody shrieked and wrapped his arms about her hips.

"We're going about it the wrong way again," Vicky said. "Chris, you and I stay here. Byron can get the bag."

"Bring the two green bags," Chris said.

Byron soon returned from the truck.

"Cody, I'll need my hand to look for the clothes." Chris was unsure of how to handle a six-year-old child. Cody accepted to let go of her hand.

"How about slipping the long pants and the sweater on first?" Byron said.

When it came to take off his shorts, Cody balked until Chris stood him on the chair and they shielded his thin body with theirs.

Chris pulled out her fleece jacket. It wasn't bulky, being designed to be worn under a coat. Cody tried it on and giggled. The jacket fell to his ankles. When the sleeves were doubled back, they were of reasonable length.

"At least it will keep him warm," said Byron. "You look great, Cody."

The child lifted his head from inspecting his strange new garment.

"This is your daddy's wooly toque," Chris said.

That caught the boy's full attention.

"It's a one-size-fits-all, which is handy. And I have those miracle gloves which look so small a baby could wear them, yet stretch to a man's size."

"All he needs now is a parka," Byron said.

"He can have mine," Chris said.

"Maybe he should wear my parka, since I'm shorter," Vicky said.

"That might work. Let's try."

Cody wrinkled his nose. "I don't want to wear pink."

Byron looked away to hide his amusement.

Chris pressed her lips together. "Mine's blue. You'll wear it?"

"Yes."

The parka trailed on the ground and gaped at the neck. By adjusting the drawstring of the hood and closing the tabs, Chris and Vicky succeeded in making it hold onto the child. His arms disappeared inside the sleeves until they tucked them up.

"His shoes are only thin leather, but we won't have to walk far," Vicky said.

"I suggest we go and buy this young man some clothes. Then we can get that hamburger," Byron said.

"That's the best idea so far. Don't you agree, Cody? How about we buy you some warm clothes first?"

He nodded and took her hand again. Byron and Vicky picked up the bags.

Outside, the boy stopped, his eyes round with astonishment.

"It's all white!"

"It's snow," Vicky said.

Cody wrenched his hand free and rushed forward to snatch up two handfuls of snow. He looked at it before bringing it to his mouth. With a cry of surprise and he threw the white stuff back on the ground.

The three friends chuckled.

"I guess he's never seen snow before," Byron said.

"It's like ice-cream, but we don't usually eat it," Vicky said.

That satisfied the boy's curiosity. At the truck, Cody eyed the dog box with interest. Each compartment had a door decorated with a dog silhouette.

"They're for my daddy's dogs?"

"Yes. When the race is over, they jump in and we take them all home."

To stop shivering, Chris grabbed her work parka from the back seat.

About to enter the clothing store, she bit her knuckles. How was she going to pay for all this? Byron caught her movement.

"You don't have Scott's credit card?"

"No, we don't need it in Fletcher Creek. I only have enough money for gas."

"We'll put the purchases on mine. I'll square it off with Walsh later."

The shopping expedition was a success. Thanks to Vicky, Cody came out of the store looking like a true northerner, and his case was packed with adequate clothes. At the fast-food restaurant, he stuck to Chris's side.

"Cody, you're going to go home with Byron and Vicky because I have to go and help your daddy."

Cody shook his head.

"It won't take long, then daddy will be home."

Cody burst into tears. The two women looked glumly at each other.

Byron handed Cody a couple of paper napkins. "Here, son, dry your eyes. You don't want to drop tears on your smart new outfit. We'll think of something."

"Do you like school, Cody?" Vicky asked.

Between sobs, Cody nodded.

"Would you like to come and see my school?"

He shook his head again.

"Nice try, Vicky. I think he's traumatized. Leaving his mother, traveling alone to a cold place and being met by a bunch of strangers is a lot to ask."

"He seems to have taken to you, though," Vicky said.

"His mother must have told him Chris would look after him, so he hangs on to the only thing he knows," Byron said.

"You're probably right. Which means it would be better if I took him with me to Dawson."

Vicky gave her a smile. "I'm afraid so."

"On the other hand, it might be safer to go home. Scott can manage on his own since he was going to, anyway. He's not expecting me."

"No, you must go," Byron said. "It could make the difference in the outcome of the race. Better get back to the store to get Cody a sleeping bag and more clothes. He'll need them to camp out."

"I'll have to use your credit card again, Byron–"

"It's an emergency. You can repay me out of the next Boreal Dogsledding Adventures tourists. In the meantime, take my card with you. With a kid, you never know what you might need."

"Thanks."

Cody stopped crying and dried his eyes. At the outfitter's, they equipped him with a sleeping bag and a bivvy sac to last him until he'd reach a ten-year-old size, as well as some more thermal clothes. The boy was relaxed and fascinated by all the attention. When Chris suggested getting snowshoes for him, he couldn't help laughing after the store clerk had him try them in the store. But he still didn't want to go with Vicky and Byron. The clerk and the owner offered a child backpack in which to carry his new equipment.

Outside again, Vicky and Byron bagged his useless clothes and took the lot with them.

"I wish I could be there to see his face when he sees his son," Vicky said.

They hugged and said goodbye. Then Chris and Cody got into the truck. Half an hour later, they were on the Klondike Highway, heading north toward Dawson City. It was not long before Cody began asking questions about the rugged countryside on either side, and about the dogs he would see when they arrived. She described the pups back at the cabin. It was past his bedtime, but he was still talking, even though he was practically falling asleep.

At Carmacks, they stopped for gas. Before setting out again, she crammed the bags and backpacks into the well between the front and back seats. After tucking him into his sleeping bag on the makeshift bed, Cody fell fast asleep. Maybe not the safest way to travel, but there was no other choice.

It was mid-morning when they rolled into Dawson City as darkness waned. Cody had woken up and was munching on nuts and raisins.

"First, we'll have a big breakfast. Then we'll go and check out the campground."

"We're going to camp? In a tent? In the snow?"

"Well, I guess we might."

That had been her plan when, at Byron's insistence, she'd agreed to go to Dawson. Cody's appearance on the scene had altered the picture. She wasn't sure that camping with an asthmatic child in mid-winter was a brilliant idea. Scott would be provided with a billet in town, though he probably intended to stay at the campground with his dogs.

Now that she had arrived, she'd insist he had a good night's rest in a warm bed. That meant she'd sleep in the tent with Cody. The billet was obviously not expecting a young child. She rubbed her forehead. A room at a hotel was a better solution, but she cringed, thinking of the price she'd have to pay. That is, if a room was even available. Byron had said the town was invaded by eager tourists and fans.

"I want to sleep in the tent." Somewhere along the way, Cody's shyness had vanished.

"We need to check with a doctor first, okay?"

Cody frowned. "I'm not sick."

"No, you are not sick, but you've got asthma, which could be made much worse in the cold."

"It's cold, but I don't have no asthma now."

The child's logic struck her. "Indeed, you're doing well. We'll check anyway, just to make sure."

Cody turned his attention to getting down from the cab. She rushed to help him and secure his scarf over his nose and mouth. At the race center, she asked a volunteer where she could find a doctor. A tall, handsome man overheard her and breached the few steps between them.

"I'm Doctor Elliot Bungard. May I help you?"

"What a stroke of luck! I'm Chris Taylor, and this is Cody Walsh."

"I'm six."

"Nice to meet you, Cody," Dr. Bungard stooped to shake the child's hand. "Is your daddy Scott Walsh?"

"Yes, sir." Pride radiated from his young face.

"Presently I'm Cody's guardian. He has asthma, but wants to sleep in the tent tonight. It's his first time in the Yukon. He was living in California with his mother, but she's traveling."

He crouched at Cody's height. "I don't hear any distressed breathing."

She frowned. "I've no experience. I wouldn't have known if his breathing was distressed."

"Oh, yes you'd have. It's very distinctive. An attack can be triggered by exertion, especially in the cold, or by stress, or by VOCs."

"VOCs?"

He smiled. "Sorry, VOCs are 'volatile organic compounds'. Organic isn't your nice garden grown food but any elements containing carbon. And by VOCs, we really mean the nasty stuff. California you said?"

"LA."

"Plenty of pollutants there. The cold, pure air of the Yukon might be just what that young man needs. If he is kept warm and dry, I think he can camp."

"Yey!" Cody did a little dance.

"Do you have medicine for him?"

"This." She handed him the pouch. "I'm not sure how to use all this."

Dr. Bungard pulled out an inhaler. "Cody, do you know how to use this sorbitol inhaler?"

"Yes, but I don't need it."

"Good." He looked up at her. "This white inhaler is corticosteroid to be used in an emergency if the blue one doesn't provide relief. And these cromolyn pills prevent the narrowing of the bronchial tubes, but unless he has an attack, don't use them."

Relieved, she thanked the doctor.

"Oh, and a tip I think might also help a lot. Cut any bread things from his diet. I've heard many asthma sufferers who turned their condition round by cutting all gluten from their diet."

"If that's what it takes to keep him healthier, we'll do it."

"There are many gluten-free substitutes. You'll even find a selection here at the Café Auley." He pointed to a brightly lit building overlooking the river. "You might talk to the owner. He makes sourdough bread and apparently his asthma sufferers clients can eat a little of it without side effects."

"I'll get some of that too. We'll try. Thank you so much."

Next, she asked directions from a volunteer and drove across the quarter mile-wide ice bridge over the Yukon River to the campground on the opposite bank. Although the site had been plowed, the part she selected toward the back was deep in snow. Her first task, much to Cody's amusement, was to put on snowshoes and flatten a space to picket the dogs. After a few tumbles, Cody got the hang of the snowshoes and helped her shovel snow to make a low wall.

The boy looked up at her. "Are we building a fort like on the beach?"

"Sort of. It's to protect the dogs from the wind. Now, let's put the spruce boughs down for their bed."

"Why do the people over there have a big tent?"

"They've made it out of a plastic sheet so that their dogs are under cover. Your daddy's dogs prefer to sleep in the open."

"But we'll sleep in our tent, right?"

"Yes. It's a bit small, but it'll be warm."

The tent fascinated the child. He had to examine every layer of the bedrolls. His excitement rose when she lit a fire to thaw meat and fat in advance of the team's arrival.

Just as these preparations were well under way, she saw a familiar truck enter the campground. A blond-haired woman jumped down from the cab.

"Marcia!"

"Chris! I never expected to see you here. How did you manage to get away?"

"I hoped I'd meet up with you. Byron offered to look after the dogs for me."

"What a nice guy! My campsite is practically next door. Say, who's the little fella?"

"This young man is Cody Walsh. Scott's son."

"Scott's?" The announcement took Marcia's breath away. "I didn't know he was married."

"Neither did I until I got a call from his wife the other evening."

"My poor–"

"Don't worry, it's nothing. I'll get over it. I never had any ideas about him." If she repeated it often enough times, she might convince herself.

"How come you ended up babysitting the kid?"

She briefly told Marcia what had happened since the phone call and how Cody refused to go with Vicky and Byron. "And now I need to know how to proceed from here."

"I've just arrived and been told to set up camp here. Luckily, Jerome gave me a few pointers. Apart from that, I haven't a clue about what's going on."

Cody was in the tent, bouncing on the bedrolls.

"Cody, come here a minute. This is my cousin Marcia."

"What's a cousin?"

"It's almost like a sister."

"Okay. I don't have a sister."

"You can see he's not overly trusting of strangers." she said. Cody went back to exploring the camp. "If you could have heard the mother, you'd know why. He'll be fine once he gets used to you. Fortunately, he's taken to me. I find him a delightful child."

"And he's the spitting image of his father," Marcia said. "Cody, do you know you look just like your daddy?"

He giggled with pleasure.

"I'll set up our camp now," Marcia said.

When the preparations were finished, they drove back to town and strolled along the preserved buildings belonging to another era. A stuffed husky in a store window attracted Marcia's attention. She poked her cousin in the ribs.

"Do you want a puppy, Cody?"

"A real puppy?"

"Back home you'll have a real puppy, but right now, Marcia was wondering whether you're too old to have one of those stuffed huskies?"

"I'm not old. I'm only six."

"Then let's go in."

His eyes lit up when Marcia handed him the stuffed toy.

"What do you say?" Chris prompted.

"Thank you, Marcia. I'll call him... Renoir, like my daddy's dog. Are you my cousin, too?"

The two women exchanged a quick look. "I guess you can say I'm your cousin, too."

The boy smiled and immediately crouched between them to play with his new toy while Marcia paid for it.

"Thanks, Marcia. I hadn't thought about getting him a toy. We got him lots of clothes, that's all. You're good with kids."

"It's tough having the responsibility of a six-year-old foisted on you. You can't be expected to think of everything."

Moments later, they came out, with Cody clutching his gray and white husky pup clad in a red harness.

"We've got a little time. I want to find the store with gluten-free stuff for Cody."

"Uh?"

"I talked to a Dr. Bungard at the center and he recommended it. Said Cody would benefit from a change of diet."

They walked on and indeed they saw Café Auley, a store and café selling healthy foods. With a bag of gluten-free cookies, sour-dough bread and other items, the three of them went back to the campground. Marcia winked at her cousin.

"The crisp air sharpened his appetite."

"Good. I think he needs to put on a little weight. Vicky, that's the teacher in Fletcher, said he was rather skinny for his age."

They sat cross-legged on the straw, sipping coffee. A while later, Marcia elbowed her cousin, pointing to Cody, who was nodding gently. He awoke when they went to the Port-a-Potty. There he was not so sure of himself and Chris had to help him. He ran back to the tent. In minutes, he was fast asleep.

"That's the quickest bedtime I have ever seen," Marcia said.

"Sleeping in a tent for the first time in his life must be so exciting for him."

"That's obvious."

"Do you want to share? There's enough room."

"I'll get my stuff."

CHAPTER TWENTY-TWO

Next day, they walked to the town and strolled around after checking at the race headquarters. The preserved paddlewheel steamer, the S.S. Keno delighted Cody, who had trouble understanding that the ice and snow on the river became water in summer. After a late lunch at Café Auley, they went back to the brightly lit race headquarters, where officials were huddled around a radio set.

"The blizzard's dumped several feet of snow on the race trail," one of the men told them. "Now that the storm's over, we've sent out snowmobiles to flatten a track for the racers."

"Any news of the placing?"

Before he could answer, a voice came from the radio. "Hello, HQ? Ian Spencer of the Canadian Rangers here. We've just met Scott Walsh. He is carrying a media guy he found stranded in a snowdrift. My partner is transferring him to my machine, and I'm heading back to Dawson. Walsh must be in the lead because we haven't met anybody else. Over."

Chris's eyes lit up with excitement. Scott in the lead.

"What condition are he and his dogs in?" the race marshal asked.

"They all look pretty frisky. Not badly affected by the weather. Some of the other racers are not so lucky. Walsh tells me he overtook several mushers waiting out the blizzard."

"What does he have pulling his sled, a Sno-cat?"

The ranger's laugh crackled over the airwaves. "You might think so. They're big suckers with thick wooly coats. I've never seen dogs like them in all the years I've patrolled the Quest. Walsh should reach you in a couple of hours. Over and out."

Hearing the man talk about Scott and his dogs in that way sent a surge of pride through her. Pride it was, certainly, and love too. She forbade herself to use the word. He was married even though he and his wife weren't living together. And now she held his son by the hand. Pain pinched her insides and brought tears to her eyes.

Marcia pulled her over to a table. They ate the snacks they'd bought at Café Auley. Chris dozed off on her chair. Cody chatted to his puppy and played at feeding it. Marcia observed with curiosity everything in the room.

A short while later, a commotion at the door woke up Chris. A tough-looking man dressed in a military parka and fur hat came in, supporting a man whose face was pinched with fatigue and patches of white frostbite.

The race marshal directed the man to a chair and gave him steaming coffee to drink.

"I'm Rob Larter," the stumbling man said. His speech slurred. "I've got to thank Scott Walsh for rescuing me in that storm. We traveled all night through the blizzard. That took some guts, particularly, since he risked his position in the race. Said I had hypothermia and made me drink all his thermos of hot broth. I nominate him for the Humanitarian Award."

"That's in the Iditarod. In the Quest's it's called Vets' Choice," the official said, "and it's for the musher who takes the best care of his dogs."

Rob Larter attempted to sit straight. "What d'you mean? The guy risks everything to save my life and I can't vote him an award?"

"You're a journalist. Write him up in the press."

"Right! I will." Rob swayed but refused to be taken to the hospital. Finally, the ranger convinced him to go there as an outpatient to get checked over.

Broth? She suppressed a laugh. It should have been hot chocolate. That's what the plan was, but she remembered he had mentioned he's once drunk the dogs' broth. Her mirth was bubbling over.

"You're laughing?" Cody's face puckered in a frown.

"Well, I think your daddy gave that man some of the dogs' broth."

"Why?"

"Because the man was very cold and tired."

It satisfied the boy's curiosity, and since Chris and Marcia were openly laughing, he laughed too, then sat on the floor to play with his husky toy.

Her spirits lifted by the praise heaped on Scott, she joined the throng of officials and spectators on the high bank of the Yukon River to await his arrival.

A man with graying hair sticking out from underneath his toque, and a volunteer badge on his chest, bent over and began chatting with the young boy.

"Waiting for the big dogs?"

"My daddy's dogs."

"Your daddy's racing?"

"Yeah, with his dogs."

"You came to see him with your mom."

"With Chris. She looks after my daddy's dogs."

"Ah, she's a handler."

"That's what she said."

"What's your name?"

"Cody Walsh."

"Walsh. Your daddy is Scott Walsh?"

"Of course."

Chris turned her head at the mention of the name, but seeing the official badge, just smiled.

"What's your name?" Cody asked.

"Ben Kayson. Your dad is just about to arrive. Would you like to sit on my shoulders so you can see him?"

Cody promptly stood, still clutching his stuffed husky, and Ben hoisted him onto his shoulders. She thanked him.

"Leave this little man to me. You'll be busy for a while when Walsh gets in. I'll stick right behind you."

"You're so kind."

He chuckled. "I'm a grandfather."

She joined the throng of officials and spectators on the high bank of the Yukon River to await his arrival. She turned to see Cody perched on Ben Kayson's shoulders.

"Being a handler, you better get down on the river. I'll stay here where Cody has the best view. Right son?"

"Yeah. I'm the best."

Amusement rippled around them.

"Okay, Cody? I'm going down to help your daddy when he arrives."

"Okay, okay."

Marcia caught up with her and tapped her on the shoulder. "Go down. I'll keep an eye on Cody."

Chris pushed through the mill of spectators to the front and went down the snow-covered bank onto the river ice. She glanced back a few times at Cody, who was chatting away with Ben and Marcia. Ben handed a strip of dried meat to the child, who happily munched on it. Cody was going to be alright, and she relaxed. Now that he was surrounded by friendly people, and keyed up at seeing his father, he was just behaving like any other six-year-old.

A wave of excitement undulated through the assembled crowd. She hurried down the last bit of slope and strained her eyes. A black dot in the distance was growing close. As the dot took shape, she could distinguish a line of dogs and the figure of a man hunched over the sled.

The noise of the crowd rose as the team approached.

The darkness wasn't really total. The snow reflected light and she could make out the silhouettes of the dogs and sled. As for the musher, she'd have known him anywhere.

Scott!

About to jump for joy, she checked herself. He crossed the line. She ran forward. The dogs enthusiastically licked her face.

He leaped off the runners and hugged each of his dogs before turning to her. "What the hell are you doing here?"

"It's a long story."

There was no time to talk. The officials checked his sled bag for the compulsory items, such as ax, snowshoes, dog booties that all race participants have to carry. Everything was in order. Dawson City's mayor stepped forward to present him with four ounces of Klondike gold, the prize given by the city to the first musher to reach Dawson.

A Canadian Customs officer asked the ritual question, "Do you have anything to declare?" to which Scott jokingly replied, "Only these American icicles clinging to my nose since Eagle, Alaska."

"Icicles are duty free," came the deadpan reply.

Next, the race vet examined the dogs. Chris held Yannamiq's head as he pushed a cup mounted on a long handle under the dog's belly to collect a urine sample for the random drug test. She soothed Ekridi, who was reluctant to let anyone touch her feet. The vet declared the dogs' pads the largest and toughest he'd ever seen.

Scott dealt patiently with the reporters' questions and tried to ignore the TV cameras and microphones thrust at him, not to mention all the cell phones turned toward him for more photos.

Rob Larter pushed through the crowd and hugged him. "My hero!"

"Thank you everyone for that terrific welcome."

At that moment, a roar rose from those on the river bank. Another team was arriving. He waited. Spectators and officials greeted Hans Reesink.

Reesink moved over to shake Scott's hand. "Thanks for helping me out there in the blizzard."

"You'd have done the same. Ciao!"

The crowd closed in around the two rivals. Scott waved. "Now folks, if you'll excuse me, I've got to take care of my dogs." The crowd parted for him. He urged his team forward and sped toward the campsite.

Chris went to Ben Kayson.

"Thanks so much, Ben."

"My pleasure. I guess you want this little one back."

"I sure do. We'll go to the campground now."

"I asked him if he wanted to get down and greet his dad, but he wisely said no. He'd have been mobbed."

Cody took her hand as she fended her way to the truck. They made it to campground minutes before the team. Cody ran into the tent with his stuffed dog, then poked his head out.

Several days' growth gave Scott an outlawish appearance. "How the hell did you get here?"

"I came up to give you support. That's what a handler is supposed to do, isn't it?" She began unhitching the dogs, cooing to them.

"Who's looking after the kennel?"

A sigh escaped from her chest. He knew the answer, of course. She couldn't figure out why he bothered to ask.

"Byron is. I'll tell you everything in a couple of minutes."

"So, Byron is looking after the dogs. That guy will do anything for you, won't he?" He grumbled something that she didn't catch and went to unhitch Amiof and Tioralak.

His gruffness must be due to the stress of the race. "It's more complicated than that." Her voice was calm.

At that moment, Cody, wide-eyed, emerged from the refuge of the tent. Scott was bending over a dog.

"Daddy!"

He spun round. His face registered incredulity.

"As I was saying…"

He wasn't listening. Cody threw himself into his open arms.

Turning away, she finished transferring the dogs to their picket line. Giving them the broth she'd prepared and warming up their food over the fire kept her busy.

Occasionally, she'd look and see the tenderness in his eyes as he held his son. Cody was busy telling him about his trip.

The sight of a happy father and son getting reacquainted stabbed at her heart. A mixture of sadness and regret welled inside her. Love, too. No, she defended herself. He was married. She had no claim on him. Hating him might be easier, but she couldn't. He hadn't forced her to make love. But it was plain that it meant nothing much to him.

Scott took his son by the hand and introduced him to his dogs. Somehow, she was not surprised that the young boy showed no fear of the animals, even though they must have seemed huge to him. He laughed in hysterics when they licked his face.

"When you're ready, I'll drive you to your billet in town."

"One problem. They're not expecting me to have a kid in tow."

"Cody wants to sleep in the tent."

"But he can't. He's not used to camping, especially in this cold. He's got asthma."

"Dr. Bungard said it was okay. I outfitted him in Whitehorse... courtesy of Byron's credit card." She added the afterthought just to rile him, yet regretted it at the same time. "And we slept in the tent last night."

A murderous look settled on his face.

Cody looked up at the adults, a worried expression on his face. "Chris said I could sleep in the tent."

"Don't you want to go with your daddy?"

"I want to sleep in the tent." A stubborn furrow creased his brow.

A twinge of sorrow went through her heart. So much like his father.

"Then I'll sleep in the tent too."

"The tent's not very big. You're worn out. If you want to keep your lead position, you need all the rest you can get. You now have only one hour lead, and one hour lead isn't much when you're running against fast Alaskan huskies. Now that the storm has ended, the other racers will be pushing to make up for lost time."

"Okay. You win. I'll leave the dogs and Cody in your care."

Under his breath, he muttered a few words which she didn't catch except for Byron.

"This is your only chance for a hot shower and a comfortable bed. Make the most of it. I'll come and fetch you in the morning."

Cody ran and climbed in the truck with his husky toy and pretended to drive. Scott caught her arm. "Before we go anywhere, I need an explanation. Why is Cody here?"

"Your wife phoned."

"My wife. Is that what she called herself?"

"Yes. Your wife. She said she was taking a trip to New York. She needed you to take Cody while she was away."

"She is my ex-wife. We've been divorced for five years."

His words stunned her almost as much as the shock of Alina's fatal phone call.

"I'm hungry," Cody shouted.

"Let's go and eat in town."

Cody's presence made it impossible to continue the conversation. Her mind was swimming. A hundred questions clamored for answers that would have to wait.

During the Quest, Dawson City never slept. Bars, gambling casinos and Gold Rush era dance halls remained open around the clock. They found a hotel restaurant that was not too crowded. Loud cheers greeted Scott. A group of giggling young women asked for his autograph. He complied with a smile.

When they'd eaten, they got back into the truck. Cody was already asleep on his father's shoulder. "Tell me everything that happened after my former wife called you."

The stress on the word former was not lost on Chris. In as dispassionate a voice as she could manage, she related the events following the woman's bombshell. A confusing mixture of relief and anger filled her. He could have told her that he'd been married and that he had a young son. She'd have been spared the heartache. At last, she had the reason for his angry moods and his avoidance of any mention of love and commitment. The discovery offered her little comfort. The memory of his upset when she'd told him to go and play with the pups or they'd grow up without knowing him came back to her. He had thought of his son growing up without him.

He ran his fingers over his chin. "Alina was a model when I met her in L.A. I often wondered why she dated me. We came from completely different backgrounds. I was committed to a speaking tour. It wasn't long before she announced she was pregnant, so I married her. She said she was attracted by the life up here, even though I made no secret of how I lived. We spent the summer in the South. We were very happy."

He paused for a few seconds. "When we came north for the race season, I soon realized she hated the dogs even more than the isolation. She went to the city to have Cody and never came back. I collected my son at the hospital. Within a few months, she sued for divorce. It was ugly, very ugly. She got herself a slick lawyer, and a year later got all my savings and custody of Cody. She and her fancy lawyer laid down impossible conditions for visitation. I'd have had to get rid of the dogs and move to California. It was a nightmare. She had me over a barrel. Last Christmas was only the third time she let me visit."

"Is that when your racing career went down the drain?"

"Having a baby to raise wasn't helping me train the dogs, yet that first year I got some of my best wins. It's after... when she got custody."

She covered his hand with hers. He shivered. A wave of troubling heat rose inside her and she withdrew her hand. "She's obviously mellowing. If she's relented, Cody will be able to visit more often."

"Did she say how long he'll be staying?"

"I didn't have time to ask."

"It doesn't matter even if she did. He's not going back to her."

"That's not reasonable. It's not even legal."

"She can come and see him here." Fatigue sharpened the bitterness in his voice.

Her heart sank. Although this other woman was no longer his wife, she still wielded enormous control over him. She could imagine what Alina looked like. The woman, doubtless dressed in elegant designer fashions, had long red fingernails and perfumed herself. Attractive for sure. Men were influenced by the visual image. With a glance at her own functional outdoor clothes, at her trimmed, unadorned nails, she knew she could never compete.

Scott and his ex-wife had something that would tie them forever. A child. Maybe he could even be hankering after her in some way. It wouldn't be the first time a divorced couple got back together again. Maybe he had always hoped she'd come back. And if she did, he'd finish building the house for her. Winning the Yukon Quest would give him enough money to bring electricity to it. She didn't doubt he could win the Iditarod, too. Although he said Alina hated dogs as much as the isolation.

"I can't leave you to look after my son. He's my responsibility."

"You're not quitting the race, if that's what you're thinking. We hit it off. I was just a little anxious about him sleeping out because of his asthma. But a doctor I spoke to said he'd be fine. And he was."

"Why are you going to all this trouble for me?"

"It's part of my job." She nearly added, because I love you, but the words stuck in her throat just in time. She'd die of embarrassment if she said something like that aloud. "There's not much difference between a pup and a small child."

"It isn't in your contract." He thought for a moment. "You're right. It's important I finish this race, even try to win it. The prize money would help. I'll be home in a few days if I can keep up this pace."

"I heard that the trail is icy south of Bonanza Creek."

"The Yukon River was a mass of jagged ice and open water. It can't get much worse."

"Your team is strong. The dogs aren't even wearing booties."

"They did on the sharp ice, of course. I check their paws at regular intervals. Other than that, there's been no need."

"The vet was impressed with your dogs."

His smile reflected his pride. She realized that they had begun by talking about his wife and ended with dog talk.

Once she found the address and dropped him at his billet, she returned to the campground. The presence of the child prevented her from dwelling on the new knowledge of Scott's life. Excited and full of questions, Cody finally fell asleep in the middle of a sentence clutching his stuffed husky.

Chapter Twenty-Three

Jerome arrived in the middle of the night. When all the chores were done, Marcia poked her head into her cousin's tent. "Everything alright?"

"As well as can be, considering the circumstances."

"The big man happy to see his little one?"

"No doubt about that."

"Call if you need help."

"I don't think we'll see much of each other before Whitehorse."

"Guess not. Shall we travel together?"

"Of course. Goodnight."

The thirty-six-hour mandatory layover was up for Scott. He drove his team at a brisk trot along Dawson City's Front Street toward the starting line. At four in the morning, there were few spectators lining the route. The enthusiasm of those who turned out made up for the lack of numbers. Rob Larter was there taking pictures.

While the race officials made the obligatory departure check. Scott pulled Chris against him. "You're sure you'll be all right with Cody? I could scratch here."

She gave him a horrified look. "Scratch! What kind of example would that be setting for him? I'm taking care of him."

"I know."

Two words softly spoken, and if she hadn't imagined it, tenderly spoken.

He took her lips with his. A short and sweet kiss that upset her fragile calm. He hugged his son. The timekeeper gave the signal to start. He was off.

With Cody's hand in hers, they watched until the team disappeared. There had been warmth in the kiss. Hope flooded her thoughts for an instant before dimming. He was happy to have his son with him. His happiness even made him kindly disposed to the reporters. She dreaded to think about what would happen when Cody had to go back to his mother.

Time to wonder, too, what she would do at the end of the racing season. Go. That was the only sensible, healthy thing to do. You'll stay on and compromise your principles, an inner voice whispered. Cody tugged at her hand and interrupted her jumbled thoughts.

They joined the spectators waiting for the red lantern, the last team to arrive in a race. The young musher bringing up the rear finally arrived to the cheers of the few spectators courageous enough to brave the cold.

She tugged on Cody's hand. "Let's go back to the campground and have breakfast. Then we'll pack up and go home."

"My daddy's going to win the race."

"I hope so."

"I know he will."

She drove the short distance to camp.

"Can I go see the dogs under the tent?"

"Not on your own, you can't. Sled dogs are not pets. You must always ask the musher to show you his dogs. Right now, he's sleeping. It's still early in the morning."

"Okay."

Cody devoured the hearty breakfast she prepared. Marcia's truck headed off to town to fetch Jerome from his billet. It was not long before they were back. Cody sidled up to them to watch them load the sled and hitch the dogs.

"He can't get enough of it. We were up at two this morning."

"A future musher," Jerome said. "I'm seven hours behind Walsh. He'll win for sure. I'm dropping two dogs here."

"Hans Reesink is only one hour behind. Can he catch up and pass Scott?"

"Maybe, maybe not. A lot depends on the trail. Scott's dogs are strong and his team is still intact. Reesink is down to ten dogs."

"They're faster, though."

"Not in this race. We're hauling a load of some three-hundred-pound in the sled. I'd say that Scott has the advantage. His Canadian Inuit dogs are born to pull heavy loads, unlike Alaskan huskies. There's also the question of temperature. This year the temps are just murderous. Never seen anything like it. Even with thermal coats on, the light Alaskans can't stand the really cold conditions as well as Scott's dogs."

"The sled gets lighter as you approach the next checkpoint in Carmacks, doesn't it?"

"Yes, but it gets heavier again when we take on more supplies. Don't forget, there's still over three hundred miles to go. No checkpoints after Carmacks, and there are the Black

Hills and the King Solomon Dome and the Eureka Dome to climb. Tough going all the way."

"How bad are they, really? I heard they take a toll on both dogs and mushers."

"Bleak, windswept, grueling. After Carmacks, there's a treacherous stretch down the length of Lake Laberge. We've got to watch for open water. There's ice fog, glare ice and biting cold winds. Anything could happen before the end of the race."

"It makes one wonder why people want to race it."

"Some people have it their blood. It's man against nature in a very primordial way. Mushers really depend on each other and on their dogs for survival, like in this last blizzard. But I love it." An enthusiastic note crept into Jerome's voice. A frostbite on the cheek distorted his smile. "I must be crazy. I don't care whether I win, I just want to do it."

"It's enough to boggle the imagination. I think I understand. I hope Scott keeps his lead."

"Why not go and take a look at Reesink's team? That'll give you an idea what Scott is up against."

"He's left already. He arrived nose to butt."

Jerome laughed. "Atta girl! You're getting the lingo. Did they tell you yet that if you're not the lead dog, the scenery never changes?"

She punched him on the shoulder and laughed. "Good luck, Jerome!"

After his departure, Chris and Marcia set off for the long drive home. Cody crawled into the back seat and fell asleep. In spite of the darkness, the freezing cold and the slippery roads, Chris arrived safely at the cabin, having left Marcia in Fletcher Creek.

One of the first things she did was to circle on the calendar the day of Scott's estimated arrival at the finish line. His son wanted to know exactly when his father would win the race.

In the evening, she puzzled where Cody would sleep. There was a folding cot in the porch, but there was hardly room for it in the main room of the cabin. In the end, she put it beside her bed in the bedroom. It meant scrambling over him when she got up in the early morning unless she could move the big log bed. Her feet braced against the wall, she put her back to the bed and pushed. Ten minutes later, she had made enough space for the cot under the window.

A shard of anxiety went through her; she had no idea what time a child his age should be in bed. Maybe she could call Vicky. A schoolteacher was bound to know. Then he'd have to go to school. Yet another problem to solve.

Cody adapted to his new surroundings in no time. He was excellent company and shadowed her daily routine. He loved his snowshoes and wanted to wear them all the time. Every time she took a team out for an exercise run, he asked to ride in the sled. He had a naturally gentle way with the dogs, big and small. She dubbed him the pups' manager. There was never a sign of the asthma she had been warned about, and he never complained about the cold. In the evening, he'd take great care to cross off another day on the calendar, impatient for the day of his father's arrival. And after hours in the open air, he fell asleep the moment his head touched the pillow. For the time being, there was no mention of school. Why send him to school when he would be going back to his mother? He was learning at the school of nature. His insatiable curiosity wasn't satisfied until he grasped the minute details.

Being idle, Marcia spent her days helping her cousin. When Chris trained the huskies for speed, she didn't want Cody in the sled in case they took a spill. Cody was happy to stay with Marcia, whom he referred to as his cousin. Every day that she wasn't staying the night in the bush with the dogs, they took the sled with the veterans and drove to Fletcher to listen to the race results.

On the evening before they were due to leave for Whitehorse, Byron and Vicky came up to the cabin.

"Don't worry about the dogs," Byron said. "I'll take care of everything while you're gone."

"That's really good of you. If Scott makes it in on time, I should be back tomorrow night."

"No, you won't. You're staying for the banquet. He'll have to be there, and you wouldn't want him to hitchhike back on his own, would you?"

"He didn't invite me."

"Nonsense. They said on the radio that although he's been overtaken a couple of times, he got back in the lead. Though Reesink is closing on him. It's fast becoming a tight race. At last report, Walsh was less than one hour ahead. Counting in minutes now."

"Reesink may narrow the gap even more tomorrow."

Gloom settled in the room for a while.

"Reesink's pushing hard, but his dogs are tired," Vicky said. "They said he was taking frequent short rests.

Chris had noticed the sadness in Vicky's eyes whenever the three of them were together, and wished she could shake some sense into Byron's head. He was blind to the way Vicky looked at him. That's when she realized the soft looks Marcia directed to the man. The irony of the situation might have brought a smile to her lips if she hadn't felt like crying. Scott was as equally unresponsive to her love for him as Byron was to his adoring admirers. Life was nothing if not unjust.

Once more, she was driving to the capital. Cody chatted away at her side. Marcia was following with Jerome's truck. Chris had packed the clothes Scott would need for the banquet. In her own bag was her pretty green dress. In her present state of mind, she was unsure whether he'd want her there. Nothing had been mentioned. The image of his glamorous ex-wife haunted her waking hours. A model! How could she compete with a model? One thing was certain: he would want Cody to see him cross the finish line. The love she had witnessed between the two moved her deeply.

In Whitehorse, she went to the race headquarters and identified herself. Hiding her disappointment that he hadn't invited her, she bought tickets for herself and Cody. Marcia had Jerome's invitation to the banquet.

They asked where they could make camp and were given directions to the park down by the river.

In the middle of erecting their tents, Marcia paused and looked over at her cousin. "This is really crazy. A few months ago if anyone had suggested I camp out in deep snow with the mercury hovering down at minus I-don't-know-what, I'd I have told them they were nuts. Yet here I am, doing just that and willingly. I never even thought about checking into a motel."

"Not surprising, though. We were brought up in sled dog racing families. It's in your blood."

"Not the racing. Or rather, unlike you, I don't want to do it. Watching and helping, that's what I prefer."

Back at the race headquarters, the electronic display attracted people like a magnet. An official explained to Cody how it worked to give the latest placing of the race contestants. "Your dad's out in front."

"Yippee!"

While they drifted among the people in the room, Chris overheard a race volunteer talking. "Scott Walsh seems to have made a comeback. Before he had that losing streak, he was my favorite. Lots of folks are rooting for him now."

Her eyes remained glued to the lighted bulletin board. According to the latest update, he would arrive midmorning. Cody was falling asleep against her, so she returned to the camp even though she wanted to stay to track the race results.

The thought of being on hand to greet him as a winner was overwhelming. She could barely sleep. When it was time to rise, she quickly rolled up her sleeping bag and prepared breakfast. Despite her excitement, some apprehension cut her appetite, but Cody would be hungry. Marcia, yawning and rubbing her bleary eyes, joined them.

A crowd had gathered at the finish line in spite of the relentless cold. Rumor had it that Reesink had made further gains on Scott. The gap between them could now be measured in minutes. Providing Reesink's dogs still had some energy left in them, they could well make a dash for victory. A quick sprint would leave Scott plodding along behind. His Inuit dogs didn't sprint until they were close to home. A leaden knot settled in the pit of her stomach.

Cody was chatting with a gray-haired woman standing next to them.

"Don't bother the lady, Cody."

"It's perfectly all right. I'm Ann Price. I've come to meet Scott Walsh. He's billeted at our house, and this young man here tells me Scott is his father."

"That's right. I'm Chris Taylor, his handler."

"You'll be busy the moment his team gets in. Why don't you let me look after this youngster? I'll make sure he doesn't get run over by the crowd. All right, Cody?"

"Yes, and I want to see my daddy when he gets here."

"Of course. I'll make sure of that."

She thanked Mrs. Price and turned her attention back to the race. An idea born of desperation crossed her mind. She hurried to the truck and put on her old parka, the one she used for the kennel chores soiled by countless doggy paws. The unusually keen noses of Canadian Inuit dogs might scent her parka and think of home.

Whenever they were out on the trail, their pace sped up when they were homeward bound, though that may be less to do with smell than recognizing the trail or hearing the home dogs howling a welcome. If those dogs could smell a seal breathing hole, the aglu, one mile away, they could smell her parka. This talent enabled Inuit hunters to arrive unnoticed at the aglu and get the seal. And now, she'd be standing upwind from the team approach. The wind would carry her odoriferous scent. Anyway, she hoped so.

Her status as Scott Walsh's handler gave her a position at the front of the waiting crowd.

Finally, a loudspeaker announced that the lead team had been sighted. Lightheaded, she waited and watched. A roar went up when a dog team entered the straight.

It was Scott's!

Elation overcame her, soon doused off. Another team was right behind him and closing in fast. A tense hush fell over the spectators. Then, as if on signal, pandemonium broke loose. A wave of fear travel through her from head to toe.

He had to win. He mustn't let himself be beaten in the dying seconds of the race.

She crouched, knowing that at a distance dogs recognize a person low on the ground much better than standing. Her mind willed the dogs on.

The intense concentration gave her a blinding headache. Had the dogs felt her presence? A barely perceptible whistle escaped her lips, but the dogs' hearing was so acute, they might hear the familiar sound over the din and want to run to her. Capitor and Tekoone's heads lifted a fraction. And then they did it.

The whole team put on a last-minute burst of speed as the final distance shrank to a matter of yards. Unable to breathe, she saw the dogs reach inward to tap that deep source of willpower that makes their breed so endearing, and at times, so infuriating. Even above the wind and the crowd's tumult, she could hear Scott singing to his dogs at the top of his lungs.

As the two teams fought for dominance, the line of spectators shrank back to allow them to pass. Reesink's team made a valiant bid to overtake. It was too little, too late. His team, with a lame dog as passenger on the sled, lacked the reserve of power to defeat his archrival.

Scott swept to victory by a clear length.

Once assured of his first place, he called the dogs to stop and slammed his foot on the brake, which brought the sled to a dramatic halt amid a shower of ice crystals. Chris bounded to Capitor and Tekoone in the lead. The dogs swarmed around her, each one eager to see what treat she had in her hand. They wolfed down the small balls of fat she had painstakingly wrapped in rice paper. She laughed. Maybe that was what the dogs smelled in the pockets of her old parka.

Scott leaped off the runners and scooped Cody into his arms. Together, they hugged every dog on the team.

Won! Scott had won! Dazed, as race officials, media and smiling fans flocked around the champion, she held back the team. The excitement reached fever pitch. Reesink and his loyal supporters put on a brave face. It had been a bitter pill to swallow. To come so close to winning, only to be forced to accept a second place.

Reeling from fatigue, Scott answered the questions put to him by the press. His eyes met his worthy opponent's eyes. Reesink advanced through the crush and held out his hand.

"Congratulations, Walsh. The best team won. I have to thank you again for helping me during the blizzard. If you hadn't been so gracious in putting up my tent, I wouldn't have been able to give you this final run for your money."

The two men shook hands. Their raw, sleep-deprived eyes shone from unshaven faces. Both men beamed with the satisfaction of a race honorably run.

Under the glare of floodlights, a woman television reporter monopolized Scott. "Can you tell our viewers what makes you want to run this punishing dog sledding race?"

He thought for a moment. "A man alone with his dogs in the wilderness experiences the ultimate freedom. Nothing else compares with it."

Looking on with tears in her eyes, she realized that in those few spoken words, he had defined his life. His dogs, the wilderness and races, formed his world. He'd make room for Cody now that father and son had been reunited. Beyond that, nothing else mattered. There was no place for her in that closed circle.

Cody twisted in his father's arms to be let down. The young woman interviewer in her rhinestone-studded parka probed him for details. "You haven't run the Quest for several seasons. I understand you're also taking part in the Iditarod. What prompted the sudden comeback?"

"Because I've got an exceptional handler."

His eyes searched the crowd. Head down, Chris busied herself with Nanertak and Shugamee, the two hyper females who didn't want to sit. Capitor growled at them both, and the dogs finally obeyed.

The television camera turned on her. She had no choice but to stand and acknowledge Scott's compliment. She shook her head at the invitation to join him on the podium and excused herself by saying she must drive the team to the campsite.

Ann stood watching father and son. Cody left his father's side and took her hand. "Come and see my daddy's dogs." Giving the boy an indulgent smile, she allowed herself to be led into the midst of the panting team of dogs.

An excited Cody climbed on the sled and Chris set off for the campground. Ann went back to wait for Scott. The media's attention switched to Hans Reesink.

***

Scott made a move to run after his retreating team. A bone-numbing fatigue swept over him. He stood, unable to do anything except remain beside the track, watching the next team cross the finish line. Anyway, it was customary for the winner to greet the next few teams, but his eyes only saw the image of Chris standing among the dogs and laughing with Cody.

An official he knew came and slapped him on the back. "Walsh, you'd better go and take a nap. You look done in."

He acknowledged the welcome advice with a wave and stumbled away. Ann Price hurried to his side and directed him to her car.

"Where's Chris camped?"

"I'll drive you, but you're only allowed five minutes. You're asleep on your feet," Ann said.

"If you don't mind. I'd like to spend a moment with my boy."

"No problem. He can come and stay with you. I'll make a bed for him."

In no time, they reached the campsite. After kissing his beaming son, he went into the tent to collect the bag Chris had brought for him. Ann and Chris waited for him, but hearing no sound, she crawled in. a second later, she stuck her head out and laughed.

"He's collapsed on the bedroll and sound asleep."

"Well, I guess we better leave him. I'll come back later. Since you're busy with the dogs, you can leave Cody at my place. We've got lots of room and plenty of food."

"Thanks so much. I'll see how it goes. Cody, would you like to stay with Mrs. Price while you daddy is sleeping?"

"Yeah, she told me she had a box of games."

In a spontaneous move, she bent to kiss the little boy. He happily followed Mrs. Price.

She went back in the tent to pull off Scott's boots and outerwear and cover him with a Mylar blanket and tucked a sleeping bag around him. After checking the tent heater, she rejoined her cousin.

Marcia drove to the finish line to soak up the excitement side by side with her cousin. Jerome had made a comeback and arrived in the eighth place. Chris recuperated her truck from the parking lot and called on grandmotherly Mrs. Price for Cody.

Chapter Twenty-Four

Scott slept for a full twenty hours. He eventually emerged, disheveled and eyes puffed with sleep. The intense cold had eased its grip over the Yukon. A pale sun shone low in the sky. "It's positively balmy."

Cody jumped into his arms. Unshaven, his clothes wrinkled, he certainly didn't look like a triumphant winner. She took a deep breath. "Did you sleep well?"

"I wasn't aware the world was still turning. How are the dogs?"

"All in order. The banquet is scheduled for tomorrow evening at seven. I brought you some good clothes."

"How thoughtful. Only, I'm not going. Pack up. We'll head home."

"It's not good for your image to skip the banquet. Everybody expects you to be there."

"Who's everybody?"

The former surliness was back. It showed in the arch of his brows and the caustic edge to his voice.

"Your public, for starters, the officials, the volunteers who give their time day and night so that the race can run, the sponsors without whom there'd be no race, the media, and your fellow competitors. Need anyone else? You'll also collect your winnings. It's part of the ritual."

"I don't go in for rituals. They can put my check in the mail."

"Well, Cody and I are going. We bought our own tickets. I'll say you have a sore head." Defiance flared in her eyes.

An impolite growl about official functions was his only comment.

"You're not shy, are you?" It dawned on her that maybe he really was uncomfortable facing the cameras.

He pulled a face. "I don't like crowds and I hate ceremonies."

"It doesn't last long. Try to relax."

"Thanks, Dr. Taylor."

She burst out laughing. He disappeared into the tent. When he came out, he was wearing his boots and carried his bag and parka.

"Ann Price is expecting you."

A tired smile stretched his mouth. "A shower would be welcome. Will you drive me?"

Seated in the truck, Cody between them, Scott kept his silence. His grouchiness had vanished. He was intrigued by just how this petite auburn-haired woman always managed to tally the score so neatly. He stole a glance at her over Cody's head. Ever attentive to the traffic, her eyes scanned the road ahead. Her long eyelashes fluttered. Those lips he knew so well reflected her concentration. The heat inside him rose a notch.

He recalled earlier moments of shared intimacy. The loneliness of the uninhabited wilds of Alaska and the Yukon had been made worse by his longing for her. A musher constantly has to ponder his race strategy and the thousand and one details of team and trail. Yet there were long stretches when he imagined her next to him.

He couldn't picture life in the cabin before her arrival. Damn! She'd look even more beautiful in the summer. He tried to visualize her in shorts and top, with the cool breeze catching that magnificent hair of hers.

Cody's insistent questions wiped the images from his mind. While he talked to his son, he noticed that from time to time, she would smile at the boy. As if in a haze, he saw the three of them together, not simply driving side by side, as at that moment, but together in life. A family. He shook himself. The race must have taken more of a toll than he thought. He'd better quit dreaming if he wanted to keep his sanity. To add to the dilemma was the unknown factor of what Alina would do next.

The kindness with which they were received by Ann Price, one of the many people who opened their homes to the race participants, softened his agitated nerves.

"We'd love to have all three of you stay for lunch," Ann said.

"That's very kind of you," Chris said. "Cody will stay and so will his father. I have to go and look after the dogs."

He dismissed her plan with a wave of the hand. "We'll both go and take care of the team. Then we'll come back here together."

"I'll agree only on the condition you come to the awards banquet."

He grinned and turned to Ann. "She always wins."

Ann smiled. "While you attend to your dogs, Cody can stay here and watch TV or play computer games."

"I help look after the dogs, too." Cody straightened his shoulders.

"If you don't want to accept an invitation," Chris explained to him, "you must always say thank you."

"Sorry. Thank you, Mrs. Price."

The woman smiled down at the boy. "That's fine, Cody. So, you want to be daddy's helper?"

"Yes. And when I grow up, I want to have lots of dogs of my own. I'll enter lots of races. Like that, I can come and stay at your house and play your computer games."

Chris joined in the laughter. A hefty measure of pride spread across Scott's rugged face.

"Go on and use the shower." Mrs. Price said. "Then, after you take care of the dogs, come back here for lunch."

***

On the evening of the race banquet, Chris accepted Ann Price's invitation to shower and dress in comfort.

"We'll drive you in our car, since we're going," Ann's husband Kevin said. "We can't let you clamber into your dog truck in your fine clothes."

Dressed in her green dress and heeled sandals, with her hair swept up, she left the bedroom and walked into the Price's living room. Her entry made Scott gasp.

"Chris, you'll be the belle of the ball," Kevin Price said.

Scott's smile creased his wind weathered face. "You're a vision of loveliness."

Ann looked up from tucking Cody's shirt back into his pants and gave a knowing smile.

When she reached for her good parka, Ann placed a hand on her arm. "You can't wear a parka to the banquet. This the biggest event of the season. I'll give you a coat." She rushed to her bedroom.

"I think I'm going to enjoy that banquet with such a beautiful escort on my arm," Scott said.

She blushed. At that moment, Ann came back carrying an exquisite, long camel-hair coat.

"It no longer fits me. Not since I acquired extra padding," Ann said.

"Thank you, Ann. It's beautiful."

"The fake-fur collar turns up to protect your ears from the wind. And the insulated lining is a blessing in this part of the world. I want you to keep it."

"But, I can't. It's such a lovely coat."

"It fits you to a T. I'd sooner someone like you has it. You remind me of when I was a whole lot younger. Doesn't she, Kevin?"

Her husband chuckled with an approving nod. "I don't mind the padding."

"I'm so thrilled. Thank you, Ann."

"All right, let's go before the womenfolk start crying," Kevin said. He pulled on a jacket.

"Why they cry?" Cody asked.

The grown ups broke into laughter. Cody joined in, though he was still confused.

"Sometimes people are so happy, they can't help crying," Scott said.

"Oh." Cody frowned, then smiled.

The banquet was a boisterous and joyful affair. After the meal, came the speeches. Finally, the master of ceremonies called Scott up on the platform to receive his winner's check and trophy. The next twenty racers each received prizes of lesser value. Cheers and good wishes were heaped on all participants. Next came the awards.

The emcee called for quiet. "As you know, the Challenge of the North Award is voted on by the race officials, and goes to the musher, who best exemplifies the spirit of the North. Ladies and gentlemen, I'm proud to announce that this year the award goes to... Scott Walsh!"

A deafening roar of applause erupted as all heads turned toward Scott. He was at a loss for words. She prodded him to stand and walk up to the podium to receive his prize, an elegant crystal artwork and yet another check.

The Emcee retained him by the arm. "While you're up here cleaning up on the prizes, Walsh, we're going to give you the Golden Harness Award for having the best lead dogs in the race. We're talking about two dogs with such a nose they discovered a man lying off the trail in the deep snow. Their names, ladies and gentlemen, are..." The man glanced down at his notes. "... Capitor and Tekoone, two of the finest Canadian Inuit sled dogs you'll find anywhere in the North."

The emcee had trouble ending the deafening clapping. Other prizes were bestowed on various mushers.

"And our last but not least award tonight, folks, is the Sportsmanship Award. The mushers themselves decide who gets this one." The Emcee looked at his assistant. "I hope everyone kept the secret."

A smiling young woman handed him an envelope.

"You'll remember we asked all mushers not to reveal who they voted for." He waited a few seconds to allow the buzz of expectation to subside. With deliberate slowness the Emcee opened the envelope.

"The name that got twenty-four votes out of a possible twenty-five finishers is... hey, this is getting boring... Scott Walsh!"

The audience again broke into a flurry of cheers and whistles. The applause again brought him to his feet. He was acutely embarrassed as he mounted the steps to the platform.

"Congratulations, Walsh. Here's a musher's hat and a check to keep the other ones company. Please tell us the true story of the incident on Lake Laberge."

"It was nothing, really. The weather was terrible. Ice fog hanging in clouds over the lake."

"So far, so good. What about the open water?"

"There was some. A darn'd nuisance."

"So, what did you do?"

"I detoured."

"Folks, if we wait until I drag the whole story out of him, we'll be here all night. Since my lady wife warned me I had to be home by midnight, I'll take up the tale. That night, the temperature dipped to a numbing minus fifty below. Scott discovered that the break in the ice had widened and refrozen with thin ice. Our trail markers were leading directly toward it. At the risk of losing his first place position, he backtracked several miles to reroute the markers, so that there was no danger of a musher losing his way and ending up in the drink. And that wasn't the first time in the race he'd done something that cost him precious time. There are a couple of mushers in this room who can vouch for how he helped them out in the blizzard near the Yukon-Alaska border. It was during that snowstorm that Scott saved Rob Larter's life..."

A standing ovation drowned out the last of the Emcee's words.

Chris stood and applauded with the others. Her eyes softened with her love for the man who remained on the platform, shifting from one foot to the other and looking puzzled about all the fuss. He hadn't even mentioned the Lake Laberge incident to her.

In that breathless moment, she knew that she could never leave him. He did respect her. Their friendship was special. If he couldn't love her, they at least shared a love of dogs and the wild reaches of the North. If that's all she could lay claim to, she was willing to accept it.

A nagging voice in her brain told her he would reject her again. Contrary to her previous resolve to leave Fletcher Creek, she'd stay and pretend indifference, make sure she didn't let her love show. After all, she could still realize her dreams of racing. He wouldn't object to his handler racing, and would just hire a second handler, now that he could afford it.

But maybe that was just a fairy tale.

A commotion to her side shattered her daydreaming. An excited Cody had climbed onto his chair. "That's my daddy! That's my daddy!"

The surrounding guests smiled at his exuberance. A press photographer snapped his picture.

"We didn't know Scott Walsh had a kid," the man said. "How come we never heard about it?" He pointed to Chris. "Hey, young fella, is this your mommy?"

Suddenly self-conscious, Cody jumped down, ran to her, and flung his arms about her. At the same moment, Scott came back to his seat.

"Quit bothering my son!" His bark made the press man flinch.

"Still as charming as ever with the media, eh, Walsh? You never could take the heat."

He was about to take a swing at the jeering photographer, when Rob Larter grabbed the man by his lapels. "Keep your questions and photos about the race, or clear out."

Faced by two angry and determined men, the disgruntled reporter snapped the lens cover back on his camera and slunk out of the room to the accompaniment of hoots of laughter.

Rob Larter came and sat at their table and related how Scott had rescued him from near death in the snowbank. The band struck up a tune. Kevin Price led his wife onto the dance floor.

"Your turn, Scott. Chris is itching to dance," Rob said.

She protested. "I can't leave Cody alone."

"Nonsense. I'll keep an eye on the young scamp."

Scott hesitated. "I'm not much of a dancer."

She raised her eyes. "Me neither. I really don't mind if we sit this one out."

"My only chance at babysitting a super-smart young guy. Say, Cody, would you like to learn how to use a camera?"

"Yes, please."

"Scott, is it okay if he comes around the room with me to take photos?"

"Daddy... please."

"All right. But make sure you stick with Rob and do exactly what he tells you."

"Yippee!"

The music started up again. He turned to Chris. "Shall we? No excuses this time."

A shiver of apprehension at the thought of being held in his arms ran down her spine. As he led her onto the floor, his hand burned an imprint on her back. When she faced him, his smile banished her fears. He didn't hold her close. He didn't need to. A vibrant current leaped between their swaying bodies. She tingled all over. Conscious of every nerve ending having come alive to his touch, her eyes held his. When he brushed against her, she wanted him to hold her tight. An invisible veil enveloped them, shutting out the other couples and the flash of cameras. In the midst of the crowd they were alone, lost in depths which only they could measure.

The spell ended with the music. They returned to their table. They found Cody asleep on a chair, with his head on Rob's lap.

"Thanks, Rob," Scott said.

"My real pleasure. I'll send you pictures." He opened the camera and recalled the last few pictures of the two of them dancing. "This little fellow took them. They are really good."

"You're a good teacher," Chris said. "But now, I guess we better put Cody to bed."

Scott carefully lifted his son in his arms. She gathered up the trophies. The Prices stood up.

"It's almost the end, but if you two would like to stay on, we could take the youngster home," Ann said.

"Thank you so much, Ann, but I've got to get up early in the morning. I have a team of hungry dogs waiting for me."

"We've got plenty of bedrooms. Why not stay with us? I hate to think of anyone camping out in winter."

"It's sweet of you to offer. I don't like leaving the dogs alone for too long in strange surroundings."

"I understand. I'd be the same if I had dogs," Kevin said.

Back at the Prices' residence, Scott fished the truck keys from his pocket. "I'm taking Chris back to the camp."

She changed out of her dance dress. They settled the boy in the bedroom opposite Ann and Kevin's. He opened an eye and yawned.

"You're staying with Mrs. Price for tonight, okay?" Chris spoke in a soft voice.

A grunt and a big sigh were the only replies Cody made as he closed his eyes.

"I'll leave the doors open," Ann said. "If he wakes up, I'll hear him."

"Thanks again."

Ann pressed her cell phone into Scott's hand. "In case we need to call."

He climbed into the passenger seat while Chris settled behind the wheel of the truck. At the camp, they checked that the dogs were comfortable. He lit the tent heater and, carrying it in one hand, pulled back the tent flap to let her go in.

"I'm happy that you won the Sportsmanship Award, as well as the Challenge of the North."

"It would never have happened without you. As for what happened on Lake Laberge, anyone would have done the same."

"Not many mushers would have jeopardized their race to go back and shift the trail markers the way you did."

"Don't be so sure. I just happened to be in the right place at the right time."

"And as a result, you risked losing your number one place."

"That's fate for you."

He fell silent. His hand slipped into auburn hair that fell in a soft mass to her shoulders. His closeness made her weak. He'd never be satisfied with a simple goodnight kiss and beg for more, and she'd relent. She eased his hand aside. A tremulous wave of heat swept over her, sending exquisite tremors along her spine.

He leaned forward, his lids heavy with longing. Slowly, ever so slowly, his lips touched hers with infinite lightness. The tension she'd felt throughout the long evening resurfaced in a sudden, fiery explosion. Her stern resolve melted like snow in summer. He dragged her down onto the bedroll and held her close. The feverish pressure of his mouth on hers sent quivers running over her burning skin.

Breathless, eyes shut, she broke free. Her sanity screamed to stop right there, yet her wanton fingers traced the firm line of his chin.

Again, he hungrily pulled her to him.

"No, we mustn't."

There was a long, silent pause.

"I know, dammit!"

With great reluctance, he drew away. For a full minute, he rested his chin in his hands, his eyes staring unseeingly at the red glow of the heater. As if emerging from a trance, he sprang to the tent door. He pulled the pink cell phone from his pocket and handed it to her. "Sleep well, sweetheart. See you in the morning." The flap fell back into place, and he was gone.

She sat staring at the canvas long after the sound of his truck had retreated into the night.

CHAPTER TWENTY-FIVE

In the morning, she had already exercised half the team by the time he turned up with Cody. Together they finished the task, walking each dog a little way to stretch their legs.

"Have you two eaten?" She strove to keep her tone even.

"Did you imagine Ann would let us go on an empty stomach?"

"Lucky you. Then you won't mind waiting while I prepare something for myself?"

"How about having a bite in town? I could handle a second breakfast."

"What about you, Cody?"

"Oh, yes, yummy!"

"Fine. Let's go. We'll strike camp when we come back."

They found a cozy diner that specialized in home-cooked meals. Over breakfast, Cody talked nonstop about being the photographer's helper at the banquet. They listened, encouraging him from time to time with questions.

They were getting friendly glances from the other customers. She colored, knowing they must think they were two devoted parents accompanied by their bright young son.

Later, Scott swung by the bank to deposit his checks. They made a last call on the Prices, who gave Cody the linked rings puzzle that fascinated him and drove back to the camp. Scores of curious children of all ages, wanting to see the dogs and talk to the mushers, crowded the camp. When they saw Scott, they rushed to him.

"Can we have your autograph, Mr. Walsh?"

While Chris and Cody folded the tent, he satisfied the insistent demands of his fans. She came to his rescue by answering questions about the dogs. When the throng dispersed, and the packing was complete, they helped the dogs jump into their compartments. After that, nothing remained but to set off on the road home.

Many long miles later, a smiling Byron met them as they pulled into the yard. She climbed out of the truck.

"My legs are so stiff, I don't think I'll ever walk again."

"Congratulations, you two," Byron said. "What a performance! I watched it on TV. I just loved the way the team sped up at the last minute to clinch the title."

"Most of the credit goes to Chris. She drew the dogs to her like a magnet. And I must thank you, too, Byron, for looking after things here."

"Don't mention it. Come on inside. My best gourmet stew's ready on the stove."

"We must attend to the dogs first. Cody is asleep in the truck."

Chris had never seen Scott so relaxed and happy. Success agreed with him. There was no point in waking Cody to undress him, so she put him straight onto his cot in her bedroom. The three adults sat down to dinner. As soon as it was over, Byron, ever the diplomat, took his leave.

Scott wedged a cushion behind his head to be able to watch her put the dishes away. "When you're done, come and sit here with me."

"On the couch? No thanks. Too dangerous. You know very well where that would lead to. I haven't the slightest intention of tempting fate."

He sighed. "I wouldn't dream of tempting you, but I can't hide how much I need you."

Need. Desire. Fine talk, indeed. For her and Scott, there was no tomorrow. No reciprocated love. Since she'd promised herself to be happy just being in the same space as him, she choked back her bitterness. The old saying that it was better to have loved and lost than never to have loved at all might have a grain of truth in it. But only if the love was shared. The fruit of one-sided love was only tears and grief.

She believed that for him, making love, as opposed to being in love, was simply sexual gratification. To give in would make life difficult, since she promised herself to keep her love bottled up for the privilege of sharing the same space as him. She must stop dreaming. On the other hand, he might not ask her to stay on as his handler.

If he asked, she ought to be sensible and refuse. So close to him now, she admitted she'd never be able to stay and pretend indifference as she'd planned in a moment of utopia. Merely to look at him, as at that moment, his long legs stretched out, his arm crooked over the backrest, was enough to deepen the confusion in her heart, make her want him as much as he wanted her.

"I appreciate your being candid. All the same, I don't intend to burden myself with a liaison. I want to be free to move."

That was not exactly what she had meant to say. He clenched his fists, a futile gesture of frustration. His face darkened.

"Be independent then."

For one moment, she almost cried her love out loud, ready to throw caution to the winds and drag him onto the couch. Not that she'd need to drag him. He'd probably lift her up before she could move. When she spoke, she didn't know where her control had come from. "We have three weeks or so to plan the Iditarod. Let's not waste a minute." She pretended to be unaware of his inner turmoil.

"Time enough for that tomorrow."

"Sure. If you don't need anything else, I'm off to bed."

"Okay. By the way, Chris…"

She faced him.

There was no mistaking the tenderness in his voice. "Thanks… for everything."

As she retreated, he grasped his head in both hands. He was going about it all the wrong way, unlike Byron, who was always at hand, pleasant and courteous. It'd come as no surprise if one fine day she and Byron announced they were getting married. Byron was young and naïve and probably held absurd romantic notions about love and marriage. With experience behind him, he ought to tell his friend that rather than sharing troubles, a wife only doubled them. Though in that respect, Chris was different. Of that, he was sure.

***

A few days later, Byron drove up with Marcia and Jerome so they could say goodbye. They were off to Alaska to enter a training race before the main Iditarod. Byron promised to be back to care for the kennel when Scott had to leave for the Iditarod so that Chris could go along to help him. Vicky was happy to look after Cody, who had enthusiastically adapted to school. Since there had been no words from his mother, Scott saw no reason why his son shouldn't attend school.

The training routine resumed. Under her watchful eye, Scott harnessed the team of Alaskan Huskies. Chris had trained them and knew them better than he did. He no longer questioned her judgement.

Although Cody wanted to go with his father, she persuaded him to remain with her, explaining patiently that his father would be returning late in the evening, long after the youngster's bedtime. The boy accepted her explanation. The fact that she drove him to school in the sled made up for his disappointment. There was always someone to drive him home on the back of a snowmobile, and that was just as exciting for him as arriving by dog team.

After his training run, Scott took her in his arms and waltzed her around the living room. "Those dogs are incredible. They run like the wind. What did you do to them? I've never seen such obedient dogs."

"Nothing special. I took them out in small groups. As a result, I discovered several of them are natural leaders. With the full team, they react quickly to the commands. It's not a strictly orthodox method, though."

"Did you pick that up from your father?" His tone became gentle.

"No. I came up with it myself as a means of training them. You see, at the beginning, I couldn't handle all twelve huskies together. So, I asked myself how would I behave if I was in their place."

"But dogs don't think like humans."

"No, not quite like we do, but they think nevertheless. Just watch them carefully, without any preconceived notions, and you'll see what I mean."

"Their intelligence is based on their ancestral instincts and what they learn from their trainer."

"In my opinion, their brain permits them to make a choice between actions. For me, that's the same as thinking."

He looked thoughtful. "I reckon you must be right. I recall times when I had the distinct impression that my dogs used logic. I simply put it down to an intelligent use of instinct."

She smiled. "Intelligent use equals thinking."

His admiration grew. "You mean think along the same track as them? Uncanny. And, talking of tracks, tomorrow, I'm heading up to Wolf Lake."

"I admire your enthusiasm."

"You're looking at a born optimist. How can I not be with such an obedient team?" His smiling face reflected the self-confidence of his words.

"You'll win. I know you will. You'll accomplish the rare feat of placing first in the two biggest races of the North."

"The Iditarod is every musher's dream."

Cody came out of the bedroom. "What's the Iditarod?"

"You weren't sleeping?" Chris asked.

"I woke up."

"The Iditarod is a really long sled dog race. It helps us remember a real race years ago to save children's lives. Do you want to hear the story?"

"Yes, please."

"Sit next to your daddy and he'll tell you about it."

The little boy scrambled onto his father's lap. Scott frowned, looking for the words a six-year-old would understand.

"In Alaska, there's a village called Nome, a long way from anywhere." He chose his words with care. "In the old days, just like now, there was no road to it. The nearest railroad was miles away at a place called Nenana. People used sled dogs pulling toboggans to get around.

"One winter in 1925, that's a very long time before you were born, many of the kids got sick with a terrible disease called diphtheria. Children don't get it nowadays because doctors give them a needle when they are just babies."

"Did I get a needle?"

"Yes, you were vaccinated. You didn't cry, either, when the doctor poked you with the needle."

"What happened after they got sick?"

"Those children had to have the vaccine or they would die, but there was no way of getting it up to them. Because it was January, the weather was very cold, with lots of big snowstorms. The dog mushers in the area all got together and took turns carrying the medicine, called serum, from village to village by dog team. The serum arrived in Nome just in time to save the sick children. The most famous of the mushers was a man called Leonard Seppala."

He took a deep breath and looked at Chris. "How did I do?"

She chuckled. "Very well. It's difficult to explain things at a child's level."

Cody's thoughtful young face smiled up at him. "Was it a long way?"

"Yes, a very long way. Over one thousand miles by dog sled." He winked at her. He wasn't going into the fine details of how the serum had traveled from Anchorage by train and the historical mushers picked it up at the Nenana train station, a little less than half way through, and then relayed the life-saving serum to the stricken town. It was still an incredible feat.

He reached for a map from the drawer and spread it out on the table. "Here, I'll show you the route the mushers took."

Father and son pored over the map. The sight warmed her heart. If only there was some way to keep Cody here, where he belonged. Almost three weeks had gone by since his arrival, and not a word from the boy's mother. Chris suddenly realized that in all that time, Cody hadn't once mentioned his mother. He's used to babysitters, Alina had said.

In the morning, Chris and Cody helped him harness his team of huskies.

"There's no need to take much food. I'll only be gone four hours at the most,"

She disregarded his words and stowed a package in the sled bag. "I thought we'd agreed we wouldn't go out without an emergency pack."

"Okay. You're right. Somehow, I'd forgotten that clause in the contract."

With Cody at her side, she watched him head out. He turned and waved his hand. The boy pulled at her hand. "Let's go to school now."

CHAPTER TWENTY-SIX

His heart beat with a troubled emotion when he looked behind and saw them together, two silhouettes against the brilliant white snow.

When they finally disappeared from view, he turned his attention to the trail ahead. At least, he tried to concentrate on the task of driving his team. The image of Cody holding hands with Chris had imprinted itself on his mind's eye. The pair presented such a natural picture. Like himself, the woman and child belonged here in this untamed wilderness.

They belonged to him. Not true, he mentally corrected. Cody yes, not Chris. To belong meant to love. Unlike other women he had known, she never spoke of love. In fact, she never used the word at all. It was as though it scared her, just as it scared him. He hated the word. Behind it, there lurked the sinister word of marriage. He'd committed one big mistake in his life. One he had no intention of repeating. But then, she was different.

He smiled as he remembered the passion with which she had responded to his embrace. The memory flushed through him like a wildfire. Later, she was the one that said no. He didn't understand why she should be so stubborn. The pleasure they experienced in each other's arms could in no way compromise her precious independence. Unless, of course, she was saving herself for another man. The notion of her in Byron's arms wrenched at his guts.

Perhaps because he was preoccupied with his thoughts, he failed to notice until the last minute the huge bull moose that loomed squarely in the middle of the trail ahead of him.

"Whoa!" He yelled at his dogs and slammed his foot on the brake. The dogs jolted to a halt, their eyes fixed on the great beast. Low growls came from their throats. There was no doubt the moose was a fully grown adult. The right-hand side of its large antlers had fallen, the way they do in the winter after the mating season. Why did this one still carry one antler? There was no time to analyze the reason. The short-sighted moose snorted and pawed the snow. In defiance, it lowered its head at the dogs. Neither dogs nor moose backed away.

He took care not to startle his ill-tempered adversary while he leaned forward to grasp the handle of his ax protruding from the sled bag.

The animal lunged in a feint but stopped several yards short of the lead dogs. The team started howling angrily. Scott leaped off the sled and ran forward. Oblivious to his personal safety, he shouted in an attempt to deflect the animal's attention from the team. There had been tragedies when a moose had charged through a dog team.

The beast's eyes trained on the dogs had not yet seen the human.

He calmed the team with a few soothing words. If the dogs chose to attack, mayhem would break loose. "Steady now. Sit." They didn't.

The half-ton bull moose shook his massive head in anger and sniffed the air in an attempt to gauge the new threat. Scott swung his ax. The sun glinted off the burnished metal, momentarily distracting the six-foot tall wild animal. The moose bellowed and made another charge. This time straight at him.

He expected it and counted on the moose's poor vision to make his move. With the agility of a bullfighter, he ducked and ran to the sled. The way was now clear. He had only enough time to yell, "Hike!" before he was struck by the moose's solid rump. The force of the blow pitched him against the sled. His left hand closed on the stanchion.

Confused and anxious, the huskies, feeling the weight on the lines, shot ahead at breakneck speed. Now he was being dragged in the snow, he vainly tried to hold on and heave himself onto the runners. A burning pain creased his side. Despite his efforts to hang on, he fell off and landed in the snow, still clutching his ax.

Instinctively, he yelled, "Whoa! Whoa!" but the team already way down the trail paid scant heed to his cries. Again, "Itirit! Whoa!" Whether his faithful lead dog heard him or not, he never knew. It was too late. The team was in full flight. It wouldn't stop until much farther on. He didn't know whether they would turn back like his Canadian Inuit dogs did a couple of times when they had run after a mule deer while he was attending to nature.

Shock almost made him vomit. His dogs disappeared into the distance. Alone with an enraged bull moose, his only weapon was a puny ax. The dogs risked injuring themselves in the trees. Worse still, they could plunge over the icy precipice of the escarpment. It was several hours' trek back to the cabin. Lacking snowshoes, he would have a tough time of it through the snow. The pain in his side spread to his back.

He had the faint hope that his trusty Nunii and smart Itirit might slow the team and somehow urge them back to him. Given such a perilous situation, he was fully aware he had no guarantee of getting back home in one piece.

Blood throbbed in his temples. He levered himself onto his hands and knees to determine the position of the moose. The beast had turned to watch the retreating sled, but now directed its short-sighted stare on him. Its small eyes blinked and one or twice the animal appeared to frown.

He took stock of his situation. He was in a shallow depression ringed by mature pines, a frozen bog. On either side of the trail, dense brush and deep snow cut off any escape in that direction. If he could reach the spot where the trail entered the trees again, he'd be safe. The heavy animal would be slowed down by the close-packed trunks and low-hanging branches. He could always climb a tree. Scott flexed his limbs to check if any bones were broken. None were, as far as he could tell. The pain in his back burned. He inched upwards and drew himself into a standing position.

As if that was the signal it had been waiting for, the moose charged. With a superhuman effort, ignoring the intense pain in his side, he dashed for the trees.

He couldn't reach them before the moose gained on him. The ax gripped in his two hands, he turned and swung at the animal's head. The flat of the ax struck the animal on the nose. Startled, the moose sank back on its hind legs.

He took advantage of the momentary distraction to plunge into the forest. The enraged moose recovered and crashed through the brush after him. He swerved but too late to avoid the deadly lunge of the single antler. One prong caught the fleshy part of his buttock. It tore through his pants and lacerated his flesh, propelling him a few feet ahead, before he landed in the snow.

Adrenalin flowed through his veins. Blinded by his own rage and pain, he again lashed out. This time, he landed a blow with the back of the ax between the beast's eyes. The moose stopped in its tracks, bellowed and shook its head. Scott had reached the limit of his strength. The effort of wielding the ax had brought him to his knees. Using the ax handle as a support, he got to his feet again.

For what seemed an age, he lurched in a drunken dance with the stunned moose. The beast glowered at him, head hung low. His strength ebbing, he dashed for the pine trees. It was his last chance to escape. Pine branches scratched his face. His leg throbbed in excruciating pain as he zigzagged deeper into the stand of tall timber.

Panting for breath and almost too weak to run any farther, he glanced back. The moose was no longer in sight. He dropped to his knees. The cold air entered through his torn pants and began cooling his exposed flesh. He had to make a fire before he froze. He heaved himself up, and noticed the blood on the snow, and grimaced. The cold anesthetized the cut and stopped the blood flow, but could cause him a severe frostbite. He tried to take a step and fell into the deep snow.

Chapter Twenty-Seven

C hris looked up from pouring the last of the broth for the dogs and scanned the northern horizon for any sign of Scott's return. He'd been gone for more than five hours. Although the days were becoming longer, twilight had now settled over the landscape. She picked up the dog bowls and scratched Renoir behind the ears.

"I'm going to play with the pups," Cody said.

She smiled. "All right. I'll be there in a moment to refill the heater."

The youngster scampered over to the kennel house. A few minutes later, he and the pups crawled through the dog tunnel into the outdoor enclosure.

Worried, she turned her attention to the deserted trail. Come on, Scott. This isn't reasonable. You're not equipped to spend the night outdoors. I know you can survive, but you said you'd be back in late afternoon. It's now evening.

Whether in answer to her silent prayer, or purely by coincidence, she saw a dark mass moving toward her in the distance.

At last! She breathed again. After putting away the bowls and broth pail, she looked again. All her anxiety came flooding back. What was he up to? The sled was careening madly along the trail. Her heart sank when it came close enough to make out the dogs and the sled. But there was no musher.

The driverless team stormed into the yard. The dogs crowded around her, entangling themselves in the lines. A couple of dogs slipped their harnesses and raced around the compound.

In the midst of coping with the chaos, her eyes fell on the open sled bag. The ax handle that normally protruded from it was missing. She was sure something awful had happened to him.

"Okay dogs. What have you done with your master?" She kept her voice level to calm the excited animals. In time, she succeeded in leading the dogs to their pickets in their enclosure. She hastily fed and watered them. Concern for Scott made her clumsy.

While on her way to the cabin, Cody looked up at her. "Can I stay out and play a little longer?"

"That's fine, sweetheart. I've just got to go to the cabin and make a phone call."

She dashed to the radiophone to call the Wildlife Conservation Office. "Hello, Byron? Omega Beta. Chris here. Can you hear me? Over."

No answer. Still, she waited. There was no reply.

"Hello, Byron. This is an emergency. Are you there? Over."

Again, nothing but the empty crackle of static.

The office must be closed. In desperation, she put the call to Charlie. He came on.

"Is anything wrong? Over."

"I'm trying to get hold of Byron. Over."

Conrad's voice came on. "He's on his way home. Would you like me to call him on his truck radio and tell him you want to talk to him?"

"Yes, please. I think Scott has had an accident."

"Don't worry, we'll come up. Over and out."

Now everybody was going to know Scott had an accident. She gnawed at her fingernails while she waited for her friends. At the door, she called Cody in.

He skipped all the way. "Daddy's back?"

"No, not yet." She wondered what she should tell him. How to explain that the team and sled had returned, but his father was somewhere out there in the wilderness?

This was the time for a white lie, since the child hadn't noticed the return of the driverless sled.

"Some of his dogs got loose and came back ahead of the others."

"And daddy?"

"He'll be here soon. He must be going slower now that he's short of a few dogs. Go and wash up for dinner."

The radio crackled into life. "Hello, Byron here. Do you read me? Over."

She yelled into the mike. "Byron. Look, I have Cody with me. There's a bit of a problem. I can't explain fully. His T-E-A-M came back, but not H-I-M. His ax is missing."

"Stay calm. I have a hunch about what might have happened. I'll be up as soon as I can. I'll call at Vicky's. She'll come along and look after the young 'un."

"Thanks, Byron."

When she stepped away from the set, she collided with Cody. He stared up at her. There was a look of confusion in his eyes.

"Give me a hand to set the table for dinner. Byron and Vicky are on their way."

"Daddy's lost?"

"No, he's just been delayed."

"But he'll come home?"

The trust she read in Cody's eyes tweaked at her heart. The child sensed something was wrong, but she wasn't about to confirm his instinctive fear. Not until she knew. "Yes, he'll come back." Not since she was a little girl had she prayed as she did now.

The shrill sound of Byron's snowmobile broke the silence. She let out a long breath.

"Cody, open the door for Byron and Vicky, please."

They came in, still brushing snow off their suits. Vicky dropped a backpack onto a chair. "I've got enough things in there to keep a whole classroom of kids amused."

She took Vicky's parka. "I can't express my gratitude for your help at a time like this."

"Don't mention it. We do what we've got to do to help one another."

"Dinner's ready. Cody should eat."

"Leave everything to me," Vicky replied.

Chris dragged Byron down to the far end of the room. In a low voice, she said, "His team arrived about forty minutes ago. Something must have happened. Itirit is very agitated. I had in mind to put a leash on her and let her guide me."

"You say the ax was missing?"

She nodded.

"The most likely scenario is that he encountered an animal, most likely a moose, on the trail. There's lots of them about right now. They're hungry and ornery."

She'd heard stories of mushers being confronted by surly moose. The hard-packed snow of the trails was as attractive to the moose as it was practical for the dog teams.

"Does it always attack?"

"Sometimes it chooses to run and hide. If it attacked, Scott could have used the ax to defend himself. While he was doing so, his team could have bolted."

"Those dogs are usually most obedient."

"If they got scared, they'd panic. It's a good thing they got back here. They could just as well have gotten themselves tangled up someplace."

"I'm scared. He was on his way to Wolf Lake. What if he fell through the ice?"

"Relax. Wolf Lake is pretty shallow. With the kind of temperatures we've been having, it'll be frozen right to the bottom."

"Thank heaven for that."

"Mushers have been known to lose their teams when they stop for a nature call. Though the missing ax kinda rules that out."

"What are we going to do?"

"Organize a search party."

"How?"

"First, I've already got my buddy Conrad to come out with the search and rescue toboggan. You and I will scour the trail until he joins us. Let me radio him to get on the trail to Wolf Lake."

"What can I do?"

"Hitch up your most reliable team and head along the trail Scott would use on his return journey. I'll take the snowmobile and follow his outward route."

"He said he was sticking to his regular run. It was supposed to be just a short outing to keep the dogs in shape."

"Take Itirit along. She seems to know what happened."

"She's good. I don't know if my teaching her search techniques will really do any good."

"She found Aqua."

"I think the dogs have no problem following a dog's scent. I'm not so sure about a human's."

"We'll see. This will be for real."

She sighed. "Do we call the Mounties?"

"Let's do the circuit to Wolf Lake first. If we call Peter now, it becomes an official search. He'll have to call the Royal Canadian Mounted Police and it'll take till tomorrow morning before anyone moves."

"By now, everyone already knows. I called Charlie and Conrad came on."

"That's the way it works over here." Byron called Conrad on the radiophone, then said to Chris, "You'll be happy to know that both Conrad and I are qualified in advanced first aid. Get some warm clothes on. I'll give you a hand to hitch up your dogs."

"I've got some dried fruit and nuts you can take with you. Not much, but it'll keep up your energy."

"Have you got a first-aid kit?"

"Yes. It's in the sled every time I go out. I'll thrown in an extra blanket."

Cody looked up from his play. "Where are you going?"

"We're going on a night training session, darling. Vicky is here to look after you until we get back."

Cody was used to them leaving at odd hours, so he was not upset. Vicky made sure to keep his attention focused.

She chose her team with care and took six sturdy Canadian Inuit dogs. Naturally, she put Itirit and Nunii in the lead. Those two worked as one. Although all the dogs knew each other, there was a bit of growling from the Inuit sled dogs. Those primitive dogs didn't have much time for other breeds, but they had been brought up with Itirit and Nunii's pack, and the growling only served to ascertain their authority.

She had an idea. "Byron, get Renoir out of the pen for me. I'll let him run loose ahead of the team. He's deeply bonded with his master."

"Okay. Sometimes, these dogs can amaze us humans with their sixth sense."

At her signal to go, they set off, Renoir bounding ahead on his own. Noses to the ground, the dogs followed the fresh tracks of Scott's incoming runaways. Dogs trained for racing love nothing better than following other dogs' tracks. Now she was out searching, Itirit settled into a steady gait, which the others matched.

The first section of the trail was relatively hazard-free, so she gave the lead dogs their head. Renoir ran at the outer limit of her headlight. After a mile or two, she reined in the team, wanting to conserve their energy for carrying Scott back home if she found him first.

Too absorbed in scouring the trail ahead, she took no notice of the full moon emerging from behind a thick bank of cloud, but she was thankful for the clearness of the night. Scott's headlamp was in the sled bag. If he was walking, at least the moonlight would make it easier to find his way home.

The dogs kept up their brisk pace for over an hour. There was not the slightest trace of Scott. Not having had time to eat before setting out, she nibbled on dried bananas and nuts.

Soon the terrain gave way to a coniferous forest. Had she not been burdened with fear and worry, she might have enjoyed the moonlit ride through the magical landscape.

Without warning, Renoir came to an abrupt halt. Even at a distance, she saw the hackles rise on his neck.

"Steady! Whoa!" She kept her voice low to keep the dogs calm. Up in front, Itirit grew agitated. Chris's eyes followed where Renoir's nose was pointing. A bulky shadow detached itself from the dark conifers and stepped out onto the trail. It was the largest bull moose she'd ever seen. Its sheer size shocked her. It had to be a bull. Females are slender with a finer head. It was hard to tell without the animal's antlers.

Renoir gave a menacing growl and jumped forward. Her pulse raced.

With an instinct born of many hours of rigorous training, she dropped the snow hook and drove it into the frozen snow crust with her heel. Willing herself to remain calm, she tied the snub rope to the base of a thick bush. Nothing would be achieved by getting panicky. They were crossing a marsh. Low willows were reclaiming the land.

The moose was still some distance away, with Renoir circling it. The dog let out a ferocious snarl, then leaped at the moose. From the moose's angry bellow, she guessed the dog had sunk his teeth into its muzzle. Before the moose could lash out with his hooves, Renoir sprang back and resumed his circling. Fear made her heart beat hard in her chest, yet at the same time she couldn't help admire the skill of the Canadian Inuit dog. Thousands of years of hunting polar bears flowed in his veins. But this wasn't a polar bear.

Again and again, Renoir attacked and withdrew. The tactic enraged the huge animal. She wished she had a gun. If the moose charged the team, dogs would be killed, maybe herself too. Working on adrenaline, she released the sled and urged the leaders to pull farther into the willows, where she'd be hidden from view. Still, Renoir kept the moose at bay. She watched with bated breath. If only the moose would get tired of the dog's harassment and run away.

After making several attempts to gore the dog, the infuriated animal gave an earsplitting bellow and turned tail. Renoir pursued it across a small clearing until the moose plunged into the tall bush and disappeared from view.

"Renoir! Renoir! Here, boy!"

The dog didn't obey right away. For several minutes he patrolled the edge of the marsh, on the alert for any counterattack the moose might decide to launch.

She was faced with a dilemma. If she left the relative security of her hiding place, she might encounter the disgruntled animal farther along the trail. But she was on a rescue mission. She had to keep going. Although it had been chased off by Renoir, the moose could still be lurking nearby. That was a chance she had to take.

This was certainly what had happened to him, probably with this same moose. A sickening dread settled in her stomach. A man alone on foot was no match for such an animal.

A frantic series of short howls in the mid-distance brought all her faculties alert. Renoir stood sideways across the trail. Between howls, he lifted his nose to test the air. Itirit whimpered and tugged on the lines to join him. The dogs made the decision for her and pulled away.

She fumbled with the lines to untangle the dogs that had become caught in the bushes. The team launched itself ahead, and she had just enough time to lift the snow anchor and jump on the runners. They cleared the marsh and a bog choked with brush.

The trail skirted a dark stand of timber. Nerves on edge, she scanned the shadows for movement. She breathed easier when she saw no sign of the moose. Though the danger to her and her team had lessened, she must still find Scott. Itirit strained in her harness and Renoir ran faster and faster, reluctant to wait for the rest of the team.

Almost five minutes later, and just about to lose hope of finding a man alive in the middle of the wintery wasteland, she glimpsed a pinprick of light amid the trees. Renoir and the lead dogs had seen it too, or smelled something, and were running toward it. Off the beaten trail, the going was difficult because of the deep drifts and scattered brush and trees in the way.

The light came from a campfire a few paces from the edge of the forest. In its ruddy glow, she made out the figure of a man lying on his side.

"Scott!"

His unmistakable voice greeted her, "Chris Taylor, I presume?"

Laughing with relief, she anchored the sled and ordered the dogs to sit. Itirit and Nunii didn't obey immediately. They first pulled to his side and sniffed him all over. She patted the dogs and took them by the collar, then secured the sled and repeated the command to sit. This time, Itirit sat and the others followed suit. Renoir was pawing his master.

"Gently, Renoir. Sit." She held him back by his collar.

The dog sat on his haunches. She dropped to her knees beside Scott.

"You're hurt."

"I had an argument with a bull moose. He wasn't very polite."

"We figured as much. It must have been the same one I met farther back along the trail."

"Did it attack you, too?"

"Fortunately no. Renoir chased it off."

"Good dog."

"How bad is it?"

"It got me with his antler."

Her eyes widened as she noticed the blood on the snow. "The bull we met had no antlers."

"It fell off when it got into me."

"Any bones broken?"

"I don't really know. I don't think so. When I escaped from the moose, I hid here until I felt safe. Then I lit the fire. Thanks for stuffing those waterproof matches in my pocket. When I heard you coming, I thought it was my team returning. They ran off on me."

"That's how we knew you were in trouble. The dogs arrived back on their own."

"Not hurt?"

She shook her head.

"That's a relief."

"Now, what about you?"

"I packed snow against the wound. The bleeding has more or less stopped." He shifted to one side. The crimson snow increased her fear. She took a deep breath. It was one thing to care for an injured dog or an unlucky musher, as had happened in the past, but quite another when it was the man she loved.

"Don't move. I'll get the first-aid kit."

With the box in her hand, she laid the blanket in front of the fire. "If I help you, can you ease yourself onto the blanket?"

He winced while he slid himself onto the blanket. She wrapped the spare parka around him. He didn't complain, but she could see he was suffering. The rolled sleeping bag under his head made a pillow. She wrapped the Mylar emergency blanket around his torso.

Once she'd got him as comfortable as possible, she picked up the ax and waded through the snow to cut enough dead branches to keep a bigger fire going. Fueled with dry wood and pine cones, the flames gave off a comforting warmth. Hopefully, the fire would also make the moose think twice about causing more trouble.

She filled the stainless steel bowl from the first aid kit with snow and balanced it on the edge of the fire to melt. "Conrad and Byron are on their way with snowmobiles. It shouldn't take them long to find us. If you've warmed up a little, I want to examine your wound. I wished we had a locator beacon."

"Wouldn't work in the mountains."

It wasn't the time to argue about the effectiveness of satellite transmission. Every racer was equipped with an emergency beacon on the Iditarod and the Quest. He was the only one keeping his in the off mode at the bottom of his bag. "Let me look at the wound."

"Best wait for the men to arrive. The cut is on my backside. Right where I sit down."

"Come on. I've already seen your backside. This examination is strictly for medical purposes."

He burst out laughing. "Oh, hell! It hurts when I laugh."

"See, you need attention." She took the scissors out of her pack. "Don't move while I cut your pants over the affected area."

He gritted his teeth and let her treat the wound.

"Damn! It's cold! I feel I have been run over by a truck. The beast first hit me with its rump."

"That'd be like being hit by a pickup for sure."

With the second sleeping bag unzipped, she covered him as much as she could.

"It'd be best if you lay on your side. Good. Now you can relax. It's a mess down here. You've got a nasty gash across your buttock cheek. Luckily, it missed your kidneys."

"It feels like it's bleeding again."

"Yes, it is. That's because I had to cut away your long underwear. The fabric was stuck to the wound. I'm going to clean it up. Don't yell. It may hurt a bit."

Using the melt water from the bowl, she washed the gash. "I'm putting on antibiotic powder. It'll sting, so be prepared."

He stiffened when she dabbed the raw flesh, but other than a few grunts, he didn't complain.

"It's very deep. I'll put a compression dressing on it. That's all I can do for the moment. It's going to require stitches."

"Stitches? Won't it heal up on its own?"

"What's the matter? Is Scott Walsh scared of being sewn up?" Although she meant it in jest, she immediately regretted her mocking remark. He had no need to prove his courage, either physical or moral. She eased the rest of him into the sleeping bag and zipped it up.

At that moment, the dogs began to grow restless. She knew their keen sense of hearing, or smell, had detected something. Not the moose again. She moved out of range of the crackling fire to scan the woods and listen. From far away came the unmistakable whine of a snowmobile engine. Relief washed over her.

"I think help may be coming. If they stick to the trail, they're bound to see the fire."

"Chris?"

"Yes?"

"Before they get here, I just want to say I knew somehow you'd find me."

"Did you expect me not to be worried when you failed to return?"

"No. Even if the team hadn't made it back, I had the feeling you'd know that I wasn't just dawdling around, and that something had gone wrong."

"I admit that when I finished the chores, I intended setting out with a team to look for you. I'd have had to bring Cody along too."

"Cody, yes. Where's he?"

"Byron had the foresight to ask Vicky to come and take care of him, so I could join the search."

He closed his eyes and sank back on the makeshift pillow. The brilliant glare of a snowmobile headlight sliced through the darkness. Seconds later, Conrad was with them.

"You've found the old guy. How badly hurt is he?"

"The good news is that there are no apparent broken bones or internal injuries. The bad news is that the moose caught him with his antler. He's got a nasty cut."

"Where?"

"On my rear end." Scott grinned despite the discomfort.

"Okay. You'd better let me take a look at it."

"Forget it, Windett. My butt is private. Besides, Chris's done a great job cleaning it up and applying a dressing."

Conrad laughed. "You blessed swine! Lucky for you that Florence Nightingale got to you first. You'd wouldn't have received that level of TLC from me or Byron."

"Cut that out, you sadist! You're making me laugh and it hurts like hell."

Conrad stopped joking. "I've got something for the pain, if you need it."

"No thanks. I'll be okay."

"Just lie put for a while longer. I'll call up Byron and tell him where we are. As soon as he gets here, we'll settle you on the toboggan. You'll be at the nursing station in no time." Conrad returned to his snowmobile and picked up the portable radio.

Scott raised his head and smiled at Chris. "Knowing how people around here monitor the air waves, we're likely to have the entire community of Fletcher Creek arrive at any moment."

"Don't talk. It'll tire you out. You've lost quite a bit of blood. Try to relax. We'll take care of everything from now on."

"You're great, you know that?"

"Only doing my job, Mr. Walsh. Now shut up and rest."

CHAPTER TWENTY-EIGHT

"I tell you, I'm leaving as planned." Scott shifted uncomfortably in the armchair and threw her a defiant glance.

"That's out of the question, and you know it. You can't even sit properly, let alone bend down to deal with the dogs."

"What a damned waste of time and money this has been. All that good training for the Iditarod for nothing. And all that dog food already at the checkpoints in Alaska will be lost." His face reflected his intense frustration.

She put the last of the dinner dishes in the cupboard and turned to him. A smile softened her lips. "There is one solution."

"What's that?"

"I take your place."

"That's a crazy idea. You know nothing about running the Iditarod. It's not at all like the Yukon Quest, where outdoors and dog skills are most important. The competition is stiff, really stiff. Besides, you've never even run in a big race."

"True, only a couple of three-hundred mile races. But tell me who trained this Iditarod team of yours? Think of the time we've spent discussing the details. I can recite the strategy word for word."

"Okay. I'll grant you that. But how can you compete against those seasoned racers? A rookie stands no chance of coming in first. Lucky if you finished the race."

"My personal ambition tells me otherwise. I could at least place in the money. The top few finishers don't do too badly. That would be better than just dropping out."

"If only we had more time. The committee has to approve you, approve the change. It won't work."

"Listen! That's a snowmobile coming up the slope."

He grimaced. "More visitors. I'm beginning to prefer the old times better. Back then, nobody ever bothered me."

"They only want to wish you well. Everybody went out to look for you when they heard you had had an accident. Anyway, Scott Walsh is the local superstar again."

"It's probably Byron. He comes to see how I'm doing, but it's really an excuse to see you."

"You're an old cynic."

Byron's noisy arrival drowned out his reply.

"Excuse me," Byron said. "I forgot Cody must be in bed."

She smiled a welcome. "Don't worry. When he's asleep, nothing disturbs him."

Her eyes sparkled as she spoke to Byron, but she didn't miss the somber expression that darkened Scott's face.

Byron took a seat next to his friend. "You don't look altogether happy."

"Neither would you be, buddy, if you were leaving for the Iditarod in fifteen short days while still virtually bedridden."

"Then send Chris in your place."

"Are you two in cahoots?"

"Did she suggested replacing you too? It makes sense. She certainly knows dogs."

Her voice softened to a whisper. "I did offer to take his place. Only, he doubts I'm capable enough."

"No, no. That's not exactly what I said." Scott threw up his hands. "I said you lacked the necessary preparation."

She leaned toward him. "In which case, tell me everything I need to know. I could write up my race strategy according to your instructions."

"She's right, old pal. All the technical stuff about handling the sled and the team she knows already. Between the two of you, there's no reason why she can't compete in the damned race."

"It's an awful lot to ask of anyone."

"I'm not just anyone." Her eyes flashed. "If I don't try, we'll never know. To succeed, you must take risks."

Scott rubbed his chin. A reflective mood settled in his eyes. "It's not certain that the race committee will allow a last-minute change of mushers."

"I'm beginning to hope I can convince you," she said.

Byron got to his feet and reached for his parka. "I'm really glad the patient is back to his old, grouchy self. I'll tell you what I am going to do. I'll phone Herb Cochrane, my old buddy. He's head of the Iditarod Race Committee. I'll plead your case. He owes me. You might have to pay a fee for the change of musher.

"That's alright," Scott said.

"Do you think you can? Convince him to bend the rules, that is? I can't remember what the rule about emergency is."

"You're already registered Walsh, so it's only a matter of a name change on the papers."

"Even though I haven't done any of the qualifying races?"

"But you ran the Beargrease race, the U.P. 200 and the Canadian Challenge. In all of those, you finished in the top ten," Scott said.

"That was seven years ago."

He shook his head. "Pass me the Idi folder."

She handed it to him. He flipped the pages.

"There, in the rules, rookies must provide a reference. The reference must be from an Iditarod musher who is familiar with the rookie, must certify that the rookie has been informed about and understands the physical and mental aspects of the Iditarod, as well as the wilderness and mushing skills necessary for contesting the race. I didn't know that. No problem, then I can be the reference."

Byron crammed his fur hat on his head and gave them a broad smile. "We'll see what happens. I'll call you just as soon as I have a reply. Good night, folks."

The sound of his departing snowmobile faded away.

He looked at her. "Hand me that stack of old log books, please."

After slipping a cushion at his back to make him more comfortable, she perched herself on the armrest. Together, they studied the race logs.

He held up an open notebook. "This page describes the last checkpoint before Nome..." His sentence hung unfinished in the air. He glanced at her. "Something wrong?"

His leg had brushed hers and sent a shiver through her body. She fought the waves of longing that engulfed her and tried to concentrate. As she leaned over to read the entry, an auburn curl caressed his hand. With deliberate slowness, his fingers closed on the silken lock of hair and brought it to his lips.

Oblivious to the soreness of his wound, he drew her down to him. He pressed his lips against the cool skin of her temple. The throbbing pulse fluttered under his touch. His arms encircled her waist.

Successive waves of heat silenced her clamoring voice of reason. With breathless impatience, she abandoned all pretense of caution and leaned against the muscled shield of his chest. Time stood still while they forgot the mundane reality of the cabin.

She took a deep gulp of air and came to her senses. Gently, so as not to aggravate his injury, she freed herself from his embrace. "You'll hurt yourself."

"Your sweet lips will heal me."

"Be reasonable. That's a deep wound you have."

"It's nothing compared to the one in my heart."

"This is not the time to wax poetic. Do you need anything?"

"Yes, you."

"I was speaking of more material things."

"Me too."

"How about using my shoulder to help you to the bathroom?"

"Thanks. If you push the kitchen chair over here, I'll use it as a support. I'd better learn to fend for myself, since you're threatening to leave at the end of the week."

"It's not if I leave, but when."

"Seriously, you can take all my equipment. Have you got all the clothes you'll need? If not, you'd better drive to Whitehorse tomorrow and buy whatever is necessary."

"I'll go to the village. I saw that Mary had some nice native-made mukluks. I'd like to have a pair to alternate with my boots. A couple of spare toques and gloves are the only other things I need. Mary will have those in the store."

"You can charge it to my account. Oh, and I ordered a locator beacon. I lost the one I had. It's compulsory to have it. It should have arrived at the post office. "And take my credit card."

"I have a little money."

"You'll need gas and meals on the road."

"It's fine, I'll—"

"Take mine. That's an order!"

"Sure thing, boss." Her laughing eyes mocked his severity.

As punishment, he seized her about the hips and looked into her eyes imploringly. She kissed him lightly on the mouth. Then, taking advantage of his distraction, she wriggled free and ran to her room.

Sleep did not come immediately. Part of her was distressed to see him injured, yet she could not quell her excitement. On the one hand, his mood was happy, like it was before

Christmas. On the other, she was being handed a wonderful opportunity to take part in the race of her dreams.

***

Two days later, Byron called on the radio. "Walsh, you'll be happy to hear that everything is in order. Chris has been given permission to replace you under special circumstances, according to Rule Number Four. Of course, she's to attend the pre-race meeting for rookies in five days' time in Anchorage. I assured them she'd be there."

"That's great news. She is out with the dogs right now. She's going to be overjoyed."

"I'm glad to have been of help. It pays to cultivate old friendships."

"I owe you."

"I phoned Marcia last night and told her about your mishap. She sends her sympathy and says to get well soon."

"You rat! There was no need to publicize my misfortune. I'm not particularly proud of my exploits with that stupid moose."

"Don't fret. Marcia would have found out soon enough, anyway. Once she heard that her cousin was running the Iditarod, she immediately said she'd set out for Anchorage to be there to help. Her boss has agreed to do without her for a few days until he gets to Anchorage for the race."

"That takes a weight off my mind. Entering the Iditarod for the very first time is tough enough for anyone, but to do it with no backup…"

"Yeah, I agree. It takes grit. But we both know that Chris has that. I'm off now. While she's away, I'll come up and take care of the dogs until you're fit enough to handle them."

***

True to his word, Byron was at the cabin early in the morning of her departure. He helped her load the dogs into the truck.

After breakfast, she stood up to clear away the dishes.

Byron held up his hand. "Leave them! Don't waste time getting on the road. It's a long drive to Anchorage."

"I can at least wash the dishes before I go. You've got enough to do with the dogs."

"Quit fighting, you two. I'm doing the dishes," Scott said.

Byron took a stern pose. "You have to rest."

"I'm able to stand up. That's all a guy needs to wash a bunch of dumb plates."

Cody sprang from his chair. "I wash the dishes."

"Bravo! Spoken like a true northerner." Byron stifled his smile.

"With all my gallant gentlemen to take care of things here, I can see I'm not needed. Goodbye then, everyone. Be good, Cody."

Byron took down the boy's coat. "Get dressed, Cody. Come and help me warm up the truck for Chris. It'll only take a couple of minutes."

Cody scrambled into his outdoor clothes and dashed outside in Byron's wake.

She watched them go and silently thanked him. How considerate to want to give the lovers a few moments alone to say farewell. He wasn't to know that Scott stubbornly refused to love her. She tugged on her woolen gloves.

Scott stood beside her, using the back of a chair for support. His free arm snaked around her waist. His mouth descended on hers. Despite her determination not to weaken, the pressure of his lips sent a fiery current directly to the very center of her being.

She took an uncertain step backward.

He lowered his voice to a throaty whisper. "That was only a good luck kiss."

"Is that all?"

"Isn't that enough?"

For a split second, she hoped he might say something else, something akin to a declaration of love.

"I'll bring you back the winner's Golden Harness."

"Complete the course and bring back the team in one piece. I'll settle for that."

His reminder of the grueling race ahead cast a shadow over her joy. In spite of the top rate veterinary attention the dogs received during the race, there were always unexplained deaths. The thought of losing one of her precious dogs made her cringe. At that minute, she might have backed out had she been pressed.

"I put the welfare of the dogs above everything. If they get tired, we'll stop, no matter what."

"And take equal care of yourself."

His sudden tenderness made her quiver. It was genuine. She could hear it. At the same time, she told herself it was only the friendship inspired by their common interest in dogs, and running in the fabled race.

"You take care of yourself, too." She had the irresistible urge to kiss him, but she held herself back.

With a quick final smile, she went outside. Byron was waiting for her at the door of the truck. The racing sled and a spare were firmly secured on top. The excited dogs poked their noses through the vents of the transporter.

Byron opened the door for her. "All set?"

She picked up Cody and kissed him on both cheeks. "Take care of your daddy, my little man."

Before she could climb into the cab, Byron brushed the veil of hair that the breeze blew in her face, and pressed a light kiss, so laden with regret, on the corner of her mouth.

"Good luck," he whispered.

"Thanks, Byron... for everything."

***

With Byron taking care of the kennel chores, Scott listened to the sound of the truck fade away, unaware that his nails dug painfully into the palms of his hand. Sadness constricted his heart. He threw himself onto the couch. His tortured mind pictured those last tender moments outside, with Chris saying goodbye to Byron. He'd guessed right. She was enamored with him.

After those few nights of delirious passion, she had kept her distance. He was convinced that he'd been mistaken. They had established a working relationship, a friendship even. Nothing more. And that was as far as it went. Byron, on the other hand, could offer her love and commitment. How could a morose musher like him compete against that combination? In a mixture of anger and disgust, he hurled a cushion across the room.

Love! What a farce. Love was merely a figment of people's romantic imaginations. Once, as a young racer, fresh from his third Iditarod victory, he'd been naïve enough to believe he was in love. He'd been dazzled by the adulation of the fans, the lavish offers of corporate sponsorships and speaking engagements. When he met Alina at a glitzy cocktail party, he'd fallen head over heels. At that time, he had it all. The future belonged to him.

It was not long before the life that had once smiled on him turned sour. Love ceased to exist for him. He shouldn't resent Chris for seeking happiness in another man's arms. A few nights of blissful sex gave him no special hold over her.

"It all boils down to a matter of hormones," he muttered. But he wasn't entirely convinced by his own explanation.

"What's hormones?"

The childish voice startled Scott. He hadn't realized he spoke loud enough for little ears to hear. "Huh... It's... about the dogs when they're going to make babies."

Cody was still at the age when simple explanations satisfied him when he was busy, which he was as he had been entrusted to wash the dishes. To watch him getting wet in the overabundant soapsuds made his father smile. He switched his thoughts to the race ahead and chided himself for not having spent more time explaining the difficulties she'd encounter.

There was the appalling weather in the mountains, winds that could topple a loaded sled, and blowing snow that blotted out every landmark along the wide sweep of Norton Bay. On the lower reaches of the Yukon River, she'd meet treacherous overflows, those frightening undercurrents that spilled over onto the surface ice.

If he could have forewarned her a little more of these dangers, she'd have a better chance of realizing her dream of winning. There, he was talking about winning as if he really believed she would. It was not impossible, but racing had become a sophisticated sport, and rookies didn't have much of a chance against hardened veterans. Though he wished Chris could just make history.

He laughed. She had spunk. Cody scooted to the armchair, climbed on his lap and joined in the laughter.

Chapter Twenty-Nine

C hris brought the truck to a halt in the service station parking lot and cut the motor. Stiff from wrestling the tight grades over Tahneta Pass, she flexed her shoulders to ease the soreness. The mountains were behind her now. Ahead lay the descent to Anchorage. This would be her last stop to exercise and water the dogs.

She'd been there for a little while when a red and white truck, similarly laden with sleds and dogs, drew alongside. A slim woman got out, accompanied by a young man. The pair came over to her.

"Hi there!" The woman smiled and held out her hand. "I'm Lauren Kains. This is my handler, Tonio Vargas."

Chris was impressed. Lauren's reputation as a top racer was well known. She shook the woman's hand. "Pleased to meet you. I'm Chris Taylor."

"Was the late Guy Taylor your father?"

It was comforting that five years after his death, people still remembered her father. "Yes. And I'm Scott Walsh's handler."

"I thought you must be. I recognized the truck. I'm looking forward to competing against him again."

"Unfortunately, he isn't running the Iditarod."

"No?"

"I'm taking his place. He had an accident just recently and injured himself."

"Badly?"

"Enough to stop him from entering the race. Luckily, they agreed to let me step in at the last moment, under the emergency clause." Her joy was written on her face.

"That's great. Then this is your first Iditarod?"

"My first really long distance race."

"The combination of your name and Scott's is a pretty powerful one. You'll do well."

"I hope to live up to everyone's expectations."

"You will, I'm sure. If you stick close to me, I'll do my best to steer you in the right direction. If I can be of any assistance, don't hesitate to ask. You have no handler? The most important thing is not to screw up at the beginning of the race. We'll find you a volunteer to help with the dogs."

"My cousin Marcia is supposed to meet me."

"Great, but an extra pair of hands is always a good thing. Especially if she doesn't have too much experience with the Idi."

"Thank you. I'll welcome any advice you can give me."

"We women mushers have to stick together, no? Tonio, have you almost finished with the dogs? We gotta roll. Follow me. I know the way."

Enchanted at finding a friend in Lauren, Chris took to the road behind the red and white truck. Her weariness had vanished. Everything seemed too good to be true. Lauren had placed second several times in the Iditarod. To get help from her was more than she could have dreamed of.

On her arrival at the campground reserved for the race participants, Chris looked for her cousin. She didn't need to look far. Marcia came running up and threw her arms around her. Chris was pleased to see that she and Lauren had been allocated neighboring campsites. It didn't take long for an easygoing friendship to blossom among all the young racers and handlers. True to her word, Lauren found a young, but expert, volunteer to help.

Chris sailed through the necessary registration formalities and attended the rookie seminar. Unabashed, she had no hesitation in asking questions. She drew the twenty-ninth starting position, a placing that suited her just fine. Having other teams ahead of her meant she'd have no problem finding the trail.

The day of realizing her dream arrived. She was standing in the staging area before the start of the Last Great Race on earth. The ceremonial start took place along Fourth Avenue in the town center.

She confided to Lauren. "Departures make me nervous. My dogs are not used to crowds, let alone streets and houses."

"Most of the mushers here are in the same boat. We live away from towns. Don't let it worry you. Dogs are smart. Once we're beyond the city limits, it's wilderness all the way. That's where the real race begins. This is just for show."

Some distance back from the starting line, amid the frantic bustle of cameras and microphones, Chris waited for her turn. The announcement that Scott Walsh was being replaced by his handler, a rookie but not any rookie, Chris Taylor, daughter of the late Guy Taylor, a winner of several years ago, created a considerable stir. Scott's success in the Yukon Quest had heightened interest among the racegoers. Not many mushers attempted both races in the same year. The kindness of the other mushers and the behavior of the media encouraged her. The cheers of the spectators helped her overcome her jitters.

The actual start proved less of an ordeal than she'd feared. Her spirits were boosted by the banner suspended over the starting line that proclaimed the race covered no less than 1,049 miles. Although actually seeing the figure sent anxious tremors throughout her body. It was an incredible distance, but this was her dream. In the recesses of her mind, she promised her father to make him proud.

Number One was called out, but no one appeared. The number was reserved for the memory of Leonard Seppala. Then the first musher, number two, to depart drove his sled to honor a particularly deserving musher. Emotion ran high when it was announced it would honor the memory of Susan Butcher, who won four Iditarod races. Cancer had taken this vibrant young woman.

At last, number twenty-nine came up. For the start, all sleds had to carry a passenger or drag another sled behind with a musher steering it. In her sled, she carried no less than Herb Cochrane, the Iditarod race committee president. He wanted to see for himself how capable she was. Misgivings rose in her throat, but she quelled them. Her dogs would pick up on her anxiety. They weren't used to her being tense. All of a sudden, a great calm came over her. Her dogs, still bewildered by the noise and confusion, remained silent. She heard comments in the crowd that her lightweight team of twelve dogs wouldn't go far. They looked different from the others. Other teams of short-haired, slim dogs, most wearing coats and booties, were over-excited, straining forward, barking and jumping three feet in the air against the harnesses. Her dogs had thick fur, large paws, wide shoulders... and they were lying down, just as she'd taught them.

Then it was her signal, "Five... Four... Three... Two..." She called to Itirit and Nunii. In a flash, her team was on its feet. "... Go!" With a mere short howl, they lunged forward, and the sled moved on smoothly. The dogs accelerated to an effortless lope. She heard the whoosh of astonishment among the spectators so used to see the big teams of the fourteen dogs frantically gallop from the starting lines. On paper, twelve or fourteen didn't appear to make much difference. On the ground, however, it was striking. What spectators saw was a short string of dogs.

As they passed the last houses, Herb Cochrane twisted in the sled to look at her. "Chris Taylor, I'm so impressed. When we decided to let you in, we did it out of kindness, in the memory of your father, to let you get a taste of the Iditarod for as far as you could go. But I believe you'll make it to Nome. You've got a winning team and an indomitable spirit."

"Thanks so much, Herb. I'll do my best to win, believe me."

Two hours later, now on her own, she was in Eagle River. There, she met Marcia, along with Alec, the dashing young volunteer. Together, they loaded the dogs into the truck for the ride to Willow.

"Why don't they start the race in Willow for good?" Marcia asked.

"I guess the ceremonial start in Anchorage draws more spectators and more media attention."

"Don't forget the sponsors' publicity," Alec said. "Actually, in the origin, the race started right in Anchorage. With the growth of the race and spectators, and the fact that the ice on Knick River could no longer be trusted, it was decided to have a ceremonial start in Anchorage, and the real start would be in Wasilla, which is like an Anchorage's suburb. Over the last couple of decades, there hasn't been enough snow around Wasilla, so it was moved to Willow. The climate has changed."

"Alas, you're right!"

Chapter Thirty

Her team was toiling up the impressive slope of the Alaska Range. She concentrated on finding the best pace for the dogs. To her surprise, even on some of the steepest sections, they didn't show signs of undue fatigue. Earlier, her confidence had been tested when strings of fourteen dogs had overtaken her. Then, she too had taken the lead over some slower competitors. This show of stamina by her dogs helped restore some of her confidence.

At her last rest stop, she'd consulted her notes. In her head, Scott's voice reminded her to take it slow and easy through the mountains. The Dalzell Gorges are dangerous, so when you reach them, you want to have your dogs in good condition. Take them there at a walking pace. Never mind the clock. Go slow. Those gorges now lay ahead of her. After that, it was the Rohn checkpoint, where a good many mushers took their compulsory twenty-four-hour layover.

Once again, he was on her mind. This was not the time to anguish about the love she carried in her heart, a love he'd spurned. Instead, she dwelt on his advice, as if he were there with her, riding the runners. Thanks to him, she tackled the gorges and their notorious switchbacks, and snow bridges over the fast running creek during daylight hours. Her team negotiated the roller-coaster difficulties with a mastery that astonished her.

With a deep sigh of relief, she pulled into Rohn. Lauren was already there.

"Your dogs look in great shape," Lauren said. "Keep going. Take your twenty-four later. When you see them flagging, that's the time to give them a long rest."

"I found the mountains pretty tough going."

Lauren's laugh attracted other mushers. "That's because you chose not to ride the runners. I saw you back there pedaling and running to help them. You've got a great team of dogs. Trust them. I've not made up my mind about pushing on or not. My team is quite strong, but I see signs of fatigue in a couple of dogs. I might drop them here and head out again."

Chris had no such hesitation. She pushed on. The race trail was unrelenting, a never-ending routine of eating, sleeping, examining dogs' paws, checkpoint stops and fresh departures.

The scenery wasn't too much different from home. A small sigh was all she allowed herself. Fletcher Creek, or rather a cabin in the woods, had become home, but would never be hers. Her mind back on the arduous trail, she kept going. She never grew discouraged, never failed to pat her dogs to instill them with her own enthusiasm.

"Scott is expecting you to do a good job, dogs. So, let's go!"

With seven hundred and ninety-six miles still to be covered, she reached the village of Nikolai just in time to wave farewell to Lauren, who was pulling out. Chris finally decided to take the required long rest, and so set about organizing her camp.

That night, the temperature took a steep dip. Next day, while waiting for her departure time, she noticed the wind had picked up. Each time a team left the village, her own dogs showed impatience to be off, too. The exception was Tioralak. He lay utterly relaxed on his back, with all four paws in the air. In contrast, Itirit anxiously raised her muzzle each time she took a step.

At last, she was able to leave. She signed the official's time sheet and resumed the trail. By now, the wind was driving the snow horizontally over the ground. Snow clung to the dogs' fur. Deep drifts rendered the going painfully slow. To keep up her spirits, she sang to the dogs.

They trotted with renewed vigor and made good time into the McGrath checkpoint. She had no intention of stopping there longer than was necessary, but she did ask a race official what time had Lauren come through.

"She's here still, taking her twenty-four hours. Heading out now?"

"Yes, I am." Chris wondered why her new friend was not making better time. But then, she'd probably overtake her tomorrow.

"Everybody's stopping. There's a real blizzard raging out there in the mountains."

"Could it be over when I get there?"

"Could be."

Although Chris was standing on the brake, the dogs, impatient to get going, were beginning to drag the sled.

In the Kuskokwin Mountains, blowing snow reduced visibility down to a few yards. The wind shrieked through the high valleys. More than once, she felt the sled tip sideways. But the dogs plodded onward, nose down, shoulders hunched. After many weary hours, she arrived at Iditarod, the mining ghost-town that gave its name to both the trail and the race.

To her astonishment, she discovered she was among the group of front runners. Three of the veteran racers were taking their long rest. Not daring to hope she was gaining on them, she halted only long enough to water her team. Already, they had been running six days, another four or five to Nome, depending on the trail conditions. The excitement kept a smile on her slightly frostbitten face while she applied a balm.

Tradition had it that the first musher to reach the Anvik checkpoint was regaled with a gourmet banquet prepared by a cordon bleu chef from the Regal Alaskan tourist hotel on the banks of the Yukon River. Phil Richter was that lucky musher.

A more immediate concern was the reports of another fierce blizzard raging along the Alaskan coast. Praying that it would end before she found herself engulfed by it, she set up camp in Anvik to take the eight-hour required rest. At first, she was tempted to postpone the layover until later. Then she told herself that a good rest in these stormy conditions would permit the dogs to travel faster over the frozen river, where the going would be hopefully smooth. Perhaps by that time the blizzard would have blown itself out.

***

Ready to leave the next day, her assurance was shattered when she found that snow had obliterated the well-marked trail. There were now only a few mushers ahead of her, and for the first time since starting the race, she saw a faint possibility of finishing in the top ten. Winning was on her mind, and she kept reviewing the strategy. It didn't help. Sled dog racing had been made into a science, but on the ground, battling the blasting snow, it reverted to being an art.

Present standings meant little because the race was only half over. Until now, she had not made any great demands on her dogs. She could always drive them harder. The moment the thought formed into her head, she dismissed it. She would never push the dogs and risk harming them. But they were used to deep snow, so she would let them set their own pace.

Okay, Scott, what would you do in my place? As much rest as hours of running. No compromising on rest for the dogs. Right?

She took her time in hitching up her team before she signaled her readiness to depart. The race marshal grinned over his clipboard. "You're in luck. The trail-breaker is going out ahead of you. You'll think you're sledding down Main Street."

The man's news boosted her morale. Of course, the mushers behind her would also be sledding on a well-flattened trail.

Although battling gale winds all the way, she kept up a brisk pace to Kaltag. From there, the route quit the Yukon River and struck out toward the coast.

On the way, she passed a musher resting on the side of the trail. He might still overtake her later. The White Mountain checkpoint was a compulsory stopover. When she got there, the only musher she saw was Phil Richter. He'd been leading the race for the past five hundred miles. There was no question he was a strong contender for the first place. At the checkpoints, she had heard murmurs that he would win.

Now she was hoping she could finish in the top five. Scott didn't expect her to win a prize, only to finish the race. None of their friends did think she had a chance, but they all believed she'd finish the race well. If he were here now, Scott would know how to place himself in a strong position to win. Her lack of experience was going to rob her of victory. Even favoring her team the way she did, she had made it to the very front of the pack. And she still had her full complement of twelve huskies. Happiness sang in her heart. The dogs loved it. She loved it. Stern and savage Alaska enfolded her and defied her to succeed.

Three other leading mushers arrived at the control minutes after her. Being experienced racers, they were sure to overtake her. Yet, for the first time, she had an advantage over her competitors. Already, they'd been obliged to drop off dogs along the way and were down to eleven apiece. Of course, one dog really wasn't enough to make or break the result. It did indicate, though, that their teams were getting tired. The finish line at Nome still lay more than seventy miles to the north.

Resigned to a fourth or fifth place, she went outside to massage the shoulders of her dogs. Thinking they were about to set off, they jumped to their feet, full of vigor.

"Okay, my darlings. We're not doing so badly. Thanks to you, I'm going to finish this race with a respectable placing."

A man's cheerful voice behind her added, "For a rookie, you're doing just great."

She glanced over her shoulder. Phil was busy fitting booties to the feet of several of his dogs. In her sled bag, she, too, had a supply of booties. Her dogs' feet remained in perfect condition. The trail was no rougher than the trail network back home. Besides, her huskies hated booties. But on the river ice, she persuaded them to wear the beige booties.

Back home, she had tried fluorescent pink and blue booties. Invariably, the dogs shook them off until she made beige ones with only a reflective tape at the top. The team had accepted those. It gave rise to a lot of merriment about dog fashionistas.

"Thanks for your vote of confidence."

Phil pointed with his chin at the resting mushers. "You'll have to drive your team flat out if you intend to stay ahead of those guys."

"But I'll be behind you."

"I leave first. I'll be first over the line. Good luck to you!"

"Break a leg!" she shouted as he sped off. The silly logic of the traditional theater wish made her smile. But in the best sporting spirit, she'd meant it as a sincere expression of goodwill.

She gave her dogs the signal to start. The remaining mushers gathered to see her off. They shouted good nature promises to catch up to her later. Although tired beyond belief, she felt her exhilaration rise now that the end of the race was so close. When she began to sing, Itirit, out in front with Nunii, quickened the pace.

Total darkness fell. She looked behind. Nowhere in the inky void could she see the telltale flicker of a musher's headlamp. That was nothing to draw any comfort from. Her pursuers would doubtless catch up to her sooner or later, but she was determined to make them sweat first.

"Keep going, dogs. At the end of this trail, you'll get all the food and rest you want." As if they understood, the team broke into a gallop before dropping back to their cruising speed.

Lulled by the smooth pace, she half-dozed. All of a sudden, something in the beam of her headlamp jerked her to full consciousness. At the end of the dancing beam, the light caught a reflection. She peered into the darkness. Whatever it was, the team was closing in on it fast.

Her foot on the brake, she called to her leaders. Not a moose at his latitude. No reflective tape shone in her light. A man. As she drew closer, she recognized Phil Richter, her archrival, walking on the trail.

As if resenting having to break their rhythm, the dogs took a long time to come to a full stop. She had to twist to look behind.

"Phil, what happened?"

"Call of nature. I shouldn't have drunk all that coffee. Damned dogs! They didn't listen to me and took off dragging the anchor. I caught up but fell off the sled."

"Climb up behind me. We'll catch up with them."

"I'm going to delay you."

"Then hurry up."

In one bound Phil was on the runners. He snaked one hand around her to grip the sled's handlebar.

"Thanks. This is really good of you. You know you're under no obligation to give me a ride? You could simply sled on by and anchor my team when you catch up with it."

"I know. But it could be another twenty miles before that happens. You're not going to hoof it for that distance, are you?"

"I'm dropping from lack of sleep."

"We don't get much shut-eye during this race."

"I thought I pushed the anchor deep enough." Phil's tone was dull. "And now I'm slowing you down. Those guys behind are catching up. No, this is no good. Let me get off here. My team can't be far ahead now."

"Phil, I think you're having hallucinations from lack of sleep. Stay where you are."

The light from Phil's lamp bobbed up and down over her shoulder, an indication he was getting woozy. In stark contrast, she was fully alert thanks to the adrenalin pumping through her veins. If she could maintain her lead over the others, there was a chance for her yet.

Several miles along the trail, they came across Phil's team. The dogs had been fighting, and the lines were tangled.

"Thanks. Get on your way now."

"I can lend you a hand."

"Go! I'll manage. And Chris?"

"Yes?"

"You're going to win if you don't slow down from now on. Your dogs can do it. This is the time to ask them to give their all."

In a state close to shock, she realized that she was out in front. Nome lay no more than thirty miles ahead. Less than three hours of sledding.

"Hike! Hike!" The energy in her voice communicated itself to the dogs. They needed no urging. Lighter now without the passenger, the sled skimmed over iron-hard snow whipped clean by the wind off the Bering Sea.

An unexpected burst of applause greeted her as she stopped at the last checkpoint village with the lovely name of Safety. She remained only long enough to check in and tell the officials about Phil's mishap.

It was with a pounding heart that she set out once more. The team sensed her urgency. They ran proud, their heads high, bushy plumed tails curled over their backs.

Soon the lights of Nome glittered on the horizon. More ominous, though, were the headlamps closing in behind her. Using her foot to pedal the sled, she put all her efforts into getting the most from her dogs. She tried to forget what was behind. Her eyes were fixed in front. Her approach had been spotted. The clamor of shouts reached her ears when she approached the town's limits. She burst into a yodeling song, and her dogs responded by running ever faster.

CHAPTER THIRTY-ONE

With his little helper at his side, Scott, still limping, went about the kennel chores. Since he'd become the primary guardian of his son, he was in high spirits.

"Daddy, why Chris is still away?"

"She's running the Iditarod Trail race."

"It's a long time."

He sighed. It was a long time. The days were so much longer without her sunny personality around. He was missing her. For the first time, he recognized it wasn't just the desire to make love to her that he was missing, but a whole unknown need.

"When she comes back?" Cody frowned. "She will come back, right daddy?"

"Yes, pumpkin, she'll come back at the end of the race."

"Forever?"

He stopped short and winced, his backside still sore. Forever. His heart beat faster. A glimmer of joy grew and enveloped him. Forever. The darkness of the evening disappeared. Warmth spread into his limbs. Forever. He'd have her at his side, friend, lover. Love. He was in love.

"Daddy?"

He bent down just enough to pick up his son. "You'd like her to stay with us?"

An anxious look came over Cody's features. "I want her to come back."

"Then I will have to ask her to marry me."

Cody laughed. "Go ask her, daddy."

"Do you think you can stay with Vicky while I go and ask Chris?"

His son swatted his face with his mittened hand. "Then you come back and stay forever, right?"

"Right. We will."

A state of inner panic stayed with him while he drove to Fletcher Creek to make arrangements for his absence. What if she rejected him?

Byron greeted him with more good news. Chris was in fifth place. They rejoiced together.

"I don't want to ask and impose on you, Byron, but I was wondering if..."

"Now, let me think. Maybe you'd like to fly to Nome to propose to Chris, hey?"

Scott's cheeks reddened. "How... What the heck, yes."

Both men laughed. Cody happily ensconced in an armchair with his stuffed husky joined in the merriment.

"About time, buddy. Yes, leave everything to me. I'll call Vicky. She'll be happy to take care of Cody."

"She already has him all day in school."

Busy dialing, Byron didn't respond. Moments later, Vicky burst in.

"Great, I'll have my favorite student all the time now. Bring his case tomorrow morning just before school. And Scott, congratulations."

"Go pack, my friend. I'll make the plane reservation for you," Byron said.

"I want a bit of spare time in Whitehorse before the flight."

Vicky tugged on his sleeve. "Size seven for the ring."

Still laughing, Scott helped his son into the truck and drove home. He was in love. He was going to convince her to love him.

Chapter Thirty-Two

C hris hit the brilliantly lit Front Street at full speed. Her laughter brought tears to her eyes. She and her team streaked toward the burled arch that marked the finish line.

The finish line! She couldn't believe she had actually won. Chris Taylor, the rookie of the Iditarod, had won! Ten days on the trail, and now it was over.

A delirious crowd swarmed about her. Helping hands grasped the sled lines and brought the team to a halt. She jumped from the runners and dashed forward to hug her lead dogs, Itirit and Nunii, then all the others. Oblivious to the flash of cameras, she let the tears of joy and relief stream down her cheeks.

A tall figure pushed through the crowd toward her.

"Chris!"

She rubbed her reddened eyes. Her jaw sagged.

"Scott!"

He opened his arms wide. The next instant she threw herself into them, hugging him, not believing that any of this was actually happening. Swept her off the ground by his powerful arms, her feverish lips found his. In that passionate kiss, the crowd melted away, the rest of the world ceased to exist.

He set her on her feet and helped her up to the winner's podium. A race volunteer led Itirit and Nunii on either side of her. Race officials and reporters pressed forward. The race marshal placed a garland of silk flowers over the heads of her two gallant lead dogs.

Being the focus of so much attention from television cameras and reporters' questions made her head spin.

Her eyes met his. A radiant smile lit his face. She noticed that the officials were moving her team aside to make way for the next arrival.

She stood and waved a greeting to the second place winner as he crossed the line. The man raised his hand to acknowledge her greeting. No words were needed. His face showed the annoyance of losing to a rookie, a woman rookie at that.

"I must take care of my dogs," she said.

Scott placed a restraining hand on her shoulder. "Stay. You're the celebrity. I'll take care of them."

She heard the tenderness in his voice. Her heart was filled with renewed hope. He had come to her.

"Can you? Your wound…"

"It's fine. The stitches are out. I'm almost back to normal. I've recruited a couple of young fellows to help."

Pride filled his eyes. There was something else too, something undefinable but wonderful. A tremor agitated her, but they were swallowed up by the sea of people.

Arms linked, they greeted the third place winner to cross the finish line. Phil came in a close fourth.

Phil Richter had no reservations about her achievement. In front of the assembled spectators and media, he announced, "More than simply winning hands down, Chris Taylor showed a great sporting spirit by giving me a ride for several miles to catch up with my runaway team. She and her dogs deserved to win. They're magnificent."

His short but fiery speech whipped up the crowd's fervor even more. Eventually, Scott was able to lead her through the smiling and cheering throng.

In the lobby of the finest hotel Nome possessed, they were greeted by the staff. With great pomp, they showed her to her room.

"Knowing from experience what you must feel like, I guess your wish right now is for a hot bath and a soft bed, in that order." He threw his fur hat and parka onto a chair.

"Your guess is right."

With infinite gentleness, he helped her undress. Breathless, she waited. Unable to resist, he took her in his arms. Their lips met in a passionate kiss. She pressed her trail weary body to him against his muscled frame. Trembling with anticipation, she raised her face to him.

He straightened. His strong hands turned her and firmly propelled her toward the bathroom.

"Go and take care of yourself while I'm still in control of myself."

She hesitated part way across the room. "The bath can wait."

"No, sweetheart. Take care of yourself first." He carried her bag and placed it on the bathroom vanity.

When the door closed behind him, she traced a nail over lips still tingling from the imprint of his kiss. He had called her sweetheart. Did that signify anything? Probably not. It was the same as Byron calling her honey. An affectionate word offered in the heat of the moment.

There was no mistaking his joy in her win. With a sigh of delight, she ran a steaming bath and lay back to savor its luxury.

Dressed in a satin robe, she came from the bathroom to find Scott seated in an armchair.

"You've never been so beautiful."

Color suffused her cheeks.

"I'd better go before I tire you further," he murmured.

"I feel better now, after the bath."

"Your eyelids are drooping. I'll be back this evening."

"Where's Cody?"

"He's staying with Vicky. Good news. Alina finally broke down and phoned. The dear gal is getting married again. Cody stays with me. She gets him for vacations if she isn't off visiting some country."

His rugged face shone with a newfound happiness. She was too tired to grasp the full significance of what he was saying. Her mind vaguely registered that all his happiness was because his son was staying with him. Nothing to do with her. But exhaustion prevented her from elaborating.

"You must rest now."

***

A soft touch on her cheek woke Chris from her deep sleep. Without moving, she opened her eyes. For several seconds, she had no idea where she was.

"Time to wake up, beautiful." He leaned over and helped her into a sitting position. Her hair tumbled about her shoulders in splendid disarray. He put his arms about her and held her close.

Hungrily, he took her trembling lips. Hers responded with even greater fervor. He trailed a path downward to tease the fragrant softness of her neck.

Her laughter echoed in the room. "I won. I can't believe it."

"You did. I'm so proud of you. I think you took the right decision when you set out despite the storm. Most of the others waited till it abated a little."

"I remember reading about the first woman to win the Iditarod. Libby Riddle set out in the middle of the storm when, like now, everybody waited."

"Setting out despite the storm clinched the first place."

"If she could do it, then I could as well. Serendipity. If Phil hadn't lost his team, I'd be second."

He chuckled. "My spirited Chris. You must be hungry."

"Hungry for..?"

"For food, of course. What did you think? Shall we go and eat?"

"I'd like to take a short walk first. I need some fresh air."

He smiled. "I need to cool down, too. Let's go."

With stolen kisses and much silly laughter, they dressed to go out. The festive air along the busy street intimidated her after ten whole days of utter wilderness silence. Back on the frozen trails, alone with her dogs, she had belonged to another time and place. Indeed, the Iditarod trail belonged to a world apart.

He guided her to where the ground sloped down to the edge of the frozen sea, well removed from the noise and lights behind them.

"Look." She motioned upward. Immense veils of emerald green hung in giant curtains against the night sky. Across the vast heavens the aurora borealis undulated, caressed and withdrew before hurling itself against the starry dome.

"Some call it the sky's lover," he murmured.

Spellbound by the breathtaking sight, she nodded. He crooked an arm about her shoulder and turned her to face him.

"Now that you've proved yourself, you must continue. There are other races to be won."

Her tone became serious. "I intend to. Next summer I'll put together a team of my own."

"No. I mean, continue as of now. This season. I spoke to Lauren Kains while you were resting. That lady is full of praise for how you ran the race. You'll get all the help you need from her in the next races."

"What about you? Don't you want to help me?"

"Me? I want to love you." His warm lips grazed her forehead.

Her heart skipped several beats.

"One doesn't preclude the other, does it?" All she could manage was a faint whisper.

"Not if you accept to marry me. There, I've said it."

His heart pound wildly against his chest. He waited for her answer before releasing his breath.

Her mind swirled in a warm mist. Had she heard correctly? It was some time before emotion let her speak again. "Marry you..? You mean you want me to be your wife?"

He gave her a confused look. What a mistake! She didn't want him. "Forget it. I must be babbling. Just forget what I said."

He released his hold on her and took a small step backward. Her hand shot out and grabbed the front of his parka, as usual, open to the wind.

"Wait a minute, you want me to become your wife? Wife, as in marriage?"

"Yes, that was my idea, but I know how much you cherish your freedom. So, let's forget it. I should never have–"

She didn't allow him to finish his sentence. Her mouth closed over his in a long, unhurried kiss that left them both gasping for air.

"I do want to be your wife."

"Do you really love me?"

"I love you with a passion that knows no bounds. And have done from the very beginning."

He squeezed her tightly. "It took my enforced immobility to discover I didn't want to lose you. You've become a part of me. I didn't know it was love. I must have been in love with you all along, but was too stupid to admit the truth, too scared that you might love someone else. I was terrified. I didn't know how to handle all those feelings. I must have been such a boorish guy, but you put up with me."

She chuckled. "Let's remember only the good times."

He fished a small box from his pocket. "I hope it's your size."

Her throat constricted by emotion, she opened the velvet jeweler's box. The facets of a diamond reflected the colorful lights from above. He didn't let her speak, but slipped the ring on her finger.

"I love you," they whispered together.

In the starlit sky, the northern lights worked their silent magic, and in the distance huskies howled.

****

About the author

Born and raised in France, she was involved in writing from an early age, Geneviève has written a score of books: children's fiction in French and English, romances and historical novels published in France, Canada and the US, non-fiction books and numerous articles for Dogs in Canada. Her poetry has appeared in the Anthologie de la poésie Franco-Manitobaine, and in several short stories anthologies. She also worked as a translator.

In 2003 she received the Queen's Jubilee Medal

In 1983 she was nominated for YWCA Women of the Year

Also by

TRANSLATIONS

L'héritage de la guerre, translation from A Touch ofMagic, June Gadsby.

Quand la nuit tombe, translation from When DarknessFalls, Rachel Wesson

Lorsque l'aube se lève,translation from Light Rises, Rachel Wesson

OTHERS

Where the River Narrows, with Kathy Fisher-Brown